SUPERLUMINAL

SUPERLUMINAL

Vonda N. McIntyre

[signature: Vonda N. McIntyre]

Houghton Mifflin Company
Boston 1983

A portion of this book appeared in the story "Aztecs," originally published in 2076: *The American Tricentennial*, edited by Edward Bryant and published by Pyramid Books. Another portion, entitled "Transit," appeared in the October 1983 issue of *Isaac Asimov's Science Fiction Magazine*.

Library of Congress Cataloging in Publication Data

McIntyre, Vonda N.
　Superluminal.

　　I. Title.
PS3563.A3125S9　1983　　813'.54　　83-8568
ISBN　0-395-34942-7

Printed in the United States of America

D　10　9　8　7　6　5　4　3　2　1

FOR CAROLYN

1

SHE GAVE UP HER HEART quite willingly.

After the operation, Laenea Trevelyan lived through what seemed an immense time of semiconsciousness, drugged so she would not feel the pain, kept almost insensible while drugs sped her healing. Those who watched her did not know she would have preferred consciousness and an end to her uncertainty. So she slept, shallowly, drifting toward awareness, driven back, existing in a world of nightmare. Her dulled mind suspected danger but could do nothing to protect her. She had been forced too often to sleep through danger. She would have preferred the pain.

Once Laenea almost woke: She glimpsed the sterile white walls and ceiling, blurrily, slowly recognizing what she saw. The green glow of monitoring screens flowed across her shoulder, over the scratchy sheets. Taped down, needles scraped nerves in her arm. She became aware of sounds, and heard the rhythmic thud of a beating heart.

She tried to cry out in anger and despair. Her left hand was heavy, lethargic, insensitive to her commands, but she moved it. It crawled like a spider to her right wrist and fumbled at the needles and tubes.

Air shushed from the room as the door opened. A gentle voice and a gentle touch reproved her, increased the flow of sedative, and cruelly returned her to sleep.

A tear slid back from the corner of her eye and trickled into her hair as she reentered her nightmares, accompanied by the counterpoint of a basic human rhythm, the beating of a heart, that she had hoped never to hear again.

Pastel light was Laenea's first assurance that she would live. It gave her no comfort. Intensive care had been stark white. Yellows and greens brightened this room. The sedative wore off and she knew she would finally be allowed to wake. She did not fight the continuing drowsiness, but depression prevented anticipation of the return of her senses. She wanted only to hide within her own mind, ignoring her body, ignoring failure. She did not even know what she would do in the future; perhaps she had none anymore.

Yet the world impinged on her as she grew bored with lying still and sweaty and self-pitying. She had never been able to do simply *nothing*. Stubbornly she kept her eyes closed, but the sounds vibrated through her body, like shudders of cold and fear.

This was my chance, she thought, but I knew I might fail. It could have been worse, or better: I might have died.

She slid her hand up her body, from her stomach to her ribs, across the bandages and the tip of the new scar between her breasts, to her throat. Her fingers rested at the corner of her jaw, just above the carotid artery.

She could not feel her pulse.

Pushing herself up abruptly, Laenea ignored sharp twinges of pain. The vibration of a heartbeat continued beneath her palms, but now she could tell that it did not come from her own body.

The amplifier sat on the bedside table, sending out a steady low-frequency pattern. Laenea felt laughter bubbling up. She knew it would hurt and she did not care. She dragged the speaker off the table. Its cord ripped from the wall as she flung it sidearm across the room. It smashed in the corner with a satisfying clatter.

She pushed aside the sheets. She was stiff and sore. She rolled out of bed because it hurt too much to sit up. She staggered and caught herself. Fluid in her lungs coarsened her breathing. She coughed, caught her breath, coughed again. Time was a mystery, measured only by weakness. She thought the administrators fools, to force sleep into her, risk her to pneumonia, and play recorded hearts, instead of letting her wake and move and adjust to her new condition.

Barefoot, Laenea walked slowly across the cool tile to a warm patch of sunshine. She gazed out the window. The day was variegated, gray and golden. Clouds moved from the west across the mountains and the Sound while sunlight still spilled over the city. The shadows moved along the water, turning it from shattered silver to slate.

White from the heavy winter snowfall, the Olympic mountains rose between Laenea and the port. The approaching rain hid even the trails of spacecraft escaping the earth, and the glint of shuttles returning to their target in the sea. She would see them again soon. She laughed aloud, stretching against the soreness in her chest and the ache of her ribs, throwing back her tangled wavy hair. It tickled the nape of her neck.

The door opened and air moved past her as if the room were breathing. Laenea turned and faced Dr. van de Graaf. The surgeon was tiny and frail looking, and her hands possessed strength like steel wires. She glanced at the shattered amplifier and shook her head.

"Was that necessary?"

"Yes," Laenea said. "For my peace of mind."

"It was here for your peace of mind."

"It has the opposite effect."

"The administrators feel there's no reason to change the procedure," she said. "We've been doing it since the first pilots."

"The administrators are known for continuing bad advice."

"Well, pilot, soon you can design your own environment."

"When?"

"Soon. I don't mean to be obscure — I decide when you can leave the hospital, but when you may leave takes more than my word. The scar tissue needs time to strengthen. Do you want to go already? I cracked your ribs rather thoroughly."

Laenea grinned. "I know." She was strapped up tight and straight, but she could feel each juncture of rib end and cartilage.

"It will be a few days at least."

"How long has it been?"

"Since surgery? About forty-eight hours."

"It seemed like weeks."

"Well . . . adjusting to all the changes at once has proved to be quite a shock for most people. Sleeping seems to help."

"I'm an experiment," Laenea said. "All of us are. With experiments, you should experiment."

"We've made enough pilots so your group isn't an experiment anymore. We've found this works best."

"But when I heard the heartbeat," Laenea said, "I thought you'd had to put me back to normal."

"It's meant to be a comforting sound."

"No one else ever complained?"

"Not quite so strongly," van de Graaf said, then dismissed the subject. "It's done now, pilot."

It *was* finished, for Laenea. She shrugged. "When can I leave?" she asked again. The hospital was one more place of stasis that Laenea was anxious to escape.

"For now, go back to bed. Morning's soon enough to talk about the future."

Laenea turned away. The windows, the walls, the filtered air cut her off from the gray clouds and the city.

"Pilot — "

Rain slipped down the glass. Laenea stayed where she was. She did not feel like sleeping.

The doctor sighed. "Do something for me, pilot."

Laenea shrugged again.

"I want you to test your control."

Laenea acquiesced with sullen silence.

"Speed your heart up slowly, and pay attention to the results."

Laenea intensified the firing of the nerve.

"What do you feel?"

"Nothing," Laenea said, though her blood, impelled by the smooth rotary pump, rushed through what had been her pulse points: temples, throat, wrists.

Beside her the surgeon frowned. "Increase a little more, but very slowly."

Laenea obeyed. Bright lights flashed just behind her vision. Her head hurt in a streak above her right eye to the back of her skull. She felt high and excited. She turned away from the window. "I want to get out of here."

Van de Graaf touched her arm at the wrist; Laenea laughed aloud at the idea of feeling for *her* pulse. The doctor led her to a chair by the window. "Sit down." But Laenea felt she could climb the helix of her dizziness: She felt no need for rest.

"Sit *down*." The voice was whispery, soft sand slipping across stone. Laenea obeyed.

"Remember the rest of your training. It's important to vary your blood pressure. Sit back. Slow the pump. Expand the capillaries. Relax."

Laenea called back her biocontrol. For the first time she was conscious of a presence rather than an absence. Her pulse was gone, but in its place she felt the constant quiet hum of a perfectly balanced rotary machine. It pushed her blood through her body so efficiently that the pressure would destroy her, if she let it. She relaxed and slowed the pump, expanded and contracted arterial muscles, once, twice, again. The headache, the light flashes, the ringing in her ears faded and ceased.

She took a deep breath and let it out slowly.

"That's better," the surgeon said. "Don't forget how that feels. You can't go at high speed very long, you'll turn your brain to cheese. You can feel fine for quite a while, you can feel intoxicated. But the hangover is more than I care to reckon with." She folded her arms. "I want to keep you here till we're sure you can regulate the machine. I don't like doing kidney transplants."

"I can control it." Laenea began to induce a slow, arrhythmic change in the speed of the new pump, in her blood pressure. She found she could do it without thinking, as was necessary to balance the flow. "Can I have the ashes of my heart?"

"Not yet."

"But — "

"I want to be sure."

Somewhere in the winding concrete labyrinth of the hospital, Laenea's heart still beat, bathed in warm saline and nutrient solution. As long as it existed, as long as it lived, Laenea would feel threatened in her ambitions. She could not be a starship pilot and remain a normal human being, with normal human rhythms. Her body still could reject the artificial heart; then she would be made ordinary again. If she could work at all she would have to remain a crew member, anesthetized throughout every journey in transit at superluminal speeds. She did not think she could stand that any longer.

"I'm sure," she said. "I won't be back."

On the exposed side of a tiny, rocky island with a single twisted tree growing at its summit, Orca, the diver, lay in a tide pool, letting waves splash against her and over her. She needed a few minutes of concentration, calm, and the sea to wash away her anger. She did not want the long and pleasant swim to the spaceport spoiled, as it would be if she replayed the fight with her father again and again, trying to think of how she could have kept discussion from turning into disagreement, or how she could have made him understand her position.

The sun spread an evening dazzle across the water, reddening the clouds that concealed Vancouver Island.

In the midst of the bright waves, Orca's brother surfaced. Treading water, he gestured to her. She shook her head and beckoned to him to come to her. His patience was ten times hers, but he was too inexperienced, too naive, to suspect she wanted him to join her because it was easier to argue about air things in surface language, or, rather, because it was easier for her to win the argument. Finally he dove again, and a moment later snaked up beside her on the rocks. Like Orca, he was small and fine boned, dark skinned and fair haired.

"Dad's upset," he said.

"I figured."

She loved her younger brother, and she felt sorry for him at times like these. He had spent most of his life trying to be the intermediary between Orca and their father. Orca had long ago resigned herself to never having anything more than superficial contact with the elder diver, but her brother never gave up trying to reconcile them. Their father had been a youth during the revolution; he had fought in it. He had to accept her choosing an outside profession, one that put her in close contact with landers, but he could never be graceful about it. He was indifferent to her coworkers' being, as she was, members of the starship crew. They were all landers to him.

Like many of his generation, though more vehemently than most, he disapproved when younger divers took salvage or exploration jobs with lander companies. He knew they needed the money for lab equipment and research materials, yet he loathed every contact divers had with ordinary people. He despised Orca's profession, and sometimes she felt he despised her as well.

"Can't you give in just a little?"

"Give in! He as much as called me a coward!"

"He knows you aren't that."

"I think it's his turn to apologize for a change."

"He doesn't understand your objections."

"He *won't* understand," Orca said. "There's a difference."

"Maybe there is," her brother said. "Would you be mad at me if I told you I don't understand, either? I'm trying, please believe me. But if you disagree with the change, why have you worked outside for so long? You make more money than anybody else in the family, you're the one who's paid for most of the research."

"I just didn't expect it to be done so soon," she said, knowing the excuse to be a lame one. She had tried before to explain to members of her family that she had joined the starship crew for itself, not for the pay. Her mother understood, but her father thought she said so just to make him angry, and her brother thought she only said so to keep everyone from feeling guilty because she had to spend so much time away from home.

"If I get back in time, I'll come home for the transition meeting," Orca said.

"Wouldn't it be easier to stay till afterwards? If you go, and you're late getting home, you won't be able to say what you think about the change."

Orca sighed and said nothing. She was sick of the argument. She had answered all the questions twenty times. It was six weeks until the meeting. If she took more leave from the crew, she would fall even further behind on the seniority list. The longer she took to work her way up, the longer before she could get on a mission more interesting than a milk run.

"I can't *talk* to you up here," her brother said plaintively. "Come back into the water."

"When I get back in the water," Orca said, "I'm going to start swimming and I'm not going to stop till I get to the port. If you want to come along, *petit frère,* that's fine." She wished he would join her; she thought it would do him good.

He let himself slide into the tide pool until only his head

and shoulders rose above the water. He acted as if he might turn around and swim angrily away. But he never got angry. He found anger incomprehensible, as far as Orca could tell. Of all the divers, her younger brother was the most distant from being human. He had never been to a lander city, never worked for one of their companies, never attended a main-land school. He had met perhaps three ordinary humans in his whole life. Her brother had never even adopted a surface nickname. He and her father acted the same way, when it came to land dwellers. But their reasons were as completely different as it was possible to be. Father avoided landers be-cause he hated and despised them. Her brother was simply disinterested.

"You spend too much time with the cousins," Orca said.

"You spend too little time with them," he replied. "They miss you. They ask about you when you're gone."

And, too, whenever she returned, they asked about where she had been. They listened to her descriptions of working on the crew, of being in space, of visiting alien worlds. At first they asked how it felt to travel faster than light. She re-gretted being unable to tell them: She, too, would have liked to know. But she was not a pilot, so she had to sleep when her ship entered transit. She could not experience superlu-minal travel, and survive. Though the cousins never criti-cized her for leaving, she often doubted that she explained her reasons as comprehensibly as she described her actions.

Her brother said sadly, "I don't understand why you go."

"I have to," Orca said. She pushed herself down into the warm salty pool. "This isn't enough for me."

"How can't it be? Not enough? We haven't learned ten percent of what the cousins are trying to teach us."

Orca sometimes wondered if that was exactly the reason she fled to space. Her family lived among aliens, and it was clear to her, if to no one else, that the cousins were so far beyond the family that understanding them was impossible. In their presence she had always felt like a child, and she knew she always would. On the starship crew she was an adult.

She pushed off toward her brother and glided past him underwater, turning over and blowing a stream of bubbles up against his chest, his stomach, his genitals. He was terribly ticklish: He doubled over laughing and turned the motion into a dive. He streaked around to chase her. Orca dove out of the tide pool, into the sea. The cold water hit her like a shock. Her brother was right behind her. She surfaced; he came straight up from the bottom and propelled himself out of the water, half his height, before falling back.

Orca scooped water up in her webbed hand and flung it playfully at him. He sputtered and shook his head, flinging his pale hair back from his face.

Orca kissed him. He embraced her, then let her go.

"Do you want company?"

"Only if you'll come all the way."

He hesitated. "No. Maybe sometime, but not now."

She nodded; he sank down under the surface. As he passed beneath her he spun around, letting his hand flick up and slide along the length of her body and legs.

Then he was gone.

Orca turned in the other direction, dove, and struck out down the strait, heading for the spaceport.

Though Laenea felt strong enough to walk, a wheelchair carried her through the halls as tests and questions and examinations devoured several days in chunks and nibbles. The boredom grew more and more wearing. The pains had faded, the accelerated healing was nearly complete, and still Laenea saw only doctors and attendants and machines. Her friends stayed away. This was a rite of passage she must survive alone.

A day went by in which she saw neither the rain that passed, nor the sunset that was obscured by fog. She asked again when she could leave the hospital. The answers were evasions. She allowed herself to become angry, and still no one would respond.

Evening, back in her room: Laenea was wide awake. She

lay in bed and slid her fingers across her collarbone to the sternum, along the shiny red line of the long scar. It was still tender, covered with translucent synthetic skin, crossed once just below her breasts with a wide bandage to ease her cracked ribs.

The efficient new heart intrigued her. She consciously slowed its pace, then went through the exercise of constricting and dilating arteries and capillaries. Her biocontrol was excellent. It had to be, or she would not have been approved for surgery.

Slowing the pump should have produced a pleasant lethargy and eventual sleep, but adrenaline from her anger lingered and she did not want to rest. Nor did she want a sleeping pill. She was done with taking drugs. Dreamless drug sleep was the worst kind of all. Fear built up, undischarged by fantasy, producing a great and formless tension.

The twilight was the texture of gray watered silk, opaque and irregular. The hospital's pastels turned cold and mysterious. Laenea threw off the sheet. She was strong again; she was healed. She had undergone a year of training, major surgery, and these final days of boredom to free herself from biological rhythms. There was no reason in the world why she should sleep, like others, when darkness fell.

The hospital retained a few advantages of civilization. Her clothes were in the closet, not squirreled away in some locked room. She put on black pants, soft leather boots, and a shiny leather vest that laced up the front, leaving her arms and neck bare. The gap between the laces revealed the livid pilot's scar from one sharp tip at her throat to the other below her breastbone.

To avoid arguments, she waited until the corridor was deserted. Green paint, meant to be soothing, had gone flat and ugly with age. Her boots were silent on the resilient tile, but in the hollow shaft of the fire stairs the heels clattered against concrete, echoing past her and back. Her legs were tired when she reached bottom. She speeded the flow of blood.

Outside, mist obscured the stars. The moon had risen, full and haloed. Streetlights spread Laenea's shadow out around her like the spokes of a wheel.

A rank of electric cars waited at the corner, tethered like horses in an old movie. She slid her credit key into a lock to release one painted like a turtle, an apt analogy. She got in and drove it toward the waterfront. The little beast rolled along, its motor humming quietly on the flat, straining in low gear on the steep downgrades. Laenea relaxed and wished she were back in space, but her imagination could not stretch that far. The turtle could not become a starship; and the city, while pleasant, was of unrelieved ordinariness compared to the alien places she had seen. She could not, of course, imagine transit, for it was beyond imagination. Language or mind was insufficient. Transit had never been described.

The waterfront was shabby, dirty, magnetic. Laenea knew she could find acquaintances nearby, but she did not want to stay in the city. She returned the turtle to a stanchion and retrieved her credit key to halt the tally against her account.

The night had grown cold; she noticed the change peripherally as fog, and cobblestones slick with condensation. The public market, ramshackle and shored up, littered here and there with wilted vegetables, was deserted. People passed as shadows.

A man moved up behind her while she was in the dim region between two streetlamps. "Hey," he said, "how about — " His tone was belligerent with inexperience or insecurity or fear. Looking down at him, surprised, Laenea laughed. "Poor fool — " He scuttled away like a crab. After a moment of vague pity and amusement, Laenea forgot him. She shivered. Her ears were ringing and her chest ached from the cold.

Small shops nestled between bars and cheap restaurants. Laenea entered one for the warmth. It was very dim, darker than the street, high ceilinged and deep, so narrow she could have touched both side walls by stretching out her arms. She did not. She hunched her shoulders and the ache receded slightly.

"May I help you?"

Like one of the shop's indistinct masses brought to life, a small ancient man appeared. He was dressed in ill-matched clothes, part of his own wares. Hung up like trophies, feathers and wide hats and beads covered the walls of the secondhand clothing store. Laenea moved farther inside.

"Ah, pilot," the old man said, "you honor me."

Laenea's delight was childish in its intensity. He was the first person outside the hospital, in the real world, to call her by her new title.

"It's cold by the water," she said. Some graciousness or apology was due, for she had no intention of buying anything.

"A coat? No, a cloak!" he exclaimed. "A cloak would be set off well by a person of your stature." He turned; his dark form disappeared among the piles and racks of clothes. Laenea saw bright beads and spangles, a quick flash of gold lamé, and wondered uncharitably what dreadful theater costume he would choose. But he held up a long swath of black, lined with scarlet. Laenea had planned to thank him and demur; despite herself she reached out. Velvet silk outside and smooth satin silk within caressed her fingers. The cloak had a single shoulder cape and a clasp of carved jet. Though heavy, it draped easily and gracefully. She slung it over her shoulders, and it flowed around her almost to her ankles.

"Exquisite," the shopkeeper said. He beckoned and she approached. A dim and pitted full-length mirror stood against the wall beyond him. Bronze patches marred its face where the silver had peeled away. Laenea liked the way the cape looked. She folded its edges so the scarlet lining showed, so her throat and the upper curve of her breasts and the tip of the scar were exposed. She shook back her hair.

"Not quite that," she said, smiling. She was too tall and big-boned for delicacy. She had a widow's peak and high cheekbones, but her jaw was strong and square.

"It does not please you." He sounded downcast. Laenea could not quite place his faint accent.

"It does," she said. "I'll take it."

He bowed her toward the front of the shop, and she took out her credit key.

"No, no, pilot," he said. "Not that."

Laenea raised one eyebrow. A few shops on the waterfront accepted only cash, retaining an illicit flavor in a time when almost any activity was legal. But few even of those select establishments would refuse the credit of a crew member or a pilot.

"I have no cash," Laenea said. She had stopped carrying it years ago, since the time she found in various pockets three coins of metal, one of plastic, one of wood, a pleasingly atavistic animal claw (or excellent duplicate), and a boxed bit of organic matter that would have been forbidden on earth fifty years before. Laenea never expected to revisit at least three of the worlds the currency represented.

"No cash," he said. "It is yours, pilot. Only — " He glanced up. His eyes were very dark and deep, hopeful, expectant. "Only tell me, what is it like? What do you see?"

He was the first person to ask her that question. People asked it often, of pilots. She had asked it herself, wordlessly after the first few times of silence and patient head-shakings. The pilots never answered. Machines could not answer, pilots could not answer. Or would not. The question was answerable only individually. Laenea felt sorry for the shopkeeper. She started to say she had not yet been in transit awake, that she was new, that she had only traveled in the crew, drugged near death to stay alive. But, finally, she could not say even that. It was too easy; it was an untrue truth. It implied she would tell him if she knew, while she did not know if she could or would. She shook her head; she smiled gently. "I'm sorry."

He nodded sadly. "I should not have asked . . ."

"That's all right."

"I'm too old, you see. Too old for adventure. I came here so long ago . . . but the time, the time disappeared. I never knew what happened. I've dreamed about it. Bad dreams . . ."

"I understand. I was crew for ten years. We never knew what happened either."

"That would be worse, yes. Over and over again, no time between. But now you know."

"Pilots know," Laenea agreed. She handed him the credit key. Though he still tried to refuse it, she insisted on paying.

Hugging the cloak around her, Laenea stepped out into the fog. She fantasied that the shop would now disappear, like all legendary shops dispensing magic and cloaks of invisibility. But she did not look back, for everything a few paces away dissolved into grayness. In a small space around each low antique streetlamp, heat swirled the fog in wisps toward the sky.

The midnight ferry sped silently across the water, propelled through the waves by great silver sails. Wrapped in her cloak, Laenea was anonymous. She put her feet on the opposite bench, stretched, and gazed out the window into the darkness. Laenea could see her own reflection, and, beyond, the water. Light from the ferry wavered across the long low swells.

The spaceport was a huge, floating, artificial island. It gleamed in its own lights. The solar mirrors looked like the multiple compound eyes of a gigantic water insect, an illusion continued by the spidery reach of launching towers. The port's other sea-level buildings curved like hills, like sand dunes, offering surfaces that might have been smoothed by the wind. Tall, angular buildings suitable to the mainland would have presented sail-like faces to the northwest storms.

Overhead, a small, silver-blue blimp passed by, driven by quiet engines. Laenea remembered arriving once a few hours before a storm hit, when all the airships on the port launched simultaneously in a brilliant multicolored cloud and vanished toward the horizon to escape the weather.

Beneath the platform, under a vibration-deadening lower layer, under the sea, lay the tripartite city. The roar of shuttles taking off and the scream of their return would drive mad anyone who long remained on the surface. Thus the northwest spaceport was far out to sea, away from cities, carrying a city within its underwater stabilizing shafts.

The ferry furled its sails, slowed, and nestled against the ramp that met it at the waterline. Electric trucks hummed into motion, breaching the silence. Laenea moved stiffly down the stairs. Pausing by the gangway, watching the trucks roll past, she concentrated for a moment and felt the increase in her blood pressure. She could well understand how dangerous it might be, and how easily addictive the higher speed, driving her high until like a machine her body was burned out. But for now her energy began returning and the stiffness in her legs and back slowly seeped away.

Except for the trucks, which purred off quickly around the island's perimeter and disappeared, the port was silent, so late at night. The passenger shuttle waited empty on its central rail. When Laenea entered, it sensed her, slid its doors shut, and accelerated. A pushbutton command halted it above stabilizer #3, which held quarantine, administration, and crew quarters. Laenea felt good, warm, and her vision sparkled bright and clear. She let the velvet cloak flow back across her shoulders, no longer needing its protection. She was alight with the expectation of seeing her friends, in her new avatar.

The elevator led through the center of the stabilizer into the underwater city. Laenea rode it all the way to the bottom of the shaft, one of three that projected into the ocean far below the surface turbulence to hold the platform steady even through the most violent storms. The shafts maintained the island's flotation level as well, pumping sea water into or out of the ballast tanks when a shuttle took off or landed or a ferry crept on board.

The elevator doors opened into the foyer where a spiral staircase reached the lowest level, a bubble at the tip of the main shaft. The lounge was a comfortable cylindrical room, its walls all transparent, gazing out like a continuous eye into the deep sea. Floodlights cast a glow through the cold clear water, picking out the bright speedy forms of fish, large dark predators, scythe-mouthed sharks, the occasional graceful bow of a porpoise, the elegant black-and-white presence of a killer whale. As the radius of visibility increased, the light filtered through bluer and bluer, until finally, in violet, vague shapes eased back and forth with shy curiosity between dim illumination and complete darkness.

The lounge, sculpted with structural foam, then carpeted, gave the illusion of being underwater, on the ocean floor itself, a part of the sea. It had been built originally as a public lounge, but was taken over by unconscious agreement among the starship people. Outsiders, gently ignored, felt unwelcome and soon departed. Journalists came infrequently, reacting to sensation or disaster. Human transit pilots had been a sensation, but the novelty had worn away. Laenea did not mind a bit.

She took off her boots and left them by the stairwell. She recognized one of the other pairs: She would have been hard put not to recognize those boots after seeing them once. The scarlet leather was stupendously shined, embroidered with jewels, and inlaid with tiny liquid crystal disks that changed color with the temperature. Laenea smiled. Crew members made up for the dead time of transit in many different ways; one was to overdo all other aspects of their lives, and the most flamboyant of that group was Minoru.

Walking barefoot in the deep carpet, between the hillocks and hollows of conversation pits, was like walking on the floor of a fantasy sea. Laenea wondered if the attraction of the lounge was its relation to the ocean, which still held mysteries as deep as any she would encounter in space or in transit. Laenea had often sat gazing through the shadowed water, dreaming. Pilots and divers could guess at the truth of her assumption.

Near the transparent sea wall she saw Minoru, his black hair braided with scarlet and silver to his waist; tall Alannai hunched down to be closer to the others, the light on her skin like dark opal, glinting in her close-cropped hair like diamond dust; and pale, quiet Ruth, whose sparkling was rare but nova bright. Holding goblets or mugs, they sat sleepily conversing, and Laenea felt the comfort of a familiar scene.

Minoru, facing her, looked up. She smiled, expecting him to call her name and fling out his arms, as he always did, with his ebullient greeting, showing to advantage the fringe and beadwork on his jacket. But he looked at her, straight on, silent, with an expression so blank that only the unlined long-lived youthfulness of his face could have held it. He whispered her name. Ruth glanced over her shoulder, saw Laenea, and smiled tentatively, as though she were afraid. Alannai unbent, and, head and shoulders above the others, raised her glass solemnly to Laenea. "Pilot," she said, and drank, and hunched back down with her elbows on her sharp knees. Laenea stood above them, outside their circle, gazing down on three people whom she had kissed good-bye. Crew always said good-bye, for they slept through their voyages without any certainty that they would ever awaken. They lived in the cruel childhood prayer, "If I should die before I wake . . ."

Laenea climbed down to them. The circle opened, but she remained outside it. She was as overwhelmed by uncertainty as her friends.

"Sit with us," Ruth said finally. Alannai and Minoru looked uneasy. Laenea sat down. The triangle between Ruth and Alannai and Minoru did not alter. Each of them was next to the other; Laenea was beside none of them.

Ruth reached out, but her hand trembled. They all waited, and Laenea tried to think of words to reassure them, to affirm that she had not changed.

"I came . . . " But nothing she felt seemed right to tell them. She would not taunt them with her freedom. She took Ruth's outstretched hand. "I came to say good-bye." She embraced them and kissed them and climbed back to the main level. They had all been friends, but her friends accepted her no longer.

The first pilots did not mingle with the crew, for the responsibility was great, the tensions greater. But Laenea had thought it would be different for her. She cared for Ruth and Minoru and Alannai. Her concern would remain when she watched them sleeping and ferried them from one island of light to the next. She tried to understand her friends' reserve, and hoped perhaps they only needed time to get used to her.

Conversations ebbed and flowed around her like the tides as she moved through the lounge. Seeing people she knew, she avoided them. Her pride exceeded her loneliness.

She put aside the pain of her rejection. She felt self-contained and self-assured. When she recognized two pilots, sitting together, isolated, she approached them straightforwardly. She had flown with both of them, but never talked at length with either. They would accept her, or they would not: For the moment, she did not care. She flung back the cloak so they would know her. Without even thinking about it, she had dressed the way all pilots dressed. Laced vests or deeply cut gowns, transparent shirts, halters, all in one way or another revealed the long scar that marked their changes.

Miikala and Ramona-Teresa sat facing each other, elbows on knees, talking together quietly, privately. Ramona-Teresa touched Miikala's hand, and they both laughed softly. Even the rhythms of their conversation seemed alien to Laenea, though she could not hear their words. Like other people they communicated as much with their bodies and hands as with speech, but the nods and gestures clashed.

Laenea wondered what pilots talked about. Certainly it could not be the ordinary concerns of ordinary people, the laundry, the shopping, a place to stay, a person, perhaps, to stay with. They would talk about . . . the experiences they alone had; they would talk about what they saw when all others must sleep near death or die.

Human pilots withstood transit better than machine intelligence, but human pilots too were sometimes lost. Miikala and Ramona-Teresa were ten percent of all the pilots who survived from the first generation, ten percent of their own unique, evolving, almost self-contained society. They had proven time-independence successful by example; it was up to the pilots who came after, to Laenea, to prove it practical.

control. Slow the pump. Someone bathed her forehead with a cocktail napkin dipped in gin. Laenea welcomed the coolness and even the odor's bitter tang. The pain dissolved gradually until Ramona-Teresa could ease her back on the sitting shelf. The jet fastening of the cloak fell away from her throat and the older pilot loosened the laces of her vest.

"It's all right," Ramona-Teresa said. "The adrenaline works as well as ever. We all have to learn more control of that than they think they need to teach us."

Sitting on his heels beside Laenea, Miikala glanced at the exposed scar. "You're out early," he said. "Have they changed the procedure?"

Laenea paled: She had forgotten that her leavetaking of the hospital was something less than official and approved.

"Don't tease her, Miikala," Ramona-Teresa said gruffly. "Or don't you remember how it was when you woke up?"

His heavy eyebrows drew together in a scowl. "I remember."

"Will they make me go back? Will you?" Laenea said. "I'm all right, I just need to get used to it."

"We won't, but they might try to," Ramona-Teresa said. "They worry so about the money they spend on us. Perhaps they aren't quite as worried anymore. We do as well on our own as shut up in a hospital listening to recorded hearts — they still do that, I suppose."

Laenea shuddered. "It worked for you, they told me — but I broke the speaker."

Miikala laughed with delight. "Causing all other machines to make frantic noises like frightened little mice."

"I thought they hadn't done the operation. I've wanted to be one of you for so long — " Feeling stronger, Laenea pushed herself up. She left her vest open, glad of the cool air against her skin.

"We watched," Miikala said. "We watch you all, but a few are special. We knew you'd come to us. Do you remember this one, Ramona?"

"Yes." She picked up one of the extra glasses, filled it from a shaker, and handed it to Laenea. "You always fought the sleep, my dear. Sometimes I thought you might wake."

"Ahh, Ramona, don't frighten the child."

"Frighten her, this tigress?"

Strangely enough, Laenea was not disturbed by the knowledge that she had been close to waking in transit. She had not, or she would be dead; she would have died quickly of old age, her body bound to normal time and normal space, to the relation between time dilation and velocity and distance by a billion years of evolution, by rhythms planetary, lunar, solar, biological: subatomic, for all Laenea or anyone else knew. She was freed of all that now.

She downed half her drink in a single swallow. The air felt cold against her bare arms and her breasts, so she wrapped her cloak around her shoulders and waited for the satin to warm against her body.

"When's your training flight?"

"Not for a whole month." The time seemed a vast expanse of emptiness. She had finished the study and the training; now only her mortal body kept her earthbound.

"They want you completely healed."

"It's too long — how can they expect me to wait until then?"

"For the need."

"I want to know what happens, I have to find out. When's your next flight?"

"Soon," Ramona-Teresa said.

"Take me with you!"

"No, my dear. It would not be proper."

"Proper! We have to make our own rules, not follow theirs. They don't know what's right for us."

Miikala and Ramona-Teresa looked at each other for a long time. Perhaps pilots could speak together with their eyes and their expressions, or perhaps Ramona and Miikala simply understood each other in the way of any ordinary long-time lovers. But they excluded Laenea.

"No." Ramona's tone invited no argument.

"At least you can tell me — " She saw at once that she had said the wrong thing. The pilots' expressions closed down in silence. But Laenea felt neither guilt nor contrition, only anger.

"It isn't because you can't! You talk about it to each other, I know that now at least. You can't tell me you don't."

"No," Miikala said. "We will not say we never speak of it."

"You're selfish and you're cruel." She stood up, for a moment afraid she might stagger again and have to accept their help. Ramona and Miikala nodded at each other, with faint, infuriating smiles. A surge of brittle energy raised Laenea far beyond needing them.

"She has the need," one of them said, Laenea did not even know which one. The ringing in her ears cut her off from them. She turned her back, climbed out of the conversation pit, and stalked away to find a more congenial spot.

She chose a sitting place nestled into a steep slope very close to the sea wall. She could feel the ocean's coolness, as though the cold radiated, rather than heat. Grotesque creatures floated past in the spotlights. Laenea curled up and relaxed, making her smooth pulse wax and wane. If she sat here long enough, would she be able to detect the real tides? Would the same drifting plant-creatures pass before the window again, swept back and forth by the forces of sun and moon?

Her privacy was marred only slightly, by one man sleeping or lying unconscious nearby. She did not recognize him, but he must be crew. His dark, close-fitting clothes were unremarkably different enough, in design and fabric, that he might be from another world. He must be new. Earth was the hub of commerce; no ship flew long without orbiting it. New crew members always visited earth at least once. New crew usually visited every world their ships reached at first, even the ones that required quarantine and vaccinations, if they had enough time. Laenea had done the same herself. The quarantine to introduce null-strain bacteria, which could not contaminate exotic environments because it could only reproduce inside the human body, was the most severe and the most necessary, but no quarantine was pleasant. Laenea, like most other veterans, eventually remained acclimated to one world, stayed on the ship during other planetfalls, and arranged her pattern to intersect her home as frequently as possible.

The sleeping man was several years younger than Laenea. She thought he must be as tall as she, but that estimation was difficult. He was one of those uncommon people so beautifully proportioned that from any distance at all their height can only be determined by comparison. Nothing about him was exaggerated or attenuated; he gave the impression of strength, but it was the strength of agility, not violence. Laenea decided he was neither drunk nor drugged but asleep. His face, though relaxed, showed no dissipation. His hair was dark blond and shaggy, a shade lighter than his heavy mustache. He was far from handsome: His features were regular, distinctive, but without beauty. Below the cheekbones his tanned skin was scarred and pitted, as though from some virulent childhood disease. Some of the outer worlds had not yet conquered their epidemics.

Laenea looked away from the new young man. She stared at the dark water at light's end, letting her vision double and unfocus. She touched her collarbone and slid her fingers to the tip of the smooth scar. Sensation seemed refined across the tissue, as though a wound there would hurt more sharply. Though Laenea was tired and getting hungry, she did not force herself to outrun the distractions. For a while her energy should return slowly and naturally. She had pushed herself far enough for one night.

A month would be an eternity; the wait would seem equivalent to all the years she had spent crewing. She was still angry at the other pilots. She felt she had acted like a little puppy, bounding up to them to be welcomed and patted, then, when they grew bored, they had kicked her away as though she had piddled on the floor. And she was angry at herself: She felt a fool, and she felt the need to prove herself.

For the first time she appreciated the destruction of time during transit. To sleep for a month: convenient, impossible.

She first must deal with her new existence, her new body; then she would deal with a new environment.

Perhaps she dozed. The deep sea admitted no time: The lights pierced the same indigo darkness day or night. Time was the least real of all dimensions to Laenea's people, and she was free of its dictates, isolated from its stabilities.

When she opened her eyes again she had no idea how long they had been closed, a second or an hour.

The time must have been a few minutes, at least, for the young man who had been sleeping was now sitting up, watching her. His eyes were dark blue, flecked with black, a color like the sea. For a moment he did not notice she was awake, then their gazes met and he glanced quickly away, blushing, embarrassed to be caught staring.

"I stared, too," Laenea said.

Startled, he turned slowly back, not quite sure Laenea was speaking to him. "What?"

"When I was a grounder, I stared at crew, and when I was crew I stared at pilots."

"I *am* crew," he said defensively.

"From — ?"

"Twilight."

Laenea knew she had been there, a long while before; images of Twilight drifted to her. It was a new world, a dark and mysterious place of high mountains and black, brooding forests, a young world, its peaks just formed. It was heavily wreathed in clouds that filtered out much of the visible light but admitted the ultraviolet. Twilight: dusk, on that world. Never dawn. No one who had ever visited Twilight would think its dimness heralded anything but night. The people who lived there were strong and solemn, even confronting disaster. On Twilight she had seen grief, death, loss, but never panic or despair.

Laenea introduced herself and offered the young man a place nearer her own. He moved closer, reticent. "I am Radu Dracul," he said.

The name touched a faint note in her memory. She followed it until it grew loud enough to identify. She glanced over Radu Dracul's shoulder, as though looking for someone. "Then — where's Vlad?"

Radu laughed, changing his somber expression for the first time. He had good teeth, and deep smile lines that paralleled the drooping sides of his mustache. "Wherever he is, I hope he stays there."

They smiled together.

"This is your first tour?"

"Is it so obvious that I'm a novice?"

"You're alone," she said. "And you were sleeping."

"I don't know anyone here. I was tired," he said, quite reasonably.

"After a while . . ." Laenea nodded toward a nearby group of people, hyper and shrill on sleep repressors and energizers. "You don't sleep when you're on the ground if there are people to talk to, if there are other things to do. You get sick of sleep, you're scared of it."

Radu stared toward the ribald group that stumbled its way toward the elevator. "Do all of us become like that?"

"Most."

"The sleeping drugs are bad enough. They're necessary — everyone says. But that . . ." He shook his head slowly. His forehead was smooth except for two vertical lines that appeared between his eyebrows when he frowned; it was below his cheekbones, to the square corner of his jaw, that his skin was scarred.

"No one will force you," Laenea said. She was tempted to touch him; she would have liked to stroke his face from temple to chin, and smooth a lock of hair rumpled by sleep. But he was unlike other people she had met, whom she could touch and hug and go to bed with on short acquaintance and mutual whim. Radu had about him something withdrawn and protected, almost mysterious, an invisible wall that would only be strengthened by an attempt, however gentle, to broach it. He carried himself, he spoke, defensively.

"But you think I'll choose it myself."

"It doesn't always happen," Laenea said, for she felt he

needed reassurance; yet she also felt the need to defend herself and her former colleagues. "We sleep so much in transit, and it's such a dark time, it's so empty . . ."

"Empty? Don't you dream?"

"No, never."

"I always do," he said. "Always."

"I wouldn't have minded transit time so much if I'd ever dreamed."

Understanding drew Radu from his reserve. "I can see how it might be."

Laenea thought of all the conversations she had had with all the other crew she had known. The silent emptiness of their sleep was the single constant of all their experiences. "I don't know anyone else like you. You're very lucky."

A tiny luminous fish nosed up against the sea wall. Laenea reached out and tapped the glass, leading the fish in a simple pattern drawn with her fingertip.

"I'm hungry," she said abruptly. "There's a good restaurant in the point stabilizer. Will you join me?"

"A restaurant — where people . . . buy food?"

"Yes."

"I am not hungry."

He was a poor liar; he hesitated before the denial, and he did not meet Laenea's gaze.

"What's the matter?"

"Nothing." He looked at her again, smiling slightly. That at least was true; he was not worried.

"Are you going to stay here all night?"

"It isn't night, it's nearly morning."

"A room's more comfortable — you were asleep."

He shrugged; she could see she was making him uneasy. She realized he must not have any money.

"Didn't your credit come through?" she asked. "That happens all the time. I think chimpanzees write the bookkeeping programs." She had gone through the red tape and annoyance of emergency credit several times when her transfers were misplaced or miscoded. "All you have to do — "

"The administrators made no error in my case."

Laenea waited for him to explain or not, as he wished. Suddenly he grinned, amused at himself but not self-deprecating. He looked even younger than he must be, when he smiled like that. "I'm not used to using money for anything but . . . unnecessaries."

"Luxuries?"

"Yes. Things we don't often use on Twilight, things I don't need. But food, a place to sleep — " He shrugged again. "They are always freely given, on colonial worlds. When I got to earth, I forgot to arrange a credit transfer. I know better." He was blushing faintly. "I won't forget again. I miss a meal and one night's sleep — I've missed more on Twilight, when I was doing real work. In a few hours I correct my error."

"There's no need to go hungry now," Laenea said. "You can — "

"I respect your customs," Radu said. "But my people prefer not to borrow and we never take what is unwillingly given."

Laenea stood up and held out her hand. "I never offer unwillingly. Come along."

His hand was warm and hard, like polished wood.

2

AT THE TOP of the elevator shaft, Laenea and Radu stepped out into the middle of the night. It was foggy and luminous, sky and sea blending into uniform gray beneath the brilliant moon. No wind revealed the surface of the sea or the limits of the fog, but the air was cold. Laenea swung the cloak around them both. A light rain, almost invisible, drifted down, beading mistily in tiny brilliant drops on the black velvet and on Radu's hair. He was silver and gold in the artificial light.

"It's like Twilight now," he said. "It rains like this in the winter." He stretched out his arm, with the black velvet draping down like quiescent wings, opened his palm to the rain, and watched the minuscule droplets touch his fingertips. Laenea could tell from the yearning in his voice, the wistfulness, that he was painfully, desperately homesick. She said nothing, for she knew from experience that nothing could be said to help. The pain faded only with time and fondness for other places. Earth as yet had given Radu no cause for fondness. But now he stood gazing into the fog, as though he could see continents, or stars. She slipped her arm around his shoulders in a gesture of comfort.

"Let's walk to the point." Laenea had been enclosed in testing and training rooms and hospitals as he had been confined in ships and quarantine: She, too, felt the need for fresh air and rain and the ocean's silent words.

The sidewalk followed the edge of the port. A rail separated it from a drop of ten meters to the sea. Incipient waves caressed the metal cliff obliquely and slid away into the darkness. Laenea and Radu walked slowly along, matching strides. Every few paces their hips brushed together. Laenea glanced at Radu occasionally and wondered how she could have thought him anything but beautiful. Her heart circled slowly in her breast, low pitched, relaxing, and her perceptions faded from fever clarity to misty dark and soothing. A veil seemed to surround and protect her. She became aware that Radu was gazing at her, more than she watched him. The cold touched them through the cloak, and they moved closer together; it seemed only sensible for Radu to put his arm around her, too, and so they walked, clasped together.

"Real work," Laenea said thoughtfully.

"Yes . . . hard work, with hands or mind." He picked up the second possible branch of their previous conversation without hesitation. "We do the work ourselves. Twilight is too new for machines — they evolved here, and they aren't as adaptable as people."

Laenea, who had endured unpleasant situations in which machines did not perform as intended, understood what he meant. Methods older than automation were more economical on new worlds where the machines had to be designed from the beginning but people only had to learn. Evolution was as good an analogy as any.

"Crewing's work. Maybe it doesn't strain your muscles, but it is work."

"One never gets tired. Physically or mentally. The job has no challenges."

"Aren't the risks enough for you?"

"Not random risks," he said. "It's like gambling."

His background made him a harsh judge, harshest with himself.

"It isn't slave labor, you know. You could quit and go home."

"I wanted to come — " He cut off the protest. "I thought it would be different."

"I know," Laenea said. "You think it will always be exciting, but after a while all that's left is a dull kind of danger."

"I did want to visit other places. To be like — in that I was selfish."

"Ahh, stop. Selfish? No one would do it otherwise."

"Perhaps not. But I had a different vision. I remembered . . ." Again he stopped himself in midsentence.

"What?"

He shook his head. "Nothing." All his edges hardened again. "We spend most of our time carrying trivial cargoes for trivial reasons to trivial people."

"The trivial cargoes pay for the emergencies," Laenea said.

"That isn't true!" Radu said sharply, then, in a more moderate tone, "The transit authority allows its equipment to be used for emergencies, but they're paid for it, never doubt that."

"I suppose you're right," Laenea said. "But that's the way it's always been."

"It isn't right," he said. "On Twilight . . ." He went no further.

"You're drawn back," Laenea said. "More than anyone I've known before. It must be a comfort to love a place so much."

At first he tensed, as if he were afraid she would mock or chide him for weakness, or laugh at him. When, instead, she smiled, his wariness decreased. "I feel better, after flights when I dream about home."

If Laenea had still been crew she would have envied him his dreams.

"Is it your family you miss?"

"I have no family — I still miss them sometimes, but they're gone."

"I'm sorry."

"You couldn't know," he said quickly, almost too quickly, as though he might have hurt her rather than the other way around. "The epidemic killed them."

Laenea tightened her arm around his shoulder in silent comfort. She regretted her thoughtless question. She should have expected that Radu had lost family and friends during Twilight's plague.

"I don't know what it is about Twilight that binds us all," Radu said. "I suppose it must be the combination — the challenge and the result. Everything is new. We try to touch the world gently. So many things could go wrong."

He glanced at her, the blue of his eyes deep as a mountain lake, his face solemn in its strength, asking without words a question Laenea did not understand.

They walked for a while in silence.

The cold air entered Laenea's lungs and spread through her chest, her belly, arms, legs . . . she imagined that the machine was cold metal, sucking the heat from her as it circled in its silent patterns. She was tired.

"What's that?"

She glanced up. They were near the midpoint of the port's edge, approaching lights that shone vaguely through the fog. The amorphous pink glow resolved itself into separate globes and torches. Laenea noticed a high metallic hum. Within two paces the air cleared.

The tall frames of fog-catchers reared up in concentric circles that led inward to the lights. Touched by the wind, the long wires vibrated. Touched by the wires, the fog condensed. Water dripped from wires' tips to the platform. The intermittent sound of heavy drops on metal, like rain, provided irregular rhythm for the faint music.

"Just a party," Laenea said. The singing, glistening wires formed a multilayered curtain, each layer transparent but in combination translucent and shimmering. Laenea moved between them, but Radu, hanging back, slowed her.

"What's the matter?"

"I don't wish to go where I haven't been invited."

"You are invited. We're all invited. Would you stay away from a party at your own house?"

"I don't understand what you mean."

Laenea remembered her own days as a novice on the crew. Becoming used to one's new status took time.

"They come to the port because of us," Laenea said. "They come hoping we'll stop and talk to them, and eat their food and drink their liquor." She gestured — it was meant to be a sweeping movement, but she stopped her hand before the apex of its arc, flinching at the strain on her cracked ribs — toward the party, lights and tables, a tasseled pavilion, the fog-catchers, the people in evening costume, the servants and machines. "Why else come here? Why else bring all this here? They could be on a tropical island or under the redwoods. They could be on a mountaintop or on a desert at dawn. But this is where they've chosen to be, and I assure you they'll welcome us."

"You know the customs," Radu said, if a little doubtfully.

When they passed the last ring of fog-catchers the temperature began to rise. The warmth was a great relief. Laenea let the damp velvet cape fall away from her shoulders, and Radu did the same. A very young man, still a boy really, smooth-cheeked and wide-eyed, approached and offered to take the cloak. He saw the tip of the scar between Laenea's breasts and stared at her in curiosity and admiration. "Pilot . . ." he said. "Welcome, pilot."

"Thank you. Whose gathering is this?"

The boy, now speechless, glanced over his shoulder and gestured.

Kathell Stafford glided toward them, followed by her white tiger.

Gray streaked Kathell's hair, like the silver thread woven into her silk gown. Veins glowed blue beneath her light brown skin.

"I'm flattered that you came," she said. "I heard you were in training."

Laenea heard in Kathell's voice the same tone that had been in the shopkeeper's, a note of awe and deference. She grasped Kathell's hands.

"I'm just the same," she said. "I haven't changed."

Kathell's tiny, fragile hands trembled in Laenea's strong grip.

"But you have," she said. "You're a pilot now."

Discomforted, Laenea let her go.

The other guests, quick to sense novelty, began to drift nearer, most seeming to have no particular direction in mind. Laenea had seen all the ways of approaching crew or pilots: the shyness or bravado or undisguised awe of children; the unctuous familiarity of some adults; the sophisticated nonchalance of the rich.

Laenea recognized few of the people clustering behind Kathell. She stood looking out at them, down a bit on most, and she almost wished she had led Radu around the fog-catchers instead of between them. She did not feel ready for the effusive greetings offered pilots; they were, for Laenea, as yet unearned. The guests outshone her in every way, in beauty, in dress, in knowledge; yet they wanted her, they needed her, to touch what was denied them.

She could see the passage of time, one second after another, that quickly, in their faces. Quite suddenly she was overcome by pity.

Kathell introduced them all to her. Laenea would not remember one name in ten. Radu stood alone, slightly separated from her by the crowd, half a head taller than any of the others. Someone handed Laenea a glass of champagne. People clustered around her, waiting for her to talk. She found that she had no more to say to them than to those she left behind in the crew. She smiled, doubting that the expression masked her unease.

A man came up to her and shook her hand. "I've always wanted to meet an Aztec . . ."

His voice trailed off at Laenea's frown. She did not want to be churlish, so she put aside her annoyance. "Just 'pilot,' please."

"But Aztecs — "

"The Aztecs sacrificed their captives' hearts," Laenea said. "We aren't captives, and we certainly don't feel we've made a sacrifice."

She turned away, ending the conversation before he could press forward with a witty comment. Laenea shivered and wished away the dense crowd of rich, free, trapped human beings. She wanted quiet and solitude.

Suddenly Radu was near. Laenea grasped his outstretched hand. He said something to Kathell, which the ringing in Laenea's ears blocked out. Kathell nodded and led the way through the crowd. The guests parted like water for Kathell. For Kathell and her tiger, but Kathell was in front. Laenea and Radu followed in her wake. They moved through regions of fragrances: mint, carnation, pine, musk, orange blossom. The boundaries were sharp between the odors.

They entered the pavilion. Radu pulled the front flap closed before anyone else could follow. Laenea immediately felt warmer. The temperature was probably the same outside in the open party, but the luminous tent walls made her feel enclosed and protected from the cold vast currents of the sea.

She sat gratefully in a soft chair. The white tiger laid his chin on her knee and she stroked his huge head.

Kathell took the empty champagne glass and gave Laenea a different drink. Laenea sipped it: warm milk punch. A hint that she should be in bed.

"I just got out of the hospital," she said. "I guess I overdid it a little. I'm not used to — " She gestured with her free hand, meaning: everything. My new body, being outside and free again, Radu. Her vision began to blur, so she closed her eyes.

"Stay awhile," Kathell said.

Laenea did not try to answer; she was too comfortable, too sleepy. She slowed her heart and relaxed the arterial constricting muscles. Blood flowing through the dilated capillaries made her blush, and she felt warmer.

Laenea thought Kathell said more, but the words drowned in the murmur of muffled voices, wind, and sea. She felt only the softness of the cushions beneath her, the warm fragrant air, and the fur of the white tiger.

Time passed, how much or at what rate Laenea had no idea. She slept gratefully and unafraid, deeply, dreaming, and hardly roused when she was moved. She muttered something and was reassured, but never remembered the words, only the tone. Wind and cold touched her and were shut out. She felt a slight acceleration. Then she slept again.

Orca felt tired after the long swim from Harmony to the spaceport. She swam into the ferry dock, pausing where water and air and the metal ramp intersected. The air world began to come back to her. Her metabolism slowed and she felt chilly. She never noticed the cold, deep in the sea.

She stood and shook the water from her short, pale hair. She had arrived just ahead of a ferry. Its sails furled softly and its hull sighed as it settled lower in the water. Orca hurried toward the deck. Swimmers, even divers, were not supposed to come on board this way, but her people used the pier as if it had been built for them. They stayed out of the way of arriving and departing ferries, but that was only common sense.

Whenever the port authorities roused themselves to complain, the divers' council renewed its application to build an underwater hatchway in their quarters in the stabilizer shaft. The fight over the permits had been going on for years. For herself, Orca ignored the dispute and came on board whatever way was most convenient at the time, whether it was ferry dock or access ladder or a fishing pier's elevator.

The afternoon breeze slapped small waves against the sides of the port and dried the droplets of water clinging to the fine hair on Orca's arms and legs. She stretched, spreading her webbed hands to the sun.

She was well clear of the ramp by the time the ferry eased

away. Naked and barefoot she padded into the blockhouse and pushed the button for the elevator. It was midafternoon, so quite a few people were around. Port workers and other crew members found the sight of an unclothed diver unremarkable, but some of the tourists stopped and stared. Orca ignored them. The only way to get from the surface of the port to divers' quarters was to use the elevator, and the only way to get to the elevator was to cross areas frequented by the public. Orca was not about to wear a wet suit, or anything else, on a long-distance swim. For a diver, the idea was ridiculous.

Sometimes a tourist complained to the port authority, and the port authority complained to the divers' council. The council considered the objection gravely — and renewed the application for the underwater entrance. By this time, the sequence was practically a game.

Public nudity never bothered Orca. She knew some people objected, but she found their reasons absurd. She had worn nothing more concealing than a knife belt until she was thirteen years old and taking her first trip into the human world. It had taken her years to get used to clothing. Even now she wore clothes more as decoration than as covering.

The elevator arrived and Orca entered the cage. She was anxious to get to divers' quarters. She was famished. She wanted half a kilo of broiled salmon and some French pastries. Coming across from the mainland, the fishing had been terrible. She had heard reports of several shoals of fish, but they were all well off a direct course to the port.

Now that her metabolism had slowed to surface normal, Orca felt chilly in the air conditioning. Gooseflesh hardened her nipples. She folded her arms across her small breasts.

Ever since she had left the water, her message signal had been glowing, a pinpoint of light just behind her eyes. Granting acceptance, she received the messages through her internal communicator. They scrolled across a screen she imagined in her mind, and she scanned each one quickly.

A note from a friend pleased her; junk announcements broadcast to everyone on the port irritated her. She killed each one as soon as she had read far enough to identify it. The people who wrote them got cleverer and cleverer. Orca's message bank contained a strong filter that was meant to discard most advertising and other solicitations. Some of the circulars had confused the program enough to make it let them through. Orca would have to rewrite it and strengthen its criteria. The escalation never ended.

One message made her angry: "The pilot selection committee has scheduled an appointment . . ."

Oh, leave me alone, she thought without transmitting. She signaled the message bank to kill that note, too. The administrators thought she would make a good pilot. She was tired of declining their invitations; now she simply ignored them. She wished she could filter them, but refusing messages from one's employer was not the most politic thing to do.

She was tired of being tempted. And she *was* tempted, she never denied that.

Orca could be on the crew and remain a diver. She doubted, though, that a pilot would still be capable of withstanding the physical stress a diver needed to take. Since no diver had ever become a pilot, the administrators could only offer Orca guesses and simulations about whether a mechanical heart would tolerate deep dives. Their guess was that it would fail, and Orca's guess was that they were right. She chose to remain as she was, and she wished they would stop trying to change her mind for her.

The elevator stopped at the divers' floor, the doors opened, and Orca stepped out into the foyer. The carpet was soft against her bare toes. She fetched some clothes from the locker room, left the clothing and her knife in an empty bedroom, and wandered down to the kitchen. A friend of hers, a member of another diving family, sat at the table munching on a sandwich and watching TV, an old flat-screen rerun.

"Hi, Gray."

"Hi," he said with his mouth full.

Orca liked Gray. He was quite beautiful, too. He was taller than average for a diver. His eyes were pale green, and he wore his sunstreaked brown hair unfashionably long, tied

at the nape of his neck with a silver ribbon. Orca felt a familiar and pleasant surge of sexual desire. Whenever two
families of divers met, it was the custom for the young adults
to go off in a group and play. The custom continued out here,
when divers from different families visited the spaceport.

Orca could imagine Gray's hair fanned out against a pillow,
or drifting loose in the water.

She pulled a couple of salmon steaks out of the refrigerator,
slapped them on the grill, opened a bottle of champagne,
poured herself a mugful, and sat down. "Can I have a bite?"

Gray grinned and handed her half his sandwich. "Anybody who would drink champagne out of a mug *ought* to
have peanut butter and jelly as an appetizer."

She took a bite of his sandwich and a sip of the champagne.
"Not bad." She offered him the mug. "Want to try it?"

He shook his head. "*Man from Atlantis* is on in a minute."

"Oh yeah? Which one is it?"

"The one with the giant flying octopus."

Orca refilled her mug, flipped the salmon to grill on the
other side, and settled down to watch the ancient show. It
had been filmed before any divers existed, and it had everything wrong. Orca loved it. She had never met a diver who
did not enjoy it, except her father, who considered watching
it to be insufficiently dignified and politically incorrect. When
they projected it underwater the cousins sometimes joined in
watching, but their reaction was one of bemusement.

"He *is* pretty," she said during a pause in the dialogue,
when Mark Harris, the hero, was persuading the giant flying
octopus not to help Mr. Schubert, the villain, take over the
world, and the giant flying octopus was sending small
squeaky noises of affection toward Mark Harris.

Orca liked the episodes in which Mr. Schubert appeared
much better than those in which the Navy demanded that
Mark Harris perform some military task, and he unquestion-
ingly obeyed. When they were little, Orca and her brother
had made up stories in which Mark Harris told the military
what it could do with its silly plots, then swam away and
conducted guerrilla warfare against the landers until he had

freed all the imprisoned cetaceans, scuttled all the whaling ships, and mobilized public opinion to ban propellor-driven craft so the sea regained its peace. That matched her people's history more closely. But even as a child she had forgiven Mark Harris for failing to accomplish all those tasks. Unlike the real divers, he was all alone.

Orca slid her salmon off the grill onto a plate and settled down to eat in front of the TV. She took a sip of champagne, savoring the bubbles that sent the alcohol straight to her head. *The Man from Atlantis* was best watched slightly drunk.

"Want to sleep in my room tonight?" she said to Gray.

"Sure," he said, and speared a bite of her fish.

Laenea half woke, warm, warm to her center. A recent dream swam into her consciousness and out again, leaving no trace but the memory of its passing. She closed her eyes and relaxed, to remember it if it would come, but she could recall only that it was a dream of piloting a ship in transit. The details she could not perceive. Not yet. She was left with a comfortless excitement that upset her drowsiness. Her heart purred fast and seemed to give off heat, though that was as impossible as that it might chill her blood.

The room around her was dim. All she could tell about it was that it was outside the hospital. The smells were neither astringent antiseptics nor cloying drugs, but faint perfume. Silky cotton rather than coarse synthetics surrounded her. Between her eyelashes reflections glinted from the ceiling. She must be in Kathell's apartment in the point stabilizer.

She pushed herself up on her elbows. Her ribs creaked like old parquet floors, and deep muscle aches spread from the center of her body to her shoulders, her arms, her legs. She made a sharp sound, more surprise than pain. She had driven herself too hard; she needed rest, not activity. She let herself sink slowly down into the big red bed, closing her eyes and drifting back toward sleep. She heard the rustling of two different fabrics sliding one against the other.

"Are you all right?"

The voice would have startled her if she had not been so nearly asleep again. She opened her eyes and found Radu standing near, his jacket unbuttoned, a faint sheen of sweat on his bare chest and forehead. The concern on his face matched the worry in his voice.

Laenea smiled. "You're still here." She had assumed without thinking that he had gone on his way, to see and do all the interesting things that attracted visitors on their first trip to earth.

"Yes," he said. "Of course."

"You could have gone . . ." But she wanted him to stay.

His hand on her forehead felt cool and soothing. "I think you have a fever. Is there someone I should call?"

Laenea thought about her body for a moment, lying still and making herself receptive to its signals. Her heart was spinning much too fast. She calmed and slowed it, wondering again what adventure had occurred in her dream. Nothing else was amiss. Her lungs were clear, her hearing sharp. She slid her hand between her breasts to touch the scar: smooth and body temperature, no infection.

"I overtired myself," she said. "That's all . . ." Sleep was overtaking her again, but she said, drowsily and curiously, "Why did you stay?"

"Because," he said slowly, sounding very far away, "I wanted to stay with you. I remember you . . ."

She wished she knew what he was talking about, but at last sleep was the stronger lure.

Radu sat on the edge of the bed and brushed a lock of Laenea's hair from her forehead. She remained soundly asleep. He was glad she had wakened, though, however briefly, for he had been getting worried. Since Kathell's aide brought them here, Laenea had barely moved.

Radu had barely moved, himself, since putting her to bed. Now that he knew she would be all right, he stood and stretched. The enormous bedroom was more than spacious enough to walk around in, but Radu wanted to let Laenea sleep undisturbed. He opened the door. The hallway was deserted.

The apartment was so large he had to be careful to keep his bearings. He paused before a wall of photographs: Kathell's crippled white tiger, signed portraits, a small airship. Her blimp's envelope was gold, its gondola black. It was a far cry from the patched and ancient craft Radu used to fly on Twilight, but the picture brought back pleasant memories. That summer, the year before the plague, had been the happiest of his life. At fifteen he had had the responsibility for the airship for a whole season. He had traveled all over the western continent, freer than he had ever been before or since, even on the starship crew. He wondered if Laenea liked blimps.

He looked around the apartment for a while longer, but found no one to talk to. Surrounded by unrelenting luxury, he felt uncomfortable. He returned to Laenea's room, sat near her bed, and waited.

When Laenea woke again, she woke completely. The aches and pains had faded in the night — or in the day, for she had no idea how long she had slept, or even how late at night or early in the morning she had visited Kathell's party.

She was in her favorite room in Kathell's apartment, one gaudier than the others. Though Laenea did not indulge in much personal adornment, she liked the scarlet and gold of the room, its intrusive energy, its Dionysian flavor. Even the aquaria set in the walls were inhabited by fish gilt with scales and jeweled with luminescence. Laenea felt the honest glee of compelling shapes and colors. She sat up and threw off the blankets, stretching and yawning in pure animal pleasure. Then, seeing Radu asleep, sprawled in the red velvet pillow chair, she fell silent, surprised, not wishing to wake him. She slipped quietly out of bed, pulled a robe from the closet, and padded into the bathroom.

After she had bathed, she felt comfortable and able to breathe properly for the first time since her operation. She had removed the strapping in order to shower, and as her cracked ribs hurt no more free than bandaged, she did not bother to replace the tape.

Back in the bedroom, Radu was awake.

"Good morning."

"It's not quite midnight," he said, smiling.

"Of what day?"

"You slept what was left of last night and all today."

"Where's Kathell?"

"I don't know. Her party was being packed up to go somewhere else. She said you were to stay here as long as you liked."

Laenea knew people who would have done almost anything for Kathell, yet she knew no one of whom Kathell had ever asked a favor. This puzzled her.

"How in the world did you get me here? Did I walk?"

"We didn't want to wake you. We cleared one of the large serving carts and lifted you onto it and pushed you here."

Laenea laughed. "You should have folded a flower in my hands and pretended you were at a wake."

"Someone did make that suggestion."

"I wish I hadn't been asleep — I would have liked to see the expressions of the grounders when we passed."

"Your being awake would have spoiled the illusion," Radu said.

Laenea laughed again, and this time he joined her.

As usual, clothes of all styles and sizes hung in the large closets. Laenea ran her hand across a row of garments, stopping when she touched a pleasurable texture. The first shirt she found near her size was deep green velvet with bloused sleeves. She slipped it on and buttoned it up to her breastbone.

"I still owe you a restaurant meal," she said to Radu.

"You owe me nothing at all," he said, much too seriously.

She buckled her belt with a jerk and shoved her feet into her boots, annoyed. "You don't even know me, but you stayed with me and took care of me for the whole first day of your first trip to earth. Don't you think I should — don't you think it would be friendly for me to give you a meal?" She glared at him. "Willingly?"

He hesitated, startled by her anger. "I would find great

pleasure," he said slowly, "in accepting that gift." He met Laenea's gaze, and when it softened he smiled again. Laenea's exasperation melted and flowed away.

"Come along, then," she said to him for the second time. He rose from the pillow chair, quickly and awkwardly. None of Kathell's furniture was designed for a person his height or Laenea's. She reached to help him; they joined hands.

The point stabilizer was itself a complete city in two parts: one, a blatant tourist world, the second, a discrete permanent supporting society. Laenea often experimented with restaurants here, but this time she went to one she knew well. Experiments in the point were not always successful. Quality spanned as wide a spectrum as culture.

Marc's had been fashionable a few years before, and now was not, but its proprietor seemed unaffected by cycles of fashion. Pilots or princes, crew members or diplomats could come and go; if Marc minded, he never said so. Laenea led Radu into the dim foyer of the restaurant and touched the signal button. In a few moments an area before them brightened into a pattern like oil paint on water.

"Hello, Marc," Laenea said.

Only the imperturbable perfection of Marc's voice revealed its artificial nature. At first Laenea had found it discomforting to speak with someone so articulate, but now she unconsciously thought of Marc simply as someone slightly over-concerned with precision.

The display brightened into yellow. "Laenea!" Marc said. "It's good to see you, after so long. And a pilot, now."

"It's good to be here." She drew Radu forward a step. "This is Radu Dracul, of Twilight, on his first earth landing."

"Hello, Radu Dracul. I hope you find us neither too depraved nor too dull."

"Neither one at all," Radu said.

The headwaiter appeared to take them to their table.

"Welcome," Marc said, instead of good-bye, and from drifting blues and greens the image faded to nothingness.

Their table was lit by the reflected blue glow of light diffused into the sea, and the fish groaked at the window like curious hungry urchins.

"Marc has ... an unusual way of presenting himself," Radu said.

"Yes," Laenea said. "He never comes out, no one ever goes in. I don't know why. Some say he was disfigured, some that he has an incurable disease and can never be with anyone again. There are always new rumors. But he never talks about himself and no one would invade his privacy by asking."

"People must have a higher regard for privacy on earth than elsewhere," Radu said drily, as though he had had considerable experience with prying questions.

Now that Laenea thought about it, Marc had never spoken to her until the third or fourth time she had come.

"It's nothing about the people. He protects himself," she said, knowing it must be true.

She handed Radu a menu and opened her own. "What would you like to eat?"

"I'm to choose from this list?"

"Yes."

"And then?"

"And then someone cooks it, then someone else brings it to you."

Radu glanced down at the menu, shaking his head slightly, but he made no comment.

Laenea ordered for them both, for Radu was unfamiliar with the dishes offered.

Laenea tasted the wine. It was excellent; she put down her glass and allowed the waiter to fill it. Radu watched scarlet liquid rise in crystal, staring deep.

"I should have asked if you drink wine," Laenea said. "But do at least try it."

He looked up quickly, his eyes focusing; he had not, perhaps, been staring at the wine, but at nothing, absently. He picked up the glass, held it, sniffed it, sipped from it.

"I see now why we use wine so infrequently at home."

Laenea drank again, and again could find no fault. "Never mind, if you don't like it — "

But he was smiling. "Twilight is renowned for making the worst wine in the settled worlds. I'll have to stop being offended when someone says so, now that I've tasted this."

Laenea smiled and raised her glass to him. She was so hungry that the wine was already making her feel lightheaded. Radu, too, was very hungry, or sensitive to alcohol, for his defenses began to ease. He relaxed; no longer did he seem ready to leap up, grab the waiter by the arm, and ask him why he stayed here, performing trivial services for trivial reasons and trivial people. And though he still glanced frequently at Laenea — watched her, almost — he no longer looked away when their gazes met. She did not find his attention annoying, only inexplicable. She had been attracted to men and men to her many times, and often the attractions coincided. Radu was extremely attractive. But what he felt toward her was obviously something much stronger; whatever he wanted went far beyond sex. Laenea ate in silence, finding nothing, no answers, in the depths of her own wine. The tension rose until she noticed it, peripherally at first, then clearly, sharply, almost as a discrete point separating her from Radu. He sat feigning ease, one arm resting on the table, but his soup was untouched and his hand was clenched into a fist.

"You — " she said finally.

"I — " he began simultaneously.

They both stopped. Radu looked relieved. After a moment Laenea continued.

"You came to see earth. But you haven't even left the port. Surely you had more interesting plans than to watch someone sleep."

He glanced away, glanced back, slowly opened his fist, touched the edge of the glass with a fingertip.

"It's a prying question but I think I have the right to ask it of you."

"I wanted to stay with you," he said slowly, and Laenea remembered those words, in his voice, from her half-dream awakening.

" 'I remember you,' you said."

He blushed, spots of high color on his cheekbones. "I hoped you wouldn't remember that."

"Tell me what you meant."

"It all sounds foolish and childish and romantic."

She raised one eyebrow, questioning.

"For the last day I've felt I've been living in some kind of unbelievable dream..."

"Dream rather than nightmare, I hope."

"You gave me a gift I wished for for years."

"A gift? What?"

"Your hand. Your smile. Your time..." His voice had grown very soft and hesitant again. "When the plague came, on Twilight, all my clan died, eight adults and four other children. I almost died, too..." His fingers brushed his scarred cheek. Laenea thought he was unaware of the habit. "But the medical team came, isolated the cryptovirus, and synthesized a vaccine. I was already sick, but I recovered. The crew of the mercy mission — "

"We stayed several weeks," Laenea said. More details of her single visit to Twilight returned: the settlements near collapse, the desperately ill trying to attend the dying.

"You were the first crew member I ever saw. The first off-worlder. You saved my people, my life — "

"Radu, it wasn't only me."

"I know. I even knew then. It didn't matter. I was sick for so long, and when I came to and knew I would live, it hardly mattered. I was frightened and full of grief and lost and alone. I needed...someone...to admire. And you were there. You were the only stability in my chaos, a hero..." His voice trailed off in uncertainty at Laenea's smile. "This isn't easy for me to say."

Reaching across the table, Laenea grasped his wrist. The beat of his pulse was as alien as flame. She could think of nothing to tell him that would not sound patronizing or parental, and she did not care to speak to him in either guise.

He raised his head and looked at her, searching her face. "I joined the crew because it was what I always wanted to do, after... I hoped I would meet you, but I don't think I ever believed I would. And then I saw you again, and I realized I wanted . . . to be someone in your life. A friend, at best, I hoped. A shipmate, if nothing else. But — you'd become a pilot, and everyone knows pilots and crew stay apart."

"The first ones take pride in their solitude," Laenea said, for Ramona-Teresa's rejection still stung. Then she relented, for she might never have met Radu Dracul if the pilots had accepted her completely. "Maybe they needed it."

Radu looked at her hand on his, and touched his scarred cheek again, as if he could brush the marks away. "I think I've loved you since the day you came to Twilight." He stood abruptly, but withdrew his hand gently. "I should never — "

She rose too. "Why not?"

"I have no right to . . ."

"To what?"

"To ask anything of you. To expect — " Flinching, he cut off the word. "To burden you with my hopes."

"What about my hopes?"

He was silent with incomprehension. Laenea stroked his rough cheek, once when he winced like a nervous colt, and again: The lines of strain across his forehead eased almost imperceptibly. She brushed back the errant lock of dark blond hair. "I've had less time to think of you than you of me," she said, "but I think you're beautiful, and an admirable man."

Radu smiled with little humor. "I'm not thought beautiful on Twilight."

"Then Twilight has as many fools as any other human world."

"You . . . want me to stay?"

"Yes."

He sat down again like a man in a dream.

"Have you contracted for transit again?"

"Not yet," Radu said.

"I have a month before my proving flight." She thought of places she could take him, sights she could show him. "I thought I'd just have to endure the time — " She fell silent, for Ramona-Teresa was standing in the entrance of the restaurant, scanning the room. She saw Laenea and came toward her. Laenea waited, frowning; Radu turned and froze, struck by Ramona's compelling presence: serenity, power, determination. Laenea wondered if the older pilot had relented, but she was no longer so eager to be presented with mysteries, rather than to discover them herself.

Ramona-Teresa stopped at their table, ignoring Radu, or, rather, glancing at him, dismissing him in the same instant, and speaking to Laenea. "They want you to go back."

Laenea had almost forgotten the doctors and administrators, who could hardly take her departure as calmly as did the other pilots. "Did you tell them where I was?" She knew immediately that she had asked an unworthy question. "I'm sorry."

"They always want to teach us that they're in control. Sometimes it's easiest to let them believe they are."

"Thanks," Laenea said, "but I've had enough tests and plastic tubes." She felt very free, for whatever she did she would not be grounded: She was worth too much. No one would even censure her for irresponsibility, for everyone knew pilots were quite perfectly mad.

"Be careful using your credit key."

"All right . . ." One was supposed to be able to keep one's files private, but enough power and money could, without doubt, overcome the safeguards. Laenea wished she had not got out of the habit of carrying cash. "Ramona, do you have any cash? Can you lend me some?"

Now Ramona did look at Radu, critically. "It would be better if you stopped being so willful and came with me."

Radu flushed. She was, all too obviously, not speaking to him.

"No, it wouldn't." Laenea's tone was chill.

The dim blue light glinted silver from the gray in Ramona's hair as she turned back to Laenea and reached into an inner pocket. She handed her a folded sheaf of bills. "You young ones never plan." Ramona-Teresa hesitated, shook her head, and left.

Laenea shoved the money into her pants pocket, annoyed

more because Ramona-Teresa had brought it, assuming she would need it, than because she had had to ask for it.

"She may be right," Radu said slowly. "Pilots, and crew — "

She touched his hand again, rubbing its back, following the strong fine bones to his wrist. "She shouldn't have been so snobbish. We're none of her business."

"She was . . . I never met anyone like her before. I felt as if I were in the presence of someone so different from me — so far beyond — that we couldn't speak together." He grinned, quick flash of strong white teeth behind his shaggy mustache, deep smile lines in his cheeks. "Even if she'd cared to." With his free hand he stroked Laenea's green velvet sleeve. She could feel the beat of his pulse, rapid and upset. As if he had closed an electrical circuit a pleasurable chill spread up Laenea's arm.

"Radu, did you ever meet a pilot, or a crew member, who wasn't different from anyone you had ever met before? I haven't. We all start out that way. Transit didn't change Ramona."

He acquiesced with silence only, no more certain of the validity of her assurance than she was.

"For now it doesn't make any difference anyway," Laenea said.

The unhappiness slipped from Radu's expression, the joy came back, but the uncertainty remained.

They finished their dinner quickly, in expectation, anticipation, paying insufficient attention to the excellent food. Though annoyed that she had to worry about the subject at all, Laenea considered available ways of preserving her freedom.

But the situation was hardly serious; evading the administrators as long as possible was a matter of pride and personal pleasure. "Fools . . ." she muttered.

"They may have a special reason for wanting you to go back," Radu said. Anticipation of the next month flowed through both their minds. "Some problem — some danger."

"They'd've said so."

"Then what do they want?"

"Ramona said it — they want to prove they control us."
She drank the last few drops of her brandy; Radu followed
suit. They rose and walked together toward the foyer. "They
want to keep me packed in foam like an expensive machine
until I can take my ship."

At the front of the restaurant, Laenea reached for Ramona-
Teresa's money.

Marc's image glowed into existence.

"Your dinner's my gift," he said. "In celebration."

She wondered if Ramona had told him of her problem. He
could as easily know from his own sources, or the free meal
might be an example of his frequent generosity. "I wonder
how you ever make a profit, my friend," she said, "but thank
you."

"I overcharge tourists," Marc said, the artificial voice so
smooth that it was impossible to know if he spoke cynically
or sardonically or if he were simply joking.

"I don't know where I'm going next," Laenea told him,
"but are you looking for anything?"

"Nothing in particular," he said. "Pretty things . . ." Silver
swirled across the air, like a miniature snowstorm falling
from a cloudless sky.

"I know."

The corridors dazzled Laenea after the dim restaurant; she
wished for a gentle evening and moonlight. Between cold
metal walls, she and Radu walked close together, warm, arms
around each other. "Marc collects," Laenea said. "We all
bring him things."

" 'Pretty things.' "

"Yes . . . I think he tries to bring the nicest bits of all the
worlds inside with him. I think he creates his own reality."

"One that has nothing to do with ours."

"Exactly."

"That's what they'd do at the hospital," Radu said. "Iso-
late you, and you disagree that that would be valuable."

"Not for me. For Marc, perhaps."

He nodded. "And . . . now?"

"Back to Kathell's, for a while at least." She reached up

and rubbed the back of his neck. His hair tickled her hand. "The rule I disagreed with most was the one that forbade any sex while I was in training."

The smile lines appeared again, bracketing his mouth parallel to his drooping mustache, crinkling the skin around his eyes. "I understand entirely," he said, "why you aren't anxious to go back."

Entering her room in Kathell's suite, Laenea turned on the lights. Mirrors reflected the glow, bright niches among red plush and gold trim. She and Radu stood together on the silver surfaces, hands clasped, for a moment as hesitant as children. Then Laenea turned to Radu, and he to her; they ignored the actions of the mirror figures. Laenea's hands on the sides of Radu's face touched his scarred cheeks; she kissed him once, lightly, again, harder. His mustache was soft and bristly against her lips and her tongue. His hands tightened over her shoulder blades, and moved down. He held her gently. She slipped one hand between their bodies, beneath his jacket, stroking his bare skin, tracing the taut muscles of his back, his waist, his hip. His breathing quickened.

At the beginning nothing was different — but nothing was the same. The change was more important than motions, position, endearments; Laenea had experienced those in all their combinations, content with involvement for a few moments' pleasure. That had always been satisfying and sufficient; she had never suspected the potential for evolution that depended on the partners. Leaning over Radu, with her hair curling down around their faces, looking into his smiling blue eyes, she felt close enough to him to absorb his thoughts and sense his soul. They caressed each other leisurely. Laenea's nipples hardened, but instead of throbbing they tingled. Radu moved against her and her excitement heightened suddenly, irrationally, grasping her, shaking her. She gasped but could not force the breath back out. Radu kissed her shoulder, the base of her throat, stroked her stomach, drew his hand up her side, cupped her breasts.

"Radu — "

Her climax was sudden and violent, a wave contracting all through her as her single thrust pushed Radu's hips down against the mattress. He was startled into a climax of his own as Laenea shuddered involuntarily, straining against him, clasping him to her, unable to catch his rhythm. But neither of them cared.

They lay together, panting and sweaty.

"Is that part of it?" His voice was unsteady.

"I guess so." Her voice, too, showed the effects of surprise. "No wonder they're so quiet about it."

"Does it — is your pleasure decreased?" He was ready to be angry for her.

"No, that isn't it, it's — " She started to say that the pleasure was tenfold greater, but remembered the start of their loveplay, before she had been made aware of just how many of her rhythms were rearranged. The beginning had nothing to do with the fact that she was a pilot. "It was fine." A lame adjective. "Just unexpected. And you?"

He smiled. "As you say — unexpected. Surprising. A little . . . frightening."

"Frightening?"

"All new experiences are a little frightening. Even the very enjoyable ones. Or maybe those most of all."

Laenea laughed softly.

3

LAENEA AND RADU DOZED, wrapped in each other's arms. Laenea's hair curled around to touch the corner of Radu's jaw, and her heel was hooked over his calf. She was content for the moment with silence, stillness, touch. The plague had not scarred his body.

In the aquaria, the fish flitted back and forth beneath dim lights, spreading blue shadows across the bed. Laenea breathed deeply, counting to make the breaths even. Breathing is a response, not a rhythm, a reaction to the build-up of carbon dioxide in blood and brain. Laenea's breathing had to be altered only during transit itself. For now she used it as an artificial rhythm of concentration. Her heart raced with excitement and adrenaline, so she began to slow it, to relax. But something disturbed her control. Her blood pressure slid down slightly, then slid slowly up to a dangerous level. She could hear only the dull ringing in her ears. Perspiration formed on her forehead, in her armpits, along her spine. Her heart had never before failed to respond to conscious control.

Angry, startled, she pushed herself up, flinging back her hair. Radu raised his head, tightening his hand around the point of her shoulder. "What — ?"

He might as well have been speaking underwater. Laenea lifted her hand to silence him.

One deep inhalation, hold; exhale, hold. She repeated the sequence, calming herself, relaxing the voluntary muscles. Her hand fell to the bed. She lay back. Repeat the sequence, and again. Again. In the hospital and since, her control over involuntary muscles had been quick and sure. She began to be afraid, and had to imagine the fear evaporating, dissipating. Finally the arterial muscles began to respond. They lengthened, loosened, expanded. Last, the pump answered her commands, as she recaptured and reproduced the indefinable states of self-control.

When she knew her blood pressure was no longer likely to crush her kidneys or mash her brain, she opened her eyes. Above her, Radu watched, deep lines of worry across his forehead. "Are you — " He was whispering.

She lifted her heavy hand and stroked his face, his eyebrows, his hair. "I don't know what happened. I couldn't get control for a minute. But I have it back now." She drew his hand across her body, pulling him down beside her, and soon they fell asleep.

Later, Laenea took time to consider her situation. Returning to the hospital would be easiest; it was also the least attractive alternative. Remaining free, adjusting without interference to the changes, meeting the other pilots, showing Radu what was to be seen: Outwitting the administrators would be more fun. Kathell had done her a great favor, for without her apartment Laenea would have rented a hotel room. The records would somehow have been made available; a polite messenger would have appeared to ask her respectfully to come along. Should she overpower an innocent hireling and disappear laughing? More likely she would have shrugged and gone. Fights had never given her either excitement or pleasure. She knew what things she would not do, ever, though she did not know what she would do now. She pondered.

"Damn them," she said.

Radu sat down facing her. The couches, of course, were both too low. Radu and Laenea looked at each other across their knees. They both wore caftans, whose colors clashed violently. Radu lay back on the cushions, chuckling. "You look much too undignified for anger."

She leaned toward him and tickled a sensitive place she had discovered. "I'll show you undignified — " He twisted away and batted at her hand, but missed, laughing helplessly. When Laenea relented, she was lying on top of him on the wide, soft couch. Radu unwound from a defensive crouch, watching her warily, laugh lines deep around his eyes and mouth.

"Peace," she said, and held up her hands. He relaxed. Laenea picked up a fold of the material of her caftan and compared it with one of his. "Is anything more undignified than the two of us in colors no hallucination would have — and giggling as well?"

"Nothing at all." He touched her hair, her face. "But what made you so angry?"

"The administrators — their red tape. Their infernal tests." She laughed again, this time bitterly. " 'Undignified' — some of those tests would win on that."

"Aren't they necessary? For your health?"

She told him about the hypnotics, the sedatives, the sleep, the time she had spent being obedient. "Their redundancies have redundancies. If I weren't healthy I'd be out on the street wearing my old heart. I'd be nothing."

"Never that."

But she knew of people who had failed as pilots, who were reimplanted with their own saved hearts, and none of them had ever flown again, as pilots, as crew, as passengers.

"*Nothing.*"

He was shaken by her vehemence. "But you're all right. You're who you want to be and what you want to be."

"I'm angry at inconvenience," she admitted. "I want to be the one who shows earth to you. They want me to spend the next month shuttling from one testing machine to another. And I'll have to, if they find me. My freedom's limited." She felt very strongly that she needed to spend the next month in the real world, neither hampered by experts who knew, truly, nothing, nor misdirected by controlled environments. She did not know how to explain the feeling; she thought it might be one of the things pilots tried to talk about during their hesitant, unsyncopated conversations with their insufficient vocabularies. "Yours isn't, though, you know."

"What do you mean?"

"Sometimes I come back to earth and never leave the port. It's my home. It has everything I want or need. I can easily stay a month and never have to admit receiving a message I don't want." Her fingertips moved back and forth across the ridge of new tissue over her breastbone. Somehow it was a comfort, though the scar was a symbol of what had cut her off from her old friends. She needed new friends now, but she felt it would be stupid and unfair to ask Radu to spend his first trip to earth on an artificial island. "I have to stay here. But you don't. Earth has a lot of sights worth seeing."

He did not answer. Laenea raised her head to look at him. He was intent and disturbed.

"Would you be offended," he said, "if I told you I am not very interested in historical sights?"

"Is that what you really want? To stay with me?"

"Yes. Very much."

Laenea led Radu through the vast apartment to the lowest floor. There, flagstones surrounded a swimming pool formed of intricate mosaic that shimmered in the dim light. This was a grotto, more than a place for athletic events or children's noisy beachball games.

Radu sighed; Laenea brushed her hand across the top of his shoulder, questioning.

"Someone spent a great deal of time and care here," he said.

"That's true." Laenea had never thought of it as the work of someone's hands, individual and painstaking, though of course it was exactly that. But the economic structure of her world was based on service, not production, and she had always taken the results for granted.

They took off their caftans and waded down the steps into body-warm water. It rose smooth and soothing around the persistent soreness of Laenea's ribs.

"I'm going to soak for a while." She lay back and floated, her hair drifting out, a strand occasionally curling back to brush her shoulder, the top of her spine. Radu's voice rumbled through the water, incomprehensible, but she glanced over and saw him waving toward the dim end of the pool. He flopped down in the water and thrashed energetically away, retreating to a constant background noise. All sounds faded, gaining the same faraway quality, like audio slow motion. She urged the tension out of her body through her shoulders, down her outstretched arms, out the tips of spread fingers.

Radu finished his circumnavigation of the pool; he dove under her and the turbulence stroked her back. Laenea let her feet sink to the pool's bottom. She stood up as Radu burst out of the water, a very amateur dolphin, laughing, hair dripping in his eyes. They waded toward each other through the chest-deep water, and embraced. Radu kissed Laenea's throat just at the corner of her jaw. She threw her head back like a cat stretching to prolong the pleasure, moving her hands up and down his sides.

"We're lucky to be here so early," he said softly, "alone before anyone else comes."

"I don't think anyone else is staying at Kathell's right now," Laenea said. "We have the pool to ourselves all the time."

"No one else at all lives here?"

"No, of course not. Kathell doesn't even live here most of the time. She just has it kept ready for when she wants it."

He said nothing, embarrassed by his error.

"Never mind," Laenea said. "It's a natural mistake to make." But it was not, of course, on earth.

Laenea had visited enough new worlds to understand how Radu might be uncomfortable in the midst of the private possessions and personal services available on earth. What impressed him was expenditure of time, for time was the valuable commodity in his frame of reference. On Twilight everyone would have two or three necessary jobs, and none would consist of piecing together intricate mosaics. Everything was different on earth.

They paddled in the shallow end of the pool, reclined on the steps, flicked shining spray at each other. Laenea wanted Radu again. She was completely free of pain for the first time since the operation. That fact began to overcome a certain reluctance she felt, an ambivalence toward her own reactions. The violent change in her sexual responses disturbed her more than she wanted to admit.

And she wondered if Radu felt the same way; she discovered she was afraid he might.

As they lay on the warm flagstones edging the pool, Laenea moved closer and kissed him. He put his arm around her and she slid her hand across his stomach and down to his genitals, somehow less afraid of a physical indication of reluctance than a verbal one. But he responded to her, hardening, drawing circles on her breast with his fingertips, caressing her lips with his tongue. Laenea stroked him from the back of his knee to his shoulder. His body had a thousand textures, muted and blended by the warm water and the steamy air. She pulled him closer, grasping him with her legs. This time Laenea anticipated a long, slow increase of excitement.

"What do you like?" Radu whispered.

"I — I like — I — " Her words changed abruptly to a cry. Her climax again came all at once in a powerful solitary wave. Radu's fingers dug into her shoulders, and Laenea knew her short nails were cutting his back. Radu must have expected the intensity of Laenea's orgasm, but the body is slower to learn than the mind. He followed her to climax almost instantly. Trembling against him, Laenea exhaled in a long shudder. She could feel Radu's stomach muscles quivering.

Laenea enjoyed taking time over sex, and she suspected that Radu did as well. Yet she felt exhilarated. Her thoughts about Radu were bright in her mind, but she could put no words to them. Instead of speaking she laid her hand on the side of his face, fingertips at the temples, the palm of her hand against the scars. He no longer flinched when she touched him there. He covered her hand with his own.

He had about him a quality of constancy, of dependability and calm, that Laenea had never before encountered. His admiration for her was of a different sort entirely from what she was used to: grounders' lusting after status and vicarious excitement. Radu had seen her and stayed with her when she was helpless and ordinary and as undignified as a human being can be; that had not changed his feelings. Laenea did not understand him yet.

They toweled each other dry. Radu had scraped his hip on the pool's edge, and Laenea had raked long scratches down his back.

"I wouldn't have thought I could do that," she said, glancing at her hands. She kept her nails cut to just above the quick. "I'm sorry."

Radu reached around to dry her back. "I did the same to you."

"Really?" She looked over her shoulder. The angle was wrong to see anything, but she could feel places stinging. "We're even, then." She grinned. "I never drew blood before."

"Nor I."

They dressed in clean clothes from Kathell's wardrobe and went walking through the multileveled city. It was, as Radu had said, very early. Above on the sea it would be close to dawn. Below only street cleaners and delivery carts moved here and there across a mall. Laenea was more accustomed to the twenty-four-hour crew city in the third stabilizer.

She was getting hungry enough to suggest a shuttle trip across to #3 where everything would be open, when ahead they saw waiters arranging the chairs of sidewalk cafés, preparing for business.

"Seven o'clock," Radu said. "That's early to be open around here, it seems."

"I thought you said you didn't have a communicator."

"I don't."

"Then how do you know what time it is?" Laenea glanced around for a clock, but none was in sight.

He shrugged. "I don't know how, but I always know."

"Twilight's day isn't even standard."

"I had to convert for a while, but now I have both times." He shrugged. "It's just a trick."

"Useful, though."

A waiter ushered them to a table. They breakfasted and talked, telling each other about their home worlds and the places they had visited. Radu had been to three other planets before earth. Lacnea knew two of them, from several years before. They were colonial worlds, which had grown and changed since her visits.

Laenea and Radu compared impressions of crewing, she still fascinated by the fact that he dreamed.

She found herself reaching out to touch his hand, to emphasize a point or for the sheer simple pleasure of contact. He did the same, but they were both right-handed. Flowers occupied the middle of the table and kept getting in their way. Finally Laenea picked up the vase and moved it to one side, and she and Radu held hands across the table.

"Where do you want to go next?"

"I don't know. I haven't thought about it. I still have to go where they tell me to, when there's a need."

"I just . . ." Laenea's voice trailed off. Radu glanced at her quizzically, and she shook her head. "It sounds ridiculous to start talking already about tomorrow or next month or next year . . . but it seems all right — it seems like I should."

"I feel . . . the same."

They sat in silence, drinking coffee. Radu's hand tightened on hers. "What are we going to do?" For a moment he looked young and lost. "I haven't earned the right to make my own schedules yet."

"I have," Laenea said. "Except for emergencies. That will help." She smiled. "Besides," she said, "we have a month. A month not to worry."

Laenea yawned as they entered the front room of Kathell's apartment. "I don't know why I'm so sleepy." She yawned again, trying to stifle it, failing. "I slept the clock around, and now I want to sleep again — after what? Half a day?" She kicked off her boots.

"Eight and a half hours," Radu said. "Somewhat busy hours, though."

She smiled. "True." She yawned a third time, jaw hinges cracking. "I've got to take a nap."

Radu followed as she padded through the hallway, down the stairs to her room. The bed was made, turned down on both sides. The clothes Laenea and Radu had arrived in were clean and pressed. They hung in the dressing room along with the cloak, which no longer smelled musty. Laenea brushed her fingers across the velvet.

Radu looked around. "Who did this?"

"What? Straightened the room? The people Kathell hires. They look after whoever stays here."

"Do they hide?"

Laenea laughed. "No — they'll come if we need them. Do you want something?"

"No," he said sharply. "No," more gently. "Nothing."

Still yawning, Laenea undressed. "What about you, are you wide awake?"

He was staring into a mirror. He started when she spoke, and looked not at her but at her reflection. "I can't usually sleep during the day," he said. "But I am rather tired."

His reflection turned its back; he, smiling, turned toward her.

They were both too sleepy to make love a third time. The amount of energy Laenea had expended astonished her. She thought perhaps she still needed time to recover from the hospital. She and Radu curled together in darkness and scarlet sheets.

"I do feel very depraved now," Radu said.

"Depraved? Why?"

"Sleeping at nine o'clock in the morning? That's unheard of on Twilight." He shook his head; his mustache brushed her shoulder. Laenea drew his arm closer around her, holding his hand in both of hers.

"I'll have to think of some other awful depraved customs to tempt you with," she said sleepily, chuckling, but thought of none just then.

Something startled Laenea awake. She was a sound sleeper and could not think what noise or movement would awaken her when she still felt so tired. Lying very still she listened, reaching for stimuli with all her senses. The lights in the aquaria were out; the room was dark except for the heating coils' bright orange spirals. Bubbles from the aerator, highlighted by the amber glow, rose like tiny half moons through the water.

The beat of a heart pounded through her.

In sleep, Radu still lay with his arms around her. His hand, fingers half curled in relaxation, brushed her left breast. She stroked the back of his hand but moved quietly away from him, away from the sound of his pulse, for it formed the link of a chain she had worked hard and wished long to break.

The second time she woke she was frightened out of sleep, confused, displaced. For a moment she thought she was escaping a nightmare. Her head ached violently from the ringing in her ears, but through the clash and clang she heard Radu gasp for breath, struggling as if to free himself from restraints. Laenea reached for him, ignoring her own racing heart. Her fingers slipped on his sweat. Thrashing, he flung her back. Each breath was agony just to hear. Laenea grabbed his arm when he twisted again, held it down, seized the other flailing hand, partially immobilized him, straddled his hips, held him.

"Radu!"

He did not respond. Laenea called his name again, then shouted for help. She could feel his pulse through both his wrists, and she felt his heart as it pounded, too fast, too hard, irregular and violent.

"Radu!"

He cried out, a piercing and wordless scream.

She whispered his name, no longer even hoping for a response, in helplessness, hopelessness. He shuddered beneath her.

He opened his eyes.

"What . . ."

Laenea remained where she was, leaning over him. He tried to lift his hand. She was still forcing his arms to the bed. She released him and knelt beside him. She, too, was short of breath, and hypertensive to a dangerous degree.

Someone knocked softly on the bedroom door.

"Come in!"

One of the aides entered hesitantly. "Pilot? I thought — pardon me." She bowed and backed out.

"Wait — you did the right thing. Call a doctor immediately."

Radu pushed himself up on his elbows. "No, don't, there's nothing wrong."

The young aide glanced from Laenea to Radu and back at the pilot.

"Are you sure?" Laenea asked.

"Yes." He sat up. Sweat ran in heavy drops down his temples to the edge of his jaw. Laenea shivered; she was sweating, too.

"Never mind, then," Laenea said. "But thank you."

The aide departed.

"Gods, I thought you were having a heart attack." Her pulse began to ease in rhythmically varying rotation. She could feel the blood slow and quicken in her temples, in her throat. She clenched her fists. Her nails dug into her palms.

Radu shook his head. "No, it wasn't illness. As you said — we're never allowed this job if we're not healthy."

"What happened?"

"It was a nightmare." He lay back, his hands behind his head, his eyes closed. "I was climbing, I don't remember what, a cliff or a tree. It collapsed or broke and I fell — a long way. I knew I was dreaming and I thought I'd wake up before I hit, but I fell into a river."

Laenea heard him and remembered what he said, but knew she would have to make sense of the words later. She remained kneeling and slowly unclenched her hands. Blood rushed through her like a funneled tide, high, then low, and back again.

"It had a very strong current that swept me along and pulled me under. I couldn't see banks on either side — not even where I fell from. Logs and trash rushed along beside me and past me, but every time I tried to hold onto something I'd almost be crushed. I got tireder and tireder and the water pulled me under — I needed a breath but I couldn't take one . . . Have you felt the way the body tries to breathe when you can't let it?"

She did not answer, but her lungs burned and her muscles contracted convulsively, trying to clear a way for the air to push its way in.

"Laenea — " She felt him grasp her shoulders: She wanted to pull him closer, she wanted to push him away. Then his touch broke the compulsion of his words and she drew a deep, searing breath.

"What — ?"

"A . . . moment . . ." She managed, finally, to damp the sine-curve velocity of the pump within her. She shivered. Radu pulled a blanket around her. Laenea's control returned slowly, more slowly than any other time she had lost it. She pulled the blanket closer, seeking stability more than warmth. She should not slip like that: Her biocontrol, to now, had always been as close to perfect as anything associated with a biological system could be. But now she felt dizzy and high, hyperventilated, from the needless rush of blood through her brain. She wondered how many millions of nerve cells had been destroyed.

She and Radu looked at each other in silence.

"Laenea..." He still spoke her name as if he were not sure he had the right to use it. "What's happening to us?"

"Excitement — " she said, and stopped. "An ordinary nightmare — " She had never tried to deceive herself before, and found she could not start now.

"It wasn't an ordinary nightmare. You always know you're going to be all right, no matter how frightened you are. This time — until I heard you calling me and felt you pulling me to the surface, I knew I was going to die."

Tension grew: He was as afraid to reach toward her as she was to him. She threw off the blanket and grasped his hand. He was startled, but he returned the pressure. They sat crosslegged, facing each other, hands entwined.

"It's possible..." Laenea said, searching for a way to say this that was gentle for them both, "it's possible... that there is a reason, a real reason, pilots and crew don't mix."

By Radu's expression Laenea knew he had thought of that explanation, too, and only hoped she could think of a different one.

"It could be temporary — we may only need acclimatization."

"Do you really think so?"

She rubbed the ball of her thumb across his knuckles. His pulse throbbed through her fingers. "No," she said, almost whispering. Her system and that of any normal human being would no longer mesh. The change in her was too disturbing, on psychological and subliminal levels, while normal biorhythms were so compelling that they interfered with and would eventually destroy her new biological integrity. "I don't. Dammit, I don't."

Exhausted, they could no longer sleep. They rose in miserable silence and dressed, navigating around each other like sailboats in a high wind. Laenea wanted to touch Radu, to hug him, slide her hand up his arm, kiss him and be tickled by his mustache. Denied any of those, not quite by fear but by reluctance, unwilling either to risk her own stability or to put Radu through another nightmare, she understood for the first time the importance of simple, incidental touch, directed at nothing more important than momentary contact, momentary reassurance.

"Are you hungry?" Isolation, with silence as well, was too much to bear.

"Yes ... I guess so."

But over breakfast (it was, Radu said, evening, so perhaps it was really dinner), the silence fell again. Laenea could not make small talk; if small talk existed for this situation she could not imagine what it might consist of. Radu pushed his food around on his plate and avoided looking at Laenea. His gaze jerked from the sea wall to the table, to some detail of carving on the furniture, and back again.

Laenea ate fruit sections with her fingers. All the previous worries, how to arrange schedules for time together, how to defuse the disapproval of their acquaintances, seemed trivial and frivolous. The only solution now was a drastic one, which she did not feel she could suggest herself. Volunteering to become a pilot might be as impossible for him as returning to normal would be for Laenea. Piloting was a lifetime decision, not a job like crewing that one could take for a few years' travel and adventure.

Radu stood up. His chair scraped against the floor and fell over. Laenea looked up, startled. Flinching, Radu turned, picked up the chair, and set it quietly on its legs again. "I can't think down here," he said. "It never changes." He glanced at the sea wall, perpetual blue fading to blackness. "I'm going out on deck. I need to be outside." He turned toward her. "Would you — "

"I think ..." Wind, salt spray on her face: tempting. "I think we'd each better be alone for a while."

"Yes," he said, with gratitude. "I suppose ..." His voice

grew heavy with disappointment. "You're right." His footsteps were soundless on the thick carpet.

"Radu — "

He turned again, without speaking, as though his barriers were forming around him again, still so fragile that a word would shatter them.

"Never mind . . . just . . . Oh — take my cape if you want, it gets cold on deck at night."

He nodded once, still silent, and went away.

In the pool Laenea swam hard, even when her ribs began to hurt. She felt trapped and angry, with nowhere to run, knowing no one deserved her anger. Certainly not Radu; not the other pilots, who had warned her. Not even the administrators, who in their own misguided way had tried to make her transition as protected as possible. The anger could turn inward, toward her strong-willed stubborn character. But that, too, was pointless. All her life she had made her own mistakes and her own successes, both usually by trying what others said she could not do.

She climbed out of the pool without having tired herself in the least. The warmth had soothed away whatever aches and pains were left. Her energy returned, leaving her restless and snappish. She put on her clothes and left the apartment to walk off her tension until she could consider the problem calmly. But she could not see even an approach to a solution; at least, not to a solution that would be a happy one.

Hours later, when the grounder city had quieted to night, Laenea let herself back into Kathell's apartment. Inside, too, was dark and silent. She could hardly wonder where Radu was; she remembered little enough of what she herself had done since he left. She remembered being vaguely civil to people who stopped her, greeted her, invited her to parties, asked for her autograph. She remembered being less than civil to someone who asked how it felt to be an Aztec. But she did not remember which incident preceded the other or when either had occurred or what she had actually said. She was no closer to an answer than before. Hands jammed into her pockets, she went to the main room, just to sit and stare into the ocean and try to think. She was halfway to the sea wall before she saw Radu, standing silhouetted against the window, dark and mysterious in the black cloak, the blue light glinting ghostly off his hair.

"Radu — "

He did not turn. As her eyes grew more accustomed to the dimness, Laenea saw his breath clouding the glass.

"I applied to pilot training," he said softly, his tone utterly neutral.

Laenea felt a quick flash of joy, then uncertainty, then fear for him. She had been ecstatic when the administrators accepted her for training. Radu did not even smile. Making a mistake in this choice would hurt him more, much more, than even parting forever could hurt both of them.

"What about Twilight?"

"It doesn't matter," he said, his voice unsteady. "They refused" — he choked on the words and forced them out — "they refused me."

Laenea went to him, put her arms around him, turned him toward her. The fine lines around his blue eyes were deeper, etched by distress and failure. She touched his cheek. Embracing her, he bent to rest his forehead on her shoulder. "They said I'd never even make it through the training. I'm bound to our own four dimensions. I'm too dependent . . . on night, day, time . . . My circadian rhythms are too strong. They said . . ." His muffled words became more and more unsure, balanced on a shaky edge. Laenea stroked his hair, the back of his neck, over and over. That was the only thing left to do. There was nothing at all left to say. "If I survived the operation . . . I'd die in transit."

Laenea's vision blurred, and the warm tears slipped down her face. She could not remember the last time she had cried. A convulsive sob shook Radu and his tears fell cool on her shoulder, soaking through her shirt.

"I love you," Radu whispered. "Laenea, I love you."

"Dear Radu, I love you too." She could not, would not, say what she thought: That won't be enough for us. Even that won't help us.

She guided him to a wide low cushion that faced the ocean; she drew him down beside her, neither of them really paying attention to what they were doing, to the cushions too low for them, to anything but each other. Laenea held Radu close. He said something she could not hear.

"What?"

He pulled back and looked at her, his gaze passing rapidly back and forth over her face. "How can you love me? We could only stay together one way, but I failed — " He broke the last word off, unwilling, almost unable, to say it.

Laenea slid her hand from his shoulders down his arms and grasped his hands. "You can't fail at this, Radu. The word doesn't mean anything. You can tolerate what they do to you, or you can't. But there's no dishonor."

He shook his head and looked away.

Laenea wondered if this were the first time he had ever failed at anything important in his life, at anything that he desperately wanted. He was so young . . . too young not to blame himself for what was out of his control. Laenea drew him toward her again and kissed the outer curve of his eyebrow, his high cheekbone. Salt stung her lips.

"We can't — " He pulled back, but she held him.

"I'll risk it if you will." She slipped her hand inside the collar of his shirt, rubbing the tension-knotted muscles at the back of his neck, her thumb on the pulse-point in his throat, feeling it beat through her. He spoke her name so softly it was hardly a sound.

Knowing what to expect, and what to fear, they made love a third, final, desperate time, exhausting themselves against each other beside the cold dark sea.

Radu was nearly asleep when Laenea kissed him and left him, forcibly feigning calm. In her scarlet and gold room she lay on the bed and pushed away every concern but fighting her spinning heart, slowing her breathing. She had not wanted to frighten Radu again, and he could not help her. Her struggle required peace and concentration. What little of either remained in her kept escaping before she could grasp and fix them. They flowed away on the channels of pain, shallow and quick in her head, deep and slow in the small of her back, above the kidneys, spreading all through her lungs. Near panic, she pressed the heels of her hands against her eyes until blood-red lights flashed; she stimulated adrenaline, until excitement pushed her beyond pain, above it.

Instantly she forced an artificial, fragile calmness that glimmered through her like sparks.

Her heart slowed, sped up, slowed, sped (not quite so much this time), slowed, slowed, slowed.

Afraid to sleep, unable to stay awake, she let her hands fall from her eyes, and drifted away from the world.

4

WHEN RADU WOKE, Laenea had gone. He slid his hand across the cushions. The place where she had lain was cold. Radu got up. Slowly, he dressed.

Outside Laenea's room, he hesitated. He opened the door very quietly. Laenea slept soundly, dappled in blue by the light of the aquarium. When she was ill he had sat by her side for hours, watching her sleep, but now he felt like an intruder. In silence, he moved into the room and picked up his duffel bag.

He hesitated, wanting to kiss her one last time, wanting her to awaken and tell him she had magically discovered a way for them to stay together. But there was no point in waking her, no point to prolonging their good-byes. Nothing he and Laenea could say to each other could change anything now. Pilots did not mix with ordinary human beings. Laenea was a pilot, and Radu was an ordinary human being. The documents from the pilot selection committee proved he would never be anything more.

So Radu Dracul closed the door and walked away from Laenea Trevelyan, whom he had known for such a short time yet loved for so long.

He left Kathell Stafford's apartment and entered the elevator. It rose smoothly toward the surface of the sea. No one joined him, for which he was grateful. He felt incapable of even civility, much less conventional social pleasantries.

He felt more alone than he had at any time since Twilight's plague. After it, he had grown so used to being alone that loneliness had ceased to bother him; and he had had his dreams. All that was changed. Reality had overtaken the dreams, fulfilled them, then shattered them completely.

Outside, in the dark, the sea wind caressed Radu's scarred face and ruffled his hair. The smell of rocket fuel tinged the breeze, but not too strongly to destroy its freshness. The tangy and, to him, quite alien winds of earth made him homesick for the deep forests and cloud-laden, crystalline atmosphere of his home world.

He felt he *had* to get away from the spaceport and away from earth.

A tram waited for passengers on the perimeter track, but Radu decided to walk. He had plenty of time to get to the control office before the next shuttle liftoff to Earthstation. He set off down the footpath.

Damp metal surfaces gleamed beneath the powerful lights. Radu moved from areas of harsh illumination toward patches of pure dark grazed by moonlight. He was glad of the long walk. It helped him think — though he knew he would not suddenly come upon some magical idea that would allow him and Laenea to remain lovers. Nothing would help him do that, but walking fast, pushing himself, stretching his muscles, felt far better than sitting at the shuttle gate, waiting and chasing himself in mental circles. Besides, he needed the exercise. He was used to much more physical labor than he ever did as a member of a ship's crew.

He brushed his hand across his hair and his fingers came

away damp with dew or sea spray. That brought him a sudden vivid image of Laenea, her long dark hair glistening as they walked together through the fog, their arms around each other, wrapped in her velvet cape. They had stopped at Kathell Stafford's party —

Radu halted abruptly, blinking, suspecting a hallucination. Kathell had packed up the fog-catchers and gaudy pavilions, her friends, and her servants, and taken the whole party to some other unlikely spot. Yet a single black-and-silver tent, alone and forlorn, still stood on the gray deck. The faint night breeze swayed its heavy fringe.

Radu walked toward the tent. It was real. A silver cord held the front flap open. Inside, Kathell knelt on the satin floor next to her white tiger.

The great creature's rough breathing filled the tent. Radu's shadow fell over Kathell. She looked up.

"Hello, Radu Dracul," she said, without surprise. Radu wondered if anything ever surprised her, or if she had seen and experienced everything he could imagine, and many things he could not.

Radu entered the tent and sat on his heels beside her. She stroked the tiger's shoulder, but it did not respond.

"Why are you out here all alone?" Radu said.

She gestured toward the tiger. "As you see."

"I mean, why didn't you come back to your home?"

"My home?" she said, her voice distracted. "Do you mean the apartment? But I loaned it to you and Laenea."

Her matter-of-fact reply prevented Radu from questioning a statement he thought distinctly odd. He let the subject drop.

"Do you need help?"

Kathell shrugged. "I made everyone else go away, because I didn't want them to have to see him die. But I don't want him to die, either."

Kathell's white tiger was the only member of the species Radu had ever encountered, so when he had first seen it, he assumed its color was normal. Perhaps for that reason he noticed the animal's more serious mutations, while others saw only its unusual coloring. No healthy creature walked as the white tiger did, with poor control of its hind legs and its spine very much too curved; and no carnivore would evolve cross-eyed. To Radu, the tiger was another example of the extravagance of earth, of things valued for their appearance rather than for their usefulness or efficiency. He could not now think of anything to say. His sympathy would sound insincere, for while he was sorry for Kathell's distress he saw no reason to regret her deformed pet's death. Its passing would release it.

The tiger's breathing grew rougher and more labored.

"My friends won't understand," she said. "I could still keep him alive — "

"No, you mustn't!" Radu felt his face and throat color with embarrassment. If she talked herself into keeping the animal alive, what business was it of his? Yet he could not stand the thought that the creature, who should be so magnificent, might be forced to stumble through its life for another year, or two, or ten, because people wanted to absorb its uniqueness.

"I'm sorry," Radu said.

"No," she said. "Don't be. You're right."

The tiger stopped breathing. Radu and Kathell both stared at it. Radu held his breath. All he could hear was the passing of the sea.

The white tiger shuddered and convulsed, jerking its hind feet up against its belly. Foam dripped from its mouth. Then its muscles slackened and it lay motionless. It breathed only intermittently. Kathell did not move or speak while its life was passing. Radu flinched every time the creature gasped for one more straining breath. The intervals lengthened.

The tiger took so long to die that Radu wanted to grab Kathell and shake her and demand that she call a veterinarian, even a doctor, to put the animal out of its pain. But finally, just when he thought he could stand it no longer, Kathell felt for the creature's pulse. She let her hand drop; her shoulders slumped.

"Poor damned thing," she muttered. Her voice shook. Her face was nearly in darkness, but tears glistened on her cheeks.

Radu laid his hand over hers in the comforting, asexual way by which one crew member helped another wake. Kathell stiffened and pulled away. Radu drew back in turn, a little hurt, but embarrassed, too, feeling that she must have mistaken his gesture.

"I'm all right," she said. "I've known long enough that this had to happen." She looked over at him, her movement abrupt. "I shouldn't have let you stay," she said. "I shouldn't have inflicted this on you." She sounded neither regretful nor sad, but angry and frightened. Laenea had said Kathell never asked anything of anyone, but surely she would accept sympathy freely given.

"You've shown me only kindness," he said. "Staying was little enough for me to do."

"I didn't ask you to do anything!" She got up and loosened the tent's heavy satin floor, detaching it from the walls. Radu got up to help, but she motioned him back.

"I'd like to help," he said. "I've taken things from you, it's only fair — "

"If you can't take what I offer without burdening me with gratitude," she said, ripping the last corner from its fastenings, "there's no need for you to take it at all!"

She took a vial from her pocket, opened it, and spilled its contents over the tiger's body. A thin film of dust dulled its coat.

"It's different where I come from," Radu said. "We have to depend on each other more."

She gathered up a corner of the satin. Radu stepped over the edge of the floor and found himself ankle deep in crushed bracken.

"I depend on no one," Kathell said. "I never accept gratitude."

"You'll have to excuse an ignorant barbarian," Radu said with irritation.

Kathell flung the thick material around the tiger's body.

"Nor guilt." Even her tone did not relent. "I don't want your gratitude and you have no right to try to make me feel guilty." She folded her arms. Head down, she gazed at the tiger's shroud.

Speechless, Radu waited beside her, slightly hunched in the low tent. He searched for something to say. The temperature began to rise.

"Come outside," Kathell said.

She led him onto the deck, then turned back to face the tent's dark interior.

Sudden intense flames erupted from the shadowed shroud, spilling down its sides like liquid. The bracken ignited, burning with a dry, harsh crackle. Radu stepped back from the heat, but Kathell did not move. Smoke billowed out, and the tiger's body imploded. The fire died.

The heat faded rapidly; the night breeze dispersed the smoke.

The tent itself remained unscorched. Kathell went back inside and unfolded the satin shroud. In its center lay a scattering of gray dust. She gathered it up in a small cloth bag.

"Go away now." She was shivering. "Go — " The bravado trembled and broke. She turned away, silently crying, fighting for control.

Radu touched her shoulder, brushing the soft fabric of her gown with his fingertips. She flinched away from him, then abruptly flung herself around and against him. Radu held her, stroking her hair and comforting her as he might a child. She felt like a child, she was so small and frail. For a moment he was back on Twilight, hugging his younger sister, who had come to him terrified and ill with the plague's first symptoms. She died the next day. The fear and pain and grief of those terrible weeks returned.

Kathell struggled against every tear she shed. Then, in a change as abrupt as all her other changes, she shrugged Radu's hands from her shoulders and stepped out of his reach. Silhouetted by the light behind her, she wiped her face roughly on her sleeve.

"I told you to leave me alone!" she said, angry and resentful. "I never asked for your help. What do you want?"

Radu shook his head, startled and confused. "I don't want anything."

"I owe you now! I won't leave debts unpaid!"

"I want nothing from you," he said, feeling as if he had given an unwelcome gift, then demanded reciprocation. "You are Laenea's friend, and you were kind to me as well."

"That wasn't kindness," she said sharply. "I didn't even notice it. That has nothing to do with this."

"Nonsense," Radu said. "If you feel that a few minutes of time and sympathy need to be repaid, then *I* am repaying *you.*"

"I don't permit anything I give to be repaid!" she said.

"Then permit me the same courtesy." The conversation had evolved into a strange and disquieting game, which he expected at every move to be ended with Kathell's being convinced that he had no secret motives.

"No," Kathell said. "Courtesy has nothing to do with it. I owe you. I do not like to be in debt. Is that so hard to understand?"

"You are not in my debt," Radu said. He felt as if he had been repeating himself for a long time. "This is trivial. This is silly! Why are you insisting that I demand something of you when I want nothing?"

"Because if once I accept something, I'll never stop!" she shouted. She took one quick step toward him with her fists clenched and her eyes narrowed to slits. "I'll not be accused of that ever again!"

The outburst shocked him. "Who accused you of such a thing? And why would you believe it?"

"You don't know me," Kathell said. "You never will, and gods willing neither will anyone else."

"I ask you to forgive me this debt," Radu said. "That's all I want, for you to believe I want nothing."

"Don't insult me!" she cried. "You're saying my reasons are meaningless and *they are not!*"

Radu reached out to her, in supplication, but she struck his hand away. Angry at her for misunderstanding his motion, Radu stepped back and gradually unclenched his fists.

"I want nothing from you," he said again. "I will accept nothing. I'm leaving earth. With any luck I'll never see it, or you, again." He walked around her, staying well out of reach, to continue on his way.

"I owe you. And I intend to pay you and be done with it."

Radu flushed scarlet in anger and humiliation, but he kept on walking.

"Choose," Kathell said behind him. "And pick something soon, or you'll have made yourself an enemy."

Radu did not look back.

Trams passed him several times, moving silently through the darkness along their magnetic tracks. Toward the center of the spaceport bright lights waxed and waned among clouds of vapor from supercooled fuel.

He was still angry and upset when he reached the control office, which lay nestled in a low complex of buildings at the corner of the landing port. Radu reserved a place on the next shuttle to Earthstation, then requested the transit schedule. Several flights listed crew berths open. As Radu was about to apply to a ship traveling as far as New Snoqualmie, a colony world not unlike Twilight, he noticed the ship was piloted.

He cursed. The last thing Radu wanted right now was to travel in the company of a pilot. But only a few of the available automated ships offered crew positions. Since automated ships still held the numerical majority, this was a fluke, a coincidence of his misfortune.

None of the other destinations particularly appealed to him. Since one of Radu's excuses for leaving Twilight was that his home world needed the foreign exchange he would earn, he chose the automated flight that paid the most. He would crew it on its outbound stops, then, if he could, transfer to another ship traveling even farther. He wanted to travel as close to the limits of explored space as possible. He had applications in for exploratory missions, of course, but so did almost every other crew member he had ever met. They applied out of curiosity, for the excitement, for the money. Radu had very little seniority and it would be quite a while before he could hope to win such an assignment.

Instead of an electronic approval, the response to his query was a personal reply.

"Radu, how are you?" The crew member whose translucent image formed before him was a normal-space navigator with the credentials to prepare an automated ship for transit. Atnaterta looked much older than the last time Radu had seen him. The time since they last had flown together was only a few weeks, for Radu, but might be of much longer subjective duration for Atna. The lines in the navigator's ebony face were more heavily sculpted, and he seemed exhausted in a way that could never be eased by transit sleep. His hair was graying from a black as deep as that of his skin and eyes. Radu trusted his ability and his experience. Most of all he valued his serenity. He was glad to see him.

"I'm fine, Atna." It would be too complicated to reply to a purely social question with the convoluted truth.

Atna's response took a moment to relay from Earthstation to a satellite to Radu.

"Can you catch the next shuttle? We need a third."

"Yes, I already have a reservation." Again, the awkward pause of light-speed's limits.

"Good. I'll put you on the roster."

An approval notice formed the air into small lighted letters.

"Thanks, Atna."

"Good to have you."

He signed off.

The trick of Radu's mind that let him always know what time it was, anywhere he was, did not help him know when the sun would rise. Looking toward the east, he searched for a glimmer of light, even false dawn. In the few days he had been on earth he had never seen the sun; he had never been outside in daylight. But until right now he had neither noticed that nor cared. He would have liked to see earth illuminated by its sun, but he would be gone too soon. Perhaps he would never come back.

He hurried to the shuttle, boarded it, and waited for liftoff.

Acceleration pressed him into his seat, back toward the

earth. But the shuttle escaped, as it always did, and while it did not leave behind his hurt or his memories, it was taking him to a place where he would be busy enough, at times, to forget both for a while.

Laenea staggered out of bed, aching as if she had been in a brawl against a better fighter. In the bathroom she splashed ice water on her face; it did not help. Her urine was tinged but not thick with blood. She ignored it.

Radu was gone. He had left no message. Nor had he left anything behind, as if wiping out all his traces could wipe out the loss and pain of their parting. Laenea knew nothing could do that. She wanted to talk to him, touch him — just one more time — and try to show him, insist he understand, that he had not failed. He could not demand of himself what he could break himself — break his heart — attempting.

She called the crew lounge, but he did not answer the page. The computer crosschecked and told Laenea that Radu Dracul was on board transit ship A-28493, preparing for departure.

There was still time to reach him before he had to go to sleep, but he had chosen an automated ship on a dull run, probably the first assignment he could get. Nothing he could have said or done would have told Laenea more clearly that he did not want to see or touch or talk to her again.

She could not stay in Kathell's apartment any longer. She threw on the clothes she had come in; she left the vest open, defiantly, to well below her breastbone, not caring if she were recognized, returned to the hospital, anything. At the top of the elevator shaft the wind whipped through her hair and snapped the cape behind her. Laenea pulled the black velvet close and waited. When the tram came she boarded it, to return to her own city and her own people, the pilots, to live apart with them and never tell their secrets.

Laenea knew where the pilots stayed when they were on the spaceport, but she had never been inside their quarters. She had taken her training on the mainland, and, as far as she knew, no one not a pilot was permitted on their floor. She stepped into the elevator and touched the proper button.

The cage fell. When it stopped, the doors remained closed.

"What is your name, please?" The voice had the artificial smoothness created only by machine.

"Laenea Trevelyan."

Machine response ordinarily occurred instantaneously, as far as human beings could tell. Laenea expected instant acceptance or instant refusal.

Nothing happened.

"My name is Laenea Trevelyan," she said again.

The pause continued.

She was about to give up and go away when the doors slid quietly open.

"Welcome, Laenea," Ramona-Teresa said. Her voice held just that: welcome, without any hint of satisfaction or censure. "Welcome."

She stretched out her hand to Laenea, who hesitated, remembering how it had felt, the last time, to touch Radu. But she and Ramona were of a kind. She grasped Ramona's warm, pulseless wrist.

Several other pilots joined them, welcoming Laenea into their company. She wondered if pilots always hugged to say hello.

She laughed.

By hurrying through Earthstation from the shuttle to the transit dock, propelling himself recklessly through the freefall of the old station's central corridors, and barely pausing long enough to show his ID at the transit dock, Radu managed to reach Atna's ship before its departure. He stepped into its self-contained gravity field.

He paused in the control room long enough to regain his equilibrium and to say hello. The older man stood up to greet him. Atna was nearly as tall as Radu, but very slender. His skin had begun to acquire the papery softness of old age.

"I'm glad to have you on board," he said. He stood back, his hands on Radu's shoulders, and smiled. "But I'm afraid you've come in low again."

"I don't mind," Radu said. He was used to having the least

seniority and to drawing most of the ship's housekeeping tasks.

Atna gazed at him more intently. "Are you all right?"

"Yes," Radu said. "Of course. What do you mean?"

"I don't want to invade your privacy," Atna said with an embarrassed shrug. "But you know the grapevine. Your name has been . . . frequently mentioned on it, in the last few days. I've been concerned for you."

As a very new member of the crew, and as someone who was solitary by nature, Radu had little experience with the grapevine, either as recipient of its information, or — so far as he had known till now — its subject. He felt uncomfortable, knowing he and Laenea must be the focus of gossip. He supposed he should have realized before now that they would be.

"Yes," Radu said. "I'm all right."

"I apologize," Atna said, and then, with considerable relief, "Ah, Orca. Come and meet Radu."

Radu turned. He had not heard the other crew member arrive, she walked so softly in her rubber-soled red deck shoes. Like many crew members she dressed flamboyantly. She wore silver pants, a silver mesh shirt, and a spangled jacket with a pattern like fish scales: silver, gold brass, red copper. Her skin, set off by her very short, pale, fine hair, was smooth mahogany tan, and her eyes were black. Her hands were rather large in proportion to the rest of her.

Radu glanced at her hands again, surprised. She was a diver.

"Hi," she said, extending her hand. They clasped wrists, and the translucent webbing between her fingers darkened against the black cuff of his shirt.

"Radu Dracul, of Twilight," Radu said.

"Oh," she said, and Radu had the impression that she, too, had heard things about him on the grapevine. If she had, she refrained from asking him any questions. "Orca, of the Harmony Isles, on earth." She grinned. "I'm afraid my given name is nearly impossible to say, out of water."

Radu had very little time to wonder about a diver's being on the crew. Atna sent them both off to finish preparing the ship for transit. While Orca made the last checks on the engines and Radu shut down all the semi-intelligents, Atna undocked and eased away from Earthstation. Then Radu and Orca prepared themselves, and their sleep chambers, and hugged each other, as crew members always did, to say good-bye.

"Sleep well," Orca said, and closed herself in. Radu climbed into his body box, lay back, and pulled the lid shut. The ship would float gently toward its transit point and pause just long enough for Atna to shut down the cerebral functions of the navigational computer and send himself into deep, sound sleep. Then the ship would vanish, diving into transit. But transit was something Radu knew he would never see.

He caught the familiar sweet smell of the anesthetic, and fell instantly asleep.

As he awakened, Radu remembered his dreams fondly. He had dreamed of Twilight, and of his clan, and of the few days, the time he could count in hours, that he and Laenea had spent together. It seemed as much fantasy as the dreams themselves.

Then he was fully awake, and he remembered that his home was far away and all his family dead of the plague that had only scarred him; he remembered that he and Laenea were now and forever beyond each other's reach.

Sometimes, coming out of transit, Radu woke before the lid of his sleep chamber unlatched, but this time it was already ajar. He pushed it up as he rose.

Someone touched his arm.

Radu started violently.

"I beg your pardon," the pilot beside him said quizzically. He was small and frail looking, with very fine black hair and very pale translucent skin. Radu remembered having seen his picture, and of course he knew Vasili Nikolaievich by reputation. He was the first person ever to become a pilot without having served on the crew. And he was a very good pilot.

"You — startled me," Radu said. He would have been startled to meet Vasili Nikolaievich at all, much less to find

him, unannounced, on a ship that was supposed to be automated. The administrators generally sent Vasili on important
flights that required fast round trips: diplomatic missions, or
emergencies. "I didn't expect a pilot, and I'm usually the first
to wake up."

"You are this time, too, but I thought you might need help."
Unlike every other pilot Radu had ever seen, he wore his
shirt buttoned high, covering all but the tip of the pilot's scar.

"This was supposed to be an automated ship," Radu said.
He immediately regretted his churlish tone, but the last thing
he wanted to see right now was a pilot. He rubbed his face
with both hands, as if he could wipe away the last languor
of transit sleep. "This *was* supposed to be an automated ship,"
he said again. For any pilot to be reassigned so late was unusual; for *this* pilot to be sent hinted at extraordinary circumstances. "What happened? Were we diverted? Is this an
emergency flight?"

"I don't know," the pilot said. "Nobody said it was."

"Didn't you ask?" Radu glanced at the other sleep chambers, but only the two cradling his fellow crew members were
in use. The ship carried no passengers, no medical people.

"No," the pilot said.

"Do we have medicine in the cargo? Hospital equipment?"

"We don't have any cargo at all," the pilot said. "They
switched the full module for an empty one."

"But why?"

"I told you. I don't know. To tell you the truth, I don't
much care." He scowled. "My bid was up for exploration
when the administrators ordered me onto this milk run, and
there isn't another x-team mission scheduled for six months."

"Perhaps this isn't a milk run," Radu said.

"Compared to an x team?" Vasili's laugh was sarcastic.
"Look, I only came in here because I thought you might need
a hand. The crew usually does after a long trip. But you don't,
do you?"

Radu's momentary flash of excitement and anticipation
subsided. He felt he owed someone, somewhere, the same
kind of risk that Laenea and the others had taken to come to

Twilight. But this trip was like all the others, neither danger nor heroic rescue, merely the transportation of frivolous goods for the profit of the transit administrators.

"No, I need no help," he said to the pilot, and, after too long a pause, "thank you." He sat down to put on his boots, and pretended to be concerned with a worn place on his right sock. His hands were shaking, not because he had been startled or because he had thought, if only for a moment, that he was by chance on an important or dangerous mission. He was trembling because the pilot was so near. His heart beat faster. He tried to control his pulse. He knew that his discomfort would continue as long as Vasili Nikolaievich stayed beside him.

Despite the danger, his adverse reaction to Laenea had until now caused him only grief, not fear. But if their intimacy had sensitized him to the presence of *any* pilot, then he might eventually have to quit the crew. That did frighten him.

The silence lengthened. Radu did not look up. The pilot turned away and left the box room.

Radu released the breath he had unconsciously been holding. He heard the pilot continue on into the crew lounge, to the passageway beyond, and to the pilot's cabin. The door opened, and closed solidly.

Ignoring his worn sock, Radu pulled on his boots and stood up. His heartbeat slowed to a more normal rate. He wiped his forehead on his sleeve. He had never heard of a crew member who responded to a pilot the way he did. But, then, the pilots never spoke of their incompatibility with other human beings, either. They simply kept to themselves. Maybe that prevented ordinary people from reacting to them.

Radu checked the other body boxes. Neither Atna nor Orca had yet reached a state approaching consciousness, so he left them alone. He walked quietly through the lounge and past the pilot's cabin, to the control room beyond.

At the sight of the viewport he stopped, astonished.

An emerald green, cloud-wisped world hung just above them. The ship had surfaced out of transit with accuracy impossible for an automated ship and unusual for a piloted one.

Most ships returned to normal space in more or less the correct region, too close for another dive but far enough away
that the crew had to travel in real time at subluminal speeds,
for a week, or a month, unable to escape the boredom even
with transit drugs. They were too toxic for any use but sleeping through transit.

Sometimes a ship surfaced so far off its course that it had
to dive again. And sometimes the ships went so far astray
that no one on board could figure out where they were, and
so they were lost. At least that was what everyone assumed
happened to lost ships; there was no real evidence that they
did not remain in transit forever, and some theoretical evidence that they did.

Radu glanced again at the bright world above, impressed
despite himself by the pilot's skill. Vasili Nikolaievich's
reputation was well earned.

Curious about the changes in the flight, Radu requested
the ship's log. The main computer responded immediately;
Vasili had already awakened it from transit mode.

Not only had they given up their cargo and acquired a
pilot, but even their destination was new: Ngthummulun.
Radu might as well not have bothered to look it up: He had
no idea how to pronounce it. He frowned. The word was so
strange to him that for an instant he suspected the ship had
been diverted to an alien rather than a human planet. In
quarantine before his first visit to earth, he had received
the null-strain bacteria that prevented cross-ecosystem con-
tamination. But Radu needed more experience before the
administrators would approve him for alien-contact training. And in addition to training, he lacked the proper im-
munizations. If Ngthummulun were an alien-inhabited
world, the first he had ever encountered, he would be forbidden to land.

The précis dispelled his moment's disappointment.
Ngthummulun's colonists were human, from Australia, on
earth. Radu thought he could probably even pronounce the
original name.

The schedule showed a brief stopover here and a direct

route back to earth. The bonus offered for a fast trip was so large that it easily explained the last minute changes as well as Vasili's reassignment. The crew's bonus, which was generous enough to surprise Radu, would be only a fraction of the amount the transit authority collected for itself. Nevertheless, Radu did not want to go back to earth. He could return without landing, of course; he could sign onto another ship immediately. But this unexpected change in his ship's course made his abrupt departure nothing more than foolish.

Radu cursed softly. He had too little seniority even to complain, as if a complaint after the fact would do him any good at all.

The potential profit caused the diversion, that was clear. But the log neglected to mention what cargo or what mission was worth the extra cost.

Radu verified their destination and for practice checked for a better orbit. He knew that the pilot would already have changed whatever needed changing. Piloting, like mathematics, was an art as well as a science. Radu had never tried to fool himself about his own mathematical talents. He saw what anyone saw; he handled the factors anyone could handle. Going beyond, into mathematical originality and intuition, was not something he was capable of doing. He was good crew, but in more ways than one he was not, and never would be, a pilot.

He returned to the lounge. It was a comfortable sitting room, one wall all tiers of plants, the other walls bright colors. Without checking — though he looked at the sensors anyway, out of habit — Radu could tell that the environmental controls were working properly. However efficient the air circulation, a slightly higher concentration of oxygen always lingered around the plant banks. He gave the ferny leaves a spray of water, then started a pot of coffee. He had drawn cooking duty, of course, as usual, but he enjoyed it and never understood why it was assigned by default.

He looked through the stores, which were adequate if unexciting. If their return were as accurate as their arrival,

Radu would have only a few meals to prepare, and he would be able to use fresh food for all of them.

Only the pilot had registered dislikes and allergies. Vasili Nikolaievich had a long list of things he would not eat. That would restrict meals to blandness, unless Radu fixed two versions of everything.

He put together an ordinary stew that everyone could season as they preferred. Then he poured himself a mug of coffee and returned to the crew lounge to wait for the others to revive.

Stretched out on a chair with his feet propped up, he thought about what he should do next. Earth had lost its luster for him and even travel did not seem nearly as inviting as it had when he joined the crew. As for exploration — Vasili's experience proved how little chance Radu had of fulfilling that ambition.

He was homesick, but he did not want to go home. Though he loved his world, its ghosts haunted him. The ache of his family's passing had diminished, but it would never go away. Before the emergency team arrived and synthesized a vaccine, too many people had died while Radu, by chance and luck, had lived. The plague killed those it touched; Radu had never met anyone else who caught it and survived, though he supposed there must be a few. But everyone who avoided infection, through natural immunity or good fortune, and then by vaccination, looked at Radu and wondered why someone they had loved was dead, instead of him.

He rubbed his face, smooth forehead and scarred cheeks, the soft scratchy bristle of his heavy mustache. Perhaps he should let his beard grow. He had, once before, but it came in in different colors and made him look like a jester. The beard hid the scars, but he preferred looking ugly to looking a fool, so he had shaved it off.

He did not have to leave it the color it grew. He could as easily change it to the same dark blond as his mustache. His reasons for leaving it alone seemed absurd even to him. He preferred to present himself to the world as he was,

without a façade. Hiding never worked. He had tried hiding
for two years, up in the mountains alone on Twilight. Hiding his physical scars behind a beard — or even hiding his
mental scars behind regenerated skin — would not help him
either.

At a sudden noise he jumped to his feet. He had forgotten
about the others. Hurrying into the box room, Radu found
Atnaterta pulling himself upright.

"Atna, wait, let me help."

Radu took him by the shoulder and arm and eased him
from his sleep chamber. The navigator was shivering, deeply
and steadily. Radu hugged him, rubbing his back, until after
a few moments the older man responded with a brief, sleepy
embrace. Gradually, his shivering subsided.

"Thanks," he said. "I'm awake now." He looked tireder
and older than before the journey. He picked up his thick
sweater and zipped himself into it. He was always cold on
the ship.

Radu helped him to the lounge. Instead of stopping when
they reached it, the navigator kept on going toward the control room.

"We're on course," Radu said. "There's a pilot on board."

"Oh." Atna stopped. "Yes. The pilot. I'd forgot the pilot."
Then his expression brightened. "Come to think of it, I'd
even forgot that this trip I'm just a passenger." He stepped
into the control room and gazed up at Ngthummulun.
"Vaska did it again, I see. How far out are we? Two hours?"

"Even less," Radu said.

Atna returned to the lounge and lowered himself stiffly
into a chair. Radu fetched him some coffee and sat down
across from him.

"What happened?"

Atna wrapped his long fingers around his cup, savoring
the warmth. "They flew him out to us. We were nearly at
the transit point when the listing came through. Some ship
was going to be ordered to take it, so . . . I volunteered us.
I hope you don't mind."

Radu shrugged. Anger was pointless; the deed was done. "Why?" he asked.

"Ngthummulun is my home world, so I suppose I have to say pure selfishness," Atna said smiling. "We don't buy many offworld goods, so ships don't come here often. I haven't been home for a long time."

"Why are we going there now?" Radu tried to memorize how the planet's name was pronounced.

"I can't be certain," Atna said. "But as it isn't an emergency, I think I know. Perhaps I'll get a chance to show you."

Radu was curious to hear more, but he heard the sharp click of a sleep chamber lid. Atna moved to get up but Radu put out one hand to restrain him. "I'll help her. You finish your coffee."

"All right. Thanks."

Radu opened Orca's sleep chamber. She shifted, regaining consciousness. He took her hand gently, afraid he might injure the delicate swimming membranes. But when she closed her fingers the web folded back out of the way. He helped her up. She smiled sleepily and slid her arms around his waist, hugging him tight while he enfolded her in his arms and stroked her back and shoulders, easing away the cramps. Her long sleek swimmer's muscles tensed and relaxed beneath his hands.

She sighed deeply. "Thanks." She let him go and rubbed her eyes with her fists, then combed her short, pale hair with her fingers. It fell back into place exactly as it had been, nearly smooth, not quite rumpled.

"You're welcome," Radu said.

"How did Atna come through?"

"Fairly well. He seems tired, but I think he's all right." He explained about the ship's being diverted, the pilot, Atna's home world.

"Every time I see him, transit's taken a little more out of him." Orca shook her head, flinging away the worry, and grinned. "I'm glad he's finally decided to take a vacation."

Orca tolerated transit sleep as well as anyone Radu had ever met. She stretched luxuriously. "Is that dinner I smell? I'm starved."

"It'll be ready soon."

They returned to the lounge, where Atna sat hunched over his coffee.

Everything about Orca — her prominent canines, her lithe walk, her narrow hips and small breasts and large eyes and hands — all her features were at one end or the other of a normal range, so except for the swimming webs Radu could not tell what about her was inherent and what intentionally changed. He admitted his fascination to himself. Whatever factors had formed Orca, they combined into a being of ethereal grace. She was not by any classical definition beautiful, but she was striking. Somehow it made Radu uncomfortable to find her so attractive, because he felt as if he were betraying Laenea.

He reached up absently to touch his rough, scarred face. He had been with Laenea too short a time to get used to her not caring about the marks. He had been away from Twilight too short a time to find out if hers was the usual reaction, or if most people off his home world as well as on it thought him ugly. He assumed they did.

"Hi, Atna." Orca kissed the navigator's cheek. He patted her hand. Radu set another cup of coffee on the table. Orca took it gratefully and sipped it, black.

She was about to sit down when the intercom clicked on. "One hour to pre-orbital check." The computer's voice gave no indication of the urgency its message implied. The crew had more than an hour's work to do. Radu stood up quickly, thinking, A lot of good it does you to know what time it is if you don't pay attention.

Atna pushed himself to his feet; Orca glanced wistfully at her coffee, shrugged, and left it behind. She vanished into the engines while Radu and Atnaterta carried out the systems checks. Used to having plenty of time between transit and orbital insertion, they had to push hard to perform all their tasks. Vasili Nikolaievich maintained his silence and his seclusion. Radu wondered if he had offended the pilot even more seriously than he had thought. It was too late to do anything about it now. They could certainly have used his help. Radu regretted his own surly behavior as he tried to complete the technical work, assist Atna, and, in the few minutes in between, finish putting together a reasonably edible dinner, which they ate on the run.

Water dappled and streaked the surface of Ngthummulun in thousands of rivers and millions of lakes that touched the infinite shades of green with blue and blue gray and silver. Ngthummulun had only primitive landing facilities, so the cargo truck had to be taken down by hand. Atna had turned the controls over to Radu, and Radu was nervous. Vasili had made it clear that he expected the cargo back through the first launch window. That meant no aborted landing approaches, no second tries.

Radu drove the truck closer to the surface, diving in at a steep, fast angle. The paisley patchwork of the land stretched and spread. All the separate shades of green and blue, mottled specks from high overhead, grew into discrete spots, then, as the truck neared the ground and the horizon flattened and receded, the little ship skimmed over a single color at a time and the borders whipped past as blurred uneven lines.

Radu concentrated on controls and signals. The forest swept away beneath him, deep green velvet streaked here and there with sparkling patches as bright as snow. The landing strip appeared suddenly, a violent slash, a dark-rimmed canyon.

"You're fine," Atna said. "Quite nice."

The truck slid between the trees; Radu slowed it and touched down as smoothly as he ever had in the simulator. Easing on reverse power, he braked the ship and it glided to a halt. He hesitated for a moment, leaning tensely over the controls, then sat back and let out his breath.

"Very good," Atna said. "Couldn't have done better if we carried gravity."

"Thanks," Radu said. Delayed tension took over. Until now, Atna's easy manner had kept him from noticing how severely his competence was being tested. It had sufficed. He had made no mistakes. If the cargo was ready, the truck could catch the next window back to the ship. Radu was happier to have pleased Atna than he was relieved to have kept, so far, to Vasili's timetable.

Radu opened the hatch. The hot, humid air rolled in on him. Tropical regions always surprised him with the force of their climates.

He jumped to the runway and glanced back, ready to give Atna a hand. But the older man moved freely and with more animation. He looked around at the rain-dazzled forest and took a deep, slow breath of the air of his home world.

A large ground truck approached them, its wheels spraying sails of water from every puddle. Atna took off his sweater. Radu was tempted to take off his shirt, but he wore nothing under it and he did not know if it would be proper.

When the ground truck stopped, Atna greeted the loading crew fondly in a language Radu had never heard. Atna introduced him to his friends, and they all switched back to speaking Standard.

"What are you shipping?" Atna asked.

"Wyunas," said the loading crew chief. "The first crop."

Atna laughed. "So that *is* what all this is about! Sending a message probe, hiring a pilot, diverting a ship —" He laughed again, an amused low chuckle.

The crew chief laughed too. "I suppose they think they ought to start out with some fanfare."

"It gave me a start at first, I don't mind telling you."

"We had good growing weather, and an early harvest. There's a major holiday cluster on earth that the first shipment will catch, if the ship makes the deadline."

"It will make it, with Vaska piloting — but the express charge will eat up the profits," Atna said drily.

His friend shook her head. "If they sell the wyunas for what they expect to, the cost of the ship and the pilot will be negligible in comparison."

Atna gave her a quizzical glance.

"Don't look so skeptical—hope they're right," she said. "We need the currency." She clasped his hand. "It's good to see you home, Atna. Can I give you a ride to town?"

"Thanks, yes."

"Good. Till we're done, then." She patted his arm, then she and the others opened up the cargo hatch and began transferring small boxes marked FRAGILE from the ground truck to the ship.

"What are wyunas?" Radu asked.

"Come along. Perhaps I can show you."

Atna led the way through a forest bordering the field. A path crossed marshy ground between huge fern trees. Radu followed up a gentle rise to the far bank of a narrow valley. The path grew drier and the trees shorter, but the fronds still reached well over his head. He brushed against one thick stem and the tree showered him with droplets of water.

Atna peered through branches into a clearing.

"Good," he said. "This field's still unharvested." He pushed the ferns back and stood aside.

It was as if he had broken through into a winter forest after an ice storm. The trees' bare limbs sparkled like diamonds. Radu followed Atnaterta into the ice forest until they were surrounded by silver and black. Fallen leaves lay mushy and rotting on the ground, but the bark of the trees sprouted thousands of marble-sized transparent spheres, all intricately patterned inside and out in loops and swirls, shaped by the uncertainties of their growth. Each was slightly different, like a snowflake or a fingerprint.

The trees sang, so delicately that their wind-chime whisper was inaudible anywhere but among the shimmering crystals.

Atna stripped several from the end of a branch and handed

them to Radu. They fractured the sunlight into a hundred tiny rainbows, sparkling among the arches and prisms.

"Are they seeds?"

Atna laughed. "To tell you the truth they're more like warts. Tree warts. That's something we don't intend to mention too prominently in the advertising. They aren't infectious, of course — the host organism has to be specially adapted and sensitized or the wyunas won't grow at all. But 'tree wart' isn't an aesthetically pleasing name."

"You're right. 'Wyuna' is better. But what are they for?"

"They're our cash crop. We needed one, so we invented it."

Radu nodded. Twilight exported the hardwoods that grew in its high forests. But Ngthummulun was terraformed. It had started out a dead world. Everything growing on it had been brought from earth or hand evolved here.

"I mean, what do they do?" He imagined some complicated electronic function that could be attained only by enzymatic manipulation of matter into forms too delicate and precise to be created by mechanical technology.

"Do? They don't do anything. They're jewels, if you like. They're decorative. That's the sort of thing that succeeds in the earth trade."

"Oh." Radu felt vaguely disappointed. Electronic components would all have been the same. He should have thought of that. Each wyuna was unique: Success rewarded uniqueness in the earth trade. Most imported items were merely decorative. The wood Radu's home world exported was beautiful, but it could be put to useful purposes. Still, for all Radu knew, once it reached earth it was carved into meaningless trinkets.

He held a jewel up to the light, for one last glimpse of its spectral colors. Then he lowered it and extended his hand to Atna, to return the wyunas.

Atna stared at them, his face expressionless. He did not move.

"Atna? Are you all right? What's the matter?" Radu touched Atna's arm.

"What?" Atna looked up, stepped back, shook his head, and gazed again at the jewels Radu was trying to return. "No," he said. "Keep them." His voice was distant. "Give some to Orca and Vaska, if you like. They'll be a curiosity when you go back to earth. For a few days, anyway."

Radu nearly gave them back anyway. He had no use for them. Then he remembered Laenea's friend Marc, and his "pretty things." Radu closed his hand around the wyunas. He could give them to Laenea, for Marc.

Do I need an excuse to see her? he wondered. Will we never even be able to speak to each other, if not as lovers, at least as friends?

"Thank you," he said to Atna. He put the organic jewels in his pocket. "Are you sure nothing's wrong?"

"Yes."

It was time to go back to the landing field; Radu felt the minutes flowing gradually toward takeoff. Back in the forest, the pale ferns concealed the iridescent orchard.

Atna led in silence, staring at the ground, his shoulders hunched. Even his footsteps were noiseless. Sunlight passing through foliage dappled his dark skin with gold and green. At the edge of the runway, among uncleared stumps and weeds, he stopped. The truck had been wheeled out to the end of the landing strip again, ready to take off.

"Good-bye, Atna."

They embraced, as crew members always did when parting. Atna put his head on Radu's shoulder and hugged him tightly, and Radu rubbed his hands up and down the older man's back, just as if he were helping him awaken. When Atna drew back, he held Radu by the shoulders as if unwilling to let him go.

"Something is wrong," Radu said.

"Don't leave," Atna said. "Don't go back to earth. Something's going to happen."

Radu frowned, curious, confused.

"You're in danger."

"In danger? What — ?"

"In the orchard, I saw . . . I can't explain to you what happened. You didn't grow up here, you wouldn't understand. I dreamed . . . I had a vision. I'm afraid for you."

Radu stared at him blankly. "I don't . . ."

"Something's going to happen to the ship and you're part of it," Atna said desperately. "You're in the middle of it. I think perhaps you *are* it."

Radu shook his head.

"Don't dismiss me!"

"But I have to go back to the ship."

"Of course you have to take the cargo back, but Ngthummulun has a shuttle truck. I can send it for you. And for Orca. Tell her there's a lovely place to swim, a deepwater mountain lake — "

"It's impossible." Radu stepped away from him. "The ship can't fly without a crew."

"Vaska can get the ship from orbit to a transit point. After that it doesn't matter. I don't think it will ever come out again."

"I'm to warn Orca, but desert the pilot?"

"You can tell him if you want. But he won't pay any attention. Pilots never think they can fail. I can't save him. I can't save the cargo. You and Orca are the only ones I can warn."

"But you *know* it's impossible."

"At least give Orca a chance to decide for herself. Will you tell her what I've said?"

"When you know she'll have no choice, either?"

"Please tell her, Radu."

"All right!" In his confusion, he spoke harshly. He regretted both the harshness and the agreement instantly. Badly shaken, Radu reached out and clasped Atna's hand; he touched his forehead. "Atna, do you feel well?"

Atna's vision was all too similar to the desperate fantasies of plague hallucination, but the navigator had no fever, nor any of the other symptoms Radu would quickly have recognized.

"Do you mean, am I ill? Am I crazy? No, neither, I understand what I'm asking. I don't want to frighten you — " He spoke quickly and urgently. "No, I do. Please do as I ask."

"I have to leave."

Atna hesitated. "You're sure?" The tension had gone from his voice.

"Yes."

"Then good-bye."

They hugged again, briefly and without intensity. Atna behaved as if he thought of Radu as already dead, already lost.

Atna turned and walked into the forest without another word.

Making the last-minute checks of the shuttle truck's systems, Radu tried to push away the grim, cold feeling Atna's words had given him. Things happened to ships in transit — sometimes things happened to ships even in normal space. Atna's fear and agitation had infected him, and reminded him of experiences he had tried to forget. He found concentrating difficult.

Atna had given him an impossible demand. Without the navigator the ship was short-handed to begin with. Besides, Radu had already taken as much time off as he dared. If all he did was take vacations, he should go back to Twilight. His home needed either his labor or the currency he earned on the crew.

What troubled Radu most was the possibility that Atna might be ill. Not with Twilight's plague: He had none of those symptoms and the cryptovirus that caused it had been, it was claimed, eliminated. But some other disease . . . He asked a few questions of the shuttle's computer; finding no useful information in its limited records, he directed it to tap into the transit ship's database. No epidemics were on report, here or elsewhere; the computer could not find a disease that matched the information Radu offered it.

Vasili broke into the flow of data.

"What are you doing with the computer? Do you realize what time it is?"

Radu noticed with a shock how close he was to the end of the launch window. Vasili's irritation was justified.

"Something's wrong here, Vasili Nikolaievich," Radu said. "Atna just said some very odd things to me. I'm worried that — "

Vasili cut him off, laughing. "You mean he told you your fortune?"

"Well . . . I wouldn't put it quite that way."

"People from Ngthummulun are always claiming to know the future."

"Oh," Radu said.

"Come back to the ship, right now. We don't have time to waste with this nonsense."

A few minutes later, Radu put power to the cargo truck. It lumbered down the runway, faster and faster, and hoisted itself forcibly into the air.

After an unexciting flight, Radu docked well, sliding the shuttle against its fittings with a satisfying sharp snap that rang through the craft's skin. He relaxed his hold on the controls. His knuckles were white and his palms damp.

He had wanted to dock perfectly, but did not quite know why it was so important. To prove he had never thought they were all exposed to a serious illness? To prove he thought nothing of Atna's visions? To show off? If so, to whom? Orca? Vasili Nikolaievich?

"Hurry in," the pilot said over the radio. "I want to leave orbit immediately."

Amused despite himself, Radu realized that the pilot would hardly even notice anything as trivial as a good manual docking in normal space.

He shut down the controls and the onboard computer, preparing it for transit. He spoke soothing words to it. Though it was not self-aware, he always talked to it when he was alone. It could hear him, it could understand the patterns of his words, but whether it understood words spoken as if to a child going off to sleep, he did not know.

Unfastening his harness, he floated out of his chair, opened the roof hatch, and pulled himself from the region of freefall into artificial gravity. He felt the familiar lurch and strain, but now the unsettled feeling did not linger, as it had when he first encountered it.

I wonder if I'll ever get too used to it to notice? he thought.

Radu went reluctantly into the control room to speak to Vasili. The pilot lay back in his chair, watching the computer display as it changed in colors and waves before him.

"Are you all calmed down now?" he said, without looking around.

"I had good reason for being worried," Radu said.

"Maybe someone should have warned you that the inhabitants of Ngthummulun can be quite strange. But I thought you knew Atna."

"I've crewed with him before. Apparently I don't know him as well as I thought."

"You were concerned about him, and about us as well, I assume. That's commendable, even if it wasn't necessary. Stop worrying about it."

Radu fingered the wyunas in his pocket, drew one out, and offered it to Vasili.

"Atna asked me to give you one of these, if you want it."

Vasili glanced at it with disinterest. "Thanks, but I don't wear jewelry. Can you find out how long Orca will be? We're near a transit point."

Feeling that he had behaved stupidly ever since waking up, Radu shoved the wyuna back into his pocket and left.

Radu climbed down into the engine room. The high and low notes of the resting transit engines beat together around him. The amber light of an information display glowed beyond banks of control nets. He started toward it.

"Orca?"

"Just a sec."

Kneeling beside one of the nets, reaching deep into its interstices, Orca watched the display that hung in the air beside her. She was forcing the repair of a broken connection. The information she was reading looked, to Radu, like numbers studded along a tangle of electric-orange string. From his point of view the numbers were backward.

Radu watched quietly, until Orca sat on her heels with a sigh, freed her hands from the net, and stretched. The data block faded out.

"Nice docking," she said cheerfully.

"Thanks," Radu said, pleased she had noticed.

"How's Atna?"

"He sent these." Radu handed her several of the wyunas.

"So that's why we're here," she said. She looked at them closely. "They're even prettier than he said. Thank you. But how is he?"

"He looked much better after he landed..." After what Vasili had told him, it seemed hardly necessary, indeed foolish, to tell Orca of Atna's fears. Even if he had promised.

"I've been worried about him," Orca said. She raised one eyebrow, silently questioning the uncertainty in Radu's tone.

"He's worried about us," Radu said. Because he *had* promised.

"Why?"

"He had ... a premonition, I suppose ... that something will happen to the ship in transit. He wants us to stay behind with him."

Orca cupped the wyunas in her webbed hand, shook them so they rang together softly, and stared at them intently.

"He was very upset," Radu said. "He made me promise to tell you and Vasili Nikolaievich. The pilot said it was nothing." When Orca did not reply, he continued. "If you want to stay — "

She touched his hand without looking at him, and he fell silent. He watched her, disturbed by her reaction. Two short vertical frown lines deepened on her forehead, then smoothed and vanished. The engine's eerie pulsations continued; the wind-chime touch of the wyunas reminded Radu of Ngthummulun's forest.

Orca took a breath, exhaled, and closed her hand into a fist.

"All right," she said. "It's all right. What were you saying?"

"Do you want to go down to Ngthummulun?"

"No. Do you?"

Radu shook his head. "Then you agree with Vasili, that there's nothing to Atna's dream?"

"On the contrary. Atna's dreams are as real as this world. They're another level of reality. Another way of perceiving things. I'm not explaining this right. I'm not sure you can, in Standard. If we were underwater — " She shrugged helplessly.

"You're staying on the ship."

"I don't get any resonances from his perception. I don't feel a threat. To me, I mean."

"I would have assumed you'd dismiss it out of hand."

"No — and I would have assumed you'd take him more seriously."

Radu shivered suddenly.

"I'm sorry," Orca said, in response to his silence. "I didn't mean that as an insult."

"No, I — I didn't take it as one. I just can't . . ."

Again she waited for him to finish his thought; again he failed to speak.

"Atna's frame of reference is a whole lot different from mine, and I suppose from yours," Orca said. "But I've learned to take it seriously."

They walked together back to the crew lounge, to report to the pilot, to make the final preparations for transit, to ready themselves for sleep. At a porthole, Orca paused and looked out at Ngthummulun.

"Besides," she said, "this place has a million lakes and no ocean. I'd sooner vacation in a bathtub."

In the box room, Radu and Orca hugged each other good-bye. Orca lay down and positioned her face mask. In a few seconds she was asleep. Radu closed her in.

The computer spoke softly to remind Radu of the time.

"I know the time!" he said, angry for reasons he did not understand. He sat on the edge of his chamber, pulled off his boots, and flung them into a corner. Bending down, he rested his forehead on his crossed arms for a moment. Then, calmly and surely, for his life depended on it, he prepared himself for transit and went to sleep.

5

*Laenea was calling to him, she needed him, as he had needed
her —*

A raucous siren penetrated the last thin haze of transit
sleep, dissolving Radu's frightening dream. He fumbled for
the latch on his body box. The lid clicked open and he
pushed it aside and climbed out, made awkward by the remnants of anesthetic chemicals, and confused by memories
recalled by his dream.

The dim light faded, and in the twilit last moment the
ship began to spin. Its motion threw Radu against his sleep
chamber. He struggled to his feet, reaching out to get his
bearings in the darkness. But as he oriented himself toward
the control room the synthetic gravity contracted, twisted,
and flung him down.

This time he lay still, waiting for the ship's convulsions to
end. Waves lapped over him, slow and dry, not of water but

of weight and weightlessness. His heart pounded and his vision turned scarlet against night. If the waves rose higher, they would crush him as easily as any angry sea.

But the oscillation slowed, gentled, and finally ceased. A circle of light from the port brightened the room: strange that the darkness before had appeared so complete. The ship had been spinning ... now the patch of light remained in one place. Radu climbed to his feet. Beyond the port spun a red-orange star.

It should be yellow, he thought with a shock. It should be earth's sun. But it's a red giant.

The siren moaned to silence. Radu's shirt was soaked at the armpits, and drops of sweat ran down his sides. Footsteps hurried down the corridor, but halted outside the box room.

Radu waited a moment, but nothing happened. He opened the door and came face to face with Vasili Nikolaievich.

"What's wrong?"

The pilot gazed up at him in silence. His black eyes glittered as he searched Radu's face, and his pale skin was flushed.

"What's wrong?" Radu said again. "What's the matter?"

"How do you feel?"

"How do I feel!" Perhaps transit *did* make pilots unstable, as rumor would have it. "I feel I ought to be responding to the emergency, if you'd tell me what it is."

"The emergency is that you started to wake up in transit."

Radu stared at him, all his reactions clamped into a tight ball in his chest. His heart pounded. The pilot's pulse throbbed irregularly at the corner of his sharp jaw.

"The sensors protected you. They threw us back into normal space," Vasili said calmly. "Don't look so worried — you're all right, they worked in time."

Radu gazed down at his hands. They looked no different, but now he knew why the pilot had stared at him so intently, and why he had hesitated until Radu opened the door. They both knew how normal people died in transit.

"How could I wake up?"

Vasili shrugged. "A mistake in the anesthetic. An obstruction in the gas line. I don't know."

He no longer sounded upset, and Radu permitted himself to relax, too. He was, after all, alive, and apparently unchanged by his experience.

"Where are we?"

The pilot shrugged again, left Radu in the hatchway, and went to inspect the information panel of Radu's body box.

"Then we're lost?"

"I haven't checked yet," Vasili said without turning toward him. "I came to see what happened as soon as I got the ship stabilized. I've never left transit quite so abruptly before."

Radu had never experienced leaving transit at all, having always gone through it sound asleep. He had wondered — as all crew members did — what he might see if he regained consciousness before he was supposed to. Now he had the evidence of his own confusion and bruises that the emergency sensors would prevent him from catching even a glimpse, at the risk of his life, of the spectacle the pilots kept so secret. If a crew member started to wake up, or slept too lightly, the sensors would always throw the ship out of transit and return it to normal space. The absolute certainty made Radu feel relieved, yet envious.

Vasili glanced at the display again. "I'll chart our position. You do a blood chemistry and check the anesthetic feeds. Do it quickly — I want to get back on our way."

He left Radu alone with the blinking machine that was supposed to protect him during flight. Radu set to work.

After several hours, his frustration increased as he looked for and failed to find any malfunction. The anesthetic, a gas, flowed smoothly and at the upper limit of concentration for someone of Radu's size and age. His blood chemistry was well within normal limits except for high readings of adrenaline and its breakdown products. He had expected that. After what had happened, low or normal levels would have been unusual.

The shreds of his dream kept distracting him. Never before

had he experienced a nightmare while he was asleep in transit. This was frighteningly like his hallucinations back on Twilight, just before he had become ill.

Stop scaring yourself, he thought. No wonder you're having nightmares.

He frowned over the blood analysis. His knowledge of biochemistry was only superficial; he had to accept the information the programs gave him. The body sometimes rejected one drug and had to be switched to another. That was the only suggestion the computer offered. Radu could think of no other likely supposition.

This ship carried supplies of two other transit drugs. Radu factored the second choice for stress and noted the upper dosage limit. He left the information drifting above his box, set up the equipment, and returned to the control room.

"I'm ready."

"Good," Vasili said. "Did you find the problem?"

"Reaction against the anesthetic, I think."

"That's unusual."

"It's the only explanation that makes sense." He paused. "Unless Atna was right. Or unless he really was sick and I'm coming down with whatever he had."

Vasili snorted. "He wasn't right, and you aren't sick. Let's go."

In the box room, Radu rolled up his sleeve, exposed his wrist to the antiseptic light, and climbed into his box.

"The IV is ready," he said. "It works quickly so I'll wish you well now."

Vasili knelt and picked up the IV needle in its sterile covering. His hand trembled, and he looked, if possible, even paler than usual.

"What's the matter?" Radu asked.

Vasili hesitated. "I'm not very fond of needles, I thought I was done with them . . ."

Though Vasili did not show his scar, Radu had seen Laenea's, and the other marks from the operations that had made her a pilot. He did not blame Vasili for his dislike of the needle. For a moment, Radu considered waking Orca up to help with the anesthetic. But that was ridiculous. Time aside, it would put her under a strain that was completely unnecessary.

"Can't you use another drug?" Vasili tried to smile but succeeded only in looking faintly ill.

"I'd prefer to avoid it," Radu said. The third-choice drug, though taken by mouth, had a range of unpleasant side effects. Radu wished for a transit drug that would migrate through the skin, but they all consisted of large organic molecules too complex for that procedure.

Vasili shook his head quickly. "Of course. I'm sorry." He took Radu's wrist in one hand, and steadied the needle.

The IV's built-in topical anesthetic tingled against Radu's inner arm, then numbed the skin. Vasili uncertainly guided the needle into a vein, digging so deep that the insertion hurt. Radu gritted his teeth.

The drug affected him almost instantly. He tried to lie down and felt himself falling.

The crystalline blackness of transit sleep formed solid around him.

Radu dreamed, as always; he dreamed again of Laenea. He could feel and smell and taste her. His hand slid gently from her breast across the ridged new scar. She whispered something that he could not quite hear, that he could not quite understand, and she laughed in the wonderful soft low way she had. Her hair swung down and caressed his shoulder and he twined the locks in his fingers.

She whispered again. "I love you." His whispered back, "I love you." She said a few more words. He thought she said, "I need you." She leaned down and kissed him, on the lips, at his throat, on the palm of his hand. Then, suddenly, she bit him hard on the wrist, slashing tendons and arteries.

"I'm sorry," she called to him. "I didn't want to — "

She was very far away. Tears streaming down her face, she vanished. Radu struggled up, clutching at his wrist to stop the blood.

He woke expecting the dream to vanish, too, but blood ran

down his hand and between his fingers. The world spun, as it had before. He scrabbled for the lock on his box and flung the lid open. The lights flickered and dimmed; the gravity pulsed in waves.

Dangling from his wrist by a crumpled piece of tape, the bloody needle dripped fluid from its point.

Radu jerked it loose and flung it away and clamped his left hand across the long gash where the needle had torn out. His head throbbed: He had come out of unconsciousness far too quickly.

Unable to use his hands to push himself out of the box, he braced his elbow on the chamber's edge, rolled over, and landed on his knees on the floor.

Vasili Nikolaievich slammed open the door.

"What in the bloody flaming hell is happening?"

Radu managed to rise to one knee. He lurched to his feet. Vasili caught him and supported him. Radu's dark shirt stayed the same color, where blood stained it, but the spots were shiny. Blood oozed between his fingers. He was surprised at the warmth.

He had ripped out the needle from base to tip, cutting a long gash. A good suicide cut. It would leave a scar, unless he went to some trouble to have it removed. Anyone who saw it would assume he had tried seriously to take his own life. The thought angered and embarrassed him.

"I taped the needle in!" Vasili said.

Radu took an unsteady step forward. "I tore it out myself, I think. I must have. I couldn't stay asleep. I can't — "

"You have to," Vasili said.

By the time Vasili finished cleaning the gash on Radu's wrist, Radu feared the pilot was near fainting. He worked with his teeth clenched, in silence, a little clumsily, as if his eyes were focused just to one side of the gash. Radu put pressure on it while Vasili fetched bandages. Tissue repair would have to wait, for Vasili could not even try it. The bleeding stopped, but the stinging pain continued.

Holding the bandage, Vasili stopped an arm's length from Radu.

"Give it to me." Radu took the package. But when he tried to tear it open, he dropped it on the floor. He gazed at it stupidly. His strength continued to drain away.

The pilot closed his eyes for a moment, opened them, scooped up the bandage, and tore off its covering with a violent jerk.

Once he had covered the wound he was able to work more easily. He bound it too tightly, but Radu did not have the heart to ask him to do it over. He was obviously being affected by Radu's presence. The longer he stayed near, the more uncomfortable Radu felt, too. His pulse began to speed up again, and each beat of his heart made the deep cut throb.

Vasili finished the bandage and stepped back, looking as relieved as Radu that he was done.

"Thank you," Radu said.

Vasili went quickly to the sink and washed away the blood.

Radu stood shakily, flexing his fingers. The needle had missed all the tendons, but the troubling dream forced him to keep reassuring himself that he could still use his hand. The dream confused him. His dreams in transit had always been pleasant, except these two times when he had awakened.

He tried to push Atnaterta's vision from his memory. He failed.

"Vasili Nikolaievich, can you contact earth?"

"Of course not. Don't be ridiculous."

"I don't mean now, of course. I meant from transit. I — "

No, he could not tell Vasili what he had dreamed. "A friend of mine, Laenea Trevelyan — "

Vasili sighed. "You have to leave her alone," he said. "If she weren't so damned stubborn you two would never have got together, it would have been better if you hadn't. But if you don't stay away from her, you'll destroy her. Can't you understand that?"

"I understand perfectly!" Radu said angrily. He hated to be reminded of what common knowledge, and common talk, he and Laenea were. "Our friendship is none of your business, but all I wanted anyway was to find out . . . to find out . . ." He tried to explain what he did want to find out. ". . . if her first transit flight went well," he said lamely.

"I can't call earth, or anyplace else, from transit," Vasili said. "In any case, you'll be asleep. You'll just have to wait till we get home."

They went back to work, maintaining an irritable silence. Neither Radu nor Vasili could discover why Radu had awakened this time. Perhaps blood had clotted in the needle; if so, the clot had dislodged when Radu ripped the IV out. Perhaps the open tip had pressed against the inside of the vein. The computer made the same suggestion it had before: anesthetic rejection. Discomforting to have that happen twice in a row.

Radu opened the drug locker and took down a vial of capsules, the third transit drug.

"Do you know where we are?" he asked the pilot.

"I haven't had a chance to plot our location," Vasili said, his voice strained. He avoided Radu's gaze, but added quickly, "I'm sure I'll have a course by the time you're asleep."

All Radu could do was take the drug. He stepped into the body box, sat down, opened the vial, and poured pills into his hand. His dose was five. He counted carefully, as if it were a difficult task.

He swallowed the capsules dry and lay down. As his shoulders sank into the padding, he felt the drug begin to work.

Again, he woke from the nightmare; again, everything went wrong. He came to awareness retching and screaming, clawing at the top of his sleep chamber without even the wit to reach for the latch. Laenea cried out in his mind, and he knew that she was dying.

As so many he had dreamed about had died.

Radu saw Vasili's pale face through the thick glass above him.

"Stay asleep! Don't wake up!" The pilot's terrified voice penetrated the heavy lid. "Damn you, stay asleep!"

The latch popped open, but Radu could not lift the lid and Vasili's weight too. He fought to escape and he knew he could not succeed. He was going to faint, but the unconsciousness would not be deep enough to shield him from transit. This time, he would die.

With his last bit of strength he lurched against the chamber lid and flung it open. Struck by its edge, Vasili reeled back and fell, thudding hard against a bulkhead.

On his hands and knees beside his box, Radu coughed and panted. Bile stung sour and hot in his throat and tears of rage and frustration and relief streamed down his face. He was shaking violently.

When he finally got control of himself, he forced himself to stand. Vasili stood pressed against the wall, his hands spread on the smooth metal surface. Saying nothing, Radu went to wash his face and rinse the foul taste from his mouth.

When he glanced up, dripping, into the mirror, he was surprised that he still looked very much the same as always. His hair was more rumpled than usual. Random damp locks, darkened by the water, clung to his forehead. His shirt was filthy, and it stank. He took it off and flung it toward the cleaner. It fell into the bin, but nothing happened. Most of the ship was still in transit mode, so even the semi-intelligent machines were down. The air felt chilly on his bare chest and arms. He stripped and put on clean clothes from his locker. The familiar tasks eased his agitation; even the nausea slowly went away.

What's happening to me? he thought.

In the control room, Vasili gazed into the course computer's display. He looked up, his expression troubled.

"The ship can't go through that again."

"No more can I," Radu said.

They stared at each other, neither knowing what to say.

"Well. Maybe once more," Vasili said.

"Once more! With what? That was the last transit drug!"

"I know it's impossible to take two at once — but could you raise the dose of one of them?"

"My dose is already calculated at the threshold of toxicity. If I took more — if I woke up at all, I'd wake up as a vegetable."

Vasili glanced toward the computer display. It disintegrated and reformed into a sphere representing the ship's immediate surroundings. A star burned brightly just off center, and around it crept its inner family of planets, their sizes exaggerated, their colors enhanced.

Vasili pointed to a tiny sapphire point, the second world from the sun.

"That one — " The star dissolved through the edge of the display, the planet's image grew, and the world's parameters formed above it. "That one is habitable," the pilot said.

"No doubt you'll get a discovery bonus," Radu said.

Vasili ignored the anger and sarcasm in Radu's tone. "That wasn't what I was thinking of," he said mildly, "though for all of that you may be right." After a long silence, he continued. "With some luck," he said, "with as much luck as I have ever had at one time in my life, I'll be able to get this ship home. We went in and out of transit so fast . . . I've looked for this star. The constellations aren't mapped. We're lost. When the ship dives I may be able to figure out where we are then. There are . . . landmarks? Anomalies and patterns. I can't describe them to someone who hasn't seen them. It's hard enough to talk about them to someone who has seen them. Never mind. It doesn't matter. I'm afraid to try to take you back in there. I'm afraid to try to take you home."

Radu stared into the translucent image of the planet. "You could . . . leave me in the truck. I could wait. They're always looking at new drugs, surely they have some in test that would work." He looked at Vasili. "They'd send someone back for me — wouldn't they?"

"I've never heard of this happening before — but I'm sure they would," Vasili said quickly. "If they can, they will . . ."

"But — ?"

"I could take us home fairly easily if I had this system's coordinates. I don't. The first time we surfaced out of transit the system was chartered. Just barely, but I found it. The second time I had to extrapolate — and I had my fingers crossed I'd done it right. I don't even know if I did or not, we fell out too fast for me to get my bearings. Now . . . I don't know where we are. There's so much interstellar dust, I can't find any of the standard markers. I can't match up any of the star patterns or pulsars or anything else. This isn't an exploration ship, it isn't prepared for involved analysis. Even with an x ship, it's safest to go in small steps. We've taken a couple of very large ones." He sounded more and more tense. "Exploration isn't as easy as going down a path and then turning around and coming back. You can't do that because when you turn around it doesn't look the same. Do you see?"

"No."

Vasili lifted his hands, then dropped them, his shoulders slumping. "It's transit," he said. "I can't explain it. I shouldn't even try."

"No trail looks the same coming back, but you can still follow it. It's harder work, but you can still swim up a river after you float down."

"Not if there are rapids — that's exactly it!" His expression brightened, then went grim again. "No, it isn't. It isn't anything like that. It's . . ." He spread his hands helplessly.

"What you are telling me," Radu said, "is that since you don't know where we are, even if you succeed in returning to earth you may not be able to find your way back here."

"I'll take back all the normal space data. It should be possible to figure out where this place is."

"But you can't be sure of that."

Vasili hesitated. "I'm afraid not," he said reluctantly.

"I can stay behind in the truck and take the chance of dying of starvation or asphyxiation, or I can try to go home, and die in transit."

"There's a habitable planet — "

Radu glowered. "How stupid do you think I am? I'm a colonist! I'm not such a fool to expect to survive on a new world alone! Even if I could — why would I want to?"

"Are you such a fool to think you can survive transit?"

"I'd rather die quickly than slowly." He spoke in anger, and only then realized he meant it.

"It isn't that quick, as I understand it."

"If I stay, what are the chances that someone will ever come back for me?"

Vasili looked at the deck. "Getting home — I can't say. Maybe ten to one. Maybe a hundred. But the chances of finding my way back here, if the position can't be charted . . . that's nearly random."

"Random!"

"I'm sorry. Transit — "

"Transit! Never mind. There is no chance at all. Nothing."

"I'm sorry!" Vasili cried. "I don't know what to tell you." He turned away, and whispered, "Maybe this is what happens to all the ships that are lost. Maybe transit spits them out and never lets them back in." He spoke like a hurt, abandoned child, and Radu saw that never getting home again was not what the pilot feared. His terror was the thought of never seeing transit again.

Radu reached out, but stopped before his hand brushed Vasili's shoulder. "You are the best pilot I've ever heard of. Even Atna never saw one better, and he was in the crew since before there were any pilots. You can take this ship home."

"What about you? Getting back here doesn't depend on me," Vasili said miserably. "Only on whether the system can be charted. What about you?"

When Radu joined the crew, he knew ships were sometimes lost. He knew people sometimes died in transit despite the drugs, and he knew that the drugs themselves could kill. Like everyone else, he had prepared himself for the possibility that he might die. His only choice now was the time and place, and where he would be buried.

"I've written my letter," he said. "There's nothing I want to add to it." He wanted to go home. He wanted his ashes to be taken back to Twilight.

Vasili nodded, without turning around.

"Then we will try . . . when you are ready."

Radu gazed through the port at the crowded stars around

them, at nothing. He wanted someone to be with him if he was going to die. He wanted someone to hold his hand, to embrace him, to comfort him. He leaned against the cool clear glass.

"Do you want me to stay here?" Vasili said.

Embarrassed by Vasili's pity, and his own, Radu felt the blood rising to his face.

"I think it would be better if you didn't," he said. He wanted someone, but not a pilot — not this pilot.

"All right," Vasili said. He had waited a decent interval to agree, but relief crept into his voice. Radu did not blame him for being glad to stay away. Radu did not want to see how an ordinary person died in transit either.

The pilot took his hand out of his pocket and awkwardly laid a vial on the table.

"They give us that," he said reluctantly. "In case the ship gets lost and there's no chance of getting home or anywhere. If it gets too bad for you — " He stopped.

Radu nodded. A quick and easy suicide sounded tempting just now. Perhaps the temptation would overcome him.

"Will I know? How long — "

Vasili laughed sharply.

In fury, his fists clenched, Radu took a quick step toward him. Vasili held up his hands in defense. But Radu had already stopped.

"I'm sorry," Vasili said. "I'm terribly sorry. I didn't mean that the way it sounded. It's only that there's no answer to your question. You can't answer questions like that about transit."

Radu found Vasili's statement hard to believe; he thought it was just another way pilots had of keeping their secrets. But he would not beg for an answer.

"I won't start until you tell me," Vasili said.

"Just go on!" Radu yelled. "Hurry up! It's bad enough without having to wait for it." He clenched his hands around the rim of the port. After a moment, he heard the door close as the pilot went into the control room.

In the port, the bright unfamiliar constellations blurred

and swam like the fish in the sea the last time Radu had pressed up against a thick glass wall. That time he knew he must part with Laenea. This time he did not know what would happen.

The ship vibrated against his fingers. He flattened his hands against the wall, feeling the power of the engines. Fascinated in spite of himself, he waited for whatever change would come. A drop of sweat trickled down the side of his face. He ducked his head to wipe it off on his sleeve. Unless he died instantly, he would at least have a few minutes to see what the mystery was about transit. Though he had wondered, he had never asked. It did not take much intuition or observation to discover that the pilots would not tell.

The vibration of the engines rose to a peak. Radu's heart pounded. He cupped his hands around his face, shielding the port from the room's glare. Nothing outside changed: The stars, of course, did not move. But slowly Radu did detect an alteration in the state of the universe outside. The great jeweled white mass of stars around him shifted, brightened, and intensified to brilliance so abruptly that Radu stepped back startled. He blinked, and the universe faded to gray.

Radu touched the glass with the tips of his fingers. It remained smooth and cool. But nothing lay beyond it, nothing at all. Radu strained his eyes for any hint of movement, any unusual scene, the embodiment of fantasies or nightmares, the perception of hidden truths. He closed his eyes and concentrated on his other senses, waiting for some revelation, or even for a warning of his own impending death.

But there was nothing.

Radu sat down again and waited. He looked at his hands, watching for the skin to age and wrinkle. But they remained the same, brown and square, peasant's hands. Despite his name, if his family included high-bred nobility, it was many generations back. His fingernails were short and rough, and sometimes he bit them.

The vibration of the engines continued, smooth and steady;

otherwise Radu felt no sensation of movement. He let himself feel his time sense, which had always expanded to include wherever he was at the moment. He had never paid much attention to the ability: It was a party trick, at most an anomalous and occasionally useful convenience. He could not teach anyone else to do it, nor could he explain it.

Relativity required that time, as Radu perceived it, pass at different rates in different places. He was used to that, and he was used to feeling the changes intensify whenever he was on an accelerating ship. Here, in transit, the underlying order had dissolved into chaos. Time passed in one place at one rate, in another at another, but when he thought about the first again the hierarchy had changed. How he perceived that there was a change, he did not know. It was like being in a dark room, surrounded by moving sculptures, able to look at each piece only for a moment as a single light rested on one, blinked off, and blinked on illuminating another in a random order, at dizzying speed.

He stopped trying to sort out his perceptions and waited quietly until he regained his equilibrium. Then he focused his attention on subjective time alone. To his surprise, it felt and behaved exactly as it would have if he had been in any other place. Pilots were said to experience a perturbation of their time sense in transit, but perhaps that was the result of the changes they submitted to in freeing themselves from the disparity between relativistic time in normal space, and the nonrelativistic universe of transit.

However ordinary transit felt to Radu, it was profoundly unknown, and he was in danger. He could do nothing; he could not even reassure himself. He could only wait, without knowing how long the wait would be.

So he waited, drenched in slow cold sweat, staring out the porthole at the infinite blank grayness. Once in a while he thought he saw a flash of color outside, but the flashes were always at the edge of his vision, and disappeared before he could look at them directly. He decided they must be his imagination.

Hugging his knees to his chest, he put his head down. Comforted by darkness, he waited.

Time passed. His mind counted it as hours, but tension made it feel like days. When he nearly dozed, he jerked awake, afraid. Why should he be afraid to sleep? He felt groggy, and the fragments of a dream swirled around him — he heard Laenea's voice — and vanished. He shook his head, stood, and paced across the crew lounge and back again.

He went down the hall and flung open the door to the control room.

At the console, the pilot stared out the sweeping forward port. The sound of the door disturbed him, or he saw Radu's reflection distorted in the glass. He spun toward him with a cry. Vasili Nikolaievich's horror gradually changed to shock. After a moment he exhaled sharply, fumbled for his breathing mask, and fitted it over his mouth and nose. He drew in pure oxygen from the tank slung over his shoulder. When he took the mask away he had composed himself.

"Do you know where we are?" Radu asked. "Are we still lost?"

The pilot gazed at him; he blinked once, exhaled again, took another breath, and answered. The faint tremor in his voice betrayed his apparent calm.

"I know where we are," he said. "I've found the way."

"How much longer do we have to stay in transit?"

Vasili breathed deeply from his mask. "I tried to explain that the question isn't answerable, we've got about the same distance still to go as we've already been, but that doesn't mean the time will seem the same." He spoke all in one breath, then put the mask back to his face. Breathing was the last normal rhythm pilots gave up in order to survive transit: They took irregular gulps of pure oxygen and exhaled only when the carbon dioxide level in their blood began to interfere with the exchange of oxygen.

"Something would have happened by now if it were going to, wouldn't it?"

"I guess so," the pilot said, "at least I think so, I'm sorry to keep saying this but I don't know because we haven't got any clear idea how things happen to normal people in transit." He paused for breath. "The ones who were still alive couldn't describe the sequences, and something that looks solid and sensible in transit will be something even a pilot can't explain afterwards, you'll see . . ." He ran out of breath and returned to his mask.

"I don't feel any different," Radu said, then realized what Vasili had been trying to avoid saying. "You mean there's no way to tell if something will happen to me until we leave transit."

The pilot kept the mask to his face much longer than necessary. Finally he took it away. He stretched his free hand toward Radu, as if in supplication. "I'm no expert, I haven't studied what happened in the early days, besides, nothing happened to you the times you woke up."

Radu slumped down in the other seat, resigned to more uncertainty. The pilot glanced briefly over the instruments and immediately returned his attention to the blank gray port. He breathed occasionally from the mask, but so seldom that he obviously did it only in response to real need.

Radu watched the digital numbers on the clock flick by, less evenly than the seconds ticked past in his mind. He tried to compare them for reference. After a while he shook his head in irritation. Something peculiar was going on, but he could not figure out what it was because he had forgotten what the clock had said when he first started watching it. That had nothing to do with the vagaries of transit: He was too distracted to be able to concentrate.

"Now that you've seen it," Vasili said, "what do you think of it?"

"I beg your pardon? Think of what?"

"Transit!"

Radu frowned. "I think it's excessively dull. But if you want to invent mysteries about it, I won't tell the secret."

The pilot's expression was nearly as surprised as when Radu appeared awake and alive and unchanged.

"You mean you don't see it — you don't feel it?"

"See what? Feel what?"

The pilot flung out his arms, pointing to the viewport. "See that — and feel . . . its presence, all around you, palpable, it's indescribable, it's different for everyone."

"But there's nothing there," Radu said.

Vasili Nikolaievich did not reply for a moment. Then, "What did you say?"

"There's nothing there. A blank gray fog. No space, no stars. Just nothing."

"You see nothing?"

"Are you trying to make a fool of me? Shall I put my fantasies up there for your entertainment?" Radu spoke in anger. His fantasies were too painful even for him.

"What are you?" the pilot whispered. "Are you some disguised machine, are you being tested, am I?"

"What?" Radu almost laughed, but the pilot was deadly serious, and frightened. "I'm a human being, just like you." He stretched out his arm, and his sleeve hiked up above the bandage on his wrist. "Pilot, you've seen me bleed."

The pilot shrugged. "Easy enough to counterfeit."

"This is ridiculous," Radu said. "Intelligent machines don't function properly in transit. Everyone knows that."

"Nor do ordinary human beings."

"If they invented such a machine there'd be no reason to keep it secret."

"Pilots would be obsolete — we may be anyway, because of you, no matter what you are, despite all the effort that's gone into making us . . . acceptable."

"This conversation makes no sense, pilot," Radu said. He could think of no gentler way to put it. "If someone went to all the trouble of making a human machine this would be a purely idiotic way to test it. And if someone made a human machine they'd choose a better face than mine to put it behind."

The pilot's tension eased slightly. "That's true," he said with childlike cruelty, "that last, at least, is true, but machine or not, you're immune to transit — you're oblivious to it! — and whatever you are, you make pilots redundant."

"I'm no pilot," Radu said. "I haven't the ability or the skills. And I haven't the desire. I'm no threat to you."

Facing the blank window, the pilot took a deep, slow breath. "Maybe you really believe that," he said, his back to Radu so his voice sounded remote, "or wish you did, but you're wrong."

Radu folded his arms, glowering. "Or you could be wrong," he said sarcastically. "I still could die."

"No," the pilot said softly, "it will be a long time before your bones go to dust, you'll live . . . unless I kill you myself."

Astonished, Radu made no response.

"Go away," the pilot said, "please go away."

Radu left the control room, though the tortured plea asked far more of him than that.

6

PILOTS HAD THE REPUTATION of being not completely stable. Radu had never paid the idea much attention. He did not know why talented people often fostered rumors of madness; truly insane people were unpleasant to be around. The only pilot Radu knew at all closely was Laenea Trevelyan, and she was exceptionally sane. Vasili was a bit eccentric, surely, but — mad? Radu tried to dismiss the pilot's threat to kill him. No one had ever threatened him before. Back on Twilight, people lucky enough to escape the plague had resented him for contracting it and recovering. He was marked by his scars, and some people hated him for living while their own families died. But even in grief and fury, no one back home had ever threatened his life.

The suicide pills remained on the table in the crew lounge. Radu picked up the vial, threw it down the disposal, and tried to persuade himself that he was not afraid of the pilot.

As Vasili Nikolaievich predicted, when the ship surfaced from transit, Radu did not die. He did not even notice the transition. He was sitting in the lounge, bored and tired but still unwilling to allow himself to sleep. For no good reason he was afraid to give up his consciousness, however naturally.

Once in a while he glanced at the port, but the dead gray expanse, never mysterious, grew tedious. He began to ignore it; he began deliberately to avoid looking at it. But when he nearly fell asleep and roused himself, startled and disoriented and searching wildly for the fragments of another dissolving dream, he stared around the room and his gaze stopped at the port. Space had returned, normal space and a pattern of widely scattered stars. Earth, very close, blue and white and brown, loomed lazily above.

The door opened behind him. Radu faced Vasili Nikolaievich, who nodded once without smiling. As he turned away, Radu took a step forward.

"I want to call Laenea," he said.

"You can't."

"You have no right — "

"You can't, because she's out on her first transit flight." Vasili Nikolaievich closed himself into the control room alone.

The tension Radu had been under for so long drained slowly away. Between exhaustion, hunger, and the three different sleep drugs he had taken, he felt shaky and nauseated. His slashed wrist ached fiercely..

He wished his dreams of Laenea in distress would fade away and vanish in the way of most dreams, but this they refused to do. Nothing would make him feel easy about her safety until she returned and he could speak to her. His nightmares, the hallucinations he remembered from Twilight, and Atna's vision all twisted together, mixing reality and fantasy. Atna's premonition of danger had too many connections to everything that had happened for Radu to be able to dismiss it so easily anymore.

He felt trapped and uncertain, helpless to confront important matters, yet confronted by the trivial chores of preparing the ship for its return to Earthstation. He cursed, and got to work.

As the other chamber cycled Orca back toward life, Radu returned resentfully to his own body box and cleaned up after himself where he had retched. In the bathroom he washed his hands and splashed cold water on his face.

Did you expect the pilot to wipe up your vomit? he asked himself sarcastically.

As he prepared a quick breakfast — they would not have time for anything more — he drank a mug of coffee, wondering if the caffeine would make him sick. But it helped.

When he heard Orca trying to get up, he hurried to her side and helped her out. Her fingers were cold, the translucent swimming webs nearly colorless. He hugged her, stroking her neck, rubbing her sides and back to warm her. She shivered violently.

"Damn," she said. Her teeth chattered. She hugged Radu tightly, leaning her forehead against his chest. "I feel awful."

"It's all right. We're only two hours out from earth."

He held her until her shivering subsided.

Orca laughed shakily. "Thanks. I'm okay now." She drew away from him, embarrassed. "I never reacted like that before."

Radu kept on lightly stroking her arms, for she did not look fully recovered.

"Did something happen?" she asked. "Do you feel any different than usual?"

"No," he said automatically, then, trying to take back the lie, "well, yes. It was more uncomfortable to wake up this time." That, at least, was an accurate statement. He wanted to tell her the truth, but he was afraid to. He did not want to see the same look in her eyes that he had seen in the pilot's.

"I'm glad Atna stayed home," Orca said. "That was a hard dive. I don't know what it would have done to him. I think he was right to be afraid."

"Yes," Radu said slowly, reluctantly. "Yes. His vision was correct."

Orca went below to check out the transit engines and prepare the ship for refueling. Radu tuned in a data signal from Earthstation, then, without waiting for the information to arrive, reset the clocks in the lounge. He had been reprimanded once for doing a reset before checking local time. The senior crew member had not bothered to notice that his reset was accurate. The record of a data signal contact saved trouble.

The ship had been out six weeks earth subjective time. It would dock well within the deadline for the bonus. Vasili might even be able to rejoin his exploration team.

Now that he had a moment to himself in the control room, Radu tried to call Laenea, hoping she had returned since Vasili asked about her. But her ship was still out. As far as he could tell, it was an even bet whether he or Laenea had been awake in transit first.

He hoped she had found it more interesting than he had.

She had been gone for quite a while. Radu wondered just how long training flights were meant to be. He tried to put off his worry by reminding himself that time in transit, at superluminal speeds, had no correlation with time in Einsteinian space, where all travel was slower than the speed of light. Against the six weeks that had passed on earth, Radu counted that the normal space segment of the trip to Ngthummulun had taken less than forty-eight hours, and he had been awake in transit barely a day.

Radu watered and fed the life-support system. Both the instruments and his own senses indicated that the catalyzed photosynthesis was performing with efficiency.

"What do you plan to do?"

Radu started at Vasili's sudden appearance.

"I don't know," Radu said. "I'd planned to find another automated ship and go back out again, but — "

"You can't fly on an automated ship anymore. You'll blast it out of transit every time."

"I realize that!"

"Tell me something. Do you dislike me in particular, or pilots in general?"

"Neither," Radu said. "It's only that I react to pilots the same way pilots react to normal people when they're too near."

"What!"

Radu shrugged.

"I never heard of that happening before," Vasili said.

Radu sighed. The last thing he wanted was to be told something else about himself that was unusual.

"You'll have to stay here," the pilot said.

"On Earthstation? Why?"

"You can go to earth if you want. But you can't go any farther without the cooperation of a pilot, and no pilot will let you fly until we've decided what to do with you."

"Vasili Nikolaievich," Radu said, trying to keep his tone reasonable, "something very odd has happened. We need to talk to the administrators about it — "

The pilot strode toward him with such fury that Radu backed up a step.

"And then what? If you ever got away from them — if they don't take your brain apart cell by cell to find out what makes it work — "

Radu felt no inclination whatever to laugh at the ludicrous idea.

" — you'd still have to ship out with a pilot. And if you betray us . . ." He let his words trail off. The threat was all the stronger for only being implied.

"Pilot, I'm not your enemy. I'm not your rival. We ought to find out if anyone else is like me. I could have caused our ship to be lost — maybe this is what happened to other lost ships."

"What to do isn't your decision."

"I think that it is."

"If you say anything to anyone without the consent of the pilots, you'll regret it."

Radu gazed down at him. "You know," he said suddenly, "Atna's premonition was right."

"Don't be absurd," Vasili said. He turned abruptly and left the room.

Radu swore under his breath. Losing his temper was a bad mistake: Now he had complicated matters even worse. And it had been completely unnecessary to remind Vasili of Atna's warning. He did not even know why he had done it.

Orca climbed up from the engine room and slammed the hatch shut.

"What was that all about?"

Radu hesitated, wondering how much she had heard. He had to put aside the temptation to retract his earlier lie and explain everything. But that would put Orca in danger to no purpose.

"Vasili Nikolaievich was just . . . making clear the relative status of pilots and crew." Almost worse than telling a lie was inventing such a feeble one.

Orca glanced at him quizzically, but if she had more questions she kept them to herself.

The ship docked at Earthstation. Before the last remnants of artificial gravity faded and the radial acceleration of the satellite took over, the chief marketing agent from Ngthummulun banged energetically on the outer hatch. Radu opened it, and the agent bounded in.

"I'm amazed at your speed," she said. "And very pleased." She grabbed Vasili's hand and pumped it. Looking extremely uncomfortable, the pilot extricated himself as quickly as possible.

"I've credited your accounts," the agent said cheerfully, not even noticing Vasili's distress. "I have a certain amount of authority in determining the bonuses, which I've used."

Radu felt too tired to react. Besides, most of his pay went directly to Twilight's account; he never even saw it. Vasili muttered something and returned his attention to the message flowing in above the controls.

Orca gave both Vasili and Radu a disgusted look. She gripped the agent's hand warmly. "We appreciate it. Thank you. Radu will have your cargo module freed up and ready for transfer in a couple of minutes."

Radu heard a subtle "or else" in her tone.

"Fine," the agent said. "I have space reserved on the four o'clock shuttle — I may just make it." She clasped Orca's hand again, and hurried off as quickly as she had arrived.

Orca swung around on Radu and Vasili. She folded her arms across her chest. "That was about as rude a performance as I ever saw," she said. "I don't care how mad you are at each other — or why. It's no excuse for the way you behaved to her."

Radu stared at the deck. Vasili looked over his shoulder at Orca, then turned away again.

Orca made a sharp noise of irritation and anger and strode out of the room. Her shoes made no noise, but the engine room hatch clanged loudly when she threw it open, and again when she banged it shut.

At that moment Vasili snarled a curse and jumped to his feet, plunged out of the control room and into his cabin, and slammed his door behind him.

Radu stood alone, upset, angry, and confused. He glanced over at the control panel, where Vasili's message hung fading in the air. Perhaps he was invading Vasili's privacy, but before it disappeared, he read it. Then he understood the pilot's reaction. He had been replaced on the exploration team, and even though it was not scheduled to leave for several days, his request for reinstatement had been turned down.

Orca and Radu worked apart and in silence, Radu transferring the cargo module and shutting down the ship, Orca finishing with the engines. When he was less than halfway done, Radu heard Vasili leave. The pilot had no obligation to stay, no captain's duty to help his own crew or to turn the ship over to its next users.

By the time Radu finished work, he felt groggy. He gingerly opened the hatch to the engine room.

"Orca? Can I help?"

She climbed up the ladder. "No, I'm all done." She sat on the edge of the hatchway, rubbed her eyes, and yawned.

"You were right," Radu said. "About the way I behaved, I mean. I'm sorry."

"Most of those agents are such sharks, we ought to at least be civil to the ones who act human."

"Vasili had an excuse," Radu said. "He was waiting for the reply for his x team."

"Did he get it?"

"They turned him down."

She snorted. "He didn't really expect them to give it back to him, did he?"

"I think that he did."

"Radu, the administrators do as little as possible to interfere with their profits." She stood up, stretched, and dogged the hatch shut. "They never change anything that works, even for the chance to do it better. Vaska's broken the elapsed time record for every round trip he's ever piloted. He can't earn express bonuses for the transit authority if he's off exploring."

"But he'd be helping find new planets — "

"They don't make as much as you'd expect off new worlds. They can't claim them, they can't own them. They wouldn't even look for them if there weren't a subsidy and a reward."

"But they gave Vasili the assignment at first — "

"And he never got to go on it, did he?"

"That's a very cynical way to look at things," Radu said.

"Tell me that again after you've been on the crew a little longer," she said.

He would have liked to point out an explanation for the sequence of events that had some more altruistic structure behind it, but he could come up with nothing better than coincidence and bureaucratic thoughtlessness.

"You look like I feel," Orca said, "and I feel like hell. Let's get out of here."

In the locker room, Orca held a wyuna up to the light, gazed into it, and put it in her duffel bag. Then she stuffed clothing, bright wrinkled bits of gold and metallic rainbows, in on top. Subjectively the trip had been so short that a change of clothes had hardly been necessary. Radu retrieved his other shirt from the cleaner and flung it into his bag.

They left the ship and checked into Earthstation. Their accounts were, as promised, credited with a substantial bonus, and Radu's was already debited with a transfer of funds to Twilight's trade balance. He wondered if his contribution made even a blip in the debt his world had incurred as a result of the plague.

Radu glanced at the shuttle schedule when Orca called it up. No seats were available until the next day. Radu clenched his fist around the handle of his duffel bag. All he wanted was to get away from Earthstation, away from the pilots, to a place where he could think.

Orca made a reservation for herself; Radu reserved a place and put his name on the waiting list for any opening, to any landing port. Orca wanted to go to North America Northwest, but for Radu it held too many memories of Laenea. He would prefer to go elsewhere.

He and Orca stepped onto the moving ramp that led to the station's crew section.

"Are you going out again?" Orca asked.

"Not immediately," Radu said. "And you?"

"No. My family's having a . . . a meeting. I promised to go if I possibly could."

"Where do you live?"

"In the Strait of Georgia. Do you know where that is?"

"Approximately." He had studied the areas around the landing platforms before his first trip down; he had chosen North America Northwest because the climate seemed most like Twilight's. But he had never seen the mainland or the inland waters that lay east of the port; he had never even left the artificial island.

"It's beautiful," she said. "When I'm gone, I do miss it. I even miss my family." She grinned ruefully. "When I'm home, I don't get along with some of them all that well."

Perhaps that explained why Orca, a diver, was working on the crew. He had wanted to ask her, but it was the custom, on Twilight and most colony worlds, to be satisfied with the information people volunteered about themselves. Besides, if Radu questioned Orca she could do the same to him, with the right to expect an answer. He could give whatever lame explanations he pleased about his home world's need for hard currency, but he preferred to keep to himself his real reasons for leaving. And his reasons for staying on earth right now he *could* not talk about.

Radu and Orca stepped off the ramp and through the entrance into the crew sector.

Six pilots stood in a semicircle waiting for them. Ignoring the diver, they stared at Radu. At one end of the line, Vasili Nikolaievich watched Radu coldly, as if they had never met, as if they had never spoken together civilly. Orca took Radu's hand. He grasped her long, strong fingers gratefully.

She stepped hesitantly forward. Repressing an urge to pull her back and flee, Radu followed. The pilots stayed in their unwavering line — and they *were* all pilots: Only Vasili among them did not show a scar.

"Hello, Vaska," Orca said to him. He did not move or speak or look at her; he simply kept staring at Radu.

"Vasili Nikolaievich, I promise you — " Radu cut off his words when the pilot's expression hardened from warning to anger.

"You're to come with us," Vasili said, and, to Orca, "You've had your chances. Your presence won't be required."

"Who says?" Still holding Radu's hand, pulling him along behind her, Orca shouldered her way forward.

"Don't make trouble, Orca," one of the other pilots said. "This has nothing to do with you."

"Oh? What does it have to do with? What the hell is going on?" She did not even slow down.

The pilots turned and moved with them, surrounding them again, closing in.

Radu felt his pulse quickening. He hoped it was only fear, but as the circle finished forming his heart began to pound, clenching in his chest like something trapped, sending his blood in a rush through his veins, so fast that his vision dimmed in a scarlet haze and a phantom wind roared in his ears. He stumbled after Orca, trying to calm himself, but his control was gone. He could no more slow his pulse and lower his blood pressure than he could grow a pair of wings and glide from Earthstation to earth itself. He walked faster — he tried to run but almost fell — and the pilots kept up easily. Orca glanced back at him. Radu could not speak. They were only a short way from a common room, where they would find other crew and station personnel. Radu set himself to get that far. Surely, in so public a setting, the pilots would have to leave him alone.

He stumbled again. His knee hit the metal floor hard and his fingers slipped from Orca's hand. He knelt, gasping for breath, his heart laboring. He could hear nothing but the roar of his pulse. There was nothing to hear. He raised his head slowly. The pilots stared down at him, still without speaking, fading in and out through his obscured vision.

Orca tried to hold him up. He heard her, very far away, shouting.

"Call a doctor! Damn you all, will you help!"

Radu collapsed, but the diver kept him from falling and eased him to the deck. He felt cold metal against his back, against his quivering hands. The lights above him stretched away in infinite glowing lines. He felt the vibrations of footsteps through the floor and flung his arm across his eyes. He did not want to see the pilots gazing down at him, willing him to die.

Then, almost imperceptibly, his heartbeat slowed. The pain clamped around his chest lessened, and he could breathe more easily. He let his arm fall to his side and opened his eyes. Orca knelt beside him, bending over him with her fingers at the angle of his jaw.

The pilots were gone.

"Don't move," Orca said. "I'll get help."

Somehow he managed to grasp her wrist before she stood.

"No, wait." He stopped to catch his breath. He could only fill his lungs halfway, and his fingers trembled feebly.

"You're having a heart attack!"

Radu shook his head. "It was . . . something else."

Orca frowned. "You're nuts, I'm calling somebody. I'd've done it before only I was afraid you'd need resuscitation."

Radu had an overpowering urge to laugh, which made him gasp and giggle weakly.

"What the hell is so funny?"

"A diver knowing how to give artificial respiration." He laughed again.

"We're not the only people in the water," she said, "and sometimes the landers get into trouble. Good gods, who cares? Lie down." She started away.

Radu's laughter trailed off, but he pushed himself up and tried to stand. Orca's spangled jacket slipped from his shoulders where she had thrown it. His fingers felt numb; he had to concentrate to make them grasp it. Orca heard him, stopped, and turned back. He held her jacket out to her.

Watching him, worried, she took it and absently slipped it on. She glanced down. There was a run in her sleeveless knitted shirt, where the gold thread had parted and the fabric unravelled in a line up her ribs and the side of her small breast. She jerked the front edges of the jacket together, hiding the flaw in irritation.

"You're all right?"

"Yes."

"What happened?"

"I react badly to pilots. I don't understand why. I think it's getting worse."

"Did they know? Did they do it deliberately?"

"I guess they did." He had, after all, told Vasili Nikolaievich.

"What did they want?"

"They wanted . . . to convince me not to tell anyone what they want."

She scowled at him. "All right. Forget it." She turned and started away. He tried to follow, but stumbled and nearly fell. She caught him and slipped his arm over her shoulders to let him lean on her. "Come on."

Radu would not have gotten very far without her. She helped him along to the station's section of small crew rooms. Finding an empty cubicle, she unlatched the door, got him inside, and eased him down on the narrow bed.

"Want your boots off?"

"I can do it." He bent his knee, drawing one foot toward his hands as he lay flat on the hard mattress. He did not feel as if he could sit up again.

"Don't be stupid." Orca grasped his boot and pulled.

"Be careful of your hands — "

Orca gave the boot a solid jerk and it slid off. She dropped it and held up her hand, spreading her fingers so the translucent webbing showed.

"I know it looks fragile," she said. "But it isn't. It's very tough." Then she showed him a long, jagged scar between the second and third fingers of her left hand. "And it heals fast when something does happen." She grabbed his other boot and pulled it off. "Besides, it doesn't make that much difference swimming."

"Then why do you have it?" he asked, surprised.

"Because when people thought about what divers would be like, even before anybody could create us, they always imagined us looking like this. So that's how they designed us. We decided to stay this way."

"Are your feet like that too?" Radu never would have asked such a question if he were not so tired. He blushed. "I'm sorry — "

"I have foldover toes, like a platypus," she said. "With webs between." Then she grinned. "No, my feet are pretty much the same as anybody's, except for the nails. Want to see?"

He nodded, curious, and glad she was not offended by his prying.

"There's nothing secret about being a diver, you know." She sat on the edge of his bed, pulled off her red canvas shoes, and wiggled her toes. They were long, but not abnormally so, and they were not appreciably webbed.

Radu pushed himself up on one elbow and took her foot in his other hand. Her toenails were like claws, cat claws, tiger claws, retractable and heavy and quit sharp. Orca flexed her foot and the claws extended. One dimpled the flesh of his hand, very gently.

"Good protection," she said. "You need it sometimes, in

the sea. They aren't much against sharks, but then there aren't many dangerous sharks where I live." She retracted her claws and reached for her shoes.

Radu lay back on the bed as she stood up.

"Do you think they'll come after you again?" she asked abruptly.

Radu shook his head. "I don't know." His reasoning was none too clear right now; he did not want to think about pilots. He could not. Surrounded by normal space time, he wanted only to sleep.

Orca stood gazing at the closed door, silhouetted against its dirty white surface. She shrugged, an action more like shaking off doubt than expressing it, and put her hand up against the panel to seal the room against outside intrusion. She turned around.

"I'm not so recently out of the water that I think this is a clever line. But I don't want to leave you alone tonight, and to tell you the truth I'm not anxious to be alone myself. Do you mind if I stay?"

"No," Radu said. "Of course not."

She kicked off her shoes again and dropped her spangled jacket on the floor. "Is there room? Not that there's much difference between floors and beds in these places."

"There's plenty of room." Radu moved over and Orca lay down beside him, between him and the door. He was as glad of her company as he was grateful for her concern.

She smelled like no one he had ever been close to before, cool and salty, like the sea's morning mist. He wondered if he smelled, to her, like forest or earth or alien ground.

"Lights out, please," Radu said. The lights obeyed, leaving the room completely dark.

Radu lay in the narrow bed for nearly an hour, unable to rest, trying not to toss and turn.

"You can't sleep," Orca said softly.

"No. How did you know? Did I wake you?"

"I can see you," Orca said.

"It's pitch dark in here," Radu said. That was one of the few things Radu did *not* like about being in space. Interior rooms, rooms with no windows, were as lightless as caves. He turned his head toward the sound of Orca's voice, but he could see nothing of her, not even the glint of her pale, fine hair. The scarlet pattern of the blood vessels in his retinas flickered against blackness.

"For you it's dark," she said. "Not for me. You don't know much about divers, do you?"

"Only that they have foldover toes, like a platypus," he said. "With webs between."

Orca chuckled and dug her claws gently into the heavy fabric of his pants. He heard the quick pricking sound, but her talons never touched his skin.

"No," he said, more seriously. "I only know what you've told me."

"We see farther into the infrared, and farther into the violet, than humans do."

"Don't you consider yourself still human?"

"My father would say no," she said.

"What would you say?"

She hesitated. "I'd say we were more different than a race, but less different than a separate species. We're a transition phase."

"A transition to what?"

"I don't know," she said, and to Radu she sounded very sad.

"What's the matter?" He slid his hand up her arm to her shoulder, to her throat, to her face. He touched her cheek in the darkness and brushed the tears with his fingertips. "Orca, what's wrong?"

"I don't know what we're changing to. I'm not sure I want to know."

"But it's all speculation, it's all generations away."

"Not for us," she said. "We didn't become divers by natural evolution. There's no reason to slow down to that rate now."

"Oh." Radu felt embarrassed by his own ignorance. "Of course. Your next generation could be different."

"Or I could."

"You — ?"

"That's what the meeting's about. To decide if we should change. The techniques are easy enough. You figure out what you want, build the DNA, construct a series of carrier viruses, sensitize yourself to them — " Radu felt her shrug. "You feel like you have the flu for a few days, while the virus replicates. Then you're well, the new genes are integrated, and they slowly change you to fit."

Radu suddenly shuddered.

"Hey," Orca said. "It's not bad at all, not really. The process itself is trivial. I've done it myself, a couple of times. But just for little things. The big ones scare me, but they won't turn us into Frankenstein monsters."

"Of course not, I'm sorry — I don't know why I reacted like that. Have you ever had an experience, and in the middle of it suddenly felt you'd gone through it before, exactly as it was happening?"

"Sure. *Déjà vu*, it's called. It's just a trick your mind plays on you, like an echo. Crossed axons."

"I suppose," Radu said. "Whatever it was, it made me understand why you feel wary of the changes you might have to undergo."

"I wouldn't *have* to," she said. "It would be my choice. But if I didn't, and everyone else did . . ."

She stopped.

"You'd be left behind," Radu said finally. "Whatever it was your family was going to, you'd be left behind."

Orca nodded against his shoulder, then held him in silence for some time.

"Let's talk about something else," she said. Her voice was easy again, full of her usual good humor. "Tell me about Twilight. What did you do before this, or did you join the crew straight out of school?"

"We never formally go to school," Radu said. "But we never formally leave it, either. There aren't enough people on Twilight for many of us to spend all our time studying. So we do that, and other things too. I liked geology, so I went on surveys every summer from the time I was old enough to be more asset than liability, first with a group and later by myself. Everybody does everything on Twilight, more or less. I helped in my clan's nursery, and built houses, and I piloted one of the blimps — "

Orca made a strange noise.

"Something wrong?"

"A *blimp?*"

"Don't you like blimps?"

"The only thing I like less than blimps is boats."

"But why?"

"Because with a boat you can't see what's under you. It's like driving a ground car down the road with your eyes and ears covered."

"That doesn't explain why you don't like blimps."

"You'll laugh," she said.

"That's possible," Radu said. "I could use a good laugh right now."

Orca chuckled again. "Get ready for one, then. I get airsick. I get seasick even worse."

Radu did laugh. Orca was not offended, because she laughed, too.

"Most divers don't like boats," she said. "You need a lot of equipment to find out things that you can learn underwater by giving one good shout and listening carefully."

"What about blimps?" Radu said.

"As far as I know," she said, "I'm the only person in the world who doesn't like blimps."

"The only person in several worlds, I think. I got to fly ours for only one season because the waiting list to take it over was so long." Suddenly he yawned.

"Me, too," Orca said.

Tentatively each put an arm around the other, and then they slept.

Radu struggled up out of dreams that, instead of being distinct and vivid, were jumbled and muddy, mixing Laenea and transit and homesickness and fear. He sat bolt upright, staring in the darkness toward the door, expecting it to open and reveal a line of pilots beyond.

He pushed the paranoid thought away, muttered for the lights, and looked around the tiny windowless room. Orca was gone. He was disappointed, and rather surprised, but he could hardly blame her.

Using the communications terminal in the room, he checked the status of Laenea's transit ship. It was still out. He frowned, and rechecked, but the display gave no additional information. He shut it off.

Combing his hair with his fingers and shedding his clothes behind him, he went into the minuscule bathroom.

No one on Twilight would have taken as long or as hot a shower as he indulged in. He did not even feel guilty about it.

Earthstation has plenty of water, he thought. It has plenty of power. I know that. But that isn't why I'm standing here with luxurious amounts of water running wasted between my toes. It's because I'm changing. I'm coming to expect what this life has to offer. And I like it.

But he disliked that realization.

When Radu came out again, more relaxed but no closer than before to knowing what he should do, Orca was sitting crosslegged on the rumpled bed with breakfast spread out before her. Radu stepped back, reaching for a towel.

"I've seen naked people before," Orca said. "We hardly ever even wear clothes at home. Come and eat."

He wrapped himself up in the towel before he came out.

"I thought you'd left," he said.

"I did. But I came back."

"I mean permanently."

She stopped smiling. "I thought about it."

Radu sat on the edge of the bed. "It probably would have been better if you had."

Orca handed him a piece of fruit and began unwrapping elegantly folded paper parcels.

"You're determined not to accept any help, aren't you?"

Radu took a cautious bite of the round yellow-green fruit. It was tart and sweet.

"This is very good," he said. "What is it?"

"An apple," Orca said impatiently.

Radu took another bite, and started to comment again on the taste, but Orca's expression made him think better of any more dissembling.

"I'm sorry you've been involved," he said. "If I knew anything you could do I'd accept your help gladly. But the truth is I don't understand what's happened myself, or what I can do about it."

"Oh, come on. This is what you were arguing with Vaska about, back on the ship, wasn't it? As for that little production last night — you were scared, gods know so was I, but you weren't surprised."

"I'd be doing you an injury if I told you everything," Radu said. "I'd be putting you in considerable danger."

"Look, Radu, we're crew. We don't give that up when we leave the ship."

"It would be stupid to endanger you any more!"

She shrugged. "I'm in about as deep as I can be. They'll assume I know anything you know."

Of course she was right. If the pilots saw him as a sufficient threat, they would have to believe Orca was dangerous to them as well. It would not be safe for them to leave her alone.

"You'll have to tell them you don't," he said. "They know how to detect the truth — "

"They wouldn't even bother to try. Divers learn biocontrol as well as pilots do. Better, in some ways. We can neutralize stress so it doesn't even show. I could pretend to lie — but I can't prove it if I'm telling the truth."

Radu rubbed his face with one hand. "It's pointless," he said. "Simply pointless."

Orca crumpled a piece of wrapping paper slowly and very tightly, and dropped the wad on the bed.

as her lover. She nodded to Orca, and smiled at Radu, as if to say, So, my dear, you like your lovers exotic: but you should have taken my advice about pilots in the first place.

Radu looked away from her, blushing. He did not speak to her, and he was too embarrassed to say anything to Orca.

Neither Radu nor Orca broke the silence, all the way down. They landed on the port platform late at night. In the disorder of getting off the shuttle, Orca vanished among the other passengers. Though he was glad she would be out of his conflict with the pilots, after her departure Radu felt very much alone. He saw Ramona-Teresa in the crowd, but she paid him no attention. Radu was puzzled. She had not been with the pilots who had confronted him. Could she be unaware of what had happened?

Radu passed his hand over his eyes and rubbed his temples. She knew. He was quite sure that she knew.

He went to the nearest communications terminal and requested the status of Laenea's ship.

It was still out.

His concern increased. He needed to find someone who knew about pilot training, who knew how long the first flight usually lasted.

Why don't you catch up to Ramona-Teresa, and ask her? he thought, and laughed quickly.

"Do you wish to receive your message?" the terminal asked him.

"Do I have one?"

Taking his question as an affirmative, the terminal responded, spitting out hard copy for privacy rather than spinning the words in the air or speaking them aloud: I must see you alone as soon as you return. Come to my restaurant. Marc.

Radu touched the wyuna in his pocket. He was surprised that Laenea's mysterious friend even remembered him.

Radu shoved the message into his pocket beside the wyuna. He wondered what Marc could have to say to him, to sound so urgent. He decided he had better find out.

7

RADU'S SEAT on the earth shuttle was right next to Orca's. It would have been easier if they could have changed, but the ship was full. They strapped in without speaking as the craft prepared to undock.

Radu glanced carefully up and down the aisle, noting each passenger. No one else was crew. A few, by their ease in weightlessness, were station personnel; most were tourists or other visitors.

He wished he had something to say to Orca to ease the anger and distrust he had forced between them. She sat straight and tense. He followed her gaze toward the front of the shuttle.

A pilot had just come on board. Radu's pulse rate increased.

Ramona-Teresa paused in the aisle when she reached his place. Her glance at him was milder than when she had warned Laenea not to take Radu, or anyone else not a pilot,

Marc's restaurant was dark. Radu stood outside the closed ornamental gate, unsure what to do.

Marc's image flickered into existence before him.

"Hello, Radu Dracul."

"I hope I didn't wake you," Radu said. "But I just got your message."

"I seldom sleep," Marc said. "Come in."

The gate swung silently open. Radu peered into the dimness, seeing no one; a light came on, but no one was there.

"It's safe," Marc said. "I don't keep a nest of tigers, which is more than I can say for some other of Laenea's friends."

The reference to tigers reminded Radu of Kathell Stafford and her threat. He had barely thought of her since he left. Could Marc know of the incident? Uneasily, Radu went inside.

Ferns and vines and tropical plants lined the walls and drooped from the ceiling of the foyer. Radu had not even noticed them the first time he was here. He smiled, remembering: He and Laenea had had other things to notice than the décor.

Like the plants in a ship's ecosystem, these raised their environment's oxygen content. Radu recognized several species that were specially designed to be used in transit vessels. He had never seen them outside one before. He stopped in front of a second wrought-iron gate. Marc's indoor display formed, its colors sparkling through a rainbow.

"Not that way," he said. "In here."

A door, completely concealed by the vegetation, slipped open silently to reveal another unlit passage.

"I don't like to leave this open very long," Marc said when Radu hesitated.

Radu stepped through the foliage. The door glided shut, narrowing and then obliterating the block of light cast from behind him.

Blind, Radu waited for one of Marc's communication displays, for any glimmer of light. The echo of a large room replied to the beat of his heart.

His eyes began to adjust. A glowing ember touched the

edge of his vision. Then one indistinct shape sprang into focus, and another. He was surrounded by luminescent objects of delicate form.

The lights came up gradually. The luminescence faded, eclipsed by artifacts whose beauty was brought out by color. Glass shelves lined the walls, displaying Marc's collection of all the pretty things that people brought him.

"Do you like them?"

The voice was not the smooth production of the machine, but clear, direct, and human. Radu turned reluctantly toward it. Marc sat in an alcove at the end of the room. He was not deformed, as rumor made him. He was quite a handsome man, forty-five or fifty, with dark brown hair and eyes, and very pale skin. His face was unlined, gentle, and calm.

"It's safe," Marc said again. "I'm safe. I know the rumors about me. You don't need to be frightened."

"I'm not." Radu approached, and, at Marc's nod, sat on a bench nearby. "It's only that I didn't expect to meet you. Laenea told me no one ever did."

"That's almost true," Marc said. "Almost, but not quite."

Marc wore blue velvet pants, sandals, and a sleeveless silk shirt. He held himself motionless, but the tension in the muscles of his bare arms showed that his lack of animation was deliberate.

He isn't paralyzed, Radu thought; and then Marc slowly crossed one leg over the other. He moved as if he were afraid of what might happen if he did not stay almost perfectly quiet. Some diseases cause the bones to grow brittle and break with any exertion . . .

"Thank you for coming in," Marc said. "I hoped you would answer my message. I was extremely anxious to speak with you, before you took any action about the pilots."

Radu raised one eyebrow. "Your sources are very efficient."

"Some people bring me things," Marc said. "Others give me information."

Radu remembered the wyuna. He drew it from his pocket. Its hard opalescent ridges caught the light.

"I thought of you when I saw this."

Marc gazed smiling at Radu's offering, but he did not reach out.

"You must already have a whole shelfful," Radu said. Marc, with his connections, had probably been given wyunas when they were still an experiment. Radu closed his hand around the jewel. He seemed always to behave like a *naif,* here on earth.

"No!" Marc said quickly. "On the contrary, I've never seen anything like it. Is it a shell? A stone?"

Radu placed it on the arm of Marc's chair. Both Marc's hands covered panels of switches and buttons; he did not move from touching them, but bent down to look at his gift.

"It's a wyuna," Radu said. As he explained about Ngthummulun's new cash crop, he decided he had better tell the whole truth about it. "There's one other fact, but I don't think Atna's people want it widely known."

"Their secrets are safe here," Marc said. "As are yours."

While he explained to Marc about tree warts, Radu considered what the older man had told him in that single offhand phrase.

Marc reached out very slowly, with a visible tremor in his hand, to lift the wyuna between his thumb and forefinger. He barely raised his arm. Radu wondered if, instead of fragile bones, he had some sort of muscle ailment that prevented his moving easily.

"It's lovely," Marc said. "Thank you for thinking of me." Marc explored the wyuna with his gaze for several minutes, turning it over and over in his fingers. Finally he replaced it on the armrest of his chair and covered the control panel with his hand again.

"You've disturbed the pilots rather badly," he said.

Radu hesitated before replying, but as Marc already knew what had occurred, Radu did not see how he could get him into trouble by discussing it with him.

"How did you know what happened? They showed me they didn't want me to tell anyone — why did they tell you?"

" 'Who knows, with pilots?' "

"I'm tired of hearing that! I'm tired of thinking it — they're human beings just like you and me. I don't believe they're so different." He forced his voice to a calmer tone. "I don't think you do, either."

"No," Marc said. "You're right. And you're right that they're still very human." He smiled briefly. "They're human enough that a few are incurable gossips. But they're also human enough to be unpredictable when they're in a panic."

"I'm not a threat to them."

"That remains to be seen. There's no way to tell how the administrators will react to the news. First, they'll want to study you."

"Do they have to find out?"

"I'm afraid so. It may take a few days, but even if they don't hear directly the flight recorder will contain anomalies that the computer will flag."

"You know a great deal about this," Radu said.

"Yes . . . well . . . I used to be a pilot."

Radu sat back, astonished. "A pilot! Laenea never said — "

"She doesn't know," Marc said sharply. "Very few people know. The old pilots, but not the new ones. I wasn't even a member of the first working group. I was an experiment. Most of the people who knew me before believe I'm dead."

"Why? Why have you locked yourself up here? And why did you let me in?"

"Something happened to me in transit," Marc said. "And something happened to you. I thought I might be of help."

Near Marc, Radu felt none of the unease he felt around Vasili Nikolaievich or Laenea, and none of the terror he had experienced in the face of the imperturbable circle of pilots who had nearly killed him. Even now that he was aware of Marc's status, he felt calm in his presence.

"What should I do?" he asked. "I'm no pilot."

"Not by the usual criteria, no," Marc said. "But if you're an indication that some normal folk can withstand transit, the pilots will become curiosities. They have no society but their own. They might continue working, but they'd soon be outnumbered. They give up a great deal to become pilots. But they gain more. They cannot — they will not — go back to being ordinary people."

"Surely I'm the one who's a curiosity," Radu said.

"Perhaps," Marc said in a noncommittal tone.

"Vasili Nikolaicvich said he should kill me," Radu said. "I didn't think he would, but I didn't believe he was trying to make a joke, either."

Radu expected him to smile, but his expression remained grave.

"Do you intend to let me leave here?" Radu asked.

At that Marc did smile. "Of course I do," he said. "I'm not a pilot anymore. My loyalties are a bit wider. I confess, though, I am curious about your experience."

"I don't think I can tell you much more than you already know. I woke up in transit. I'm alive."

"There's more than that. There must be. Did you ever come out of the anesthetic early before? Did you have any indication that you were restless?"

"No. The opposite. The recordings always showed I slept more peacefully than most."

"Did anything unusual ever happen on your other flights?"

"No."

"Don't answer so quickly with such certainty. Did you awaken easily?"

"Yes."

"You were often first, then."

"Yes." He thought back over his rather small number of transit dives. The one time he had been helped from his sleep chamber, it had been by Vasili, the only pilot he had ever flown with. "Always first, so far. But I've not been crew that long."

"You felt that you slept soundly in transit."

"Yes. I used a high anesthetic level, and I dreamed."

"Dreamed!"

Radu hesitated. "Laenea was surprised, too, when I told her. Is it all that uncommon?"

"Yes. It's unique as far as I know."

"I don't see how it could make the least bit of difference."

"There is a difference. Like the difference between real sleep and the crew's drugged coma. How did you wake up when you were supposed to be drugged?"

"The first time, I thought the gas line was stopped up. I found no obstruction." He stretched out his arm so the sleeve pulled back from his wrist, revealing the bandage. "The second time, I tore loose the needle. The third time I reacted badly to the drug." He scowled and folded his arms across his chest. "Maybe there's nothing strange about what happened to me. Maybe most people can live through transit awake and it was something else that killed the first ones to try it."

"Do you think so?"

Radu did not answer for a while. Finally he said, "No. I wish I did, but I don't."

"Nor do I, and I have reasons for my opinion. What do you dream about?"

"Usually? Or this time?"

"Both. Tell me the difference."

"Before now, my dreams were always pleasant. About home, and my clan. Before the plague. And on the way to Ngthummulun, I dreamed about being with Laenea."

"And coming back?"

"I dreamed about her again, but something was wrong; she needed help, she was calling to me — " He shivered. The dreams had been very real. He would not feel comfortable, he would not believe she was safe, until he talked to her. "The nightmares woke me up."

"Did you ever have nightmares like that before?" Marc asked.

"For a while," Radu said reluctantly. "Back on Twilight . . ."

"Under what circumstances?"

"It was during the plague. I'd dream of people, and they'd die. I had nightmares, or hallucinations. Sometimes it was hard to tell the difference — "

"Wait," Marc said. "What did you say?"

"Just now? I said sometimes I was too tired to tell the dif-

ference between dreams and hallucinations. I'd have nightmares about being able to help my family and my friends
who died."

"Not exactly," Marc said. "You said, 'I'd dream of people,
and they'd die.'"

Radu hesitated, tempted to say he had misspoken himself.
"That's how it seemed, sometimes," he said. "That I'd know
someone was going to die before they got sick. You see what
I mean about hallucinations."

Marc gave no sign of immediate agreement. "Were there
similarities between those dreams and the ones you had in
transit?"

"Only superficially. The people back home really were in
danger. Laenea's perfectly safe."

"No one's ever perfectly safe in transit," Marc said.
"Laenea's training flight has lasted an exceptionally long
time."

"You don't think she might really be in trouble, do you?"
Radu asked.

"There's no way to tell, until she comes back ... or
doesn't."

Radu tried to smile. "She probably just insisted on learning
everything there is to learn, all on the first trip."

"No doubt." Marc sat very still, watching Radu and blinking slowly. "Now tell me what happened when you were
awake."

"I saw nothing. Vasili Nikolaievich asked me what I
thought of transit, and I got angry at him because I thought
he was making fun of me. But he wasn't. He perceived something."

"Yes ..." Marc said. "And you did not?"

"Just a flat gray surface, as if the port had been covered
over." He shrugged. "Oh, once in a while I thought I saw a
flash of color, but I think that must have been my imagination."

"Perhaps."

"Surely one can't fly blind in transit — what use could I
be? How could I be a threat?"

"Radu," Marc said kindly, "I think you're going to have to accept this ability, not deny it. There's a lot we don't know about transit yet. You're going to be a factor in its exploration, however uncomfortable that makes you feel."

Radu slouched down, feeling unhappy, uneasy, angry.

"Do you have any immediate plans?"

"I don't see how I can make any," Radu said. "Last night, on Earthstation, the pilots confronted me. They wanted me to go with them, and I refused. But I can't crew again without their help. I can't even go home."

"I think if you don't antagonize them, they'll come to a reasonable decision."

"What's a reasonable decision, for a pilot? That they'll deign not to kill me? Can't you help?" he asked desperately.

"They must respect you and consider your advice."

Marc gazed over Radu's head, then around the room. Radu heard his breathing deepen, as if he were working hard to control a strong emotional reaction.

"Not as much as you might think," he said.

"But you're one of the first. You made everything possible for them."

"I'm a failed pilot," Marc said. "One of the first or not, I returned and had my natural heart put back in my chest. I'm not one of them anymore, nor am I like you."

Radu waited. He asked no questions. But he waited.

Marc looked at him, his eyes half closed.

"Transit is different for everyone. The people who ask what it's like think that if they're lucky enough to get an answer, they'll understand it. But the truth is that no one, pilot or not, understands it at all. If you got a reply from every pilot you talked to, you'd still not know what transit is like, you'd only be more confused." Marc uncrossed his legs and sat with his knees together and his feet flat on the floor, his hands curled around the arms of his chair. "The way it affected me . . . was to send me into a panic." His voice shook. His eyes were wide open now, but he was not staring at anything in this room or in this universe.

"I was in terror — I hit the emergency switch. You know — "

Radu nodded, reliving a precipitous departure from transit.

"It took me some time to gather my courage enough to try to go home. It took me so long that the choice was between the terror, and starvation. I was too far from any system to try to reach a world where I could die peacefully." He smiled sadly. "And I do believe I would have chosen exile to transit, if I'd had the choice.

"The return was completely different. I can no more describe it than I could the other. I came back . . . in a daze of rapture. But I wasn't a pilot any longer. I wasn't sufficiently freed from normal space-time. Transit changed me. Not quite enough to kill me, but if I flew awake again, I'd die. I would have accepted that fate, to return. But of course they wouldn't permit it."

"When you went out," Radu said, "you had no assurance that you'd survive."

"They were still developing the parameters. They thought I fit. But I didn't. Not quite."

"But you're a hero," Radu said. "Why do you shut yourself away like this?"

Marc sighed. "Don't think I wouldn't enjoy being lionized," he said. "But I'm old history. And then there's this." He lifted his trembling hand.

"A tremor? Who would care?"

"It's more than that. I lost a lot of brain cells during the trip."

"Oh," Radu said, and then, inadequately, "I'm sorry."

"I never did see much use in regenerating a ruined brain into a new one."

"You seem far from ruined."

"Close enough to need regeneration, not close enough to have the decision taken from me. When I'm rational I'm not quite ready to lose myself."

"The damage . . . is in the cerebral cortex."

"The damage is all over." For the first time Marc's voice

held a hint of bitterness. "No worse there than anywhere — except of course that's the place it really matters."

Radu nodded. It was one thing to regenerate a lost hand or a severed nerve or a heart damaged by disease, or removed. Even large areas of the brain, the motor and sensory regions, were well worth bringing back. But what point to regenerating the gray matter, to reforming the connections until memories were stretched and fuzzed beyond recall?

"I'd be left at the level of a three-year-old," Marc said. "With great luck, four. I don't even remember being four." He shook his head. "I have some memories, you see, that I want very much to keep. Those moments in transit. A few others. No, my friend, I'm stuck with me as I am or not at all."

"I'm sorry," Radu said again.

"Never mind. It's far too easy to be maudlin about it. It's your problem that concerns us now. I'll do what I can."

"Thank you," Radu said. "Until I got your message, I had nowhere to turn. I tried to call Laenea, but she's still in transit."

"Radu — " Marc stopped. He closed his eyes, then glanced down at his hand. It trembled despite his efforts to clench his fingers over the panel of knobs and switches. He sighed, and touched one button.

Radu started violently at the abrupt sliding crystalline noise. He was on his feet, turned around and crouched, before he realized that the sound was simply the closing of glass doors over the front of each display shelf. Abashed, he turned back toward Marc.

"I apologize for startling you," Marc said. "Radu, you'll have to leave now. I've overtired myself and I won't be able to answer for what I do, in a few minutes."

"Then you'll need help — "

"No. I won't. I'll be all right if I don't have to worry about you. Please go."

"But — "

"Don't argue," Marc said sharply. "Get off the port and

stay away from the pilots till I've had a chance to talk to them. I'll do it as soon as I'm able."

"Marc . . ."

"Please, go."

He stood. Moving awkwardly, he took Radu's arm. Afraid to resist and take the chance of hurting Marc, Radu let himself be guided through the door.

"Marc — "

Marc stepped back abruptly and the hidden door slid shut between them. Radu put his hands to the wall, thrusting his fingers between the clinging vines to try to find his way back inside. He scratched for a crevice but found only smooth metal.

Marc's image formed in tenuous colors nearby.

"Believe me," Marc's electronically modulated voice said. Radu could hear the resonances of the true voice that formed its basis. "Believe me, I'll be all right. It's a matter of pride. These spells aren't pretty. Call me every day until I answer, but don't leave word where you are." The image vanished.

"But — " Radu hesitated in the foyer, disgusted with himself for having left Marc alone. He willed the image to reappear, but it remained as hidden as the doorway. Radu knew he must go.

From the alcove, he looked cautiously out at the mall. This late at night, it lay deserted and silent. Radu stepped out into the corridor and headed for the elevator. Marc had made the pilots more comprehensible to him, yet more frightening. *They* were frightened, too, which made them seem more human, but more unpredictable and therefore more dangerous. Marc's suggestion that Radu avoid them was, Radu decided, excellent advice.

He turned a corner and came face to face with Orca. Astonished, he stopped. She glared up at him, folding her arms across her chest.

"Do you *want* the pilots to follow you?" she said belligerently.

"No," he said. "No, of course not. What are you doing here? How did you know where I was?"

"Gods," she said. "They shouldn't let you off the ship. They ought to give colonists a survival manual. They ought to wrap you in structural foam. Radu, you didn't put a guard on your file. Is everybody on Twilight that respectful of privacy? What were you thinking of?"

"Wait," he said. "You read my messages?"

"Don't sound so distressed. I looked to see if you'd protected yourself, and you hadn't. The pilots wouldn't have any more trouble finding you than I did."

"I don't understand, Orca. Can anyone learn anything about me, whenever they want? How can that be?"

She unfolded her arms and shook her head. "It's practically reflex to protect your file," she said. "People's parents start doing it for them, when they're kids. But it isn't automatic, and if you don't keep track of it, then, yes, people can find out anything they want."

Radu calmed down. "Thank you for telling me," he said. "How do I fix it?"

"You don't have a personal communicator, do you?"

He shook his head. He carried none; they were rare on Twilight and unnecessary on shipboard. He had not bothered to get one when he landed on earth because he had known no one to call.

"Come with me."

She took him to a terminal and brought up his files. She did not even have to identify herself; without any question of Orca's right to the information, they revealed Radu's comings and goings, his credit balance, Marc's message.

Orca spoke a code, and a patch of light, like the image of a nova, formed before her.

"Stick your hand in there," she said.

Radu tentatively touched the boundary of the sphere of light. It tingled against his hand like a field of static electricity.

"It's okay," Orca said. "It just records your fingerprints."

Radu thrust his hand into the chaotic light. It read his handprint to the wrist; its border dimpled down where the bandage touched its surface.

Then the display faded to translucence, to transparence, to nothingness.

"Done," Orca said.

"Is that all?"

"That's it. The guard isn't foolproof, but if anybody's trying to keep track of you, it'll slow them down."

"Why did you come back?" Radu asked.

"Not to ask you any more questions, don't worry," she said. She started toward the elevator.

He reached to take her hand. "Orca— "

He heard something behind him and spun, afraid of having to face another group of pilots. But a perfectly ordinary person rounded the corner, passed him with a quizzical glance, got on the elevator, and disappeared.

Radu laughed quickly, with relief, then suddenly realized how tightly he was holding Orca's hand. He let loose his desperate grip.

"I'm sorry — are you — ?"

She flexed her long, fine-boned fingers. Radu feared he had crushed them.

"I'm okay." She put her hand back in his, a gesture of trust and perhaps even of forgiveness.

"I might have broken a bone, or torn your skin — "

Her fingers clamped around his wrist, tight, cutting off the circulation, though she did not appear to be putting much effort into the grip. She squeezed, and Radu winced in pain.

"Orca — " He tried to pull away. Orca appeared perfectly relaxed, but her hand stayed still and so did Radu's.

"I keep telling you," she said coldly, "that I'm not delicate. The webs won't tear and you'd have to work at it, hard, to break my fingers. Are we friends? I thought we were starting to be, but you don't even trust what I say."

She let him go.

Radu looked at his wrist. The white impressions of her fingers slowly turned red. He would be bruised in stripes, to match the bruise that spread around the wound on his other arm. "I believe you," he said. "I won't doubt you again."

"You can think me a liar for all I care right now. But when you treat me like a surface child, or some shell that the sand or the water could smash — " She snorted in derision.

"It's just that you're so small," Radu said. "Back home . . ." He hoped he could say what he meant well enough not to offend her again. "Ever since I left home, I've been surrounded by people who seemed fragile to me. I feel as if I could hurt them without meaning to. I felt awkward around Vasili Nikolaievich, and when I helped Atna awaken, I could have been holding a songbird in my hands, his bones seemed so frail." Radu did not mention Laenea: He had never felt that she was frail, but she was unique in his mind anyway.

"I'm third generation diver," Orca said. "That's hardly enough time for us to get decadent."

Radu rubbed the stinging marks on his arm. "I won't forget again."

She touched him, gently this time. "Sorry," she said. "Come with me for a way."

She entered the elevator; Radu got in after her. They rose to the surface and left the blockhouse. Orca faced the night's sea wind and breathed deeply. Beneath the hint of fuel and ozone lay the salt spray of half a world of ocean. Without waiting to see if he came with her, she walked along the edge of the platform for several hundred meters. Radu hesitated, then followed, and they walked together in silence. It was very late, very quiet; the brilliant spotlights fell behind and darkness enfolded and isolated them.

At the edge of the landing platform, Orca put her fingers to her lips and whistled, a piercing, carrying, complex burst of sound. She tilted her head, as if listening, and then she looked out serenely over the gentle swells. Radu saw nothing in the dark waves, and all he could hear was the soft splash of water against the port's side.

Orca faced him, serious and intense.

"When you want it, I offer my help, and that of my family. Come to Victoria, to the harbor, and ask after us. We aren't hard to find unless we wish to be."

"Thank you," Radu said again.

Orca unfastened her spangled jacket, let it slide from her shoulders, and stripped off her net shirt. She unzipped her pants, let them fall from her narrow hips, and kicked them off along with her red shoes. Her skin gleamed in the moonlight as she paused on the edge of the dock.

"What are you doing?"

"Going home."

"You're going to swim? All the way? Won't you freeze? What about your clothes?" Now that she was actually leaving, Radu found himself gripped by a feeling of loneliness as sudden as it was unexpected, unwanted, and inexplicable.

"Everything I wanted to keep, I left in my bag. My clothes will get to crew quarters, or they won't. It doesn't matter."

"I'll take them." He bent and picked them up.

Instead of replying, Orca pointed out at the sea.

The black back of a huge animal cut the surface and vanished. A few seconds later the creature breached the water in a spectacular leap. White patches on its side shone like snow. The graceful bulk sliced the water noiselessly coming down, but at the last instant the creature slapped its tail on the water. Droplets spattered Radu's cheek.

Orca laughed. "She's playing."

"What is it?"

"My name-cousin. Orca. The killer whale. She's come to meet me." The diver's voice sounded far away, as if she were already swimming naked and joyous in the frigid mysterious sea. "She's come to take me home."

"Good-bye, Orca," Radu said.

She did not answer, and she did not hug him good-bye. She was no longer crew, but a diver. She drew back her arms, and, as she launched herself off the platform, flung them forward. Her long, flat dive curved down from the high deck, and she entered the water between two swells, without a splash.

Radu watched for her to surface, but saw neither Orca nor her name-cousin again.

He searched for them for several minutes, then, finally, turned away from the sea. If he was to follow Marc's advice, which seemed very sound to him, he had just enough time to catch the early morning ferry to the mainland. He looked forward to getting away from huge metal constructions, to breathing fresh air, to watching the sun rise over a dark line of distant mountains. He wondered how fast Orca and her name-cousin traveled, and whether the ferry might sail past them; would they swim underwater all the way? He did not know if Orca could breathe water, or if she had to surface for air. But perhaps, at dawn, he might stand on the deck and see her swimming with her friend on the bright horizon.

Water slapped gently against the side of the port. The lights of the ferry dock made dim, distant stars in the fog. Radu walked along the edge of the platform. The darkness and the quiet reminded him of home, and of the two years he had spent all alone in the mountains. There he had been alone without feeling loneliness. Loneliness was much more powerful in the midst of many people.

Stop feeling sorry for yourself, he thought angrily. Orca offered you help, and friendship, and you turned her down.

Still, he wished he could dive out into the mist, into the black and soothing sea, and swim through the solitude and silence all the way to the mainland.

He knew better. Whatever permitted Orca to swim long distances in this climate and temperature, Radu lacked. In the frigid water he would last a few minutes, a half hour with great luck. After that he would lapse into hypothermia, and then unconsciousness, and then he would die.

Shadows startled him. He turned, and saw nothing.

Of course you saw nothing, he thought. Nothing's there. Why are you letting shadows scare you? If you'd behaved like this back home, you would have driven yourself crazy before a season was out.

But he could not help glancing once again toward the imagined movement.

Like a ghost, Vasili Nikolaievich appeared, only his pale face visible in the darkness. Radu gasped involuntarily. The shadows behind the pilot moved: Scattered light glinted off a long lock of blond hair here, a dark face there, a gray wolf-stone, glowing like an animal's eye. The fog draped itself around them.

"This time you'd better come with us," Vasili said.

Radu took one step forward. "Leave me alone," he whispered. "Why don't you leave me alone?"

"Please don't argue. Everything's been decided."

"Not by me!"

"I told you before, you haven't anything to say about it."

Radu panicked. He flung himself around and fled. But there was nowhere he could go, with the pilots spreading out into a semicircle around him, capturing him against the edge of the port. He glanced over his shoulder. They were coming after him, getting closer with each step. He pushed himself harder, panting with exhaustion. Being away from home was making him soft.

Suddenly, in front of him, two more pilots appeared.

Skidding on the damp deck, he stopped. He turned slowly. The blurry, backlit shapes of the pilots were all around him. When he stopped again, he faced the sea.

Radu plunged headfirst off the platform.

He would swim to the ferry ramp, he would climb up it, he would make enough noise to attract the attention of someone besides the pilots —

He hit the water.

The cold knocked the breath out of him. He floundered to the surface, cold salt water in his mouth and nose. He sputtered and coughed and struggled against the return of panic. Above him the pilots argued. The fog hid them and blotted out all but the tones of their voices. They did not shoot at him, if they had weapons, and none followed him into the sea.

The salt stung the cut on his wrist until, in a moment, the cold numbed his hands.

Twilight's icy mountain lakes held a touch of the world's

warmth, but this ocean promised only inconceivable depths of freezing, lightless water.

Radu paddled laboriously along the edge of the port. If he just kept going he would be all right. Each high swell slapped him in the face with harsh salt spray. His clothes weighed him down. He tried to kick off his boots. He failed. Shivering uncontrollably, he started swimming. He lost his grip on Orca's clothes. They drifted away. He lunged for them and grabbed them. Somehow it seemed very important to keep hold of them. Orca's jacket twisted around his arm.

His only hope was to reach the ramp before he passed out. The distance, which had seemed so short when he was running, stretched on interminably. A trick of perspective, he thought, his mind winding around the words, then losing the sense of them. A wave, rebounding from the side of the port, curled over him. He reached for the surface: He thought he knew where it was, but he stretched his arms into water like black ice, and his struggles got him no closer to the air.

A huge dark shape appeared below him. The sight of it pierced through the cold. He remembered what he had read of earth and its predators, and what Orca had said of sharks when she showed him her claws. Terrified, he flailed upward and broke the surface. He tried to catch his breath; he tried to call for help. He tried to swim harder toward the ferry ramp, but the current carried him farther and farther from the port.

The creature rose under him and he felt the turbulence of its motion. He expected slashing pain, teeth through flesh, hot blood gushing through severed arteries and veins. But he felt nothing, except the black shape pushing him. He was beyond pain, beyond panic, beyond fear. Calm settled over him. When the creature attacked, he would not feel it. He would not feel anything anymore. Radu lost consciousness.

8

RADU STRUGGLED with another nightmare. Laenea was on Twilight, a member of the crew of the emergency ship. The crew, rather than remaining safely in their orbiting ship, had landed with the medical team. They had arrived just as Radu had begun to feel, and deny, high fever and mental dissociation, the plague's first symptoms. That was the reality. But in the nightmare it was Laenea who grew ill, and instead of her caring for him, he cared for her. He was afraid she would die like the others, friends and family, whom he had known would become ill but had no way to save. In the reality of the past, Laenea had saved his life. In the past of his nightmare, he saw that Laenea was dying, but refused to accept that result.

He woke. His dream, as dreams will, began to dissolve to nothingness.

He pushed at the lid of his body box. His hand encountered

rough wood. In a moment of pure terror and resurging memory he jammed his hands up against the planks. He had been dying of the cold; he had been attacked by a creature. He had been taken for dead and no one had read his will. Instead of burning him and sending his ashes home, they had boxed him up and put him in the ground. A recurrent nightmare was coming true.

After the plague he dreamed over and over and over again that he had been buried along with the rest of his family and most of his friends. In the peculiar multiple time flow of the dreaming state, he saw himself as gravedigger for himself just as he had been gravedigger in dreams and in reality for his mother and for his other parents, for his sisters and brothers, one after another till he was alone. In his dreams they, and he, struggled to get out of the coffin, to throw off the thickening cover of soil, and to return to life.

I'll never save them now, he thought. Not them, or Laenea —

The lid stayed solid above him and he flung his hands apart, searching for some weakness in his prison. One hand hit a wall, but the other clutched only air, and the combined motions made him lurch sideways.

He fell out of bed.

The air was fresh and the echoes those of a room. So many levels of dream and nightmare, memory and reality, swept around him that he wondered if he had gone mad.

The lights flicked on, bright enough to dazzle him. A vague shape jumped down beside him.

"Radu, are you all right?"

He recognized Orca's voice. His eyes reaccustomed themselves to light. Orca sat on her heels before him, watching him anxiously.

Radu pushed himself up and looked around. Books lined two walls; the built-in bunk beds lent the cabin a nautical look. But the underwater porthole over the desk, and the chamber's dimensions and floor plan, revealed it to be one of the ocean spaceport's sleeping rooms.

"What happened?"

"I had a nightmare, and I remembered one I thought I was having again," he said. "I'm awake now." He tried to stand, but could not gather the strength. "I thought . . ." He glanced down. His legs were unwounded, unscarred.

Orca nodded toward the porthole. In the light that dissolved through the glass into the sea, the black-and-white form of Orca's friend the killer whale glided by. Radu shivered.

"My cousin heard you," Orca said. "We hadn't gone very far, we were playing. When she heard you dive she thought you might be one of us, but neither of us recognized the swimming patterns. Then you started moving like you were in trouble, so we came back."

"I'm very grateful that you did."

She shrugged, then scowled. "Did they *push* you in?"

"No," he said. "They followed me. They wanted me to come with them, but . . . I declined. I don't think they intended to drive me into the water. It's only that they scared me, and I panicked."

" 'Only' scared you? Like the other time?" Orca said angrily. "They weren't even trying to help you — and by the time I got you out of the water they'd just disappeared."

"Where are they now?"

"Some of them are waiting for you. They can't come into the divers' section without an invitation. But they're waiting outside."

"I've made a very bad mistake," Radu said. "I've put you in danger but left you in ignorance. I can try to correct that, if you still want me to."

She helped him back into his bunk, pulled a blanket around him, and sat crosslegged nearby.

"I guess you'd better." She sounded much less eager than before to hear what he had to say.

He would not have believed the simple telling of a story could exhaust him so completely, but when he reached his dive from the edge of the landing platform he was shaking with fatigue.

"Good lord," Orca said. "Awake in transit . . . no wonder."

"I don't know what to do," Radu said, pressing the heels of his hands against his closed eyes, trying to drive away some of the tension and fatigue. "Marc said to wait until he had news for me, but who knows how long it might take him to . . ." He had kept Marc's secrets and told Orca only his own, but that made some things difficult to explain. "To make any progress."

"Why don't you call him and see if he has any help for you so far? Then at least you'll know if you need to try something else."

Radu suspected that Marc's illness was too serious to be dispensed with overnight, but a call was worth a try.

"That's a good idea," he said.

"I'll wait for you in the lounge," Orca said, and left him alone.

Leaving off the outgoing video, Radu called Marc's number. If he did not answer, Radu would try to reach Laenea again. Surely she must be back by now.

The flowing colors Marc used to represent himself intertwined and separated.

"Hello." Compared to his real voice, the electronic tones were smooth and uninteresting. "Who's calling, please?"

"This is Radu Dracul, Marc. Are you better?"

"I beg your pardon? Who are you?"

Too startled to answer, Radu stared at the screen.

"Would you repeat your name, please?"

"Radu Dracul. Laenea Trevelyan's friend." But it was clear to him what had happened: The illness had wiped out Marc's memory of their conversation, and of Radu himself.

"Never mind," he said. "I'm sorry to have bothered you."

"It's only that I can't find your name. I have Laenea's, of course."

"I was with you a few hours ago, just before you became ill. I shouldn't have disturbed you so soon." Upset and disappointed, knowing he was being unfair, Radu reached to cut the connection.

"Wait," said Marc's voice. "Are you aware that Marc has

an analogue? I'm not Marc himself. I'm in use when he isn't available."

"No," Radu said. "I wasn't aware of that."

"I apologize for being unfamiliar with you, but my personal programming is several hours behind. Marc feels it is bad manners to record everything he handles himself. That sometimes creates difficulties when he is . . . called away suddenly, as he was last night."

"I know. I was with him."

"With him?"

"Yes. Is he better?"

"I'm specifically prohibited from discussing that subject," the analogue said. "May I help you in some other way? Are you calling about Laenea? Marc, too, was friends with her. I'm not looking forward to telling him she's lost."

"Lost . . . ?"

"Her ship is lost."

"How could it be lost?" Radu said, completely stunned. "I don't understand. I was just about to call her, she's out in training, there's no indication that anything's wrong — " He was babbling. He stopped.

"I'm terribly sorry," said the analogue, in a tone of sincere regret. "When you mentioned her I thought you'd heard."

"I haven't heard anything."

"Her ship has been declared lost. Her teacher's ship, I mean, of course."

"But — it's only overdue. A few days — "

"The ship is two weeks late. Dear boy, the first trip out is meant to be brief."

"How can they declare her lost? Just because someone says so — "

"The training flight Miikala chose for her takes between half an hour and half a day. Her presence introduces an unknown, of course, into an equation that is empirical at best. But they've waited a very long time — "

Radu stopped listening to Marc's sympathetic, informative, compassionless analogue, refusing to be forced to believe

Laenea was gone. He shut out the screen's decorative patterns. Laenea was too real to be lost. He had not yet even managed to convince himself they could never be lovers again, though he knew it was impossible. He would never convince himself she was lost: dead. He would never try.

He thought: She *was* in danger, and I knew it. I woke up in transit because I knew it. Then he thought: It's like the hallucinations back on Twilight. Maybe they weren't hallucinations. Maybe Marc was right... And finally: The way Atna was right. He was wrong in detail, but he was right all the same.

The silence drew his attention back to the phone. Two pools of brilliant blue, like eyes, peered out at him. Startled, he blinked, and the pattern swirled into abstract shapes again.

"I'm sorry to have been the one to tell you," Marc's analogue said. "I would have said it more gently had I realized you had no intimation."

"It isn't your fault," Radu said dully. "I'd better go."

"Do you want to leave a message? Where can you be reached?"

"I don't know," Radu said. "Tell Marc..." He could think of nothing of any substance to say to Marc. "Tell him I called."

"He will know."

"Good-bye."

"I'm sorry I didn't know who you were," said the analogue. It broke the connection and the vibrant colors faded away.

In a daze, Radu slowly drew on his clothes and went into the divers' lounge.

Orca's smile faded when she saw his expression.

"What's wrong?"

"Laenea's ship has been declared lost."

"Oh, Radu — " She took his hand in a gesture of comfort, led him to a couch, and made him sit down. "I'm so sorry... I met her, on the crew. I liked her."

"I don't believe it," he said. "I can't... I won't."

They sat together in silence for some minutes. If Orca accepted that Laenea was dead, she did not try to persuade Radu to bow to inevitability.

"Do you want me to leave you alone for a while? Or do you want me to stay with you?"

"I dreamed of her on the way back from Ngthummulun."

"When? How could you? We didn't have time for any real sleep."

"In transit, before I rejected the drugs. I usually dream in transit, but this time I had nightmares." His last image was of Laenea crying out in distress, crying out for help he could not give. He did not want that to be his last memory of her. He wanted to remember her with her head thrown back, laughing.

"Oh, gods," he groaned. He hid his face in his hands. "I thought they were hallucinations, I thought they'd stopped. Why do I dream about when my friends will die?"

Orca hesitated, then said, "You mean you dream they'll die, and they do?"

"I dream they need help, but I never know how to help them. It happened during the plague," he said miserably. "I know it sounds crazy . . ."

"Not particularly," Orca said. "But you seemed to think so, when it was Atna."

Radu drew his knees to his chest and wrapped his arms around them. "I did . . . but I didn't. I thought what happened to me was hallucination, or fever memory."

Orca stroked his arm.

"Back home," Radu said, "when people started getting sick . . . my dreams changed. After a while I began to think I knew who was going to die. I tried to warn people . . ."

"Oh, lord," Orca said.

"Yes." Radu shook his head. "It should have taught me something, but I think I learned the wrong lesson. I acted toward Atna just the way the others acted toward me."

"You can't blame yourself," Orca said. "There wasn't anything you could do back on Twilight and there wasn't anything you could do in transit. Even pilots don't look for lost ships. I'm sorry Laenea is gone, but you're the one who's in trouble now. You've got to look out for yourself."

"Why?"

"What? Do you want to just give up to the pilots?"

"That isn't what I meant," Radu said. The slash on his wrist throbbed. "I mean why doesn't anybody look for lost ships?"

"Because they tried for years to find any of them, even one, and they never did. So they stopped looking."

"They can't find them because they can't communicate with them. But Laenea did need help, and I knew it."

"Radu, she's *lost*."

"Lost — that doesn't mean she's dead. Nobody knows what it means! She could still be alive." He looked toward the exit door, thinking about what lay beyond the divers' quarters.

Orca followed his gaze. "You can't go out there!"

"I have to. I have to try to get them to listen to me. I dreamed I could help, if I only knew what to do. Now I know. I have to find her."

"What makes you think they'll believe you?"

"Nothing," he said. "They have no reason to trust me and several reasons not to. And they see me as a threat. But I have to try. Otherwise Laenea and her teacher and the people in their crew will all die." He stood up. He still felt shaky.

Orca caught his arm, gripping him just hard enough to remind him of her strength.

"What the hell did I come back for you for, if you're just going to go out and let them throw you in the ocean again? I could be halfway home by now," she said. "This is just crazy."

"I don't blame you for feeling that way," Radu said. He laid his hand gently on hers, and she relaxed her grip.

"Sorry."

"Never mind," Radu said. "You're probably right, after all."

"If you believed that, you wouldn't be going out there." She followed him into the hall and to the center of the divers' quarters, where a doorway led to the public elevator lobby.

"Thank you, for everything," Radu said.

"I don't guess you happen to be one of those people who think that since I saved your life I get to tell you what to do with it from now on."

"I'm afraid not," he said, then laughed. He hugged her, perhaps a little longer, a little more tightly, than if this had been a regular farewell between two members of a starship crew. If the pilots believed him, if he could persuade them to do as he wished, then he would have to endure their company for some inestimable time alone, without the buffer of another normal human being. He was very glad he would have the memory of Orca's friendship.

"Good-bye," he said.

"Good-bye."

He faced the door, reluctant to open it, then stepped close enough for it to sense him. It slid aside, then slid closed behind him.

The two pilots waiting for him rose. Vasili Nikolaievich, particularly, looked surprised to see him. Neither pilot appeared to have any idea what to do with him now that he had come to face them of his own free will.

"You wouldn't tell me what you wanted of me," Radu said, "so I'll say what I want of you."

Vasili scowled. "I don't think you have that choice."

Radu walked toward the pilots, feeling more and more tense.

"Laenea Trevelyan's ship has been lost," he said. "I think I can find it. I think that was what was happening to me when — "

"You . . . what?" said the other pilot. "Wait. We can't discuss this here." She reached out to take his arm. "Come along with us, will you?"

Radu drew back.

"I'll come," he said. "I don't mean to be rude. Your proximity is as uncomfortable to me as mine is to you."

"You think so, do you?" Vasili said.

"Shut up, Vaska," the other pilot said. "We've screwed this up badly enough already. Come on, let's go someplace where we can talk."

Orca let Radu Dracul leave, all alone. He was an adult; he had the right to make his own decisions, even if he did not know what he was doing, even if the decisions were stupid ones.

Her cousin glided past the porthole, brushing the glass with the tip of her fluke. The soft sound reminded Orca of her other responsibilities, and her promise to her family; it reminded her of last night, swimming free with her friend. Orca always felt isolated when she left the sea, as if all her senses had been damped down to half intensity. It was not only sound that carried much more efficiently in water than in air, but touch and scent and heat perception as well. The texture was altogether different. The density of experience increased a hundredfold. Orca cupped her hands against the port so she could see through reflections. Her cousin swooped by again.

Orca turned on the speaker. She and her friend could converse only in middle speech, when one of them was in the air. The language was denser than Standard, but filmy and insubstantial compared to true speech.

The cousins were more intelligent than human beings, though not as much more intelligent as were any of the great whales, about whom Orca felt too much awe for friendship. Yet they were naive as well. Thousands of years of predation by humans had done nothing to temper that quality into cynicism or doubt. Since the revolution, whales were no longer legal prey of humans. A few outlaw whalers had tried to defy the ban, but they disappeared and no one ever saw them again. Orca's mother knew something about that, but seldom mentioned it unless she had had a long day undersea and one brandy too many after dinner.

The differences between whales and human beings, which Orca's brother hardly noticed, seemed so enormous to Orca that she found it marvelous that the two species could communicate at all. There were great gaps in understanding. Humans could not understand the whales' acceptance of events; whales could not comprehend anger or hatred, or the even more alien emotions of ambition and fear. They had concepts so far beyond human understanding that even the descriptions made no sense, even in true speech. Orca's brother knew what they meant, but he had tried to explain them to her, both in the water and in the air, and failed every time.

Come out of there, her cousin said. I can't see you properly, I can barely hear you, I can't touch you. I want to hear about what you've been doing.

I know, Orca replied. I want to touch you, I want to feel the coldness of the sea at my back and the heat of your body against mine, but, oh, my friend, I can't come with you now.

You're going away again, to unsounded regions.

Don't worry about me, Orca said. The places I've been haven't harmed me, it's only if I can't go back that I'll be sad.

You are sad when you have to stay, her cousin said, and I am sad when you have to go.

Go, to the whales, was the same word as *disappear,* which was in turn the same word as *die.* Her cousin did not mean *die,* but the connotation of distress was unavoidable and unmistakable. The sea was a medium in which another family, the gray whales, could sing a song one day and by the next day hear its echo — echo was the nearest concept human speech possessed, though what they and the other cetaceans and the divers heard was the song's direct sound wave, stretched and changed by its circumnavigation of the globe.

In the sea, intelligent beings did not disappear from hearing unless they died.

I know, Orca said. I know, and I'm sorry. I love you.

Her cousin slid past her, wanting her to come back into the sea and play. Play, with the cousins, involved love-play and sex-play and joy-play; the same sound sequence meant all those things.

Orca wished she could be playing with her cousin, gliding around and through and between her songs.

I'm sorry, she said again. If I left now, it would be like leaving a newborn underwater...

Her cousin made a sound of surprise, for accusing someone of the ability to abandon a child to death by drowning was the worst insult one could offer.

This acquaintance of yours is not newborn, cousin. Has he so little sense that you must care for him?

If I don't help him, he'll be all alone.

There are others.

Yes. But he'll only be with — Orca combined the sound sketch of a pilot with the sound sketch of a shark. Even though the result was very crude, in middle speech, a blood cousin would have understood. But the name-cousins, having evolved in an environment where nothing threatened them, found fear incomprehensible even in true speech. There was a word for it, but it was made up as a courtesy to the divers, and it meant, to the whales, a feeling their cousins had in response to potential experiences they preferred to leave un-realized. Even that was difficult for the whales to understand, for to them all potentiality was opportunity.

I'm sorry, Orca said. He's part of my other family. Do you understand?

No, her cousin replied. I don't understand. But I accept. Good-bye.

Good-bye.

Orca turned off the speaker and sprinted out the door. The whole interchange had taken only a few moments; she hoped she still had time to catch up to Radu.

The elevator doors were sliding closed. She jammed her hands between them and forced them open again, then stepped calmly inside with Radu, Vasili Nikolaievich, and another young pilot named Chase.

"What do *you* want?" Vaska said. She had startled him, and now his surprise was turning to anger.

Orca shoved her hands into her pockets, hunching her shoulders. She spoke to Vasili with irritation equal to his own. "Since there isn't any reason Radu should trust you half as far as he could throw you, there isn't any reason why he should go with you all alone."

"You aren't needed."

"I will be, soon enough," Orca said. "No matter how small a ship you take, you'll need a crew of at least two to run it, and on this flight you might have a little trouble finding volunteers."

"What flight?"

"That's part of what you didn't want to talk about in the hall," Radu said.

"Oh," said Chase. "Then you'd better wait till we're more secure."

Like the divers, the pilots owned a floor of the stabilizer shaft. No one else was permitted inside who was not an invited and accompanied guest. The isolation was not only for physical privacy; they guarded against electronic invasion as well.

"Orca," Chase said, "we're shielded for all modes of transmission. The feedback's fairly severe. If you need to communicate with anyone, it would be safer to go outside our quarters."

"I understand," Orca said. "Thanks."

Radu whispered to Orca, "What did she mean by that?"

"About feedback? That was a tactful way of telling me not to try to use my internal communicator unless I want my skull exploded."

"What!"

"It's okay," she said. "We don't like strangers coming into our quarters and making transmissions, either."

They followed Chase through several concentric rings of chambers, deeper and deeper into pilots' quarters.

In the center of the pilots' deck, in a windowless room, more pilots than Radu had ever seen before had gathered together. He recognized several who had surrounded him on Earth-station, and many he had seen in news reports, and Ramona-Teresa.

She stood up. Beneath her shirt's red lace inset, a triangle with its base at her collarbone and its point at her navel, her scar was a vivid white slash.

"Well, Chase," she said. "Well, Vaska. You finally found him." She looked drawn and tired.

"Found him!" Orca said. "You nearly killed him twice!"

"Never mind, Orca," Radu said.

"We didn't mean to scare him, out on deck," Vasili said. "It was an accident."

"We didn't expect you to jump off the side," Chase said. "By the time we found a life ring that whale was swimming you toward the ferry dock."

"I was not anxious to be surrounded again."

"No, I guess not," Chase said. "I'm sorry, I didn't think of it that way."

Ramona-Teresa sighed with exasperation.

"Well, I apologize to you, too, then," Chase said. "None of us is exactly trained for spying and kidnaping."

"I realize that. Still, you might have handled this more gracefully. And why did you bring the diver here?"

"We didn't bring either of them," Chase said. "They brought us."

"Orca thinks she's his bodyguard," Vasili said sarcastically.

Radu felt Orca tense with anger; he curled his fingers around hers, but he doubted he could restrain her if she chose to free herself.

"As she's already saved my life twice in encounters with pilots," he said, "I'm extremely grateful to her for offering to come with me."

"Radu Dracul," Ramona said, speaking so slowly and distinctly that it was clear she would not put up with another interruption or change of subject. "It's true I . . . invited you to come to speak with us. But that was last night. Now is a bad time. A ship is lost — "

"I know. That's why I'm here. To ask you to help me find Laenea."

After the uproar — some of it laughter — died down, and

Radu explained what he believed had happened to him in transit, he had to endure an hour of skepticism, questioning, and speculations. He kept his back to a wall, and the pilots stayed farther from him than when they had been trying to frighten him. They discomforted him, but the discomfort was bearable.

At first none of the pilots believed a word he said, and then, as they began to be intrigued by the possibilities of what he told them, they asked him to repeat random bits of his story, again and again. He answered, though he refused to discuss his friendship with Laenea beyond the fact that they were friends. It was none of their business.

Ramona-Teresa, who understood that they had been lovers, hardly participated in the inquisition. She sat in a chair in the corner, watching and listening and smoking a cigar.

Clearly, something strange was going on, something that had not happened before. The speculation changed focus again and again, moving from just exactly what was happening, to why it was occurring, to the ways it might damage or benefit the pilots.

"No," Radu said for at least the tenth time. "I don't understand what relation my time perception has to my perception of transit. Probably none. I keep telling you, I don't perceive transit. But it doesn't kill me, either." The pilots, growing more and more interested, drew closer to him. Another question probed at him. He heard the inflection, but the words blended into the background like smoke into fog, and then the noise blended into the real smoke of Ramona's exceptionally foul-smelling cigar. Radu wanted to ask her to put it out but could not. He still found her as intimidating as the first time he had met her, and this was her territory. Someone else asked another question and he replied without even trying to hear or understand what had been said.

"It doesn't matter. None of this matters right now. All that matters is that I can find the lost ship, if you'll let me — if you'll help me. I don't think it's safe to waste time, either."

He pushed through the half-circle of pilots and fled to the

farthest corner of the room, fighting to keep himself under control. He wished for a window, even one peering out into the sea. He was near crying from frustration, near collapse from the concentrated attention of all the pilots. Someone touched his arm and he flinched violently.

"Sorry," Orca said. "Are you okay? Let's go out on deck for a while." The pitch of her voice was several tones higher than usual, and when Radu took her hand, her fingers were cold.

"You're shaking," Orca said. She chafed his hands between hers. "And I'm about to start. What *is* it about them?"

"Did anyone ever tell you about the safeguards ships carry, in case they get lost?"

"No. I don't know what you mean."

"When I knew I had no choice but to go into transit awake, Vasili gave me a vial of suicide pills, to use if whatever happened to me was too much to bear. But what they're for is if the ship gets lost and the only other possibility is starvation or asphyxiation." He closed his eyes, but he could feel the tears squeezing out from beneath his eyelids anyway. He could see the slender vial of shimmering translucent crystals.

Orca hugged him, offering comfort friend to friend. "I never thought about it," she said. "I guess I just thought when you get lost, you vanish, the way it seems to the people you leave behind."

"I don't know how long she'll wait," Radu whispered. "I don't even know how long 'long' is for her, in transit. But Laenea isn't someone who holds back from — from things that need to be done." He looked across the room at the cluster of pilots, who spoke in low tones and paid not a bit of attention to him and Orca.

"Did you hear me, Vasili Nikolaievich?" he shouted. "Don't you remember the pills you offered me?" The pilots turned to stare at him. "Ramona-Teresa, how long do you think Laenea will wait for us? She's too proud to choose despair."

The older pilot left the group and strode toward him, stopping just before the point at which they would be able to touch if each extended a hand to the other.

"You need more patience, my boy, and so did Laenea. If she had waited to understand herself better, it's possible she and Miikala would never have been lost. Perhaps none of this would have happened."

He was ready to fight to keep her from declaring Laenea dead and gone. He started to speak, but she silenced him with a quick, sharp motion of her hand.

"If we find them — " she said.

"Ramona," Vasili said angrily, "I think you're letting your personal feelings — "

She needed only a glance to silence Vasili. She shook her head, and began again. "If you find Laenea," Ramona-Teresa said to Radu, "she'll still be a pilot, and you — I don't know what you are, but if we tried to make you into a pilot, the process would kill you. Do you understand that? That part of it cannot change."

"I understand," Radu said. "I understand that she's suited to being a pilot and I am not. I understand that the transition back — "

Ramona-Teresa narrowed her eyes.

" — is seldom made successfully, and would not be attempted even if it were simple." That was as far as his pride allowed him to go. If the pilots thought he wanted Laenea to give up all her ambitions and all her dreams and destroy herself for him, then they did not understand why he loved her, or why — he believed — she had loved him.

Ramona-Teresa's expression cleared. "The patience will come with time. For now, you're right to be impatient." She turned her attention to Orca. "You know what's planned? You understand the danger?"

"Yes, pilot, I do."

"Yet you wish to crew this ship?"

"You can hardly take someone along who doesn't know what they're getting into."

"Ah, good. You also understand that no one else must

know of the attempt before we leave. The administrators — "
She glanced at Radu and laughed, a clear and hopeful sound
after so much silence and grim discussion. "If you think we're
slow to make decisions, Radu Dracul, you should spend some
time with the administrators. You will, if your mission succeeds. You'll learn patience then."

9

SOME DECEIT WAS NECESSARY, but Ramona-Teresa had so much seniority that by the time she, Vasili, Radu, and Orca booked passage on the shuttle and returned to Earthstation, a ship waited to take her home for the leave she had requested. Anyone on the crew, and nearly all the other pilots, would have had to wait for a scheduled flight, but this was a courtesy owed to Ramona-Teresa, which she had never before demanded. It would have been refused, of course, if the administrators had known what she really planned to do with their ship.

They would surely have suspected something if they had known about the extra equipment Vasili talked out of a friend in the x-team planning section. The administrators had given up looking for lost ships years ago and would have forbidden the waste of resources to search for one now.

Radu wished Vasili were staying behind. But Ramona had

chosen him because, of all the pilots, he was best. Officially, he was to pilot Ramona home, then fly the ship back to earth.

They boarded the transit ship and undocked from Earthstation. Vasili began working out a course to the transit point that had begun Laenea's training.

"This ship is off course," the computer's voice said, when the display lights flickered from dead center. "Shall I bring up second level navigational aids?'

"Shut down the cerebral functions," Vasili said. "The last thing I need is a lecture."

Radu obeyed, cutting off the helpful protest by shunting the computer to transit mode.

"P-2709, this is Earthstation. We show you drifting, pilot, are you having difficulties?"

"No difficulties, Earthstation, I show no drift."

"You're drifting, pilot, you're half a radian off course and several degrees above the plane."

"Don't be ridiculous."

Ramona drew Orca out of the transmitter's pickup area.

"Orca, get to sleep quickly. They'll be screaming at us in a moment, and when they realize we're going to use the wrong transit point they might even send someone after us. We won't have time to circle back."

"Okay," Orca said. "Good luck."

Radu accompanied her to her sleep chamber. She had already prepared it. Radu hugged her, memorizing the pressure of her arms around him, the touch of her strong hands on his back. She kissed him on the throat, at the corner of his jaw. His pulse beat against the light pressure of her lips. She had not kissed him before, and Radu had time only to wonder, not to ask, if she meant more by it than the customary parting.

Orca pulled away from him slowly, sliding her hands along his back and his sides and then grasping his forearms.

"Good luck," she said again.

"I'm very glad not to be all alone," Radu said.

"A big lot of good I'll be, sound asleep, but — " She

shrugged, stepped inside her body box, and sat down. "But there's no help for it." She grinned. "Unless you figure out what it is you do, and teach the rest of us." She double checked to be sure the programming was correct.

"Radu — "

"Yes?"

She glanced away, then looked at him intently. "Well, hell. It isn't as if you're a pilot. What did you see?"

Radu blinked, not understanding her. Then he laughed. Orca sat back, frowning.

"Never mind," she said. "Forget it." She reached for the anesthetic mask.

Radu stopped her. "No, don't yet, I'm sorry. I only laughed because I haven't even thought about it since— "

"Why should you? You *know*."

He shook his head. "That's just it. I don't. I didn't see anything — there was nothing to see. It was like looking out into thick fog, fog that went on forever, with nothing even concealed inside it."

"You mean it's all lies? All these years and mysteries and we've been wondering about *lies?*"

"I don't know," Radu said. "Maybe what makes us different from pilots is we can't see what's really out there. Or maybe what makes them different from us is that they create what they experience. I just don't know."

" 'Who knows, with pilots?' " Orca said softly.

Radu's sense of time tugged itself into a conscious thought. "The alarm is about to go off, Orca, you only have a few minutes to get to sleep."

"Okay," she said, and patted his arm. "Take care of yourself out there." She lay back, pulled the mask over her mouth and nose, and breathed deeply. Soon her pupils dilated, and her eyelids drooped. Radu unlaced her red shoes, slipped them off her feet, and stowed them under her sleep chamber. The boxes were of standard size, so she looked very small inside one. Radu had the momentary urge to find a blanket and tuck it in around her. Instead, he closed the lid over her and stood up.

Ramona-Teresa came into the box room as the automatic alarm chimed its warning.

"She's asleep," Radu said.

"Good. As far as the instruments are concerned, so are you." She left the room again. Radu did not take her rapid departure as an insult; she, too, had to prepare herself for transit. Neither Ramona-Teresa nor Vasili Nikolaievich could risk having their concentration or their biocontrol disturbed.

The seconds flowed away. Radu considered, one last time, what he was trying to do. It was no better than a game in which a possible solution was death, a game for which he did not know all the rules. But the prize for winning was very great, and it was too late to resign from the competition.

He spun around to face the port just in time to watch starry black space fade delicately to silver gray. He stopped moving, stopped breathing, awaiting the changes that would begin if his strange ability had only been temporary. But it was just the same as last time: Nothing happened at all. He returned to the control room.

The pilots had put on their oxygen tanks and breathing masks. Vasili was watching something move across his field of view — something invisible, as far as Radu was concerned. Ramona-Teresa focused her gaze on infinity.

"I'm going to follow the flight plan Miikala filed," Vasili said, "as near as I can, anyway." He took a breath. When he spoke again, sarcasm slid into his voice. "And then I suppose you want to take over piloting."

"I don't know yet," Radu said calmly.

"You won't have much time to decide what to do, because theirs was a short flight," the pilot said, "and we can't just keep going indefinitely, or there's no telling where we'll end up." He breathed from his oxygen mask.

"Maybe that's what happened to them."

"I keep trying to make you understand how this works," Vasili said so angrily that he had to stop immediately and take another isolated breath. "You're all right if you know your starting point and your destination, or your start and a familiar route, you can go a little way beyond, but not indefinitely without coming out and taking a look, because you get *lost.*" He turned his back on Radu and began working on the interface between the ship's computer and the computer he had liberated from the exploration team.

"Let's wait until we reach the end of Miikala's flight plan before we worry about what to do, Vaska," Ramona said mildly, then, turning to Radu, "and since if you did perceive Laenea you did it while you were asleep, I suggest you try to go to sleep now and see what happens."

"I guess I should," Radu said. He hesitated, looking out into the gray viewscreen. He felt an unreasonable reluctance to take Ramona's advice, sensible though it was. If he went to sleep and did not dream of Laenea, that would mean, to him, that she was dead.

Only when Vasili glanced at him with a quizzical expression did Radu leave the control room.

In the crew lounge, he kicked off his boots and lay on the couch. He shifted around, trying to get comfortable, but after a while he gave up trying to force himself to sleep. He got up again.

After the past few days he should feel exhausted, but he was wide awake and restless, alert and nervous. In transit, he still felt reluctant to give himself up to normal sleep.

He was tempted to make himself a cup of coffee, but that would further delay what he needed to do. And he already knew how useless sleep drugs would be.

He poked around in the galley — no matter what happened on this flight, he still had the least seniority of anyone on board and was therefore, he assumed, responsible for the cooking.

The ordinary tasks helped to relax him. He rested his elbows on the narrow ledge and stared out into the grayness. His description to Orca had been slightly inaccurate. Fog, indeed, but not a great depth of it. It had no depth. One did not so much look into it as at it. It had neither form nor texture, and only his imagination gave it the bright sparkles at the edge of his vision.

Perhaps he would see more if he stared long enough; perhaps it was sensory deprivation that created whatever the pilots saw.

He did not believe that.

Yet gradually, imperceptibly, the soft gray soothed him. He yawned, and he felt the wandering of his attention, the softly distracted state of mind, brought on by sleepiness. He breathed very slowly and regularly, long deep breaths with as little concentration as he could manage: He let his conscious thoughts sink down and away. The sounds of his body, his steady breathing, his strong, slow heartbeat, blended into the low vibration of the ship's engines. It was too much trouble to take the few steps to the couch, too much effort to fight the great lethargy overwhelming him. He sank down, sliding his hands along the cool glass and the muted swirls of color on the wall. He curled up on the deck, his back pressed into the corner's comforting solidity, his cheek resting on his arm, and, there, he fell asleep.

Radu felt cold. He shivered uncontrollably and his fingers and toes lost all feeling as he fought his way through an impenetrable snowstorm. Walking on ground that was flat and featureless, he moved slowly with his arms outstretched. He could see only as far as his hands could reach. But he encountered no obstructions, no trees, no brush, no irregularities of the land. And there was no sound: Even his footsteps were completely muffled.

The storm continued, but he could make out a faint path beneath the drifted covering.

Radu broke every rule he had ever learned about surviving in the wilderness. He was lost and he should stay still, but here he was, plowing through shin-deep powder snow to follow a nearly obliterated path. He should stay still, so he could be found.

So he could be found: He laughed.

Seconds were the only measure of the distance that he traveled, and without thinking about it he kept track of them. The path made a right-angle turn. Radu followed.

At the second turn, he stopped short.

He knew how easy it was to become confused and disoriented while lost. Without a point of reference, distance and direction were meaningless. He looked back over his track but could not see where he had turned before, and the path he had broken was rapidly filling in.

There was no way to prove it, no way even to demonstrate it to himself, but he was certain in his own mind that this third path lay perpendicular to the other two. Yet the ground was still monotonously flat, and the only dimension left over was up and down.

He turned along the third path reluctantly. It was solid and reassuring, it felt just the same; he experienced no awkward change in gravity and the snow still fell from "up."

When the fourth path appeared, perpendicular to the other three, he nearly succeeded in finding it all quite funny. When he was younger, studying elementary mathematics, he had conquered three-dimensional geometry by brute force. Four spatial dimensions had fought him to a draw; he could manipulate the formulae but not visualize what they represented. Five dimensions had ambushed him and left him so bruised he did not even have an ambition for revenge. Yet he turned onto a fifth path, which again lay perpendicular to all the rest, and he navigated it quite easily.

How long could this go on? He had heard of, though never studied, geometries with an *infinity* of dimensions.

His body was tiring. His brain began playing tricks, out of boredom, with imaginary sounds and imaginary lights. Radu wished for even so little of reality as the faint crinkle of heavy snowflakes falling.

In the quiet he thought he heard someone calling him. "Laenea?"

He received no reply.

At the same time, the blizzard thinned for a moment and he could see the next turning.

He stepped gingerly onto the sixth path, and kept on walking.

It went on so long that he began to believe he had made a mistake. The indentation in the silver surface of the snow was so faint he feared he had lost it and was following an illusion. But he had kept careful watch for another turnoff. He had seen none, and at certain angles the trace before him was plainly visible. He was a good tracker, when the skill was required, back on Twilight. The path was there. The snow had piled so deeply that it slowed his pace and tired him even more rapidly than before. By his own reckoning, he had been traveling for nearly five hours. He wondered if he had been gone that long from the pilots' point of view, and, if he had, if they could tell. Perhaps he had caused their ship to become lost.

Strangely enough, the prospect bothered Radu very little.

The snow was treacherous. He slipped and fell to his hands and knees; he struggled to rise, too fast, and slipped again, falling hard and painfully. Lying flat in the snow, he could hear his heart pounding, faster and faster. The sound filled his ears and bright lights exploded into darkness before him. He flung his arms across his eyes, crying out.

Radu made himself be calm. He dragged himself back into control of his body and he forced himself to remember where he was and what he was doing. Cautiously lifting his head from his arms, he pushed himself up on his elbows. He opened his eyes, and saw the next turn: the turn into the seventh dimension.

He struggled to his feet and looked down at the seventh path. He did not know how many more of these he could face; what made it worse was that he did not know how many he might have to face.

The voice called to him again. Despite the snow, the weight of the silence itself, Laenea's voice reached him, clear and close.

Radu sat bolt upright, wide awake, his hands flung out before him.

He blinked slowly, bringing himself back to the crew room. Shivering, he slumped against the wall and stared back at the two pilots who stood in the doorway staring at him.

"Did you call out to me?" he said stupidly.

"No," Ramona-Teresa said, "you cried out to us."

"We're near the end of the flight path, we don't have any-where to go but back to the beginning or out into normal space," Vasili said.

Radu's absurd mental clock lurched and chirped and told him he had been asleep nearly as long as he had walked in the dream. Relating dream time to real time, or time as real as time ever got in transit, he would just be turning onto the sixth track, the longest one.

"Just keep going."

"How far?"

Radu shrugged.

Vasili scowled and stalked away.

10

IN THE CONTROL ROOM, Radu tried to tell the pilots about his dream. He started twice, and stopped twice, unable to find the right words. He tried again, fumbling to express concepts for which he had no language.

"I was walking on a path," he said. "It was very precise. Each turning was a right angle, but . . ." He hesitated, certain Vasili and Ramona would laugh at him. "Every time I started on a new path, I thought it was perpendicular to all the others. I never climbed, the ground was very flat — " He stopped again. He was not conveying information, only his own tension and confusion, and that was no way to make the pilots believe him. Besides, he knew better than anyone that dreams were images. What he needed to do was understand what the images meant. "That happened for six segments. But when I got to the turning, at the seventh, I heard Laenea. That's when I woke up," he said lamely.

Neither pilot spoke. Vasili had turned translucently pale. He looked over at Ramona. The older pilot gazed at Radu, her serenity shaken by a hint of shock. She bent her head down, pinching the bridge of her nose between thumb and forefinger as if she felt very weary.

"I could have misinterpreted the extra directions," Radu said in a rush.

"Not directions," Ramona-Teresa said, "dimensions."

"*Seven* of them?"

"Seven spatial dimensions in theory, six in practice, until now."

"Seventh doesn't *exist*, Ramona," Vasili said.

Ramona managed to smile. "True," she said, "nor will it until someone perceives it."

"That's a lot of philosophical bullshit, if it were there one of us would have found it, *I've* looked for it hard enough."

"Ah," Ramona said, "you've detected a flaw in the proof?"

Vasili glowered at her. "Proofs are boring."

Ramona laughed. "This is hard on your pride, it is on mine, too, believe me."

"What difference does it make?" Radu said desperately. "It isn't another dimension we're looking for — it's Laenea's ship."

"He doesn't even understand what this means," Vasili said to Ramona, in disgust.

"If we find the lost ship? I think I do," Radu said.

"Not the lost ship — seventh."

Radu frowned.

"You can navigate our galaxy with four," Vasili said, "people who perceive four are easy to find, those of us who see fifth and sixth are a little rarer, and we don't much matter anyway because sixth only reaches empty intergalactic space — it's seventh that will open up the universe."

"We haven't even finished exploring the systems in easy reach," Radu said. "What's the difference if we can get to Andromeda, or only halfway?"

"We'd be unlimited — we could follow the history of a quasar, experimental physics can catch up to the theory, the possibilities are unimaginable." Vasili turned slowly toward the viewport. "And maybe we'll even figure out just exactly what it is we're doing in here."

"All right," Radu said softly to Vasili's back. He knew he should be excited by the idea of a tremendous gain in knowledge, but it only made him feel weary and overwhelmed. "All right," he said. "I understand."

"No, you don't, you really don't," Vasili said without looking at him, "and it's all coincidence anyway."

"Truly?" Ramona said. She watched Vasili while she breathed from her mask. He looked at her, looked away, and fidgeted. "You're willing to make yourself believe that, for your pride?"

Vasili put his own breathing mask over his face and slumped down in sulky silence.

"What you just described," Ramona said to Radu, "was a fair representation of the plan for a first training flight, in which the teacher takes the new pilot along the intersection of the hyperplane with one dimension at a time." She took a breath. "First you orient the new pilot with the normal three, then you introduce fourth, and fifth and sixth if they can perceive them." She paused to let that sink in. "As far as I can tell — assuming the usual progression, and relating your perception of time to mine of distance — you've given an accurate tracing of the path we've been following."

"I . . ." Radu shook his head.

"Yes," Ramona said, "it's a lot for us to accept, too."

"So what?' Vasili said, gesturing toward the viewport. "Can he look out there and show us where to go, to find seventh?" His tone was belligerent. "Can you even perceive fourth?"

"No," Radu said. "I can't see anything at all."

"We're still following their flight plan, but we're near the point where they should have turned back to the start, so what do we do when we get there?"

"I don't know yet," Radu said. "Please don't turn the ship. It isn't time."

"Time doesn't *mean* anything in transit!" Vasili shouted.

"It does to me," Radu said gently.

"Vaska," Ramona said, "that is enough, you agreed to come, but we aren't so far from home that we can't return and start the search over."

"You need the best pilot you can get," Vasili said sullenly.

"That's true, but I'm wondering if we have you at all." She paused, and Vasili shifted uncomfortably. "You aren't so much better that this flight would be out of the question with Chase, or Jenneth, or even me at the controls."

"We can't go back now," Radu said. "I don't care what he says to me, as long as he'll try to follow what I think I've found out."

"I would — if you'd only decide what it is!"

"Keep going," Radu said. "Just keep going."

Between the long wait and being so near the pilots, Radu found it difficult to remain calm. Until now his fragile belief in a perception he did not understand had been a desperate attempt to fend off reality, the reality of Laenea's death. Now that the perception had connected itself so neatly to something concrete, it was becoming reality itself. The scene in the viewport remained, for Radu, a plain gray fog. He was so bored by it that the imaginary flashes of color increased in intensity. He folded his arms across his chest and slumped against the wall. He wished that if he were going to hallucinate, he would do it in an interesting manner.

Vasili had left the control room for a few minutes; Radu sat in the pilot's chair beside Ramona.

"Is the ship, right now, traveling through six spatial dimensions?"

"Yes," Ramona said, "ordinarily Vasili would be piloting the ship freely within a multidimensional space, usually a hypercube." She paused to breathe. "But as we're following a training run, at the moment we're proceeding along the intersection of the fifth- and sixth-dimensional hyperplanes."

Radu tried to imagine it, and failed. "I don't see how you can even begin to handle all the variables."

"In two ways — mathematically, by approximation, by representing the hyperplanes as a combination of two-dimensional spaces, the way most of us do it."

"And the other way?"

"By conceptual purity."

"What?"

Ramona smiled at his expression of confusion. "Have you ever known someone who can always prove mathematical theorems, but who skips so many steps that no one else can understand their proofs?"

Radu nodded.

"They make an art of science, they make jumps of intuition that the rest of us can't follow: Vaska is like that."

"I'm not, though. It doesn't seem strange to me that I can't do it. But transit's *out* there, right in front of me. Why can't I see it?"

"I believe the question is not why you don't perceive it, but why we do, which no one has ever explained."

Radu shook his head.

"Does everything look the same to you, inside the ship?" Ramona asked.

Radu nodded. "Not to you?"

"Far from it, here, and back home we perceive what's called a shadow change; one must block it deliberately most of the time, or it overloads you."

Block it deliberately? Radu thought.

He realized that Vasili was standing to one side of him. He got up quickly. The younger pilot sat down in his seat without acknowledging him.

"We're well past where Miikala and Laenea should have turned back," he said, "is this familiar territory to you, Ramona?"

"No, I've not been far on this track."

"Nor have I — I *must* take a bearing, if I don't there's no telling where we'll come out, and there are a lot of anomalies in this region; I'm worried about the perturbations."

"We've got to keep going," Radu said. "We're nearly there."

"What's the point of going there — wherever *there* is — if we can't get back?"

"How can we be getting lost already? We haven't been out that long." Their expressions changed and Radu wanted to scream with frustration. "I know! I know it doesn't mean anything to you, but it's true nonetheless!"

"I told you he didn't understand about seventh," Vasili said.

"Each successive spatial dimension gives the ship an exponential increase in range," Ramona said patiently to Radu, "so it's possible to go a very short distance in transit, but a very long way in normal space, particularly when you've moved up to sixth."

"Oh," Radu said. "But — just a little farther?"

Ramona sighed. "We'd best do as he asks, Vaska."

"I won't take orders from a crew member!" Vasili fumbled for his oxygen mask and took a long deep breath.

"Can you return us exactly to this spot, going the same direction and the same speed?" Radu asked.

"I was under the impression that was what I was here for."

"All right."

The acquiescence was so sudden that Vasili looked confused.

"You have your wish, Vasili Nikolaievich," Ramona-Teresa said; "take us out of transit."

Vasili settled in at his controls. A moment later the gray of the viewport glowed to black. Each pilot took a deep breath and resumed a relatively normal pattern of breathing. Radu stopped his count of the seconds they had spent on the sixth track. He had so many different time-lines going together in his mind that he wondered if he were in danger of losing them all.

He looked outside, and gasped.

The ship lay close to the fiery disk of a forming star, so close it could be engulfed at any moment, so close Radu could see rivers and points of brilliant color in the great burning spinning central sphere —

He glanced at Vasili, at Ramona. The younger pilot looked

irritated, the older bemused, but they were quite calm. Still alarmed, Radu turned back to the port.

Perspective jolted him. It was not a single coalescing star that lay below the ship. His eyes had tricked him, following color to create motion. What he was looking at did indeed spin, at an enormous speed. But it was itself so enormous that its motion would be imperceptible if Radu watched it for his lifetime.

Feeling dizzy, he gazed down at the Milky Way. Its filmy, fuzzy edge crossed the port at a diagonal.

Ramona made a sound of mild surprise. "We *have* come a long way. Vaska, can you mark our position?"

"I think so, here, with the x team's computer. But just how much farther are we supposed to go?"

They both glanced at Radu, without asking the question that was unaskable about transit.

"About ten minutes, subjective time," he said. "But that won't match the clock. Do you want me to plan to give you a countdown?"

"Good gods, no! Haven't you learned *anything* about pilots?"

"I'm sorry," Radu said, startled by the vehemence of Vasili's reply.

"Maybe it doesn't matter to you but Ramona and I would like to get home from this alive."

"Vaska," Ramona said, "he's done nothing to upset your balance. He will not. So stop harrying him."

"I'm sorry," Radu said again. "I didn't realize just how careful you have to be."

"We're generally a bit more resilient," Ramona said. "But you put us under an extra strain, as we do you." She rubbed her hand along the side of her face, and closed her eyes; she looked as if exhaustion were about to overcome her.

Radu took the hint and left the control room.

He stopped near Orca's sleep chamber and sat beside her. The anesthetic was supposed to be relaxing, but Orca's teeth were clenched. He could see the muscles in a band down the side of her jaw, and the tendons standing out in her neck. She moved, shifting as if to wake.

He wished he *could* wake her and talk to her. But the wish was too selfish to indulge. He was worried about the delay, and he hoped the pilots would not be long at their task. It would be unfair to Orca to wake her; she would hardly be out of the box before she had to climb back in.

He watched her uneasy sleep for a long time. Her strange hands were clamped into fists. In his imagination she needed the comfort of another human being as much as he did.

He passed his hands over his eyes, and went back to the crew lounge. In front of the viewport he flung himself into a chair.

Perhaps he was doing unconsciously what Ramona had said she could do deliberately: blocking out the new perceptions. He lay back, trying to feel all his senses, to leave himself open to any sight or sound or feeling such as he had experienced in his dream.

He became hyperaware of the small sounds of the ship, the ventilation's slow drift, the stretch and turn of leaves seeking starlight. He felt the nubbly blue of the upholstery beneath his spread fingers, and smelled oxygen's occasional ionization.

A whistle lanced through his hearing.

Vasili's cheerful notes, in a random cadence, implied good news, but the sound grated on Radu's nerves. He put his hands over his ears and decided he preferred the pilot irritable, and silent. The whistling continued.

You shouldn't be bothered by it, Radu thought. It's practically imperceptible in here.

But once it had begun to trouble him he could not make it stop. He moved his hands back and forth over his ears, filling his hearing with raspy distant ocean sounds. But he could still hear the whistling.

Go and ask him to stop, he told himself.

That was as ridiculous as being troubled by the noise in the first place.

He hunched over with his head on his crossed arms. He started breathing shallowly, rapidly, and his heart pounded, drowning out the whistling and conscious thought as well. Lying down, he curled up on his side with his knees to his chest, trying to ease the pain as his pulse dissolved into a useless flutter.

He gasped for breath, rolled face downward, and spread his hands against the cool floor. Then, knowing his only hope of survival was to force away the panic, he very deliberately took control of his body's reactions.

He was adequate at biocontrol: On occasion, under ideal conditions, he could even achieve deep trance. Conditions were far from ideal, but deep trance was not what he needed. Rather, he needed to dissipate stress before its build-up destroyed him. Breathing came first: He breathed slowly, deeply, and very, very regularly.

Radu slowed and eased his heartbeat. He could feel his blood pressure falling. He pulled his knees to his chest, then straightened his legs and pushed himself to a headstand, supported in the corner. His mind grew calm and clear as he imposed upon it the patterns of relaxation.

He only noticed how long he had stayed like that when he heard one of the pilots speaking. After a while it registered that the pilot was speaking to him.

"What's the matter? Is he all right?" Ramona's voice came faintly from the control room.

Vasili paused quite a long time before replying. "I *guess* he's all right," he said with irritation. "He's standing on his head in the corner."

Radu realized how silly he must look. He opened his eyes. The pilot looked equally ridiculous, from Radu's viewpoint. Radu started to laugh, and collapsed in a heap, giggling absurdly.

"When you're finished, let me know." Vasili stalked away.

Radu climbed to his feet, still laughing. He supposed he should feel humiliated; instead, he felt calm and relaxed and in possession of himself for the first time in far too long. Whether he could maintain the fragile grasp he did not know.

He returned to the control room. "I am finished," he said to Vasili.

Ramona-Teresa gazed at him, her distress plain. "Are you all right?"

"Yes. Now."

"What happened?"

"I . . . reacted badly. The way I did on Earthstation, and when I was — when Laenea and I were together."

Ramona frowned. "Did you stop breathing? Was your heartbeat arrhythmic?"

He shrugged. "For a moment."

She hesitated for a long time. When she spoke, her voice was very low and sad. "I think we must turn back."

"What? Why? No!"

"Because our search is a long chance, one only worth taking if there isn't any risk to you."

"That's up to me."

"No," she said, "it isn't. Radu, I've seen pilots react badly to ordinaries, but not the other way around. I'm worried. If something happens to you in transit, and you can't control it yourself, neither Vaska nor I could help you till the ship returned to normal space. Restarting your heart, regulating your breathing — we simply would not be able to do it. We *could not.*" She paused. "By the time we left transit, it might be too late. Do you understand?"

"Yes," Radu said. "I do. It's all right. And *I'm* all right. We've got to keep going — we can't give up now."

She smiled slowly, sadly. "You think we'll find them, don't you?"

"Don't you?"

"I'm afraid to believe you, but I'm beginning to."

Vasili swung his chair around. "Are you two done arguing?"

"Yes, Vaska, I think that we are."

"Then I'm taking us back into transit," Vasili said. "Right . . . now."

Radu hoped — the universe turned gray — for something more. Disappointed, but resigned, he let the seconds start ticking away again, taking him closer and closer to the final intersection, where the only test that counted lay.

"How much longer?" Vasili asked.

"*What?*" Radu could not believe a pilot had asked such a question. "The last time I tried to tell you that, you screamed at me. Why do you want to know something that's meaningless to you? And dangerous as well?"

"Go ahead and tell me — if you can make sense out of space here, maybe I can make sense of time."

"Sense!" Radu burst out laughing.

"Just tell me if it's soon."

"It's soon."

The time passed, and Radu searched the viewport for anything, even a depth to the faceless gray. He began a silent countdown of the seconds in his mind.

"I'm going to have to turn," Vasili said. "We're headed straight for an anomaly."

One of the bright hallucinations glimmered, not at the edge of Radu's vision, but in the center, and this time it remained. He blinked, expecting it to vanish like the others.

Instead it widened, and at the same time its substance coalesced, the colors intensifying and thickening, intertwining and parting like the threads of a tapestry.

"Did you hear me?" Vasili cried. "If this is where Miikala and Laenea went, they're gone, forever, and we'll be lost, too!"

Radu stayed completely still, afraid that any motion, any glance away, would send the pattern to the edge of his sight, there to vanish.

"Ramona!" Vasili shouted.

"Yes, turn, quickly!"

"No, Vasili, don't!"

The younger pilot swung the ship from the shiny crazed surface. Radu lunged. He shouldered Vasili out of the way, knocking him to the deck. The controls were warm in his hands. He forced them against the whole momentum of the ship, and the lurch penetrated the artificial gravity. Radu staggered and almost fell. The enormous patch, glazed with deep color, wider and higher than the ship, opened out to receive them. It became a soap bubble, lucid, transparent, an aurora that spun curtains even more intense than those of the flaming skies of Twilight. It was a solid coruscation of curvetting fire.

Radu guided the ship straight into it.

Vasili screamed.

The transit ship shuddered. Radu expected, any moment, a breach of the hull, the shriek of escaping air, the slow end of sound. But the ship passed into the aurora, and the aurora passed into the ship. Through dimensions Radu had imagined but could not describe, the color rained upon him and passed through his skin and flesh and bones. He shivered as it touched him. He felt that he could reach out and sweep the universe up in his arms, from its beginning to its end.

For that moment, he understood what pilots knew about transit.

Radu slumped down in the pilot's chair, dazzled and confounded. He blinked, trying to clear his vision. Everything around him, machines and people, was surrounded by light and shadows. He rubbed his eyes, but the shadows remained.

Vasili pulled himself up from the deck, lurched at Radu, and grabbed the front of his shirt.

"What did you see? Tell me what you saw!"

Radu stared at his hand, fascinated by the multiple images, scared and exhilarated at the same time. He reached out to make Vasili release his grip, but as soon as he touched him, the young pilot cursed and snatched his hand away. Radu wanted to feel sorry for him, he wanted to feel anger toward him, but he could spare the attention for neither.

"Dammit, tell me — "

"Vasili, Radu," Ramona said softly, "look."

She pointed at the viewport.

Don't block it out, this time, Radu thought. Don't persuade yourself that you can't see anything.

He turned, slowly, and looked where Ramona was pointing.

A set of images like broken shards of a mirror: Before them lay the irregular silver and shadow twinkle of another transit ship.

Ramona took the controls. Intently, she guided their ship toward the other one.

Vasili snarled a curse and tried to pull Radu from the pilot's chair. Radu stood, gingerly testing his changed perceptions. He gazed down at Vasili, seeking out the true image among the multitude of similar reflections.

"I'd tell you what I saw if I could," he said. "Please believe me. It's just that I haven't figured it out myself yet."

"I *don't* believe you!"

"Stop it, both of you," Ramona said angrily, "and prepare for docking."

She docked the ship noisily, messily; the two craft clanged together and the fittings locked and held as momentum and inertia combined to give an awkward spin. Without pausing to correct, she jumped up and rushed toward the airlock. Ignoring Vasili, Radu hurried after her.

He crashed into a wall, banging his shoulder hard. Tears filled his eyes, further fragmenting the multiple visions. He shook his head, scrubbing his sleeve across his eyes. The airlock started its cycle. He moved toward it, feeling his way along the passage.

Ramona stepped into the other ship. Radu hesitated. The pilot's footsteps echoed and re-echoed. He followed.

She did not pause in the darkened box room, but Radu stopped. The sensors and instrument lights gave off a vague glow. Radu bent over a sleep chamber, trying to make out the calibration. All he could be sure of was that it registered activity.

"Ramona, the crew member's alive," he said.

She kept on going.

"Laenea — " Radu meant to shout, but her name came out in a whisper.

He followed Ramona into the crew lounge. She stopped so suddenly that he almost ran into her, then she took a few hesitant steps, and stopped again. A body lay on the couch. The sheet covering it obscured its outlines.

Radu saw a man living, a man dead, a man decayed. He gasped, watching the transition to ashes.

Ramona drew the sheet away and gazed down at Miikala's body in silence.

There was only grief in her expression, not revulsion or fear or surprise: She could not be seeing what Radu had seen. Miikala's body was reality for her. Radu could make sense of the rest of the images only as projections from the past, from the future, as if spatial dimensions and time had become equally accessible to him.

Radu was over being startled and he could not be repelled, for he had seen far worse deaths on Twilight. Trying not to shut himself off completely from what he had learned to see, but knowing he must simplify it or be as good as blind, Radu gradually projected each shadow back onto a single reality that he chose as best he could. The process was something like drawing a three-dimensional cube onto a two-dimensional sheet of paper, something like changing the focus of his eyes from very far away to very near.

Slowly he brought himself to a world where the shadows did not blot out the objects, a world less overwhelming to his senses. But it was not what it had been before. He doubted it ever would be what it had been before.

Ramona knelt at Miikala's side and touched his throat, seeking — surely not a pulse, but warmth, some sign of life. Radu wished he could touch her, draw back her hand, embrace her without causing her pain, for she could only find sorrow here. Miikala was dead.

Even if Miikala had committed suicide, Radu knew Laenea would not leave a crew member to wake up when the anesthetic ran out, to die horribly and alone.

He walked past Ramona and into the control room.

One hand dangling to the floor, Laenea lay sprawled in the pilot's chair, her breathing mask over her face, the instruments blinking around her. Radu approached, terrified, afraid of seeing again the transition to bones and ashes.

"Laenea?" His voice broke.

Her hand moved. He started violently at the faint sound of her fingertips brushing the deck.

And then she stretched, and pushed away the mask, and yawned. She shook back her hair, just the way she had during the few days they had been together, when he watched her awaken from a sound sleep.

"Laenea — "

She leaped to her feet, spinning around to face him, her long black hair tangled.

"Radu!" She looked around, still half asleep and confused. "I was dreaming about you — I'm still dreaming, I must be!"

"No, this is real. We came to find you."

He began to smile; she laughed, her wonderful, open laugh of delight and surprise; Radu's smile turned into his absurd and embarrassing giggle, bubbling up with joy. They threw themselves into each other's arms, in a long, unbelieving embrace. Neither cared that one was a pilot and the other was not.

"How can you be here?" She pulled back a little; she touched the base of his throat where the pilot's scar would end, if he had one. "You aren't a pilot, but you're awake — and alive — "

"I don't know how to explain. I woke up in transit. I knew your ship was in trouble."

"In trouble — ? But — " She ran out of breath, grabbed her mask, and took a deep gulp of oxygen. "Sorry, I'm not used to that yet."

"They declared your ship lost. But . . . something . . . happened to me in transit. I *knew* you were out here, and alive."

"How could they declare the ship lost? It hasn't been here very long. I mean it doesn't feel like very long. How long *has* it been?" She reached for her mask again; she was not yet proficient at conserving her breath and speaking in long single sentences, like the more experienced pilots.

"Your ship is two weeks late, and that's after they gave it the maximum for the trip itself."

She shook her head. "I suppose you understand how hard it is to keep track of time here."

"I've been told. Repeatedly."

"I only just sat down to sort things through, and to try to figure out how to get home," she said. "I guess I fell asleep. After Miikala..." Her voice trailed off; she glanced over Radu's shoulder. "You couldn't have come here all by yourself, surely — ?"

"No. I persuaded the pilots to help me. Vasili, and Ramona-Teresa — "

"Ramona! Is she here? Where?"

"She was with me — in the other room."

"Oh, no . . ."

"What is it?"

"Miikala's in there."

"I know. I saw . . . do you see things differently, here?"

She ignored his question. "Radu, Miikala and Ramona were lovers, they've been lovers since before they were pilots." She hurried toward the other room. Radu followed.

Of course, he thought. He felt ashamed, chagrined, and stupid. All the clues came back to him, now that it was too late to do anything about them. Until now he had been oblivious to them, and now it was too late. He had abandoned Ramona to her grief.

She was kneeling beside the couch, staring at Miikala. Laenea knelt beside her and embraced her. Radu stood helplessly nearby.

"What happened? How did you get here? What did he mean, experimenting with a novice in the ship? Did he lose hope when you were lost? Oh, *damn*."

Laenea held her. Radu, knowing how Ramona felt, how she must have felt since hearing of the lost ship, wanted to add his comfort to Laenea's. His hopes had raised Ramona's, and now she was betrayed. He remained where he was, knowing his touch would only hurt her.

"It was only supposed to be a training flight, that's true. We went into transit — Oh, Ramona!"

"I know, my dear." Ramona spoke softly, her eyes closed, tears heavy on her thick black eyelashes.

"But at the end of the flight, when he said we had to turn back, it was as if he'd let me sit at the controls of an airplane but never take off."

Ramona-Teresa drew back in surprise. "You saw it? You, Laenea? The first time?"

"I showed him, and then he could see it too. Just like that. So we went into it, to see what it was like. I saw — I felt — " She stopped. "I don't have the right words. He'd only started to teach me."

"Even Miikala didn't have the words for what you've done," Ramona said. Her voice shook. Her composure finally shattered. The stolid, independent pilot hid her face against Laenea's shoulder, and the younger woman held her, rocking her gently. Radu knew how the possibility of joy could intensify grief; joy was nothing when one was all alone.

"He was ecstatic, Ramona," Laenea said. "He explained what seventh would mean. We explored it a little way. I thought he was only getting tired. But then he . . . he had a seizure. A stroke. I don't know. I tried to revive him . . ." She looked away from Ramona, at Miikala's body. "I know he never felt any pain. But he'd still be alive, if I hadn't — "

"You don't know that!" Ramona said angrily. She dashed the tears from her cheeks with the back of her hand, and then she spoke more calmly. "Perhaps it *was* seventh that killed him, but you aren't to blame, you — tell yourself this isn't a bad place or a bad time for a pilot to die." She stopped, as her voice almost broke. "It's what I'll be telling myself."

She started to cry again, and Laenea kept holding her.

"Come away," Laenea said, "come away." She led Ramona from Miikala's side, back to the control room and to the pilot's chair.

"I'm all right," Ramona said. "I'll be all right." Laenea knelt beside her, holding her hands.

"Did you get into seventh?"

Radu started. Vasili stood in the shadows of the hatchway,

the sharp planes of his face softened by patterns of light.

"We're in it, Vasili," Laenea said, calmly, gently. "You're in it all the time."

"Then where is it, what does it look like?"

"Can't you see it? It's all around, once you've perceived it you can't lose it again." She glanced at Radu. "You can see it, Radu, can't you?"

"Yes," he said. "Yes. I can."

"You're lying," Vasili said to both of them. "Anyone can claim a perception and try to get the credit, but who'll care if you can't show it to the rest of us? I don't believe you!"

"I'm getting very tired of being called a liar!" Radu said angrily.

Laenea kept her temper. "Vasili . . . you brought exploration equipment, I assume?"

"Yes, of course, we didn't come out here to get lost along with you."

"Good." Laenea stabbed at a control. The ships fell out of transit and the universe opened out around them. "Now look."

The stars lay spread in strange patterns. Knowing they had left their galaxy, and must be in some other, made Radu feel a little frightened.

Laenea gazed quite calmly at space and the stars.

The longer Radu stared, the stranger the stars appeared. He thought, for a while, that he had lost his ability to project the new images back on themselves.

Ramona let her breath out in a long sigh. Radu looked more carefully, and overcame his misperceptions.

Each star — each patch of light, for they were patches and not points, patches indistinct around the edges where the density of matter thinned out — each was a single galaxy. And farther away . . . each of those bright patches must be a whole galactic cluster.

"Where *are* we?" Vasili whispered.

"We are," Ramona said, "where you have wished to come, for so long."

All of time and space lay beyond the port; the little ships

hung at the end of the universe, billions of light-years, billions of years, from its origins. Vasili placed his hand flat on the glass. Radu could not tell if he were reaching for the star clusters, or trying to push them away.

Radu's gaze met Laenea's.

"Do you understand?" she said softly.

"Not enough," he said.

She grinned. "Me, either. Not yet, anyway. But I will."

For the first time, for Radu, Laenea *was* a pilot. He could see the change in her bearing and her manner. Luminous, serene, she touched Radu's cheek.

It was, he feared, the last touch between them. Nothing he had done or seen could overcome the essential disharmony between pilots and ordinary human beings.

Radu covered Laenea's hand with his own. He kissed her palm, then slowly let his hand fall. She gazed at him a moment longer, nodded, and drew back as Radu, too, stepped away.

Laenea touched a control. The ship silently and smoothly rotated. The galaxies slid from the viewport.

In the other direction lay . . . nothing.

Interstellar space is deep black, touched richly with stars. Even the featureless shadows of hard vacuum could not match the complete absence of light that faced Radu now. He tried to open out the darkness, to let images expand to include a future or a past. But there was nothing there, no stars, no galaxies, no light or heat or radiation. Nothing was there and nothing ever had been there. He was looking into a place that did not yet exist and never would exist. The universe, still expanding, would engulf it, and it never would have been.

The ship continued to turn till the galaxies swept into view once more. Ramona sat back in the pilot's chair as if she were exhausted, and Vasili made an inarticulate sound of confusion and fury. Radu felt stunned. Laenea touched another control and neutralized the spin.

"That's hard to look at for long," she said. "Now do you

believe me, Vasili? We couldn't be here, except by going into seventh."

"True," Vasili said with a sort of grim and self-destructive pleasure. He turned on his heel and strode from the control room.

"Why can't he see it?" Laenea said. "All you have to do is look."

"It isn't that simple," Ramona said. "All the pilots can see fourth, but only half of us can perceive fifth, and half of those, sixth. As for seventh — I had my chance, and Vasili had his, when Radu brought us here. But we were oblivious to what he sensed, and to what you understand."

Radu rubbed his hands over his face, pressing his fingers against his eyes to shut out, for the moment, the light of the universe past and present and future. He knew the respite had to be a short one; his understanding had come more slowly, but no less surely. The implications, though, would take much longer to discover. He felt very tired.

He steadied himself and let his hands fall to his sides. Ramona stayed where she was, her shoulders slumped, while Laenea leaned over her computer, which had interfaced with Vasili's and the x team's. An enormous mass of data scrolled rapidly through the air.

When it finally stopped, Laenea whistled, a low sound of relief. "Before you came," she said, "I was afraid I'd spend the rest of my life trying to get back by successive approximation." She faced Radu. "What you must have had to go through to make them listen — thank you, Radu."

He looked into her eyes.

It isn't fair, he thought, we ought to be even closer, but we aren't, we can't be.

His love for her, and his admiration, were as strong as ever; and the physical attraction was undiminished.

"It wasn't something I thought about," he said. "It wasn't something I had to decide."

She smiled.

"Come on. Let's go home."

11

ORCA WOKE SLOWLY. At first her vision refused to clear. She blinked at the fuzzy lights overhead, trying to force them back into focus. She pushed away the anesthetic mask. The smell of the chemical had already faded, but she felt like curling up and going back to sleep. She wished she were in the sea, in a remote harbor, floating and sinking and rising with a pod of napping killer whales.

Her knees and her back felt stiff and sore. She raised the lid of her sleep chamber and climbed out, wishing as she seldom had before that someone were there to help her. She had expected to see Radu. But if something had gone wrong, if the stress of transit had suddenly caught up with him . . .

She slipped into her gold mesh vest and padded barefoot out of the box room.

Radu, hurrying down the corridor, stopped when he saw her.

"You're okay," she said with relief.

He nodded.

"Where are we?" Orca said. Her shoulders ached. She rubbed her collarbone. "It feels like we've come a long way."

"I'll show you," Radu said.

She followed him into the deserted control room. She stopped, astonished.

Galaxies spread out in clumps and clusters before her, endless concentrations of stars in hazy spirals, some of them dark red, dying. The ship had passed beyond any region of single stars.

"A long way," she said again, very softly.

The implications began to come clear. Orca walked to the viewport and leaned her forehead against it, cupping her hands around her face to screen off reflections.

"Turn down the lights, please," Radu said to the computer, and it complied. Orca stood in the dark, her hands pressed to the glass. She felt as if she could dissolve right through it, she *wanted* to dissolve right through it, to embrace the whole universe with her body and fling the molecules of her being into the void.

Her vision clouded. She blinked, but the glass had misted over. Tears ran down her face.

"Orca — don't, please, we're not lost." He put his arm around her shoulders. "I didn't mean to scare you. We aren't lost."

"I know," she said. "I mean, I wasn't afraid of that, I wasn't *afraid* ..." She stopped, unable to explain. "I don't care ..." She held him, trying to ease his concern, and needing the solidity and touch of another human being to temper her excitement. Starlight, galaxy-light, gave the only illumination. It glinted off Radu's dark blond hair and his high cheekbones. Orca wished transit ships had more ports, or that they had been built of some transparent material, so she could bathe in the light of the universe.

"You must have traveled through seventh," she said. "You must have discovered it!"

"Laenea discovered it. I only found her."

Orca drew away from Radu and turned to the port again. She looked down, nearly parallel to the ship's surface. The docking hatch lay out of sight, but she could see the curve of Laenea's training ship beyond the search craft's flank.

As Radu told her Laenea's tale, Orca listened in silence, nodding now and then, hearing and understanding what he said to her, but increasingly distracted by the sight of the universe.

"Radu," she said suddenly, "what's on the other side?"

He avoided glancing back at the port. "Nothing," he said.

"Nothing?"

"Nothing. Darkness — you can't even call it that. More than an absence of light. I can't explain. Laenea would show it to you. I'm not ready to see it again." He changed the subject abruptly. "I'd better fix lunch," he said, turning away. "Everybody must be getting hungry." He spoke as if his pedestrian duties could erase the extraordinary thing he had done.

"Radu — "

Orca reached toward him. Though she was behind him, out of his sight, he tensed before she touched him.

She let her hand fall.

"Okay. I'll see you later."

He nodded without speaking and walked away.

Orca let him go, all alone, and hoped that was the right thing to do.

After Radu had already begun chopping up the vegetables, he noticed that the meal he had chosen to prepare took longer than anything else he knew how to make. He could have put everything through the preparer in the galley, and quite probably everyone would laugh at him if they realized he had not done so. But he was beyond caring what any of the others thought. The work was comforting. Slicing through onions and bok choy in a steady rhythm gave him something to concentrate on other than seventh, other than his new perceptions, other than the edge.

He tasted the sauce. It had no taste. He added pippali, more than he should have, and a handful of chopped ginger.

He felt the radial acceleration as the linked ships slid into a slow, gentle spin. After half a turn, a counterthrust stopped them. Radu shut his eyes, then opened them again. With his eyes closed it was all too easy to let the petals of dimension open out onto an endless abyss.

Radu Dracul shivered.

When Laenea turned the ships to face the edge, Orca gazed at it, into it. It lay just beyond the port; no, it lay forever beyond vision or understanding.

"Turn the ship around." Vasili's voice was haunted and strained.

"No!" Orca said.

"Laenea — "

"Don't look at it if you don't like it," Orca said.

"It'd be there, all the same, I'd know it, I'd feel it."

"It's there, even when we aren't facing it!"

Vasili reached for the controls. Ramona put her hand over his. "Vaska, it isn't going to jump in and eat us."

His shoulders stiff with anger, Vasili strode from the control room.

Ramona hesitated, sighed, and finally got up and followed him.

"Laenea, what's out there?" Orca asked softly.

"I wish I knew," Laenea said. "I tried to figure it out, but beyond where we are, the transit equations haven't any solutions. We've come just about as far as we can."

Orca kept staring at the edge. Laenea busied herself at the control console.

Quite some time later, the ship began a slow spin. Orca made a sound of protest, or supplication.

"Sorry," Laenea said. "But I don't much like it looming over me, either. Orca, can you get your ship ready, please? We'll have to use its engines, too, to get home."

Orca stood, reluctant, still staring at the viewport. Now it held a field of galaxies.

"Yes . . ." she said. "All right . . ." She left Laenea's ship. She felt both enlarged and diminished by what she had seen, and all she knew for certain was that she wanted to explore it until she understood its secrets.

Now she knew how her brother felt when he dove into the sea until its depths sliced away all the sunlight. She knew why he loved it, and why he would never leave.

Radu felt the ships spin again, returning to their original orientation. He wondered how Orca, down in Laenea's control room, had reacted to the sight of the edge.

It will excite her, he thought. It won't surprise her any more than she was surprised by seeing constellations formed by galaxies instead of stars. She can swim across an ocean all alone, or accompanied by a predator that would terrify any ordinary human being. The edge of reality would not frighten Orca.

He scraped his knife a few times across the sharpening stone, then went back to chopping everything very fine.

Orca climbed down into the engines. She found stress wear even more severe than the damage she felt within her own body. The distance they had come had penetrated all the protective mechanisms of sleep and shielding. She signaled the computer for the schematics, replaced three circuit splinters, and reached into a net. She pushed herself into the heightened state of awareness she needed to heal the frayed luminescent connections. The energy flux tingled through her hands and along the edges of her finger webbing.

Radu flicked on the intercom.

"Lunch, everybody," he said.

Laenea came in a minute later, Ramona soon thereafter. Radu finished slicing a green onion, swept the pieces onto the edge of his knife, and scattered them across the soup for garnish.

"Smells good," Laenea said. "Is it — "

"What's that smell?" Vasili put all his disappointment and disgust over the whole trip into those three words.

"Lunch," Radu said, without apology. He was thoroughly sick of Vasili's bad humor.

"*I* can't eat it." The young pilot stormed back to his cabin.

Ramona made as if to go after him but Laenea touched her arm and she stopped.

"Let him sulk, Ramona. Come have some lunch. It smells wonderful."

Ramona allowed Laenea to lead her to her place at the head of the table.

"I'm not very hungry," she said apologetically to Radu. "But Laenea's right, it does smell good."

Laenea glanced at Radu, struggled not to laugh, and broke out giggling. He gave her a quizzical look.

"I'm sorry," she said. "You looked so funny, when Vaska said he wouldn't eat lunch. Poor Vaska, he hasn't even the sense not to insult the cook when he's holding a butcher knife!"

Radu wiped off the blade and put the knife away. "I forgot I had it," he said. "Go ahead and start. I'll get Orca."

He went to the engine room hatchway and called her. He expected to hear her climbing the ladder, but silence was the only response. He went down to look for her.

She was sitting crosslegged on the floor, her chin on her fist, faint frown lines of intense concentration on her forehead. Radu sat on his heels beside her. The light from circuit interstices flowed over her.

"Orca?"

She stayed where she was, without answering; she took a long, deep breath, and let it out again. She blinked slowly and looked at him.

"Lunch," he said lamely.

It was a quiet meal. Laenea, having recovered from her fit of laughter, complimented Radu on the taste as well as the smell of the soup, then lapsed into a thoughtful silence. Vasili remained in his cabin. Orca responded to nothing more complicated than "Pass the soy sauce." Ramona picked at her food for a few minutes, then murmured a word of apology and left the galley. Orca watched her go, and soon thereafter, without another word, got up and followed her.

"I don't think they meant it as a comment on your cooking," Laenea said.

"I know they didn't," Radu said. "It doesn't matter. I don't expect anyone to act as if this trip were ordinary. I'm surprised I feel as normal as I do."

"I feel better than normal," Laenea said. "I'm sorry about Miikala, I'm sorry Vasili is disappointed. But I can't help it. I feel wonderful."

Orca paused just inside the control room where Ramona-Teresa sat all alone with the lights out. The diver thought about seeing deeper into the infrared. Ramona became a deep glow, motionless and silent. The strangeness of pilots intensified in the darkness. At night Orca could see the pulse of ordinary people. Pilots changed their blood pressure without any definite rhythm. The bright strokes of the veins in Ramona's throat suddenly faded and her skin darkened to deep red.

"Ramona-Teresa," Orca whispered, "are you all right?"

"Yes, my dear," the pilot said sadly. Cool black tracks streaked her face, where tears had fallen and not yet quite dried. "There aren't many of us left, the first pilots. I've survived losing friends before. Never quite as close a friend as Miikala, though."

"I'm very sorry. That this happened."

"Thank you."

"Ramona-Teresa . . ."

"Yes?"

"Would you turn the ships around again? Just for a few minutes? Please?"

"If you wish." The pilot's short, square hands moved on the controls. The galaxies slid away.

Orca sat crosslegged on the deck in front of the port and let the edge engulf her and slice through her.

Someone spoke. Orca did not hear the words; she did not reply.

Ramona crouched next to her and put one hand on her shoulder.

"Orca — " she said again. The reflection of her face overlaid the edge. "Orca, what do you see in it?"

"I . . . I don't know." Using true speech underwater, she might be able to describe it. She said a few phrases in middle speech.

"Are you singing?" Ramona asked.

"No," Orca said. "I was trying to explain. But I don't have any words you can understand."

Ramona's reflection showed outrage, then she began to laugh.

"I deserve that," the pilot said. "Oh, I do deserve that, I and all the pilots."

Radu came in. Though his steps were silent, the warmth of his body reflected from the viewport and outlined him in a faint glow that brightened and dimmed with his pulse. His image combined and melded with Orca's. She met his gaze in the reflection. As quiet as his image, he crossed the floor and sat beside her, and both of them looked out, out at the edge.

When Ramona's signal came through the linked control panel, Laenea could have turned on the intercom and asked the older pilot not to change their orientation; she could even have counteracted the thrust. Instead, she ordered all the lights out and watched the edge come into view again. The viewport disappeared against black, and Laenea stared into a mystery so close she might reach out and touch it. It frightened her in a way she had never before been frightened. She had been scared before her first transit voyage, when she was still a crew member, as well as before the operation that made her a pilot and during the approach to this, her first training flight. Scared, yet excited and eager as well. This fear was of a much more intense unknown.

But it was a familiar factor that immediately threatened them. The ships were traveling at a significant percentage of the speed of light. The time distortion of transit aside, here in normal space (or was the edge normal space anymore?) they would experience relativistic effects. A minute here was some longer time back on earth. Laenea set the computer to figuring out the factor, then went looking for Radu.

She found him sitting next to Orca, both of them gazing fascinated at the edge.

"Radu — "

She thought he had not heard her, but he finally looked over his shoulder.

"Yes?"

"Can you still tell *when* it is, back on earth?"

"Of course." He paused a moment. "Oh," he said. "I see. You're right. We probably shouldn't stay here too much longer."

"How long have we been gone?"

"You'd been gone nearly three weeks when we left, and since then it's been, earth time, about eight days."

Laenea nodded. As long as they could measure their presence here in hours, their world would not outdistance them in time. But if they stayed too long, the effect of time dilation would be to transport them years into the future, when they would be not merely lost, but forgotten.

"Ramona, we really had better go home," Laenea said.

Ramona nodded. "I suppose we had. Orca, is our ship ready?"

Radu had to nudge her gently before she responded.

"Yeah," she said absently. "The repairs are done."

"Good. We'll start home as soon as you're asleep."

Startled out of her reverie, Orca jumped up and grabbed Laenea's arm.

"We're going *home?* We came all this way just to turn around and go back?"

"I came all this way by mistake — and you came all this way to find me." Laenea drew away.

Scowling, Orca kept her grip.

"I'm sorry," Laenea said. "I didn't mean to be flippant. Orca, would you please let me go?"

Orca complied without apology.

"We aren't prepared for exploration or research," Laenea said. "We need to go back and set up a proper expedition. Besides, no one on board either ship contracted to be away from home for a couple of years. That'll be the elapsed time on earth for even a short research trip."

"But — "

"I'm sorry," Laenea said again. "We have to go home."

Orca strode from the control room.

Radu helped prepare his ship for transit, shunting the computers to transit mode. When they were ready, he went to the box room to help Orca go to sleep.

She was gone.

"Orca?"

He hurried through the small ship, swung down into the engine room, searched for and failed to find her. He opened the intercom.

"Laenea, is Orca on board your ship?"

"I don't think so. Isn't she sleeping yet? I'm ready to start for a transit point."

"I can't find her."

Laenea's voice switched channels, following him automatically as he went from room to room.

"Shall I come help you look?"

Radu stopped in front of the airlock. One of the suit packs was missing.

"Laenea!"

"Yes?"

"Don't put any delta vee on the ship!" He grabbed a second pack and fastened the collar around his neck and shoulders.

"Why not? What's wrong?"

"Just don't. Don't do anything." He was afraid to take the time to explain. He turned on the suit. The fine support of an energy field enclosed him. Everything he looked at sparkled slightly around its edges. He hurried into the airlock and started it cycling.

When the exterior hatch slid aside, Radu found Orca immediately. Her suit glowed faintly blue against the formidable blackness. Lacking even a tether, she floated in space as she might float in the sea. Radu touched the lifeline plate, and a tenuous extension formed from the ship to his suit.

He pushed off toward her, toggling his radio on.

Orca was singing.

The sound made him shiver. It spoke of the whole universe behind him, and of something unknown, perhaps unknowable, before him.

Orca drifted farther and farther away. By the time Radu reached her, his lifeline had stretched far beyond its limits of safety, into a filmy, silky wisp, a filament of blue smoke connecting him to the ship. The hypnotic notes of Orca's singing drew him on.

"Orca!"

The melody never faltered. Radu reached for her. His hand passed through the skin of her suit, the two fields merged, and he grasped her arm directly.

"Orca!"

Her haunted song touched him like a lover. He turned off his radio, but the sound passed directly between them and he could not block it out. He pulled Orca around to face him. She had a strange, lost, searching look in her eyes that frightened him, because he had only seen that look before in the eyes of people who knew they were going to die. She fell silent.

Radu reached behind him and stroked the lifeline to make it contract, willing it not to dissolve from the stress and abandon them. He drew Orca closer, every moment expecting her to break loose, flee beyond his reach, and lose herself before he could call for help, as he should have done in the first place. But she remained quiescent. He embraced her and their suit fields melded together into a single entity. Orca's heart beat fast and hard.

Radu risked a glance toward the ship and saw to his relief that the lifeline was contracting and thickening slowly but steadily, pulling them back to safety.

When they had cycled back through the airlock, Radu turned off the suits.

"What do you think you were doing out there? Good gods — !" He pulled off his suit collar and threw it into its container.

"I need to get closer to it," she said. "I need to see it more clearly — "

"There isn't any 'it' to get close to!"

"You don't understand. You don't understand anything. All my senses are different from yours — "

"This is absurd. Come away."

He removed her suit collar, as gently as he had ever dressed a child in the nursery where he had worked on Twilight.

"It'll be better to come back later. We need more than just the x-team computer to study what's out here, we need the ship and the specialists, too."

"I know we do," Orca said bitterly. "But what chance do you think I've got to come back?"

"Oh . . ." Radu said. "Oh. I hadn't thought of that."

"Why should you? They'll let you go — they'll probably make you go even if you don't want to."

"I don't think — "

"Half the instruments they send will be for studying the edge, and the other half will be for studying *you!*"

"But you're here — you volunteered — "

She made a rude and derisive noise. "Who wouldn't volunteer? Ninety percent of the crew is on the exploratory mission waiting list! I've got no seniority and none of the right credentials!"

"Orca . . ." Radu stopped. She was, all too probably, quite right. He wished he could laugh off what she said. But she was right.

She cursed again and strode away. Radu waited, giving her time to regain her composure, then followed her to the box room. Her sleep chamber stood ready.

"You must go to sleep, Orca, we have to go home."

"I don't want to go to sleep, I want to stay awake — " She spun on him and grabbed his wrist, clenching her fingers around the sore, bruised slash.

Radu winced.

"Nothing would happen to me in transit, it's all mistakes, it's all lies!" Orca glared at her sleep chamber.

Lying down and letting his consciousness dissolve into the dream-filled anesthetic darkness would have been a comfort for Radu.

"If I don't get in there," Orca said, "who's to say I won't survive?"

Radu shook his head, remembering Marc. "The risks are real, Orca. I don't know why I'm immune to them, but they're real. Maybe they'll catch up to me."

"What do you see, Radu?" Orca asked softly. "What's in transit?"

"I don't know," he said. "I can't describe it. I'm sorry, the pilots are right, there aren't any words. I can't even *remember* what it looked like, what it felt like, because there aren't any words for it and I haven't got any way to set it in my mind."

Orca pushed off her right shoe with the toe of her left, the left shoe with her bare right toes. She clenched her hands and flexed her feet. Her extended claws scraped the deck.

"There are words for it," she said. "But not your words."

She hugged him tightly, desperately. He clasped her to him, feeling the long strong muscles of her back move beneath the rough texture of her vest. He touched her fine hair. She withdrew from their embrace, squeezed his hand, and faced her sleep chamber as if it were an enemy.

He stayed near, even after the instruments showed she was asleep. He waited until he was sure for himself that she was under the anesthetic. He watched her sleep, envying her and pitying her both at the same time.

He joined Laenea in her ship.

"Orca's asleep."

"Good." She waited expectantly.

"What's the matter?" Radu said.

"You tell me — you're the one who didn't want the ship to accelerate yet."

"Sorry," he said. "Orca . . . Orca needed another few minutes to look around." He said nothing of the diver's odd behavior, for he suspected that if it became known to the administrators, her future in the crew might be seriously compromised.

Laenea raised one eyebrow, then shrugged and turned on the intercom. "Ramona, Vasili, I'm going to take us home."

The other pilots' seniority meant nothing anymore. Laenea's perceptions would create another level to the hierarchy. As for Radu's ability — whatever it was — he had no idea what it would do.

Radu watched from the second pilot's place, copilot of an unplanned exploration, as the two linked ships dove down into transit. He braced himself for the change.

This time he made the transition calmly. He embraced the perceptions; he let them flow into him, and flowed around them himself. The sensation of being able to encompass and comprehend the whole universe swept him up.

His sight blurred slightly, but he could keep track of what was here and now, what was the past, what the future. Curiously, and with some trepidation, he looked at Laenea.

Her image exploded into such a multiplicity of visions that Radu shoved himself back in his chair, astonished and confused.

He closed his eyes and sorted himself back into reality, seeking an explanation of what had happened. He could not perceive Laenea the way he had Miikala. Miikala's possibilities were ended, Laenea's just begun. They increased every moment, with every decision, every subatomic interaction. He could see an unambiguous future for a living creature only from the moment of its death.

In the ordinary fashion, without trying to track her, he watched Laenea. The artificial gravity obscured changes in velocity whether the ship was in normal space or in transit.

"Tell me what you're doing," Radu said.

"I took us a little way through seventh, you can't go very far in it or you end up at the other end of the universe — or back where you started." She disappeared behind her oxygen mask for a moment. "As soon as we get back to where Miikala died, we'll retrace my training flight. I know all the coordinates; it'd be a lot shorter distance if we cut across, but I haven't enough experience and Vasili would rather sulk than pilot."

"His pride's hurt," Radu said. "He's used to being the best. Then you come along, and do something he can't . . . Even worse, I come along, a crew member — "

"Stop shrugging off what you've done, Radu! Vaska knows it's extraordinary, and I certainly know it, because you gave me back my life."

"How could I not?" Radu said, smiling. "I owed you mine. Haven't I told you people from Twilight always pay their debts?"

She grinned back at him, reached out automatically for his hand, but stopped before she touched him. She turned the movement into a shrug of inevitability.

"Is it different out there now for you?"

"No," he said, glad of the change of subject. "No, I felt — or saw, I don't know how to describe it, it was a sensation that existed inside my mind, but something, while you piloted us through seventh. But now it's just the same as before, there's nothing out there." He looked at the viewport, still somehow expecting it to change.

When he glanced back at Laenea, he found her staring at him intently.

"What's the matter?" he asked, startled by her frown.

She relaxed her concentration, shrugged, and laughed.

"I was performing an experiment," she said, "but I disproved my hypothesis."

"What was it?"

"That you found me by hearing my thoughts."

"I don't believe in telepathy."

"It was worth a try, but I thought at you as hard as I could, and nothing happened, you didn't hear anything, or feel it, or whatever you did."

"No," he said. What I did was find you again, Radu thought. I found you once, and lost you through my own failure. If I'd failed you a second time I thought it would have meant your life.

He felt embarrassed to say that out loud. Instead, he shrugged. "It doesn't matter. You weren't really lost. You would have found your way home."

"Would I? The ship was out of control the whole time I tried to help Miikala, and when it stopped, I didn't know where I was. Say it took me a year to find a way back — you can figure out better than I can how long that would have been on earth."

The information came unbidden into Radu's mind. He pushed it away. He would have been long dead when Laenea returned, far in the future and forgotten. The prospect of his own death did not trouble him — he had been on borrowed time ever since he survived the plague — but the idea of living out his life believing Laenea was dead, unable to help her while she struggled to survive, sent a shiver through him.

"Are you all right?" Laenea said.

"Yes. But I've changed . . ."

"I know," she said. "So have I."

She put her hand on his, and slid her fingers up to his wrist. He felt his pulse against the pressure, a strong, steady beat. The beat suddenly clenched into a wave of darkness. Radu gasped.

Laenea jerked her hand back with a sharp exclamation of surprise. Radu's vision cleared. Laenea rubbed her hand as if it had received an electric shock. She met his gaze, with regret.

"Neither of us has changed enough, have we?" Radu said. If anything, he was less compatible with pilots, she less compatible with normal human beings, than they had been before.

Laenea shook her head. "We've changed too much," she said. "And in all the wrong ways."

Radu looked down at his hands. Beneath the dirty bandage on his wrist, the cut itched. He rubbed it.

"I love you," he said suddenly. "None of this makes any difference, not that you're a pilot and I can't be, not that we can't be together. I still love you."

"I know," she said softly. "I'm sorry."

The transit ship shimmered into Einsteinian space. Laenea scanned for the beacon, found it, locked in and analyzed it, and felt pleased by her accuracy. She was only a few hours from Earthstation. She was, in fact, only just outside the limit at which it was felt to be safe to surface from a transit dive. She plotted a course toward the station. The two docked ships slowly spun, then gently accelerated.

Normal space seemed flat and dull to her. She could see the fourth spatial dimension of ordinary objects, and force one more perspective upon them, but sixth was lost, and seventh almost unimaginable. Seventh was what thrilled her. Laenea very nearly turned the ship around and fled back into transit.

Instead, she signaled Earthstation. Suspecting a hoax, the controller who answered reacted first with disbelief, then, when he accepted what she said, with astonishment. He disappeared from the channel; when he returned, the background noise had changed to that of shocked and excited conversations.

Despite the uniqueness of the ship's return, the ordinary work remained. Laenea roused the computers, and Radu helped Orca out of transit sleep. But Laenea's crew member woke in a state of confusion and exhaustion bordering on shock. They put him to bed, undrugged, for some real sleep.

The news of a lost ship's return was spreading rapidly. Laenea had the easy task of telling her crew member's family that he was alive, and would be well.

Ramona took the job of contacting Miikala's family. By the

time she got through to them she had to destroy their raised hopes. Nothing she could say could ease their grief; perhaps only another pilot could understand the factors that tempered it.

Two hours later Laenea docked the ships with Earthstation and logged them in. Only after she had finished did she remember that Ramona had the right and the responsibility to command the ships, and, after her, Vasili. Vasili remained in his cabin, and Ramona had hardly spoken since contacting Miikala's family. Now, in a silent depression, Ramona deferred to Laenea without comment or objection.

Laenea started to apologize, but the older pilot nodded.

"Fine," she said. Her voice held resignation. "Never mind, it was a good return."

Laenea felt uncomfortable, and a little wild.

"But what now?" When she was still in the crew she had always had several hours' work to finish after docking. As a pilot, she was at the end of her duties.

"The administrators will have plans for you," Ramona said. "But so do the pilots."

A medical team was already waiting when Laenea opened the hatch. They took Laenea's crew member off to the clinic, and carried away Miikala's shrouded body. Ramona watched them go. Laenea moved nearer to the older pilot, wondering if Ramona might break down again. Instead, she blinked quickly, raised her head, straightened up, and looked exactly her old self. Her grief concealed, she led Laenea and the others into Earthstation.

The shuttle bay, usually active and busy, was so quiet and empty that the footsteps approaching them echoed. Dr. van de Graaf, the surgeon who had performed the operation on Laenea to make her a pilot, stopped in front of Ramona and regarded her coolly. She wore a severely tailored business suit and looked, if possible, even more self-possessed than before.

"Welcome back, pilots," she said.

"Hello, Kristen," Ramona said. "Radu, Orca, this is Dr. van de Graaf, of the transit board. Kristen, I believe you are acquainted with Vasili and Laenea."

"Yes," she said. "Laenea and I have had some interesting discussions about the decisions of administrators."

Laenea said nothing. She felt annoyed not to have been told that the surgeon was also a transit administrator. Van de Graaf smiled slightly, assuming, no doubt, that Laenea regretted her remarks about the conservatism of the transit authority. Quite the contrary, had Laenea known the doctor held a position of power, she would have pressed the case more strongly.

"Please come with me." Somehow van de Graaf made the civility sound sincere, rather than a concession to good manners. "We have a lot to talk about."

Laenea glanced at Ramona, who folded her arms and shook her head. "Indeed we do," she said. "You may speak with Laenea after we do, Kri."

"No, Ramona, not this time. The event is unique."

Ramona chuckled. "It's a shame that there's no superlative for 'unique.' Believe me, Kri, for once the interests of the pilots and the interests of the administrators coincide. It's more important than ever for the debriefing to proceed as usual. What happened is exactly what the debriefing is intended to explore."

A moment of disbelief showed on van de Graaf's face before her control and serenity returned. Much more was going on between her and Ramona than Laenea observed, and she felt as if her fate were being decided in the dense silence between the administrator and the pilot.

Van de Graaf nodded abruptly. "All right."

"Don't I have anything to say about any of this?" Laenea said irritably.

"No, my dear," Ramona said easily. "Not right now."

12

LAENEA FOLLOWED RAMONA to a small cubicle supplied with voice recorder, writing and drawing terminal, even paper, pens, pencils, and a set of paints.

"What you're to do is record your impressions and your experience of transit in whatever way is most comfortable for you," Ramona said. She spoke quite formally. "If you prefer some other medium, you need only ask, and I will have the materials brought to you. Afterwards, we can talk about it, and you'll be free to look at the records all the rest of us have made. Do you have any questions?"

"I guess not."

Ramona nodded and left her alone, closing the door behind her.

"I'll speak," Laenea said.

"Ready," the recorder answered. A green light formed in

the air. Laenea stared at it for a while. "I changed my mind," she said. The light dissolved.

She stood up, but the room was too small to pace in.

She sat down at the terminal and began to type steadily and fast. After a while she lost track even of the erratic version of time pilots still could sense.

Orca followed Ramona to a second cubicle. The pilot opened the door to let the diver in.

"Orca," she said, "if you would tell us something of your perceptions of what happened — ? If you wish any other materials, you need only ask."

The transit administrator waited in silence with a quizzical expression.

Orca let herself be closed inside a tiny room crammed full of recording equipment. She was not used to making permanent material records, or records by any mechanical means. The cousins remembered everything perfectly. True speech was ideal for telling stories, true and imaginary, though the distinction meant less to cetaceans than to human beings.

Orca wondered if Ramona's offer of other materials extended as far as a filled swimming pool. She suspected not — but then again, who knew? She sang a few words of middle speech, but when she played it back, it sounded all wrong, artificial, outlandish, and stilted. The description of the edge would have to wait. She had no answers for Ramona's questions yet. But she had a question that Ramona might answer, or might, at least, want to think about. She erased the tape, started it again, and said, "What's beyond where we were?"

"Radu," Ramona said, "do you understand what we hope to learn from you?"

Radu nodded, but he was glad she did not ask him if he would be able to fulfill her hopes.

"Ramona," van de Graaf said, "why are you debriefing the crew?"

"You are asking me the wrong question, Kri," Ramona

said. "The question you should be asking me is how we found the lost ship. More accurately, who found it."

As Radu closed the door of the cubicle, he heard the doctor say, "Ramona, I think . . ." She stopped, and had to start again. "I think you'd better tell me just what the hell happened out there."

In the silence of the closed room, Radu faced the banks of machines. He sat down, picked up the pencil, chewed on its end, and scrawled a few disconnected words in his unpracticed handwriting: trees after rain, crystals, the texture of fish swimming upstream. Then he rubbed out what he had written. The paper tore. He threw it away and faced a second empty sheet. He thought of making up words, but even if he could do it, they would be only random collections of letters to anyone but him. And without definitions, without a way to set the meanings in his mind, they soon would dissolve to randomness even for him. He threw away the second sheet of paper, which had not a mark on it.

He tried the door. It remained shut, so he knocked. He felt as if he had just attempted to take a test he had known all along that he would fail.

Ramona-Teresa opened the door.

"I can't," Radu said. "I haven't anything to say about it. I'm sorry."

"Never mind," she said, with far more understanding than he ever expected. "It's all right."

"I thought you'd be angry."

"How can I be angry at you for not being able to do something I couldn't do myself?" She stood aside to let him into the corridor. "Yours is hardly a unique reaction."

Taking over for Ramona-Teresa, Dr. van de Graaf left Radu at the clinic, where a technician told him to strip and then carried away his clothes.

The battery of physical examinations he had to take was more rigorous and more tedious than what he had passed to join the crew. He remembered Laenea's reaction to her experiences in the hospital: "undignified." That was certainly true. He supposed Laenea and Orca were undergoing the same exams, but he saw neither of them, nor, indeed, anyone else he knew.

Twelve hours later, Radu had begun to understand why Laenea, when he first met her, had been so determined to stay out of the hospital. He felt exhausted and trapped. He wished he could get out, out anywhere, down to earth or back home, or even outside Earthstation in a field suit. Somewhere beyond the region of artificial colonies and space stations lived beings who had started out human but, generations ago, deliberately changed to something else. They could live in vacuum, on barren rock, on the shores of molten lakes. Radu was as strange as they — or at least that was how he felt right now — but they were free. He envied them. He was bored and so exhausted he could barely think straight.

He tried to endure what was demanded of him, but when another technician — he never saw the same one twice — left him naked and without a word of explanation in a cubicle that had no windows, no viewscreens or terminals, not even any books, he began to lose his temper. He tried the door, but it had neither knob nor interior controls. He knocked. No one replied. He pressed his hand hard against the door's surface and tried to slide it open. That, too, failed.

It occured to him that they might be watching him — spying on him — and he refused to give them the satisfaction of seeing him panic. He sat down. He let his hands lie relaxed on his knees, and waited.

Can they spy on my mind as well as my body? he wondered.

Not by telepathy, of course — he still did not believe in that. (Yet he thought: Laenea, can you hear me? and tried to project the question to her, but received no response.) It would be ridiculous to suspect the administrators of keeping some mental freak hidden away to report what other people thought. (Yet he formed a rude image in his mind; and then he wondered: How did Atnaterta know something would go wrong? How did I know where Laenea was?)

If the administrators could spy on his mind, it would be a matter of machines: sensitive recorders of electromagnetic activity, of nerve pulses and chemical changes, of the movements of his eyes.

Radu sat very still, and sought tranquility.

Another hour passed with exquisite sloth. Radu wished he could put aside his time-sense for a while, so he could pretend the time was hours on hours, even days. That was what it felt like.

When the door of his cubicle finally did open, Radu had made some decisions.

Dr. van de Graaf stepped inside and let the door close behind her.

"I have some questions to ask you," she said.

It was one thing to endure standing naked in front of a panel of anonymous physicians, quite another to be interrogated by one of his employers while stripped to the skin. The doctor had not even troubled to change to physician's garb; she was here in her position of transit administrator, not surgeon.

"I would appreciate having my clothes," Radu said.

"You'd just have to take them off again. There's another series of tests we need to have the results of."

The dismissal kindled the spark of anger that had been growing in Radu since all this began.

"I want my clothes," he said again, "and I want to leave. You have no right to keep me here."

The tone of her voice changed only a little, but it altered her manner abruptly from transparent affability to superficial courtesy backed by steel.

"On the contrary," she said. "The contract that you signed, that we signed, gave us the responsibility to treat you for any disabilities you incur in transit."

"I'm not disabled."

"That's a matter of opinion. All the evidence we've collected till now indicates that it would be unsafe for you ever to fly again."

Radu started to object, but van de Graaf cut him off.

"Until we find out if that's true, if you left here without my permission, you'd be in breach of contract with the transit authority. That in itself would make it impossible for you to work on the crew again."

"What makes you think I want to, after all this?"

"You have very little choice."

"I've had other jobs besides housekeeping duty on a starship."

"I'm sure you have. Do you have a work permit, too?"

"What is that?"

"A document that permits you to work," van de Graaf said.

Radu bristled at the sarcasm. "You need permission to work on earth? That's a stupid system."

"Perhaps. But without a permit you can't get a job. Not on earth, not in Earthstation. No one will hire you. No one *can* hire you. And there'd be no means of paying you."

"I've lived most of my life without money — "

"On a colony world," van de Graaf said patiently. "Radu Dracul, you're in a more complex society now. You can't go out and forage on a space station. It's true that back on earth, a great deal of land has been allowed to return to wilderness. But the wild areas are very strictly controlled. No one may enter them without permission."

Radu looked down at his bare hands, his bare knees.

"You don't understand that it isn't necessary to close me in on all sides until I cannot move or see or breathe," he said. "I'm as anxious as you to understand what happened to me. It *did* happen to *me*, but no one will say a word to me about what you have discovered."

Van de Graaf hesitated, then sat nearby, crossed her left leg over her right, and rested her right hand on her left ankle.

"You're right, of course," she said. She made her tone placating, and her voice much kinder. "Perhaps the difficulty is that we've yet to discover anything."

Radu waited, disbelieving.

"You're unique in our experience, but so far, physically, there's nothing to distinguish you from the usual range of human beings. The range includes ordinary people who experimented with transit, most of whom died."

Radu waited for her to go on, but the silence continued, stretching tautly between them.

"Do you think I can explain what happened?" Radu said. "I know less about it than you do. If I'm not unique then the obvious explanation is that other normal people could survive transit as well as I did."

"That may be true — though I doubt it — but I'm not willing to experiment with people's lives, at least not until we've explored other possibilities."

"I'm not opposed to cooperating with you — " Radu said.

"Good," van de Graaf said dryly.

" — but I want to know the purpose of what you're doing. I'm tired, and I'm tired of being treated as if I'm not even here."

That finally produced a reaction: The doctor looked at him as if he really were here.

"Will you accept my apology?" she said. "What's happened has put us all into quite a state of confusion. Things aren't running as smoothly as I'd like. But I will instruct the technicians to explain the purpose of each procedure. I'd like you to take just one more test, a neurological examination, then answer a few questions. After that, I'll try to answer your questions. Is that acceptable?"

"If — "

Van de Graaf's laugh was both sympathetic and charming. "If you can have some clothes. Of course."

Van de Graaf was as good as her word: The technician who came in brought a gown for Radu to wear. He even explained what was going on.

"The nerve scan is like making a giant circuit diagram of the nervous system," he said. "After I record the data I feed it into the computer, which does a statistical analysis to compare the way your brain cells interact with each other and with the rest of your body's nerve fibers. Then we look at your profile against the average."

"How often do you find differences?"

"Oh, always," the technician said cheerfully. "I've never

seen anybody who matched the average exactly. But the differences can tell a lot."

Radu submitted to the scan.

After that, they finally did give him back his clothes.

They gave him Dr. van de Graaf's few questions, too; they turned out to be a long, computer-based interrogation. The voice that spoke to him was, unlike most machine speech, so monotonous and hypnotic as to be, at times, nearly incomprehensible. At first Radu could answer most of the questions without thinking about them. He drifted in and out of paying attention. But the voice probed further and further into his past until it returned him to Twilight, to the plague. He wished he could answer those questions without thought.

The voice stopped abruptly. A few minutes later van de Graaf came in.

"I appreciate your patience," she said sincerely.

Radu was too tired to protest any more; he was so tired he even felt grateful to be treated with simple courtesy.

"Never mind," he said.

"Tell me a little about yourself," she said. "Tell me about your childhood on Twilight."

"It was the same as anybody else's," he said. "The same as that of anyone from a colony world, I imagine. You learn how to do everything adequately, and you're an expert at nothing."

"You'd say you were unexceptional?"

"Completely."

"What do you remember about having the plague?"

"Almost nothing. I remember Laenea — "

"Laenea!"

"Yes. She was on the emergency ship. Its whole crew landed and helped us. Didn't you know?"

"No. That's very interesting. Do you remember anyone else?"

"No. When the ship arrived I had just fallen ill. All I remember is that Laenea helped me. I would have died otherwise."

"What about afterwards? Did you feel changed?"

"I *was* changed," he said. "My whole family died. I buried them with my own hands. That changes you." He touched the scars on his cheeks with his fingertips. "And I'm marked. Anyone from Twilight knows immediately that I had the plague and recovered."

"Before you found Laenea, did you ever believe you could communicate with people in an inexplicable way?"

Radu hesitated, but this was no time to rewrite his history the way he wished it to be. He told van de Graaf about the hallucinations.

"And you consider this an unexceptional childhood?"

"It wasn't my childhood," he said. "It only happened a few times, just before I got sick. It may actually have been hallucinations."

She changed the subject abruptly. "Do you happen to know the plague's incubation period?"

"It's about six weeks," he said. "What has that got to do with anything?"

"Oh," she said, "probably nothing at all."

Before he could decide whether the offhand tone was a deliberate attempt to distract him from his question, her eyelids flickered in the way Radu had learned to associate with transmission by internal communicator. He waited for the administrator to return.

The idea of being able to link up with an enormous pool of data bases intrigued Radu, but not quite enough to overcome the visceral revulsion he felt at the idea of having a machine implanted in his brain. A small machine, true, mostly biological and barely the size of his little fingernail. Still he preferred not to submit to it. He suspected that if he had been accepted for pilot's training he would not have been able to go through with that operation, either, even for Laenea's sake.

The administrator opened her eyes and regarded Radu curiously.

"Did you say you knew other people who contracted the plague and recovered?"

"Not exactly. I said I didn't know any but I'm sure there must be some."

"There aren't."

" . . . What?"

"The records don't show any."

"No one was thinking about keeping records."

"True. But the census they took a couple of years later should have found other people like you, if there were any, and it didn't."

"There must be some," Radu said. "The records must be wrong."

Van de Graaf gazed at him speculatively, thoughtfully. "Perhaps," she said. "Or perhaps you really are unique." She stood up. "Come along."

She took him to a small lounge where the others were already waiting. Radu was very glad to see Orca; she was the only unambiguously friendly person he knew right now. He trusted neither the administrators nor the pilots. When Laenea smiled at him, he realized with distress that he was not even certain he trusted her.

"If you'd all come with me, please," van de Graaf said. She had an amazing facility for giving orders with the phrasing of requests.

She took them through secured doors toward the main body of Earthstation. The narrow, deserted hallway exactly paralleled the main corridors of the space station. Since returning from transit, Radu had neither seen nor spoken to anyone who was not in some way under the control of the transit authority. The secret hallway brought this fact to his conscious attention: He and the others were being kept isolated.

"Did you know these halls were here?" he asked Orca in an undertone.

"I never thought about it," she said. "But if I had, I would have suspected they were."

"Why are we being kept hidden?"

"The transit administrators like publicity if it's completely positive. Anything that's negative, or ambiguous, they try to avoid. You, my friend, are definitely ambiguous."

At the rim of the station they entered a twelve-ship shuttle extension. The long, wide dock was eerily deserted: blocked off, Radu supposed, from those inquisitive eyes of ambiguous publicity.

At the hatch of a shuttle, Orca stopped short.

"Wait a minute," she said. "Where are you planning to take us?"

"Back to earth," van de Graaf said.

"Very funny," Orca snapped. "Landing where?"

"White Sands."

"I can't land at White Sands."

"Why not?"

"Because I have no intention of being arrested and interned as a prisoner of war. Surely you know my family has never made peace with the United States government?"

After a moment of incomprehension, van de Graaf said, "Oh. I'd forgotten all about that. Surely, in an emergency — "

"No! Even if they promised me free passage I wouldn't believe them. Besides, I'd be in trouble with my own people if I accepted it."

"We all have more important things to think about than ancient history."

"Do you think this is some kind of joke?" Orca said angrily. "It may be ancient history to you, but my family has an even longer memory than the U.S. Navy — and the U.S. Navy blows us out of the water whenever they have a chance. They still consider us traitors, if not spies."

"I'll get you a world council safe-conduct on the way down — "

"Let me explain this to you in terms you may understand, doctor," Orca said. "Not landing in the United States is in my contract."

Radu could not help it: He laughed. Van de Graaf turned toward him, outraged, and Orca glared.

"Wait," he said, trying to explain. He dissolved into

laughter again. "Doctor, how can you argue with her?" he said after he managed to catch his breath. "That's exactly the threat you've been holding over me!"

Orca's anger changed to amusement and she started laughing, too.

"Kri, for heavens' sake," Ramona said. "We can as easily land at Northwest. There's no reason to put Orca in a compromising position."

"White Sands is more secure."

Ramona snorted. "Up until now it's been convenient to let you administrators indulge yourselves with your passion for secrecy, but no longer. I'll take the responsibility and fly the shuttle in myself, if you prefer."

"No," Kri said. "The responsibility is mine. We'll land at Northwest. But it'll be a zoo there by the time we get down." She glanced at the hatch and it swung open. "Will you all please get on board?"

They complied, entering a shuttle the likes of which Radu had never seen. It was as opulent as Kathell Stafford's apartment, though not quite as gaudy. Radu's boots sank deep into the carpet, the leather of the seats glowed with care and polishing, and a bar stretched all the way across the back wall of the passenger compartment.

"Is this how pilots travel?" Orca said to Laenea.

"If it is, nobody ever told me," Laenea said.

"Orca, you know very well we fly on the same shuttles as everyone else." Ramona-Teresa sat down and fastened her seat belt. She turned toward Kri. "Or almost everyone else. Just exactly who does use this one?"

Kri shrugged. "VIPs, usually."

Orca laughed. "I thought pilots were the VIPs," she said.

"Apparently not," Vasili Nikolaievich said.

Radu felt a little sorry for the young pilot, who had experienced so many affronts to his pride and his self-confidence in the past few days. This was simply one more insult, perhaps all the worse for its being, to Radu's mind, so trivial.

They felt a mild vibration as the ship undocked from the space station and accelerated gently toward earth.

Orca leaned back and stretched. "That was some day," she said.

"Not one I'd care to repeat." Radu slumped down in his seat.

"We'll probably have to, though, you know," she said. "Unless they found out what they wanted to about you."

"I don't think they did." He wished he knew more about what they *had* found out about him. Van de Graaf's interest in Twilight's plague troubled him deeply.

Orca grinned. "They discovered I'm not quite human." She laughed. "I don't think any of the techs ever had a diver to work on before. One of them was as nervous as a barracuda. He must be one of those nuts who believes they can catch the carrier virus." She bared her prominent canine teeth, then giggled. "Just like an old movie — zap! Transformed into a were-fish!"

Radu turned toward her, stunned by her chance remark. Orca stopped laughing.

"Radu," she said, "good gods, that can't happen. You can't change without being sensitized, and you can't even be sensitized until — "

"No, no, it isn't that," he said. "But you made me realize . . ." He stopped, suspicious, and lowered his voice to a bare whisper. "If I told you something . . . might other people be listening?"

She glanced around the shuttle. No one was paying any attention to their conversation.

"I haven't any reason to suspect the place is bugged," she said. "But I haven't any proof it isn't, either, so I guess the only safe assumption is that they can listen to us."

"I need to talk to you. I need to tell you what I think they want. Perhaps — if I'm lucky — you can tell me I'm crazy. But not here."

Orca nodded and took his hand between hers. The swimming webs slid across his skin like warm silk.

"Okay," she said. "We'll find a place to talk when we get down, when we get out of here."

13

THE SPACEPORT WAS CHAOS.

Radu looked through the shuttle window. The landing strip was completely overrun. Half the people out there carried cameras, from miniature instant-prints to recorder-transmitters with their own antennae. Floodlights illuminated the area as brightly as day, but much more harshly. Shadows twisted across faces; light flared off lenses and news corporation logos.

The crowd spilled onto the runway while the shuttle was still moving. The craft turned a few degrees toward the blockhouse, rolled a few meters forward, stopped, pressed forward, stopped again. The wheel motors shut down abruptly, their whine fading into silence.

Banging open the hatch between cockpit and passenger compartment, the shuttle driver stepped through.

"Sacrificial lamb time," she said. She sounded as if she had seen this sort of reaction before. "Any volunteers, or do you folks want to draw straws?"

Radu glanced out the window again. Several of the cameras pointed upward; others followed. He realized they were photographing him. Embarrassed, irritated, he drew back out of their range.

"No," the driver was saying. "I can't get any closer to the blockhouse until the runway clears. Unless you want some squashed pedestrians."

"Not a bad idea," Vasili said.

"Then you drive."

Vasili shrugged and stayed where he was.

Ramona stood up. "They will not move until someone speaks to them," she said.

"Wait," van de Graaf said. Her eyelids flickered.

"Kri — "

She lifted one hand in the "please wait" gesture of someone using an internal communicator.

"I've asked for more security," she said when she opened her eyes.

"Why bother?" Laenea said. "It never works."

"One of us must talk to the people outside," Ramona said again. She glanced at Vasili and Laenea. "Or we can go out together."

"You're on your own," Vasili said.

Radu had an irrational desire to punch him; what worried him was that the recurring impulse was beginning to seem less and less irrational.

"But what should we tell them?" Laenea asked.

"The truth. There's no reason to hide it." She gestured to Radu, inviting him, or commanding him, to join them. "You, too, are part of this."

Laenea dogged open the hatch. The crowd noise poured in. The stairs descended slowly toward the crowd. People pressed back, opening a small space, and one reporter leaped to catch the lowest rung and pull himself onto it. Laenea stepped out onto the platform. Radu hesitated.

"They're only curious," Ramona said.

"I've never seen so many people at once before," Radu said. He followed Ramona out onto the small upper landing. Reporters with cameras, already halfway up the stairs, began asking questions.

Ramona waited until the uproar quieted. The sea breeze ruffled her roan hair. Radu breathed the fresh air gratefully. He felt as if he had not taken a deep breath since Ngthum-mulun.

The older pilot's voice carried, strong and clear.

"I know some of you," she said. "Too often when we speak together it is because of tragedy. A friend has died, but his death was a natural one, and the sorrow should remain private. I want to speak to you instead of joy and discovery. The joy and the discovery are public." She drew Laenea forward to stand beside her. "Laenea Trevelyan has done what the pilots have hoped to do since there *were* pilots. On her first training flight, she discovered the transit dimension which will open the universe beyond our galaxy."

Silence dissolved in another rush of questions. Laenea and Ramona answered. Laenea's discovery overshadowed the story of the lost ship that everyone had come to hear. Perhaps they assumed the discovery explained why Miikala's ship stayed out so long. At any rate no one asked Radu anything. He wondered if Ramona-Teresa, understanding that Laenea was a hero while Radu was a freak, had planned it this way. He suspected that she had, and he was most grateful to her.

He admired her for her control of the crowd of reporters, gawkers, and passers-by. The force of her personality charmed them, much more than her status as one of the first pilots. She would have had the same effect on them if she were merely a politician or a street-corner haranguer. Though every word she spoke to them was the truth, she could easily have lied. They would have believed her.

Suddenly, Orca bolted past Radu and down the stairs.

"Orca!" Ramona shouted.

If Radu were to escape, even only long enough to tell Orca what he feared, now was the time —

At that moment Laenea plunged back into the shuttle, fighting for breath. She flung out her hands when Radu came toward her, roughly shrugging off his help.

"I'm all right," she said, her voice short and rough. "Just — don't — touch me."

Radu obeyed, unwillingly. Laenea bent down, breathing hard.

"Vasili Nikolaievich!" Radu cried. "Come help Laenea, hurry, please!"

To Radu's surprise, the young pilot, his expression and his posture as sulky as ever, appeared a moment later. He put one arm around Laenea's shoulders.

"You can't do anything for her anymore," he said. "It's other pilots she needs, now." He led her farther into the shuttle. Radu watched them go, wanting to do something, knowing he was helpless.

Ramona-Teresa joined him a moment later.

"What happened?"

"I don't know. We . . . can't even bear each other's touch anymore." He hesitated, then said, unwillingly, "You were right all along."

"Perhaps," she said, sounding distracted, and followed the others into the shuttle.

Radu was alone. He could not see where Orca had gone. The crowd had begun to disperse.

This might be the only chance he would get. With one last wistful glance after Laenea, Radu stepped out of the shuttle, hurried down the ladder, and lost himself among the spectators.

Constant, painful, beautiful dreams of outside filled Marc's fugue state. When he recovered and reoriented himself in time and space, he knew he could not continue as he was. His pretty things no longer sufficed. They never had, though he had succeeded in distracting himself with them for years.

Exhausted, emaciated, and safe for a time from another attack, he came to himself again, and knew that he must change.

He fixed himself tea and broth and settled in to catch up on what had happened while he was gone.

Marc's analogue had culled the messages from his informants, his news traces, and his data-base infiltrations. Marc's sources of information were, as Radu Dracul had said, excellent. Radu's problem was one to which he would have to set himself immediately. The analogue began the report on Laenea and Radu with reassurances: "Laenea is found again, but . . ." and ended with a very human-sounding complaint that Marc had not troubled to mention Radu. Intrigued, Marc read the report.

The day after receiving Marc's cautions, the young offworlder had shipped out, with not one but *two* pilots — so much for taking Marc's advice — and with a crew member who was also a diver. Marc had wished to meet Orca for some time. He prized unique people even over unique things.

Marc had, over the years, acquired the habit of letting his attention wander. It passed the time more quickly than most activities, and often showed him connections he would not otherwise have seen. Now he reminded himself that time, which had not mattered to him for so long, mattered once more. He concentrated on the report.

Laenea's ship, declared lost, had returned in the company of the craft that had taken Radu Dracul back into transit. Both ships had docked at Earthstation, and an unscheduled shuttle now sailed back toward earth. It would soon land on the Northwest port. Anyone with both access to a radar trace and any intuition, common sense, or curiosity could guess that the shuttle carried the people who had been on Laenea's ship and on the rescue craft.

It should be very interesting up on deck.

Marc turned off his news collation, stood, and brushed his fingertips across the controls of the door between his chambers and the outside.

It was time for his exile to end.

Marc left his rooms, walked down the corridor, boarded the elevator, rode it to the surface, and stepped out on deck for the first time in many years. Everything he was doing, he was doing for the first time in many years. He dared not let himself react with much intensity.

He walked slowly toward the shuttle and the mass of people around it. He supported himself on his favorite stick, a long polished limb with a heavy growth of textured vine entwined around its length. Though he did not feel lame just now, he was shaky and agoraphobic, severely affected by the unaccustomed noise, the tumult, and the enormous space around him. His eyes were not used to focusing at such distances.

The air, though, the air: He had forgotten how fresh and good the air smelled out here on deck, even among the machines with their tang of fuel and lubricants and ozone.

The blockhouse lay like a silent island in a pool of illumination. The shuttle formed a promontory above a sea of people, lights, and shadows. Marc hobbled through the empty darkness separating them. He heard Ramona's calm, certain voice, though he had not made out the question to which she was responding.

Laenea stood beside her, Radu Dracul a little behind them. Marc allowed himself a smile, but tried to check the joy he felt at seeing Laenea alive. Marc thought himself safe from a fit — the malfunctioning nerve cells seemed to require a period of recovery between episodes of misbehavior — but he preferred to minimize the risk by remaining calm.

He paused before he reached the edge of the crowd, reluctant to test himself against such a concentration of people. He glanced around, neither hoping for a break in the crush nor finding one. Only a single other person haunted the edge, as he did: a very young man, a boy, who might have been as old as fifteen. He was completely naked. He gazed up at the shuttle. Droplets of water glistened on his sleek body. His skin was the color of mahogany, and his hair, damp and plastered against his head, was so blond it looked like a silver helmet. He moved forward, his step hesitant. Light glowed through the tan pink webs of his hands.

A diver, Marc thought.

In the middle of answering a question, Laenea suddenly

stopped, stepped back as if from a blow, turned, and vanished into the shuttle. Amid the murmur of surprise from the crowd, Ramona picked up the reply in midphrase.

Knowing how severely Laenea reacted to ordinaries, Marc pushed forward, trying to get to the stairs. But that was the aim of everyone else, too, and he immediately realized how foolish was his attempt. He found himself crushed between a tall reporter and a short massive camera operator. He tried to back up, too late. He lost his walking stick. He stumbled; he felt himself going down as if he were diving into a warm salty sea. The reporter tried to help him, but the current pulled her away. Someone else bumped him and he fell.

He was dragged across the deck; the sound of shoes and boots on metal overwhelmed even voices. The trembling began deep inside his body, and he curled himself up, thinking only, It can't take me again, not so soon, not here among all these people.

Then he was dragged free, and the footsteps and voices receded. He lay on the deck, his arms around his head and his face hidden against his knees for protection. He peered out cautiously.

The blond dark boy, the naked diver, knelt motionless nearby, his hands, relaxed with webs and fingers spread, resting on his thighs. Marc had never read that divers had eyes any larger than the average, but the young man's extraordinary black eyes were enormous.

Marc unfolded his long, gaunt body and sat up slowly, grateful for the cold sea breeze. He shivered, but the sensation was different altogether from the trembling that warned of a fugue.

"Are you injured?" the diver asked. "I thought they'd crushed you, when you fell."

"Say I was knocked down, at least," the older man said. "I'm sorry. I don't mean to be churlish. Thank you for helping me. Do you see my stick?"

The young diver glanced around, then got up and retrieved the cane, kicked aside at the edge of a spotlight's shallow puddle of illumination. He brought it back to Marc.

"Are you a pilot?" he asked.

Marc touched the scars on his chest: two scars, not one, parallel to each other and close together, both scars old and faded to white.

"No," he said. "Not anymore. Are you a diver?"

"Yes. My name is . . . Mark Harris."

Marc smiled and extended his hand. "We should get along well, then. My name is Marc, too."

Orca used her strength and her small size to get through the crowd, bulling her way past people, slipping between them, till she reached open space.

Her brother had freed himself and now knelt beside an older man, a grounder who, by the look of him, had come to some grief in the crowd.

Orca spoke her brother's underwater name. In the air the long descriptive phonemic string came out a high-pitched garble, but he recognized it and spoke her name in reply.

"Why are you here?" she asked.

"I heard what happened. I was afraid for you."

She had never thought to see him in the human world, and so close to so many landers. He was wary of them, yet he had come to help her without so much as a knife belt. Touched, she knelt and hugged him. He put his arms around her and nuzzled the hollow of her collarbone.

"I missed you," he said softly, and drew away again. Orca squeezed his hand and let him go.

She heard the high-pitched descending whistle of a killer whale's greeting. She answered as well as she could, but did not try to explain where she had been or what had happened. It would be difficult underwater; in the air she could not even make a start at it.

A half dozen port security officers came out of the block-house. They paused to assess the crowd and to curse, though rather good-naturedly, at the thought of trying to break it up without offending tourists or earning the wrath of reporters. Ramona had vanished inside the shuttle, so the spectators at the edge of the group were drifting away. The air of expectancy was fading. A network helicopter took off with its news crew; farther away, another information corporation's microjet powered up with a sighing whine.

"This is my sister Orca," her brother said to the older man.

"How do you do," he said to her. "My name is also Marc."

She did not have a chance to wonder what he meant by "also," for he was trying to rise. He got to his knees and steadied himself with his stick; Orca helped him with a hand under his elbow.

The spot of warmth behind Orca's eyes became tinged with red; she let the emergency message through.

This is van de Graaf. Where are you?

Right outside, Orca replied. If you look you can see me.

Is Radu with you?

No.

You should have stayed here. Now stay there. If you see him, keep him there, too. The rest of us will be out in a minute.

Without replying, Orca ceased to accept the transmission. Though the crowd had thinned it would be longer than a minute before anyone — any pilots, at least — got through it from the shuttle. Orca looked around for Radu, but did not see him.

She heard her cousins calling for her to return to the sea, welcoming her, curious as always about what she had done during her absence in the air.

"Go ahead," her brother said. "I'll stay here."

"Wait — " Marc said.

Orca kicked off her shoes and her pants. "I'll be right back," she called, throwing off her vest and running for the edge of the port.

She dove. The sea closed in over her with an energizing shock. Air bubbles tickled past her body. She let her momentum carry her straight down, then swam even deeper. The conversations of her cousins showed her where they were. She was inside the delicate webbing of a three-dimensional sound net. Fifty meters underwater she arched her body and circled upward again.

Her metabolism accelerated to the higher rate. When she broke the surface she took a deep breath and felt the oxygen burning in her lungs. She dove again, humming to her cousins. Their dark shapes surrounded her. They brushed her with their bodies, their fins, their flukes, more gently than any human lover.

I'm glad you decided to come to the gathering, her closest cousin said.

I haven't decided yet, Orca said. I came out to talk to you.

But how can you think of missing it?

You sound like father, Orca told her.

Her cousin's laugh vibrated past, and then her cousin disguised her echo pattern so she really did sound like Orca's father: His voice, his swimming patterns, his outline.

You must at least come to the gathering, she said in father's voice, stern and self-satisfied, with a parodic note thrown in.

All the cousins and a few of the divers could do the same thing, a little, but her ability was uncanny.

Orca and her cousin both laughed, but Orca grew serious again very quickly.

I'm not that anxious to attend this meeting, she said.

But it will be fun.

You have a different idea of fun than I.

Aren't you excited?

No, Orca said. I wish I were. I'm frightened, my dear friend, I can't help it. I don't know if I'll be able to survive these changes.

Then you should come to the gathering and speak your mind about it.

You're right, Orca said. Of course, you're right. I'll try. Whatever happens otherwise, I will try to come to the gathering.

Come now, her cousin said.

I can't. I wish I could, but something has happened, something important.

Does it have to do with your friend the newborn?

Yes, Orca told the killer whale. He — she told them his name, a sound pattern that would immediately identify him to anyone who saw him or met him, and who spoke true speech — he took us to the edge of the universe.

The patterns the whales used for communication, the three-dimensional shapes, as transparent to sound as solid objects, could express any concept. Any concept except, perhaps, vacuum, infinity, nothingness so complete it would never become anything. The nearest way she could try to describe it was with silence. She expected them to be confused when she told them that she had gone, deliberately, to a place of silence, and that she would return to it if she could. She expected, not that they would be afraid for her, because they did not feel fear, but that they would be worried about her. The whales did know madness.

Her nearest cousin rubbed against her, spiraling around her in a warm embrace.

You have seen this, my cousin? Seen it, heard it, felt it?

Yes.

You are right, the killer whale said. You must go back.

I know it, Orca said, astonished. But I didn't think you'd understand.

Of course I understand. I've always understood. We've waited for what you are telling us. You must go back, and learn, and return to tell us more.

Radu touched the call bell at Marc's one last time, not expecting an answer, not getting any. Marc must still be taken by his affliction. Even his analogue remained silent.

Radu moved to the back of the dark, leaf-lined alcove and sat on the floor in the shadows, trying to think.

It was, perhaps, for the best. Radu had endangered Orca, earlier, with his naiveté. He did not want to do the same thing to Marc. He should have learned enough by now, he should know enough about earth, to solve his own problems without jeopardizing everyone who made the mistake of befriending him.

The pilots had made serious threats when they knew neither what they wanted from Radu, nor whether what they wanted would be important. Now the administrators knew what they wanted, and had defined it as essential. If they were willing to attempt what he feared, then they admitted no limits to the means they would use to get it.

He closed his eyes for a moment, but that made it too easy to remember Twilight, and the plague.

He had only one course left to take, one he had avoided because he had sworn never to use it. He went to Kathell Stafford's apartment.

The hour was unconscionably late, but one of her aides was always on duty. Radu put his hand to the sensor concealed in the silver filigree. When he stayed here the door had opened to his touch, but he expected no more, now, than an answer from inside.

The door opened. Lights, music, and laughter spilled out around him. Radu hesitated. He had become accustomed to silence and solitude in this place, where he and Laenea had begun to know each other. Seeing it overrun by Kathell Stafford's permanent floating party made him uncomfortable and unhappy. He moved inside. All the other guests wore gold or silver or rainbow colors with the quality of jewels. Radu felt as if he could pass among them completely unnoticed, obliterated like a drab satellite at the noon of a hundred suns.

He made his way through the smoke of cigars as heavy and pungent as any Ramona ever smoked, through the powerful artificial odors meant to represent outdoor smells. He repressed a sneeze.

Deep inside the apartment the crowd thinned slightly and the music changed from loud and atonal to delicate and melodic. The light here had a softer quality. He paused, lost, in the middle of an unfamiliar room. Some of the interior walls had been changed around and redecorated.

It would be painful bad luck to stumble upon the scarlet and gold room where he and Laenea had spent so much time.

Finally he saw Kathell, standing all alone against the curving wall of her largest living room. When she saw him, her expression hardened. He crossed the thick carpet and stopped before her.

"You took your time," she said coldly. "What do you want?"

"I need to talk to you alone," he said. "I can't tell you what I want in public."

One of her guests wandered toward them, staggering slightly, a drink in his hand. He wore an emerald-colored robe, opaque yet giving the impression that a deep jewel formed its surface.

He blinked blearily at Radu, then, with disappointment, at Kathell.

"Oh . . ." he said.

"What do you want?" Kathell was speaking to Radu but her invited guest took the question for himself.

"I thought this one had come back with the Aztec," he said.

"It's urgent," Radu said to Kathell, ignoring her guest's insulting reference to Laenea.

"This isn't one of your better parties, Kathell," the other man said querulously. "Where's the entertainment?" He looked Radu up and down. "And I don't mean the rare privilege of chatting with a novice crew member."

"Will you go away!" Radu snapped. "Can't you see we're trying to talk?"

"Last time I came to one of your parties, I didn't even get to meet the Aztec — "

"The pilot!" Radu said angrily.

"What?" He looked around. "Where?"

"She isn't here," Radu said. "Pilots don't like to be called 'Aztecs.' " To Kathell he said, "It's important."

The other guest spoke to Radu directly for the first time.

"And what makes you think you know so much about pilots?"

Radu started to get angry, but that was pointless. The question was ludicrous, yet entirely appropriate. He opened his mouth to answer, changed his mind and shut it again, and realized he must look like a gasping fish. He began to laugh.

"Nothing," he said. He chuckled. "Nothing at all." A fit of laughter overcame him. He could not stop it. He laughed till tears ran down his face, till he had to lean against the wall or risk falling down. "What makes you think I know *anything* about pilots?"

A young man, almost as plainly dressed as Radu and with the look of one of Kathell's aides about him, appeared at the edge of their small group.

"Find him something to amuse him," Kathell said to her aide, and then, to Radu, "Come along."

The aide led her drunken guest in one direction; Kathell took Radu the other way, to a smaller, quiet room.

"Now," she said, "what do you want?"

"Is one of your blimps on the port?"

"Of course," she said. "Is that *all?*"

"No," Radu said, reacting to the contempt in her voice. "It's true I want to use the blimp, but no doubt you'd consider that — or any material request my barbarian imagination could come up with — an unacceptably trivial demand."

"That is true. You're trying my patience, Radu Dracul. Are you looking for an enemy?"

"I have as many enemies as I need," he said. "It isn't just the blimp I want from you. I want something more important and more difficult."

She waited.

"I want you to lie for me."

"Explain yourself."

"I want you to loan me your blimp. I won't tell you where I intend to take it, but I will return it to you if I possibly can. When people come asking for me — and it won't be just anyone, they will be powerful, and they make threats they can carry out — I want you to tell them . . . I don't care what, but anything except that you know how I got away."

"What am I helping you run away from, Radu Dracul?"

"I don't owe you an explanation. You made the rules, and the rules say *you* owe *me*. You can either pay the debt you've imposed upon yourself, or declare yourself my enemy. But decide which, now, because I don't have time to wait."

"You're learning the ways of earth quickly," she said.

"Not with any willingness," he said.

Her eyelids fluttered.

"What are you doing?"

"Calling a pilot, of course," she said, most of her attention on her internal communicator.

"The last thing I want is a pilot!" he said, thinking, How could she know enough to betray me?

She opened her eyes again. "A *blimp* pilot," she said, smiling very slightly.

"I don't want a blimp pilot, either," Radu said. "Do you want to see my license?"

"From Twilight, no doubt."

"No doubt."

"Anyone who works for me will abide by the promises I give," she said.

Radu turned and started for the door.

"The airship and the deception are yours," Kathell said. "And then my debt is paid."

Radu went back out into the night, made his way to the airship field, and sought Kathell Stafford's blimp. No other was like it. It was a great gold oval glowing with reflected light against the sky. The breeze shifted slightly. Each airship swung a few degrees around the mast to which its nose was tethered. The tail of Stafford's craft began to rise. The fan controlling the buoyancy whirred, and the landing wheel touched down with a gentle thump of rubber on the decking.

Despite his claim to Stafford, Radu felt apprehensive about piloting a blimp here, where the level of technology was so much higher than on his own world. The controls might easily be alien. He swung up into the gondola and reached for the spot where the dashboard light switch would be, if he were back on Twilight.

The lights glowed on, illuminating a panel almost identical to the one on the airship he had piloted as a youth, directing a rudimentary autopilot, a few electronics, and simple mechanical controls for buoyancy and orientation.

And in only three dimensions, he thought.

He disconnected the sensors, started the engine and left it in neutral, then jumped back to the deck. He climbed the mast in the dark, expecting at any moment to be challenged and stopped.

Launching a blimp solo was a tricky job. Ten meters above the deck, he unfastened the line and pulled it free. The wind immediately began to blow the ship backward. Radu climbed down again, gripping the line. While he let the wind push the ship away from the mast, he moved sideways, set his heels, and pulled. Almost imperceptibly the ship swung toward him, so its nose no longer pointed directly at the mast. The wind caught its flank and pushed and lifted it like an enormous kite.

Radu sprinted for the gondola, grabbed the bottom rung of the ladder, dragged himself up, flung himself inside, and scrambled to the pilot's seat.

He tilted the airship back on its tail and threw the engine out of neutral. The propellors roared.

The airship took off, rising almost straight up into the sky.

Marc chatted with Orca's brother while they waited for Orca to return. The young man was fascinating: He had had experiences Marc had never imagined, experiences at least as unusual as those of pilots. While they talked, the crowd slowly dispersed and vanished. When almost everyone had left, a slender woman with short iron-gray hair came out of the shuttle alone and approached the bench where Marc was sitting. Marc smiled to himself, wondering if Kri van de Graaf would recognize him after all these years.

She stopped and frowned, looking at the diver.

"Sorry," she said abruptly to Mark. "I thought you were someone else."

"Are you looking for Orca? We're waiting for her, too. She just went for a swim. She'll be back soon. I'm her brother. I've come to visit."

"Oh," Kri said. Marc had seldom seen her nonplussed. He cleared his throat. She glanced at him, then took a step forward.

"Marc?" she said. "Marc, my gods, where did you come from?"

He stood to greet her. "So many interesting things have been happening, I couldn't resist."

" 'Interesting,' " she said. "Yes, indeed. As in the curse, 'May you live in interesting times.' "

"Can you tell me?"

She drew her eyebrows together. "I'm sorry. I think not, for the moment. I don't know quite what your status is."

He offered her a place on the bench and sat down beside her. Suddenly she shivered.

"Where are your clothes?" she asked Mark.

"I don't have any."

"Aren't you cold?"

"No. Are you?"

"Yes. What size are you?" she asked him.

Mark looked down at his own naked body. "I don't know. Where do you measure?"

She started to laugh, but he was quite serious. "Never mind," she said. She ran her hand through her short gray hair. "So Orca's gone for a swim, and Radu — does either of you know Radu Dracul?"

"No," Mark said.

But Marc kept his silence until he could find out what she wanted with the young offworlder. For the moment Marc felt glad that Kri did not quite trust him; it saved him from the guilt of not quite trusting her.

Van de Graaf's irritation increased the longer Orca remained in the sea. Most of the crowd had gone home, and it would be quite safe for the pilots to come out of the shuttle.

A young woman stepped out of the blockhouse, hurried across the deck, and handed a stack of folded material to Dr. van de Graaf.

"Thank you," the doctor said, handing it on to Mark.

Mark looked curiously at what van de Graaf had given him.

"Thank you," he said. "What is it?"

"Clothes. They'll fit, or close enough."

"You want me to put these on?"

"If you plan to stay here long," she said, "other people will be a great deal more comfortable if you do."

Mark shrugged, put the folded garments on the deck, and picked up the one on top. He shook it out. It was an ordinary cotton T-shirt.

"The tag goes inside and at the back of the neck," Marc said.

"Where's the neck?"

"Here." He showed him.

"That's a hole."

"It goes around your neck."

He would have ended up with the shirt wrapped around his throat like a scarf, so Marc took it from him and helped him into it as if he were a child. For all the familiarity he had with clothes, he might as well have been. They repeated the process with a pair of stiff new blue jeans.

The jeans were too tight around Mark's muscular thighs and too loose around his waist. He looked as if he were not so much wearing the clothes as existing inside them.

"That's the best I can do for now," van de Graaf said. "It's a little late to shop."

Every time Orca surfaced, the point of warmth behind her eyes, the message signal, had gained another level of urgency. It rose through the spectrum from dull red to yellow to blue to incandescent white. She knew that when she answered it she would be ordered back on deck, but when she finally chose to return it was — if it was anything in addition to her own desire — more because her cousins wanted to learn from her than because of what the administrators wanted.

Orca dove one last time, cutting through the water beneath her closest cousin, spinning over, and sliding her hands along the whale's smooth flanks as she passed her. She surfaced beside the port. She and her cousin called her brother, in harmony, then the killer whale slapped her tail against the water, sounded, and returned to the pod.

A line snaked down the side of the port. Orca climbed hand over hand to the deck.

Her brother reached down. She grabbed his hand and swung herself up. As soon as she came over the edge of the platform and Dr. van de Graaf saw her, the emergency message signal faded, leaving only the normal point of warmth that signaled regular mail. Mostly junk, no doubt, as usual.

The crowd had dispersed. The shuttle stood silent and dark on the runway. Orca had stayed out longer than she meant to, but she felt wonderful. She was full of joy and disbelief at what her cousin had urged.

Orca looked at her brother, astonished. "What's this?" she said, touching the front of his T-shirt.

"Well . . ." he said. He shrugged. "Clothes, I guess."

Orca shook the water from her hair. She put her arm around her brother and they walked back to where Marc sat on one of the benches scattered here and there beside the walkway. Dr. van de Graaf stood nearby, looking impatient.

"About time you deigned to come back," she said. Orca did not bother to answer.

"I envy your freedom," Marc said.

Orca's clothes lay in a neat stack on the end of the bench beside Marc. She felt too warm to put them on yet. She sat crosslegged near him.

"Who *are* you?" Orca said.

"I told you."

"You told me your name, that's all."

"I'm a friend of Laenea's."

Orca heard voices and glanced at the shuttle. The three pilots came down the stairs. Radu was nowhere to be seen.

"Where did Radu go?" Orca asked.

"That's what we've been wondering," van de Graaf said. "Where did *you* go? I told you to stay here. We've been waiting for you to come back for over an hour."

"I didn't realize I'd been out that long," Orca said without apology.

Van de Graaf's expression remained cool, but she scooped

up Orca's clothes and tossed them to her with a quick and angry snap of the wrist. Orca plucked them easily out of the air. She doubted that van de Graaf believed she had no idea where Radu had gone.

Despite her calm, the doctor obviously felt angry at Orca for disobeying orders. Pilots could get away with disobeying representatives of the administrators, but it was not a prudent thing for a crew member to do. A week ago that would have worried the diver, but now she felt that no one, administrator or otherwise, could threaten her.

"This is Laenea, and Ramona-Teresa, and Vasili Nikolaievich," Orca said to her brother, nodding to each pilot in turn. "I guess you've met Dr. van de Graaf." There was an awkward silence in which Orca should have introduced her brother by name, but did not. She could not. "This is my brother," she said.

Then, to her surprise, her brother said, "You can call me Mark Harris."

Startled, surprised, and delighted, Orca laughed.

"What's so funny?" van de Graaf said.

"Never mind," Orca said. "It's too complicated to explain." She started putting on her clothes.

Laenea glanced at Marc. Orca thought they must not be as good friends as the older man had implied, for Laenea's expression held more curiosity than recognition. The pilot frowned slightly, took one step toward him, and stopped.

"Marc . . . ?" she said doubtfully.

He pushed himself up, clasping both hands around the top of his stick to lever himself to his feet.

"Yes," he said.

"But how — ? Why — ?"

"It seemed like the right time," he said.

He extended one hand. Without hesitation she clasped his wrist tightly. They embraced, more like crew members than a pilot and . . . Orca could not make herself think of Marc as an ordinary, a grounder, but she had no idea at all how she should think of him.

"How did you recognize me?" Marc asked.

"I don't know. I'm changed," Laenea said, "from what I was before."

He smiled at her. "I would imagine so."

Orca finished tying the laces of her shoes.

"Are you ready?" Van de Graaf's impatience crackled like static electricity.

"Yes," Orca said.

"It was good of the two of you to welcome your friends home," the doctor said, "but we'll have to leave you now."

"I'm coming with you," Orca's brother said.

"Are you sure?" Orca said.

He nodded. "If you're not coming home."

Now that her brother wanted to enter the human world, Orca suddenly felt afraid for him. She wished he had stayed in the sea. He was too much like the cousins to get along well here. To survive, he would have to learn things that he would never need to know, in his real life.

Still, he *had* chosen the perfect surface name. Perhaps he would get along up here after all.

"It's impossible," van de Graaf said. "We're going to the administration deck. Your brother will have to stay out here."

"If he stays, I stay," Orca said.

"Out of the question."

"Surely not, Kri," Ramona said. "If it will make Orca more comfortable for her brother to join us, why forbid it?"

Van de Graaf sighed. "All right. He can come." Her eyelids flickered as she communicated with someone or something. Orca tried, rudely, to listen in, but could not break into the frequency. The doctor returned and glanced at Marc. "I suppose you want to come along, too, Marc?"

"That is true."

"Oh, what the hell," van de Graaf said, with the exasperation of someone unused to anything less than total control. "Does *anyone* have any idea where Radu Dracul might have gone?"

"You saw him the last time I did," Laenea said.

Van de Graaf glanced at Ramona, asking the same question with her silence.

"He went past me and down the ladder. I thought he was trying to help Orca."

"Obviously not," van de Graaf said. "Is there anyone else he might have contacted?"

"As far as I know, everyone on earth that he's acquainted with is right here," Laenea said. Then, a moment later, "Except . . ."

"Who?"

"He only met her once, for a few minutes, at a party."

"Who?"

"Kathell Stafford. Do you know her?"

"Doesn't everyone?" She stroked the outer curve of her eyebrow thoughtfully for a moment. "Well," she said. "Let's go."

The group made its way toward the stabilizer shaft. Marc joined the pilots, who kept their distance from the divers. Dr. van de Graaf walked by herself.

"I like your name," Orca said softly to her brother.

"I thought it might be awkward for them if I didn't have one," Mark said.

"It would have made them uncomfortable — but they often feel like that anyway. They get over it."

Mark fidgeted inside his new clothes.

"You wear this stuff all the time," he said.

"When I'm around landers," Orca said. "But when I wear jeans, I leave them in a tide pool in the sun for about a week and then wash them before I ever put them on."

"Do you have to stay here?" he said quietly.

"I have to be sure a friend of mine is okay." She was worried about Radu. Whatever it was he had discovered must have troubled him deeply, to make him disappear so suddenly and completely.

"I mean, would you be able to leave if you wanted?"

"That's a good question," Orca said. It surprised her that Mark would ask it, and made her think again that perhaps he could get along in the human world. "I'm not sure I want to.

I told the cousins what happened to me out there, and they understood. They want to know more — they want me to go back."

Mark looked at her curiously. "Really? Tell me what happened, too."

"I can't. Not up here, it's impossible. As soon as we swim, I will."

"All right." He walked beside her in silence, in patience.

Orca doubted she would be able to use her internal communicator once she was inside the administration deck, so she quickly explored several record indices. She found no trace of Radu. Orca doubted he would forget the lesson she had taught him. He would leave as little trail as if he were moving through the forest on his own home world.

They approached the blockhouse. An elevator cage, doors open, waited for them.

Orca still felt flushed and warm from the metabolic rush brought on by her swim, but the effect was fading. She would be glad to get out of the wind.

Then the obvious thing occurred to her. She accepted her ordinary mail and scanned the messages quickly.

Among the junk mail was an unsigned note.

I accept your offer, it said, and that was all.

Damn, she thought. It's the wrong time, the wrong way for all this to work out . . .

But maybe the only way, for Radu.

Orca grabbed Mark's hand.

"Let's go home," she said.

Without hesitation, without question or surprise, he turned with her and they ran toward the edge of the port. Orca heard van de Graaf curse, startled and irritated; Ramona-Teresa called her name, and Mark's.

They dove together and sank beneath the waves. Several meters down they swam close together and undressed each other, having trouble and laughing over Mark's stiff new jeans. They abandoned the clothes by the edge of the port and swam away to join their cousins.

14

THOUGH NO ONE in the group believed that Orca and her brother had gone for a quick swim, they waited a few minutes, till van de Graaf said, "Divers!" in disgust, and led everyone into the elevator. The doors closed and it slid downward. It stopped at a floor that Laenea had tried to visit a number of times, out of curiosity. The elevator controls always before had refused to acknowledge the request.

The carpet in the foyer was deep and springy; the room van de Graaf led them to exceeded the VIP shuttle in luxury.

The administrators do treat themselves well, Laenea thought.

"The bar's over there," van de Graaf said, sat in a chair in a corner, closed her eyes, and went immediately into a communications trance.

"I suppose she thinks all we do when we're not flying is

get drunk," Vasili said, and flung himself into a chair, where he sat sullenly with his arms crossed.

Ignoring him, Ramona-Teresa poured herself a straight shot of scotch and drank it. Marc found a bottle of tequila at the very back of a shelf. Laenea decided that a drink of cognac was not a bad idea.

I might have expected that Vasili doesn't drink, Laenea thought. Ah, well, he ought to be happy; at least it gives him something to sulk about.

Laenea was on her second drink and Ramona-Teresa on her fourth when van de Graaf returned.

"Radu has simply disappeared," she said. "There's no credit or transportation trace, and Stafford claimed she hadn't seen him since he was with you. I had to remind her she'd ever met him."

"It was a far-fetched idea," Laenea said. "They barely met." Still, she thought, it was not like Kathell to forget anyone.

"Maybe. But she wasn't speaking to me directly; she used a remote. She could have been lying."

"You were monitoring her!" Ramona-Teresa said.

Van de Graaf shrugged.

"I don't think you need to be so anxious about Radu," Laenea said quickly. "He's done this before, gone off alone. He just wants time to think. He'll be back."

"You seem very sure of that."

"Well, what's a few hours? It will take you a long time to turn him into a pilot."

"Radu Dracul cannot be a pilot," Ramona-Teresa said. She poured herself another drink. So far she was completely unaffected by the alcohol.

Laenea frowned. "But I thought — since he perceives seventh — "

"He does. And six other dimensions. But some are different dimensions than those you perceive, which are the dimensions of transit. The intersection is not completely congruous. Without someone to follow, he'd be lost, he'd be blind."

"Then why do you want him back so badly? Why don't you just leave him alone?"

"His perceptions are of a different worth entirely than yours."

"It ought to be obvious to you, of all people, why we want to study him," van de Graaf said to Laenea.

"Hah!" Vasili said. "She doesn't even have to think about it. She knows she's safe."

"Vaska, *what* are you talking about?"

"You can't be lost!" Vasili shouted. "If you get lost, he can find you. What about the rest of us?"

"Oh," Laenea said. "You're right, I'm sorry, I didn't think of that." The reason, though, was less selfishness than a determination to learn so much about transit that she never again would be lost, and need to be found. "I'm sure, though, if he *can* find others, he'd do it willingly."

"It seems unlikely to me that he could find anyone but you," Ramona-Teresa said.

"Then what — "

"I think," van de Graaf said, "that his abilities are unique, interrelated, and the result of a single basic change, brought about by the illness he survived. I think it likely that the viral genome integrated itself into his chromosomes."

"I disagree in part," Ramona-Teresa said. "I believe that most of his abilities are present in some percentage of the population, but that they can only be expressed in the proper environment. I believe the illness forged some perceptual link between you and him. If you look at the mathematics, you can see that anyone who is aware of seventh is very close to any other person — or any other point — in normal space-time."

Van de Graaf interrupted. "Whatever the details of the effect, the cause is the illness. It must be. But the samples I took from him — skin and blood, nothing more invasive — show no obvious alteration. I need more samples, of more tissues, nerve tissue in particular, in order to study him properly."

"No wonder he ran," Laenea said. "You want to sample his *brain?*"

"Don't be ridiculous, pilot. I'm not going to dissect him.

Any peripheral nerve cell would probably do; he wouldn't even notice it. He has no reason to fear me, and even if he did, he had no way of knowing the direction of my speculations."

"Only a couple of hours of being questioned. You can learn a lot from questions, even if you don't know the answers. He isn't stupid. He's a colonist, he may not have a fine-edged education like you do. But he isn't stupid."

"If I thought so before, I don't think so now," van de Graaf said.

"You know him better than the rest of us, Laenea," Vasili said. "Is he so selfish, does he dislike pilots so much, that he'd refuse a little more time and a few more tests, if it would save some of our lives?"

"He's the least selfish person I know," Laenea said, annoyed. "And he doesn't dislike pilots."

"That isn't my experience."

"I think you're trying to make individual dislike into something more general," Laenea said, letting the edge in her voice come through.

Vasili colored.

"You still haven't explained," Laenea said to Ramona and van de Graaf. "If you don't think he can find anybody else, why do you need him back so badly?"

"Because the change might be transmissible."

Laenea sat very still, trying to change the meaning of what she had just heard, but failing; trying to control a slowly rising fury, but failing.

"Good gods," she said, horrified. "Do you realize what you're saying?" She stood up, her fists clenched. "How could you even consider such a thing? Are you monsters?"

"What?" van de Graaf said.

"Laenea!" Ramona-Teresa said, in honest protest.

"Don't you know what that illness did to Radu's world? It killed every member of his family, and it nearly killed him. I was there, I saw it — "

They waited in patience till she finished her outburst.

Ramona chuckled, low and soft. Laenea glared at her.

"My dear," Ramona said, "if you only knew how familiar that all sounds."

"What are you talking about?"

" 'It's horrible!' " Ramona said in a voice not her own. " 'Taking young people and ripping out their hearts and putting in machines instead!' "

"But — " Laenea said, confused. "It isn't the same."

"How, not?"

"We're all volunteers, for one thing."

"Do you think we mean to recreate a plague and infect the population with it? No wonder you think us monsters!"

"Who would volunteer? It kills half the people it touches."

"More than half," van de Graaf said. "Nearly all, in fact."

"Well, then."

"Don't you see? That's why we have to study him. To find out what makes him different. Why did he survive?"

"Can you swear it will be safe?"

"Of course not. Most assuredly it won't be, not completely."

"Then he'll never let you study him, and no one will volunteer anyway."

"Some might," Marc said.

She looked at him, shocked.

"If it made me able to fly again. If Kri's hypothesis is correct, it might do that. Then," he said softly, "the regeneration might be worth it."

"The whole point is that we don't know how he can do what he does, or why — in fact we don't even know all of what he can do. We need to study him."

Laenea remained unsoothed.

"He'll let us test him if you ask him to, Laenea," Vasili said.

"I'll do nothing of the sort."

"You *are* selfish," Vasili said with contempt.

"That may be true," Laenea said, sick of the accusation. "But what I am more than anything right now is angry."

"Laenea," Ramona said, "we must study him. If we can find more people like him — "

"Or create them," Vasili said, earning himself a sharp look from Ramona.

" — we might develop the ability to communicate with ships in transit, or even directly between the inhabited worlds."

"Ramona, I can see the potential, even weighed against the risks. But you're going to have a hard time convincing Radu — *if* you can find him."

"He has to come to us if he ever wants to go home," Vasili said.

Laenea sighed. "He'd sacrifice that if he didn't believe he could trust you."

"He must cooperate with us," Ramona said. "He's the only source of information we have."

"If you've got to study something, why don't you study the virus? It might tell you all you need to know."

"Your expedition was all too efficient," van de Graaf said. "There's no record of any subsequent case of plague."

"You think it's extinct, then?" No one was allowed on Twilight without being vaccinated, but the antibody was to surface proteins, not genetic material. If the organism had disappeared, no one could reconstruct it.

"Possibly. More likely it still exists, in whatever indigenous host it occupied before people landed on Twilight. Finding it might be difficult, though. Its source was never identified."

What van de Graaf was telling her was that the most straightforward way of finding the virus would be to send unvaccinated people to the surface of Twilight and wait until they got sick.

"But you can't . . ."

"We'd prefer not to," van de Graaf said.

Marc listened to the conversation quietly, sipping tequila, conserving his strength. He had never been on the administrators' deck before; it had not yet existed when he was, so briefly, a pilot. Marc knew real antiques from reproductions, and this room's furnishings were real. Despite the glass wall looking out into the sea, the central fireplace seemed appropriate.

Kri continued to worry the subject of Radu Dracul's whereabouts, but no one had even mentioned Orca and her brother. Marc was less inclined than the others to assume their departure was a whim, unconnected with Radu's disappearance.

"Well," Kri said, "security's on it, and that's all we can do for now." She downed her drink. "We'd all better get some sleep, and start fresh in the morning."

Marc rose slowly.

"I'll bid you farewell till tomorrow," he said. "I will rest better in my own bed."

Laenea rose. "Let me walk you home," she said. "You look tired."

Marc could see Kri preparing to argue against Laenea's leaving. He suspected Kri would insist that he stay here — which he definitely did not want to do — before she would permit Laenea to go out.

"No, no," he said. "I'll be quite all right. I just want to get home before I overtire myself."

He clasped Laenea's wrist, and she gripped his. The touch felt strange, but not unpleasant.

As soon as Marc left the administration deck, he opened a communications terminal. He had never acquired an internal communicator, fearing it might further confuse the insulted tissue of his brain. He signaled his analogue, which awakened quickly.

"Where are you?" it said. Its voice remained smooth and calm.

"I'm on my way home."

"Why are you away from your home?"

"It was an emergency."

"You should have let me go on duty."

"I know," Marc said. "I'm sorry. I forgot. Would you look out in the foyer and see if anyone's there?"

"Of course." After a barely perceptible pause, the analogue said, "No one at all."

"Thank you. I'll be back soon."

Marc left the terminal and hobbled homeward, deep in

thought. If only he had turned on the analogue . . . If Radu Dracul had come to him for help, he had found nothing. Well, there was no changing what was past; the future would have to concern him now.

Marc suspected that Kathell Stafford had had good reason to speak via a voice synthesizer to a representative of the transit authority.

Orca surfaced, trod water, and contacted Harmony. She had to use a satellite to jump the communication over the mountains, but true speech adapted well to radio frequency, and no eavesdropper could decipher her family's dialect.

Her mother answered.

Hello, *chérie,* she said, mixing true speech and French as their family sometimes did. Where are you?

Halfway home, Orca said. With Mark.

She added her brother's true speech name.

Their mother laughed, understanding by the construction that Orca's brother had adopted a surface name, and understanding the joke immediately. She liked to watch *The Man from Atlantis,* too.

The news reports are intriguing, *chère petite fille,* and the gossip even more. How much of it is true?

For once what really happened is more exciting by half, Orca replied. I'll explain when I get home. My crewmate may come to stay. Has he called?

No.

I don't know where he is, Orca said. Or how he's traveling. I told him to ask for us in the harbor at Victoria. He needs our help, *mon-amie-maman.* Are you feeling revolutionary? Is father?

Your father, always. Me? If necessary.

It may be. When my friend arrives — Orca sent a sound-name for Radu; any diver or whale who heard it would recognize him immediately — he's an offworlder, she added. He's shy, and modest to several faults. His trouble isn't of his own making.

We'll make him welcome, youngling.

Thank you, *maman-amie.*

Shall I send the boat? You'll be very late for the gathering, otherwise.

Orca sent a grimace, and her mother laughed again.

Send the plane, instead, *maman!* The misery won't last so long.

I will, *amie-fille,* who loves to fly a ship from world to world, but not island to island.

The faint glow of the instrument panel gave the only light, the whisper of the noise-baffled propellors the only sound. Radu floated alone in silent darkness, waiting for the sky to lighten, looking forward to the dawn.

His eyelids drooped; he dozed. He jerked awake when his chin touched his chest. The night had retreated by a single shade of blue.

He tried to remember the last time he had slept real, un-drugged sleep. He discounted both sleeping in transit (which seemed very much something *other*), and recovering from unconsciousness and hypothermia in the diver's quarters. His last full night's sleep was on Earthstation, when Orca shared his room and his bed. His time-sense automatically sorted through all his perceptions and told him how long ago that had been, subjectively, as well as in elapsed time on earth, an objective measurement. He laughed softly: if objective measurement even made sense anymore.

He could not stay awake till dawn. He turned on the auto-pilot, glad that it contained only navigational functions. Had it possessed cognition, the computer might answer radio calls and give their position away. Flying very low, the airship would avoid both navigational radar and small craft routes that might otherwise intersect their path.

He was so tired he had to check the autopilot settings four times to get an agreement on the course.

I'll just nap for an hour, he thought, changing one of the passenger seats to its reclining position. An hour, and then I'll be able to take over from the autopilot again.

He fell instantly and deeply asleep.

Laenea woke slowly and with great pleasure, luxuriating in the warmth of the bed and the silence and the quiet blue light of her room. She stretched her bare arms wide, feeling not even a twinge of pain, feeling as if nothing could ever hurt her again.

Flinging off the bedclothes, she rose and dressed without taking time for a shower. She was eager for whatever today would bring.

In the common room of the suite given over to the three pilots, Kristen van de Graaf and Ramona-Teresa sat sipping coffee.

"Good morning," Laenea said, and poured coffee for herself.

"Good morning." The doctor sounded tired.

Instead of replying to Laenea, Ramona put aside her cup, and rose. "It's time for me to catch the ferry," she said. Her small duffel bag lay beside the door.

"Where are you going?" Laenea asked.

"To see Miikala's family. To tell them what happened."

"Should . . . should I come with you?"

Ramona hesitated. "I think . . . I think perhaps someday they'll be able to speak with you, Laenea. I think someday they'll want to. But not now. Not yet."

Laenea touched Ramona's hand. "I understand," she said. "Ramona, I'm so sorry — "

Ramona-Teresa embraced Laenea, hugging her tight. Then she pulled away, grabbed her duffel bag, and disappeared out the door without another word.

Laenea took her coffee and sat down, wishing she could be more help to Ramona. She glanced across the room at Dr. van de Graaf, whose eyes were slightly bloodshot.

"Did you get any sleep at all?" Laenea asked.

"A little, on and off."

"You look exhausted."

"I've had other things on my mind. There's still no trace of your friend."

"He came back before," Laenea said. She still believed he would return, though she wondered if he might be better off to stay away.

"I think he must have gone with the divers," van de Graaf said. "If they've taken him in, and he refuses to leave voluntarily, it will be . . . awkward."

Laenea knew as well as anyone how jealous the divers were of their sovereign territory. They fiercely protected their cousins from harassment, whether malicious or merely curious.

"I still think you should leave him alone for a while."

Van de Graaf picked up a slice of toast, bit off one corner, and chewed it thoughtfully.

"I suppose you're right," she said. "He does get rather stubborn when he's pressed far enough."

Vasili Nikolaievich emerged from his room, hollow-eyed and haunted. Laenea wondered what to say to him. His envy and disappointment saddened her.

"Vaska — "

"It's all right," he said. "I know what to do." His words were as intense as his gaze. He turned to van de Graaf. "I have to go to Ngthummulun. I have to find Atnaterta. He knew what was going to happen — "

He described Radu's experience on Atna's home world. Laenea listened without comment. She had flown with Atna. It was true that he was an excellent navigator. It was true that Ngthummulun had produced equally excellent pilots.

"If Atna can teach me what he did — how he knew what was going to happen to Radu — " Vasili's words trailed off, as if he had not quite finished imagining what it was that he wanted from Atna. He stared at van de Graaf, anxious for her reaction. "Can't you see — "

Laenea held back from saying what she thought. None of the pilots from Ngthummulun had perceived seventh, and none was as good a pilot as Vaska. Laenea herself, though she could do the one thing Vasili wished to be able to do, was not as fine a pilot as he.

Not yet, anyway, she thought.

Dr. van de Graaf stroked her eyebrow with the tip of one finger. "It's worth checking," she said.

Neither her expression nor her tone revealed whether she

believed Vasili's idea to be reasonable, or whether she simply had no more heart than Laenea for crushing out his dream. She put aside her toast and said, "I assume you're both ready to do some more exploring."

Laenea stood and put down her cup so quickly that some of the coffee splashed out onto the table.

"I am," Laenea said. "When do we leave?"

"Not quite yet," van de Graaf said.

Laenea took one step toward her, hands outspread in supplication, ready to argue against a delay of weeks or even days.

Van de Graaf smiled. "Finish your breakfast, first."

When Radu woke he thought, groggily, did I sleep? It was nearly dawn, the sky was midnight blue, and now it's no lighter.

Perhaps he had merely dozed for a moment, then awakened again. He thought about his time sense.

It was night again, not night still. He had slept the whole day; he was approaching his destination.

Victoria was a stolid, beautifully tended, rather fussy old city. The last streaks of scarlet sunset faded into the ocean. Lights flicked on here and there, illuminating windows in the ivy-covered stone of the Empress Hotel and picking out the cabins of rows of sailboats moored along the piers. Flower-beds covered the banks of the harbor. In the dusk, the colors dimmed to white and shades of gray.

Radu nosed the airship toward the landing field by the ferry dock. It was plainly marked on the chart, plainly marked against the land by several sets of concentric circles, worn into the grass by the landing wheels of different sized airships, one set circumscribing each mooring mast.

Landing a blimp solo was even more difficult than launching it. He would have to descend upwind of the mast and let the wind push the ship into position. That carried the risk of ramming the mast and puncturing the envelope. But it was his only choice. Unless the air was completely still — and it was not; he could tell from the way the blimp handled and from the ripples across the dark water — then trying to drag the ship against the wind would be sheer stupidity.

A shadowy silhouette ran across the field toward him as his craft neared the ground. Radu tensed, ready to take off again. Perhaps Kathell had failed to deceive the administrators; perhaps she had even turned him in. He found her character incomprehensible, how seriously she took her word a mystery.

Radu had left the radio off, so, for all he knew, whatever agency controlled the city's airspace might well have been ordering him all afternoon to give up and come down.

The airship dropped low enough for Radu to see that the woman running toward him, far from being dressed in the uniform of a security guard or the severe suit of an executive, wore raggy cutoffs and a tank top. She paced the airship. Radu opened the window and leaned out.

"Come down till I can reach the ladder!" she yelled. "Be ready to drop some ballast and take off again."

"Who are you?"

She raised her hand, fingers spread. Light from one of the field's floodlamps turned the thin membranes of her swimming webs pink and gold.

Radu dipped the airship sharply down and reached across to open the door. The diver grabbed the ladder and swung herself into the gondola. As it sank, and the landing wheel bounced against the grass, Radu dumped sixty kilos of ballast and gunned the engines. Lighter now than before the diver came aboard, the ship took off at a steep angle.

The diver scrambled up the tilted floor and slid into the forward passenger seat.

"Well," she said, looking him up and down, "you're definitely the person Orca sent me to meet. You can call me Wolf. What's your name?"

"Radu Dracul," he said. "Didn't Orca tell you who I was?"

"Yes," Wolf said. "And a great deal more. She gave you a true name that's a description of you. One would have to be blind and deaf not to recognize you after hearing it."

"What is it?" Radu asked.

"I can't say it out of water. It would just sound like ca-cophony, anyway. That was the idea, over the radio, if she'd used your surface name it would have been obvious who we were talking about even if no one not a diver could under-stand the whole conversation."

"Oh," Radu said. "Thank you for meeting me."

"Head north," Wolf said. "We'll be at Harmony by midnight."

He did as she said. As they passed over a tremendous domed Victorian building, strings of white light bulbs lit up, outlining it completely. Its walls vanished into darkness and it became a phantom carnival structure.

"What is *that*?" Radu asked.

Wolf chuckled at his reaction. "The Parliament building," she said.

"Why do they do that to it?"

"For tradition. For the tourists. Just for fun, I guess. They've been doing it for more than a hundred years."

The blimp sailed over the Parliament building, then north. Victoria fell behind them. The lights of small towns dotted the coast, and ground cars on the highway spread tiny mov-ing fans of illumination before them. In the Strait, a pale navigational beacon flashed strobically, streaking the water with its beam. Reflected by its own sails, chased by its phos-phorescent wake, a ferryboat glistened like an elongated carousel.

"Did Orca tell you why I've come to you?"

"No," Wolf said. "She said you needed help."

"That's certainly true," Radu said. "I wouldn't have in-volved her, or you, but she was already involved, and I couldn't see any alternative."

"She also said you were her friend. That gives us the privi-lege of helping you, if we can."

Wolf was in her midforties, perhaps, a handsome woman, taller than Orca but with similar coloring: dark skin and very pale hair. The handle of a knife strapped to her leg projected through the split side seam of her cutoffs, in easy reach.

"You'd better hear what happened, first," Radu said.
He told her everything.

"Now I see why my daughter asked if I were feeling revolutionary," Wolf said when Radu had finished.

"Will it come to that?" Radu asked. "Would they attack you, to make me go back?" He felt a deep distress at the possibility of involving the divers in warfare.

"If they do, they'll use very diplomatic violence. We keep our fights on a high plane these days." She smiled; the resemblance between her and her daughter became that much more striking. "Now let me ask you something. Do you truly believe your employers would infect people with this disease, if you let them recreate it?"

"I don't want to believe it," Radu said. "But all their questioning led in that direction. And they wouldn't tell me what they meant to do. I was afraid that if I waited too long, I wouldn't be able to stop them if that was what they planned."

Wolf nibbled on her fingernail, deep in thought, and remained silent most of the rest of the trip.

While waiting all day to catch a shuttle, Laenea had plenty of time to think. The administration had no real reason to schedule this exploratory trip so soon, and the haste with which it had been arranged insured that it would be poorly organized and result in little useful information. Laenea was anxious to return to transit, but she did not let the administrators use her eagerness or her joy to erase her suspicions.

Radu was still missing; Orca had vanished into the sea. Even Marc remained unavailable. He had set his analogue to answering his phone, and the analogue had years of experience at courteously refusing to reply to questions. Laenea was the only link to Radu the administrators had left, and she had no doubt that they wanted him back. It seemed likely to her that they hoped Radu would perceive that she had entered seventh again, fear that she was once more in danger, and give himself away.

But she let her employers think she believed what they

told her about exploration and knowledge. She had two reasons. First, she believed she had at least as good a chance of warning Radu as of betraying him.

Second — and perhaps Vasili Nikolaievich was right; perhaps she *was* brutally selfish — Laenea could not bear to be out of transit any longer.

As Wolf had said it would, the blimp reached Harmony by midnight. Radu guided the airship to a meadow on the crest of the island. Several divers grabbed its trailing lines and drew it to the mast; others came running with bags of sand to heave into the ballast compartments. Soon the blimp rolled in a gentle, narrow arc, swinging back and forth in erratic wind currents. Wolf and Radu climbed down.

To his surprise, Orca waited for him on the ground.

"Welcome to Harmony," she said to Radu. "Hi, *loup-chérie*," she said to her mother, giving her a quick embrace. She hugged Radu tightly. Instead of the bright, metal-scaled clothing she wore on shipboard, she had on a pair of faded blue cutoffs like everyone else. She still wore her red deck shoes.

"I'm very grateful to you," Radu said.

"We haven't done anything yet. You'd better wait and see if we can be of any help."

Just being among people he felt he could trust, people who had no motive to deceive him or bend him to their will, was the greatest help he could wish for right now. Just being in a real place, a place not constructed, artificial, controlled, made him happy.

"How did you get here so fast?" Radu said. "Do you ride the killer whales?"

Orca laughed. "No. They hate it when you do that. Mom sent the seaplane for us." She introduced her brother, who stood back shyly in the shadows. He resembled Orca closely, and he was naked; he did not even carry the knife belt most of the other divers wore next to their skin.

"I'm glad to see you survived the flight," Wolf said smiling.

"As well as I ever do."

"I liked it," Mark said. "I'd like to learn to fly a plane. What's flying a blimp like?"

"I'd be glad to show you, if we get a chance," Radu said.

"Forgive me, *mes petites*," Wolf said. "I'll leave you. Radu, you'll have to excuse us if we're a bit distracted tonight." She gripped his upper arm in a welcoming gesture and vanished into the darkness. Mark stayed with them a moment, then suddenly said, "I have some things to do, too. See you later," and disappeared.

Orca watched him go. "Well, he isn't very subtle yet, but he's getting the idea."

"Has anyone asked about me?" Radu said, preoccupied. "Do you think they can find out where I am?"

"They'll probably figure it out eventually." She took his hand. "Come on. I'll show you around."

"I wish I hadn't had to involve you," Radu said.

"No more apologies. They aren't necessary. I offered you our help. I'm glad you trust me enough to take it." She drew him along the dark path, down from the crest of the island toward its shore. "Stop worrying for a while."

She took him through a grove of evergreen trees. The ground was soft beneath his feet, the rocky island soil cushioned by layers of fallen needles. Radu had been so long among machines and concentrations of people, the constant background noise of civilization, that the silence of Orca's home struck him with wonder. It was a presence, not an absence. He stopped, so even his footsteps did not mar it. Orca stopped, too, and glanced back curiously.

Nothing Radu could think of to say to her expressed what he felt, so he remained silent. They continued on along the path.

Nestled against the slope, nearly concealed by trees, a low, shingled building faced the water. Orca opened the carved wooden door and led him inside, where she kicked off her shoes and set them on a shelf in the entryway. Radu followed suit.

"This is the longhouse," Orca said. "The labs are down at the other end, sleeping rooms are this way." She showed him to a room that was illuminated by moonlight streaming through the window. Tatami mats covered the floor, and a futon lay folded against one wall next to a low wooden table holding a brass lamp. The room was spare and peaceful. Radu felt immediately at home, as he had not, not anywhere, for years. He walked to the window and looked out. The hillside fell away sharply to the water; trees outlined without obscuring the wide channel between this island and the next. A white flash caught his gaze. A killer whale arced upward, then vanished beneath the water. Another followed, and a third. As Radu's eyes became more accustomed to the darkness he could see more than the bright patches on the creatures' sides. The bay and the channel beyond were full of whales and divers, playing and swimming, surfacing and disappearing again with barely a splash, barely a ripple.

In the channel, a creature bigger than anything Radu had ever seen, or ever imagined, glided in a slow and graceful curve across the surface of the water. He gasped.

The moonlight silvered Orca's pale hair. Radu had not even noticed her move beside him, but now he was acutely aware of her presence.

"What was that?" Radu whispered.

"A great whale," Orca said. "A blue. They're open ocean beings, they never come into straits or bays. But a representative came, for our transition meeting."

Radu watched, fascinated. The enormous creature spouted, then lay quiet on the surface of the water.

"There are only a few of them left," Orca said. "It's only been thirty years since they stopped being hunted — " She stopped, started again, and said with difficulty, "Since humans stopped killing them. It will take them a long time to recover, if they ever do."

"I've never seen anything like it," Radu said.

"Being near them, talking to them — it's like being at the center of the universe," Orca said. "It's terrifying, but they can't understand that. Fear is one of the few things they can't understand. The blues aren't afraid of my cousins, even though sometimes — not anymore, because of the truce, but in the past and maybe in the future — killer whales killed blues."

Radu looked down at her. She was intent on the scene below.

"You need to be down there, don't you?"

She replied, finally, after a long silence. "Yes," she said. "I really do. I'm sorry. You must be exhausted. Why don't you sleep for a while? I'll be able to spend some time with you in the afternoon."

"I don't think I could sleep," Radu said. "I'd rather — would it be impolite of me to sit on the shore and watch? I don't want to intrude on your privacy . . ."

She glanced up at him, her smile one of amusement and even glee, the somberness of a moment ago vanished.

"It wouldn't be rude at all. You're our guest, a member of my family, while you're here. Radu — would you like to come swimming with me?"

He felt as if she had offered him a new world, one he had dreamed of but could never find.

"Yes!" he said, then ruefully, "But I tried that before, remember, and it didn't work out very well."

"You just weren't properly prepared," she said. "Come on."

She took him through the hall and down a long flight of steps, wood first, then stone, that led into the living rock of the island. At the bottom, a tunnel reached out to a wooden dock that crossed the tiny, rocky beach. A small chamber had been cut near the mouth of the tunnel. Inside it, Orca chose a garment from a hook on the wall. It was black, with a white stripe up each side and down each arm.

"It's a wet suit," Orca said. "Once in a while we get a visitor who's a lander, and wants to swim. A field suit would protect you, but you wouldn't really be in the water. The wet suit is better. Ever wear one before?"

"No."

"It'll keep you warm. You've probably never worn a scuba tank — ?"

He shook his head.

"Okay. I'll teach you to use the tank some other time. Tonight you can use a snorkel."

She helped him out of his clothes and into the wet suit, then led him to the end of the dock. He entered the dark water hesitantly. After a quick shock of cold, the trapped water warmed against his skin and he felt perfectly comfortable.

"You won't want to go very deep anyway, or move around too much, just yet," Orca said. "But you can watch and listen."

They swam out into the bay.

Listening was extraordinary. He could see very little, despite the clear water and the face mask that permitted him to open his eyes beneath the surface. But the sounds — ! He was surrounded by them, engulfed and inundated, penetrated: long, leisurely songs that formed a background to it all, trains of clicks and whistles that started below his hearing range, sailed up through it like a rocket, and passed far beyond, moans and sighs and laughter. At times he felt he was at the focus of a wave of sound, as if one of Orca's cousins, or even one of the other, larger whales, were looking him over, sounding him out. Radu hung in the water, just beneath the surface, breathing through the snorkel and trying to make out the forms and shapes around him. Orca waited long enough to be certain he was comfortable, then swam to join the others. But now and again a diver passed Radu and touched him reassuringly, or waved; a few times one of the killer whales glided beneath him, and once one let its fluke curve up and stroke him from chest to toes. The touch was unbelievably gentle. Nothing in his life before, not his first trip into space, Twilight spinning slow and graceful above him, not Earthstation, not even the moment of transition into seventh, had affected him like this. He felt calm, and enchanted, and in the midst of a magic night.

For a long time nothing moved nearby, and the sounds receded. Radu moved his hands till he floated upright with his head above the surface. He barely needed to tread water,

the wet suit was so buoyant. He pushed the mask to his forehead. The group of whales — several kinds of whales, now,
besides the killers and the magnificent blue — had moved
out through the mouth of the bay, to the channel. Radu slid
his mask back down and set off after them.

The bottom dropped away sharply. Radu kept swimming.
He was not at all afraid or even apprehensive. Soon he was as
close to the group as he had been before, perhaps a little
closer, and his good sense overcame his desire actually to go
among the whales. No matter Orca's welcome, he was only
honorarily and temporarily a member of her family. He was
a landbound guest, wrapped in black rubber, while the beings
nearby frolicked naked in the freezing sea, and spoke to each
other in song.

Very slowly — so slowly he felt not the slightest fear — a
shape rose up beneath him. It was so big it lost its form in
distance and darkness.

The blue whale rose till its great eye looked him right in
the face. From a distance the blue whale had been awe in-
spiring. This close, its size was simpler: incomprehensible.
Radu reached out, as slowly as the whale had approached
him, hesitantly, in case his touch might be unwanted. The
whale closed its eye, and opened it again, and did not move.
Radu touched its skin. It was soft and smooth and warm.
Even when he took his hand away, he could feel the warmth
of the whale radiating through the water.

The great blue whale blinked at him again, embracing
Radu in sound.

I can't understand you, Radu thought. I wish I could,
but I can't. I can't even speak to you in my own language,
not around this rubber mouthpiece and through all this
water.

The blue whale blinked a third time; the caress of music
ceased. The whale moved very slowly forward, gliding past
Radu, making no more noise than a feather in air. It curved
downward, diving. The pressure of the water parting for it
pushed Radu gently back. He lay motionless, entranced by
the whale's sheer presence.

A lifetime later the creature's flukes slid by beneath him, and it vanished into depths of dark water.

Radu dove down after it and swam a few meters, fighting the buoyancy of the wet suit.

"Wait — "

Air bubbled up around his face and he got a mouthful of cold salt water. It served to bring him to his senses. He struck out for the surface, broke through, and gasped and coughed for air.

Now he knew how Orca had felt, confronting the edge; he understood why she had left the ship. He knew how Vasili and Laenea felt in transit. He knew what it was like to meet an alien.

The divers and the whales cavorted and played far off in the channel. Radu knew he could not join them. He turned and swam back into the bay, toward the lights of the divers' house.

He was halfway there when Orca broke the surface nearby and swam beside him.

"She talked to you," Orca said. Awe touched her voice.

"I guess she did," Radu said. He stopped swimming and faced her. "But I couldn't understand."

"It doesn't matter. You might not have understood her even if you could understand true speech. But the blues hardly ever speak to divers, Radu! They've never adopted any of us as their family."

Some faint ambition and unformed wish faded away just as Radu became aware of its existence. He felt tired and lonely.

"Would it be rude for me to go ashore?" he asked.

"No, of course not. Come on. I'll swim with you."

Radu set out to cross the other half of the bay, swimming slowly. Orca sidestroked alongside him, graceful even at a pace that to her must have been like creeping, or floundering.

Radu climbed up the ladder and stood dripping on the dock. Orca helped him out of the wet suit and showed him how to rinse it in fresh water, to keep the salt from damaging it. Radu hardly noticed the chill of the air on his bare skin; it was almost as if he had learned the divers' ability to stay

warm in freezing water. He and Orca walked down the dock
and into the cavern.

"Orca . . ."

"Hmm?"

"What did she say to me?"

"That's awfully hard to explain, here on the surface."

"Please," he said desperately. "Please try."

"She told you her name. Not just the sonic description, her
whole name. That's part of what's hard to explain. Your sonic
name is objective — anybody who's met you knows what it
is, and anybody who hears it will recognize you immediately.
The rest of it . . . it's a combination of your experiences and
your feelings and your beliefs. Then she asked you your
name — "

"And I couldn't answer . . ."

"She understood. I'm sure she did. She knew you weren't
a diver. She wouldn't be offended. They just aren't, not ever.
Then she welcomed you to the transition, and said you and
she would speak together some other time."

"Is that possible?"

"You'd have to learn middle speech, at least. True speech
would be better."

"They must be difficult languages."

"Well, I grew up speaking them, so I don't know how hard
they are for adults. But I've been told they're easy to begin
to learn. They're very flexible, though, and I don't think anybody — any of the divers — knows true speech completely.
Parts of it you can make up as you go along, and anyone who
speaks it will understand what you're saying."

Radu raised one eyebrow, not exactly disbelieving Orca,
but finding the description difficult to comprehend.

"I don't think anything exists that you can't describe in
true speech," Orca said.

"Not anything?"

Orca hung the wet suit up on its peg and tossed Radu his
clothes.

"I guess I'd have to see transit to prove that, wouldn't I?"
Her voice was distant and thoughtful.

She accompanied him upstairs. He felt comfortable enough in her presence now that he did not feel the need to dress himself immediately.

The simplicity of the divers' house welcomed Radu in a way that none of earth's overdone luxury could match, in a way he had not experienced since before his family died. In his room again, he looked down on the channel where the whales and divers swam.

"What are they doing out there?" Radu said.

"Playing. Talking. Loving each other. Later on, they'll vote on whether to make the transition."

"I shouldn't keep you," he said, reluctantly. "Shouldn't you be down there with them?"

"No. I'm not voting."

"Why not?"

"Because it doesn't matter. The vote will be for transition. But I'm not going through it again."

"Orca, you'll be left behind. Your whole family will change — "

"I will, too. But it will be a different kind of change, one that isn't compatible with remaining a diver. I've applied for pilot's training, and they've accepted me."

He started to protest, for he could not imagine giving up the freedom of the ocean once one had tasted it. But Orca was reaching for a different freedom.

"Soon you'll be able to find out for yourself if true speech can explain transit."

Her soft laugh held an undertone of sadness. "Yes. I'm glad you understand. Some of my blood-family thinks I'm crazy. I had an awful fight with my father about it."

"Your father sounds like a formidable opponent," Radu said.

"Yes, formidable," she said, stretching the word out in its French pronunciation. "I tried to get him to come meet you, but he wouldn't. Even after the blue talked to you. He said he hadn't spoken to a lander since the revolution, and he wasn't about to start now."

"Would he speak to me," Radu said hesitantly, "if I . . . if I weren't a lander?"

Silently, Orca reached out and brushed a damp lock of Radu's hair from his forehead.

"Is that what the blue understood?" she said. "Will you be staying here? Will the blues finally have a human cousin?"

"Is it possible?"

"That's how we all started, as landers, a couple of generations ago. And once in a while — not often, and I won't pretend it's easy — ordinary humans join us and change. To change among the blues, though . . . Radu, I'm scared for you."

He sat down on the window seat. The great mass of hope and confusion he had carried inside him since seeing and touching the great blue whale grew denser and hotter and suddenly fused into a white and glowing star. He flung his arms around Orca and held her tight. She embraced him, stroking his hair.

"Don't be afraid for me. Be happy for me, and I'll be happy for you."

She knelt beside him, and kissed him, hard. She took his hand and drew it between them so their bodies pressed their clasped hands together.

Laenea stepped on board her transit ship.

True, she would not be piloting it herself, for she had never even flown simulation on such a large craft. True, she was technically not qualified to solo even in a training ship, for Miikala had not, of course, certified her. And true, every other pilot on board had far more seniority.

Nevertheless, it was hers. It was here because of her; it was preparing for transit because of her. Kristen van de Graaf had asked her to return to transit with a group of experienced pilots, in the hope of introducing them to seventh.

She stepped on board, and a dozen pilots, who had been gathering here all day, greeted her.

She knew several of them — Jenneth, and Chase, both from

earth, and Quentin, from the same home world as Atnaterta. She paused, not knowing what to say, seeing in them the same expression she had seen in the faces of grounders meeting a pilot. She glanced quickly over her shoulder. The hatch swung slowly closed.

"Laenea —"

She faced the pilots again. Jenneth, who had spoken, came toward her, carrying a small flask of iridescent blue glass. She offered it to Laenea. Laenea accepted it.

"What is it?"

"The ashes of your heart."

Laenea looked down at the flask again, and traced a pattern of color that curved up its cool, smooth side.

She tried to say something, but joy made her speechless. She raised her head. All the other pilots watched her, smiling, remembering their own final initiation, the gift of their freedom.

"Thank you," Laenea finally managed to whisper. She laughed suddenly with joy, and the other pilots surrounded her, laughing with her, embracing her, welcoming her to their company.

Radu woke warm and content, with Orca nestled sleeping against him. The room was suffused with the midnight blue light just preceding dawn.

He stretched, happy for the moment to doze in the silence. But as midnight blue began turning to azure, he could not stay inside. He kissed Orca gently and slid from beneath the down comforter without disturbing her.

He put on his pants, picked up his boots in the foyer, and sat on the outside steps to slip into them. There was a lot of brush on the hillside, and the path was rough. Even among the divers, only Orca's brother Mark climbed around barefoot on their rocky island.

The approaching dawn turned the world a soft, misty blue-gray. The salt tang of the ocean and the spicy scent of the trees blended into one. In the bay, the killer whales lay in black patterns against the slate-colored water. He looked for the blue, but could not find her.

Radu climbed the path to the crest of the island. The blimp drifted motionless in the still air, its landing wheel a handsbreadth from the ground.

Radu clambered to the top of a projection of smooth gray lichen-patched rock, the highest point of the island, to watch the first sunrise that he had ever witnessed on this world.

The edge of the sun crept over the mountains to the east, a single point of clear yellow light. It grew to an arc, until he had to look away.

The sunlight and the colors fairly dazzled him. He took a deep breath of the sun-sharpened resiny air and stretched his arms wide. He chose, deliberately and willingly, to see this place in the manner that had been forced upon him in seventh. Since returning to earth he had been afraid to look at the world that way, afraid of being overwhelmed again by the perception of rapid change. Here, the pace would be slower and more careful.

The morning breeze touched his hair, ruffling the locks at the back of his neck, on his forehead, touching his chest and shoulders with a caress as gentle as Orca's lips.

The world opened out around him. He did not try again to see any single specific thing. He knew from trying to look at Laenea that it was impossible. But he could see and feel the multiplicity of outlines of gradual, inevitable, growth and life and change and even death.

When he heard a thought as clear as a nearby voice, he was not at all surprised.

Laenea's great ship slid into transit. All the pilots had gathered in the control room, and now they waited. They were fearful, eager, apprehensive, intent.

Laenea sat back in the pilot's chair and let herself experience transit. All the words she had used to describe it during her debriefing, the words she had imagined captured its very essence, lost their meaning and became not only inadequate, but simply wrong. Trying to define what she had missed before, she responded again to the sensation of existing within the universe and, at the same time, surrounding it completely.

"Laenea!"

She realized that Chase had spoken her name several times and received no response.

"Sorry," she said. "What?"

"No, that's my question, what are we supposed to be seeing?"

"We don't know what to look for, remember," Jenneth said, "you have to show us."

She showed them.

Chase gasped. One of the other pilots, whose name Laenea could not remember, cursed softly and joyfully, damning himself to horrible purgatories for never having seen what was right in front of him all the time. Quentin frowned slightly. Jenneth folded her arms and stared belligerently through the viewport. The others remained mystified.

"That's amazing," Quentin said.

"How do we get into it?" Chase said.

They were always in it, but Laenea knew what she meant. She found an anomaly and took them from a deep cave to the open air, from the land to the sky, from the ground to the excited state.

Jenneth cried out as they made the transition. She covered her eyes and flung herself away from the port. Quentin caught her and held her, embracing her.

"It's all right," he said, "it will be all right."

Laenea stood, worried for the other pilot.

"What did you see?" Quentin said. His tone became more insistent and he grabbed her by the shoulders. "What's out there?" He shook her.

"Quentin!" Laenea and Chase both grabbed him and dragged him away from Jenneth, who was sobbing and gasping for breath. Chase put her breathing mask to her face, and tried to soothe her.

"Quentin, what's the matter with you — you saw it for yourself!" Laenea kept her grasp on his arm.

"No," he said. Tears glistened in his eyes. "No, that's just it, I didn't, I lied."

He fled from the control room.

Laenea returned to Jenneth and Chase.

"What happened, are you all right?"

"I saw...I knew...something..." Jenneth was still crying. "Laenea, please, I want to go home."

"Soon," Laenea said, "soon, we won't stay very long, come lie down." She glanced back at Chase, who nodded and took over the controls.

Laenea helped Jenneth to the lounge, let her lie on the couch, made sure her breathing mask was easily in reach, and covered her with a blanket.

"Just rest for a few minutes, and we'll go back soon."

Jenneth turned her face toward the wall.

In the corridor, Laenea hesitated. She should go back to the control room. Instead, she slipped into her cabin and picked up the small glass jar. She hurried to the airlock and put on a field suit.

Laenea stepped into the airlock and cycled it. She linked her suit to the tether-plate, then opened the hatch.

She pushed herself out of the ship.

She loosened the flask's stopper. The air within pushed against it. She released it, and the pressure exploded the ashes of her heart into a delicate white sphere, its dust roiling and dispersing as momentum carried it away from the ship.

Laenea cast the urn after it.

She would have liked to remain where she was; instead, she stroked the tether line.

Back inside the ship, Laenea took off her field suit, closed her eyes, and attempted the task she had truly come here to carry out.

Radu?

Laenea.

The tone of his reply was calm and strong and sure.

You *can* hear me! she said to him.

We're very near each other, after all.

The administrators are looking for you.

I know it.

They're hoping you'll think I'm lost again, so when you try to find me, they'll find you.

Thank you for telling me.

Did I need to?

Maybe not. But I'm glad to be able to be close to you.

She sent him a smile. So am I. Radu — two more pilots, two who came with me, can see seventh.

Radu said, I'm glad. Is Vasili there? Did he have better luck this time? I didn't see what was right in front of me, at first. Perhaps it takes practice.

Laenea's tone was sad. He's been in transit hundreds of times. If he were able to perceive it . . . But, no, he isn't here. He went to Ngthummulun. He's convinced Atna has some clue to everything that's happened.

Vasili behaved in a manner both impulsive and compulsive, yet Radu could not convince himself that the young pilot had switched so abruptly from complete rejection to complete acceptance of Atna's beliefs.

Did Vasili go alone? he asked Laenea.

Just with a crew member. No other pilots.

Laenea, Radu told her urgently, he never meant to go to Ngthummulun. He's going to Twilight. Don't you see? He thinks the plague explains what I can do. He's never been there before, so he hasn't been vaccinated —

Oh, gods. Of course. The silly fool — !

After a moment's thought, Radu felt more disgusted than worried. After all, humans had been on Twilight for a generation before the first outbreak of the plague. Perhaps the disease was, as Radu hoped and Kristen van de Graaf feared, extinct. But even if it still existed, Vasili Nikolaievich would have to have incredible bad fortune to contract it with a single unprotected visit to Radu's home world.

But the risk, however small, was real.

Can you stop him? Radu asked Laenea.

I can try.

I love you, he said, pure and clear, without any shadow of regret or loss.

Laenea sent Radu a caress of love and affection, and vanished suddenly from his perception.

Radu gasped and nearly slid from the pinnacle to the field several meters below. He recovered himself, brought back to the world of the present. Laenea's touch had been every bit as intense and erotic as any physical contact they had ever had. It was, in some ways, even more powerful. He felt breathless and aroused, yet peaceful. Even his concern for Vasili could not mar his extraordinary sense of well-being. He reached out to Laenea again, to tell her what had happened, to see if the same thing would work for her, but when he tried to find her, she was gone. She had to leave seventh, of course, to chase Vasili to Twilight.

Never mind, for now. Laenea would return to seventh very soon, if she had her way.

They had plenty of time.

He laughed aloud, and jumped down. He turned all the way around, as if he could absorb this spot into his skin and keep it with him forever.

He saw a transparent sparkle in the sky, and heard the distant hummingbird buzz of an engine. The ultralight dipped closer, waggling its wings. Radu waved. The tiny aircraft shimmered to a crooked, bumpy landing. Radu ran after it to help tie it down; it was even more vulnerable to random winds than the blimp, and harder to moor.

He was astonished when Marc climbed stiffly from the tiny cockpit.

"Marc!"

"Good morning, Radu."

"How did you find me?"

He led the older man to a bench at the edge of the meadow. Marc sat down and stretched his legs out before him.

"I have . . . sources of information that aren't easily accessible to the administrators."

"But why did you come? What are you doing out of your home? Marc, you look exhausted."

"I know what you're afraid the pilots want to do. Radu, I understand why you're afraid, but I came to ask you, to beg you, at least give them a chance. I know there's a danger, but I promise they aren't evil people. They would not act as recklessly as you fear — " He spoke all in a rush, desperately; he stopped only when he ran out of breath.

"Why you, Marc? Why did you risk coming here?"

Marc avoided his gaze. "I tried to help . . ." He stopped. He looked up. The pupils of his pale gray eyes were very large, for such a bright morning. "That's true, but it isn't the whole truth. I told you that you could trust me, and I won't betray your trust now. If they learn what they hope to, I might fly again. I'm here out of selfishness. I want to go back into transit."

"And the memories you'll lose? What about them?"

"I'll have to relearn them, I suppose, along with everything else. My analogue will tell me."

"That would be worth it to you?"

"If I could change enough to fly again, yes, it would be worth it." He leaned forward, reaching out in supplication. "Please, Radu."

Radu took Marc's cool, frail hand and gripped it gently.

"You will come back?" Marc said.

"Yes." He would let the administrators and the pilots make their demands of him, and he would have a few demands to make of them in turn.

Marc sagged forward. Radu steadied him and helped him sit in a grassy shade-swept spot beneath a wind-gnarled evergreen.

"I've overtired myself," he whispered, staring at his hands hanging limp between his knees.

"I don't doubt it," Radu said. "Lie down. Sleep for a while."

Then he remembered that those were the same words Marc had used just before shutting himself away in his rooms, just before his last illness.

"I seldom sleep," Marc whispered, lying back on the grass.

"What should I do, Marc?" Radu said.

"Nothing," Marc said. His voice became still and breathless. "I'm sorry to expose you to this . . ."

Radu wished he had put on his jacket so he could at least wrap it around Marc's shoulders.

"It's all right," he said.

"I . . ." Marc's voice failed him and he closed his eyes.

His whole body stiffened, then began to quiver. His eyelids flickered and he muttered a few words. The quivering continued for ten minutes, then stopped, and Marc's body relaxed again.

Radu waited another ten minutes, expecting the fit to start any moment, until the movements of Marc's closed eyes showed that he was deeply asleep and dreaming.

Radu felt pity and understanding. It was not Marc's illness that had kept him so isolated for so long. It was — as he himself had said, back at the spaceport — his pride.

Radu heard footsteps on the trail.

Orca climbed to the crest of the island. She saw the ultralight, and Radu with someone lying prone beside him, and ran toward them.

Radu put his finger to his lips. "He's sleeping," he said quietly.

She saw that it was Marc, let her apprehension go, and sat crosslegged beside Radu.

"Good morning."

He leaned over and kissed her.

"It is indeed," he said. "I came up here to watch it, and look what it brought me."

"He used to be a pilot, didn't he?"

"Yes. And hopes to be one again."

"So he did come to take you back."

"To ask me to come."

"And?"

"I'm going to go."

"What about the blue?"

"I want to be able to talk to her, Orca. I want to be able to tell her the name you gave me, and find out what the rest of my name is. I need to learn true speech. While I'm doing that . . . I'll trade my time to the administrators, if they will cancel Twilight's debt. Then the pilots can try to learn . . . whatever they think they can learn from me."

"Can you trust them?"

"In general? Who knows? They're people like the rest of us, not ordinary, perhaps, but people all the same. Van de Graaf? Vasili?" He laughed. "I doubt it. But I can trust Laenea, I think I can even trust Ramona-Teresa. As for Marc . . . Marc is too honorable to lie, even for his own benefit." Radu put his hands gently on Orca's bare shoulders. "And you. I should have trusted you much sooner."

Orca gripped his forearms.

"Last night," she said, "I saw that you'd found your place, if you wanted it. Are you sure you want to go?"

"Do you remember what you said when I told you how worried Atna was for us?"

"Of course."

"Resonances make sense to me now," he said. "Mine come back here, and here they stay, but for a little while longer they blend with those of the pilots. And with yours."

"I'm glad of that."

They hugged each other, like crew members saying good-bye, like friends saying hello.